Rowan Sylva

1526

A Sword and Superstition Historical Noval

Press

Published by 99% Press,
an imprint of Lasavia Publishing Ltd.
Auckland, New Zealand
www.lasaviapublishing.com

ISBN 978-0-9951398-2-4

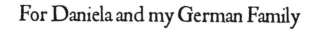
For Daniela and my German Family

Contents

Acknowledgements

I must acknowledge the work of German renaissance artist Albrecht Dürer. His work provides the basis of the cover art as well as the title images for each chapter, excluding chapter three, which is derived from a 1535 wood cut by another German artist, Niklas Store. Dürer and the other late medieval German printmakers made the early sixteenth century visually alive to me and provided valuable research for clothing and setting. In writing this book I would also like to acknowledge Giovanni Boccaccio, the fourteenth century Florentine humanist writer, who's work the Decameron provided inspiration for some of this novel's side plots and an insight into late medieval society.

Book One

Death and Fourtune

The 23rd of July, Day of the Moon, Year of the Lord 1526, on the northern frontiers of the Hungarian Empire

Manfred Lock, Lord Bishop of Eisenberg, sat reading by the window. The bundles of mint, lemon balm, and rose failed to keep out the pernicious vapours of the town – the stench of excrement, of rotten blood from the butchery, of moulding hay from the stables, of burning fat from the chandlers and of brimstone from the iron foundry. Lock put his book down to look at the city in the bright moonlight, a jagged landscape of slate roofs and spires.

Lock was lucky. His journey to Rome, that glorious den of depravity, had won him the favour of his Holiness and the support of the archbishop of Buda and, when the Bishopric of Eisenberg became vacant, Lock had been able to secure the appointment. The diocese was rich and extensive with land and mining rights that rivalled the crown's. The Bishop's dwelling, more castle than house, stood right at the top of the Eisenberg hill dominating the city bellow it. It had a walled and cobbled courtyard, from which an old ash tree grew, a row of stables containing six horses and two carriages, two stories of living quarters, extensive cellars, and a tower with a cone shaped slate roof.

At twenty-seven years old Lock was a young bishop, and could look forward to a long and affluent bachelor life, and yet he missed the intellectual milieu of home. True, Eisenberg was a thriving town, a hub of trade and industry, with its own class of burghers. It had a guild of alchemists, and it was of course famed for its engineers. But despite all this it had no university and exuded all the urban flavour of a large stone walled farm. The locals were cliquey and suspicious of Lock's foreignness, and his efforts to improve the city's hygiene had come to naught. Disease and Lord Death were ever close.

"For He hath delivered me out of all trouble and mine eye hath seen His desire, upon mine enemies." The droning voice of the girl, Sonia Muller, ceased as she completed her recitation of the fifty-fourth psalm. "Is this all I can do to become closer to God?" she asked with a hint of irritation, "saying the psalms?"

Lock picked up his book, a well-illustrated edition of Dante's Divine Comedy, and turned to look at the girl who sat on a stool by the open fireplace. "Yes, child," replied the bishop, "a life of constant prayer, studious learning of the psalms, attending mass, receiving communion, shunning vanity and having constant faith in the Lord. These things will bring you into His Kingdom."

"But," the girl's lip trembled, "I want to be close to God now. I want to feel divine ecstasy like Saint Flora. Is there nothing I can do to hasten the process?"

The bishop placed the book on his reading table and considered the girl. Her round face was the colour of milk. Her high-collared blue satin gown was laced tightly about her throat. She was the fifteen-year-old daughter of the miller, a vassal of Lock's. The miller had presented Sonia to Lock when he had visited to survey the land. Lock had been impressed with her comeliness and literacy. He had suggested to her parents that he might take her on as a student, assuring them that he believed in the education of girls. He had thought he would be glad for the company but perhaps he had made a mistake. She was excessively devout and terribly naive. Lock understood that she had had a sheltered upbringing. *But who did not know that eggs came from chickens?*

"Well," she asked impudently, "how can I get to God now?"

The bishop turned back to idly looking out the window. "There are ways of getting close to heavenly rapture that I have read about in some Augustinian texts. But the rituals, well they are unusual and you had best not worry about them. Prayer and recitation of psalms will be sufficient."

"What are they?" the girl demanded. "What are the rituals? I want to know."

Lock sucked air slowly in through his lips, "I suppose there can be no harm in explaining the theory. You see the Augustinian claimed that the Devil and Hell were not only a being and a place but existed to a certain measure in each of us. God, you see, banished the Devil to Hell and thus things were put into their place and God was happy. The Augustinian believed that by ritualistically sending the Devil to

Hell we could invite God's light within us on this earth."

At the sound of the words *the Devil* the girl's eyes widened with excitement. "Oh teach me the ritual, your Excellency. Teach me."

Countess Greta von Eisenberg stepped from her bedroom onto a colonnaded balcony that overlooked the grounds of the schloss and the wilderland beyond. The warm summer night's breeze ruffled the blue Venetian satin of her long-sleeved gown. It brought with it the smell of damp leaves and horse dung. The night was alive with the sounds of chirping crickets, cooing pigeons, and in the distance, a barking stag. The moon was full, the night was bright and she looked out over the wooded hills that advanced toward the craggy mass of the mountains. A fifth summer was passing, her thirtieth birthday was approaching, and it was yet another year without word from her husband, Peter, away with his soldiers in the south.

True, she had no time for sloth or idleness, and worked to administer the von Eisenberg estates, collecting taxes, giving alms to the poor, and hosting hunts and feasts for the nobility. She kept the king's law, and punished criminals. She should, she supposed, be grateful for her blessings. Her home, the schloss, was a wood frame palace, built by her late father in law to be the seat of the count's power. It contained guest rooms, parlours, stables, and a parade ground. Greta employed a host of servants, cleaners, cooks, footmen, maids and retainers and her husband had given her full power to act in his name. She knew that her wealth and freedom were the envy of others, and yet on nights like this she felt empty. *What was the good of being a dutiful wife if your husband was a distant memory?* Peter had not given her an heir, but it was not the absence of a child that bothered her, it was the loss of her husband's company.

"Help me, by God."

Greta looked down.

A man stood at the foot of her balcony. His hair was a tangled mass of shadow, but in the ailing twilight she could see that he was naked and dirty, and yet his dialect was not that of a peasant.

Heinrich son of Mendel, Exalarch of Eisenberg, lead his donkey along the forest path. The moon was bright and he needed no lantern. He touched the band of red wool around his wrist, a spell against evil. The forest on the night of a full moon was a dangerous place, where spirits walked and the vampires sought their prey. It was good that he knew all the spells, and, as keeper of his people's magic, he spoke the magic tongue of the ancients better than any. He should have no reason to fear, and yet he did. *Perhaps,* he reasoned, *I am just worried because of what I promised my daughter.* But it had to be more than that. His heart told him that this was an ill-fated night.

He made his way along the sandy path, deeper into the dark spaces beneath the trees. A fox crossed several feet in front of him. It turned briefly to look, before darting under the low leaves of a birch. The grunt of a wild boar in the undergrowth startled him and sharp fingers of hawthorn scratched him as he pushed forward toward the light, toward the camp of the Travellers.

The Travellers had first come in the time of Heinrich's great grandfather, Jacob, and Heinrich had heard the story of their coming from his own lips. They had ridden over the mountains bedecked with silk and jewels, selling the finest horses that had ever been seen. Their skin and hair was dark like turned earth. They prayed to deities that were part man, part animal. Jakob had received the right of the king to trade with them, and it was a right that had passed to Heinrich.

Greta was applying leaches to her wrists and ankles to balance her humours when she heard the customary soft knock of her maid on the oak door.

"Enter," she called.

Magda entered and curtseyed.

"Yes, Magda?"

Magda rose, "The man, my lady, he's eaten and bathed."

"Very good, Magda. I trust you have made lodgings suitable to his status?"

"Of course my lady. He... well..." Even in the low light of the beeswax candle Greta could see Magda blush. "We've wrapped him in a blanket but he has no clothes."

"So I saw, Magda. Was he well spoken?"

"Very," said Magda, "He is the son of a nobleman."

"Then give him some of Peter's old things. I doubt whether the loss of a doublet, shirt and hose will bother the master."

"Yes my lady. My lady?"

"What is it Magda?"

"I thought perhaps my lady might like to meet with him. I thought seeing as his lordship had been gone for so long and you were telling me of your melancholic temperament you might wish to keep the stranger company."

Greta felt her spirits lift yet feigned indifference to her maid.

"I suppose it can do no harm. Have a supper of milk and berries arranged."

Heinrich bowed to Zafir, Prince of the Travellers. He held his court outside on a divan of rugs and cushions. Surrounded by his three wives, one a child, one a maiden, and one a woman. His three sons were seated around a nearby fire, one of them playing on a Greek fiddle.

"It pleases me to see you, Heinrich," said Zafir in the tongue of the Travellers. "Be seated."

Heinrich took his place on the rug in front of Zafir.

"You have bought my payment."

"Yes," replied Heinrich in the Germanic tongue of the Jews. "A mark of the emperor's gold." This was how they always spoke, each speaking his own tongue and each knowing enough of the other to understand.

"Would you like to dance with one of my wives?" Zafir weighed the bag of gold in his hand.

Heinrich shook his head. "I shall be happy with naught but a blanket and a place by the fire."

"I take it you are well satisfied with the silk and horses."

"No better is to be found." Heinrich inclined his head.

Zafir ran his fingers through the hair of his second wife. "Yet your face tells me you are worried. There is something you wish to ask me?"

"It's my daughter," replied Heinrich.

"Ah yes, Basha the Beautiful," said Zafir, "hair black as raven feathers, and skin white as falling snow. To be possessed of such a lovely jewel must weigh heavy on a father's heart."

"She has married."

"So I have also heard," said the prince of Travellers. "To Joseph, the miller's son, a good man, but a Christian. They are married and yet they do not yet dwell together. Is it not so?"

Heinrich nodded. "The marriage was held in secret. Joseph had yet to break the news to his parents and now he is missing. He was to meet Basha two nights ago and he has sent no word. Basha is distraught and will neither drink nor eat. Joseph was known as a friend of your folk. Can you tell me anything of his whereabouts?"

Zafir was silent for a moment. "I know not," he said, "But perhaps we should ask my son Jango. He knows Joseph and your daughter well."

Hearing his name, the boy with the fiddle ceased to play.

The handsome teenager bowed to Heinrich. He had not, he explained, seen or heard word of Joseph, but he impressed upon Heinrich that he should consult his mother, the oldest of Zafir's wives. She was a seer of some ability. Perhaps she could offer insight. Heinrich had no objection to white magic and he agreed.

Greta received the man in the small parlour, a room for meetings and gatherings less formal than those held in the large parlour. It was set with a table and cushioned chairs, lit with candles and decorated with a large tapestry. She guessed the man to be in his mid twenties. He was handsome but a little shy.

"You were headed to Buda?" Greta prompted as the man sipped his bowl of strawberries and milk.

The man nodded, meeting her gaze, and licking the milk from his lips. "I am on a quest to bring the word of Luther to the lords of Hungary."

"And how did you come to be wandering about, without clothes, and close to death on my estate?"

"I was joined by two merchants on the mountain road and I shared bread with them but they were terrible scoundrels, brigands. And when they found that they could get no ransom from me they stripped me at sword point, made sport of me, and left me to the mercies of wild beasts. Surely I thought that I must die. But God saw fit to save me and lead me to your house. And for that I bless those scoundrels."

"Is that really what I must do?" asked Sonia.

"You are not compelled to do anything," replied Lock. "I'm simply explaining the theory as it was written by Pithicus the Augustinian."

Sonia seemed glued to the chair by the fireplace. "But does it work? Have you tried it?"

"Oh me?" said Lock, "Oh no, it's much too outlandish for me. I think I will prefer to reach heavenly rapture when Death takes me."

Sonia looked thoughtful, "I want to try," she said. "Will you help me?"

Lock considered her request. "The ritual is dangerous."

"I'm not afraid."

"You must do exactly as I say."

Sonia, tucked her hair behind her ears and straightened her skirts "I am ready."

Lock watched as Sonia removed her undergarments, lifted her skirts, opened her legs, closed her eyes, and placed two fingers at the gates of hell.

"Am I doing it right?"

"You are doing very well," replied Lord Bishop Lock.

Zafir's first wife sat cross-legged opposite Heinrich. She was dressed in red silk and had a gold ring in her nose. She conversed in hushed tones with her husband, and son. Before turning to Heinrich. "What did you see on your way here?"

"A fox, it ran across my path. A pig, I heard it in the bushes. And," Heinrich fell silent as he reviewed his journey. "Hawthorn, I was scratched by hawthorn."

Zafir translated the words to his wife.

She leaned forward, resting her chin on her hand, while her elbow rested on her knee. "Did it draw blood?"

"Yes," replied Heinrich, "yes it did."

"You and your family are in danger," said the seer. "Yester eve young Joseph went to the pines to search for butter mushrooms. There he met a man who had an offer to make. But Joseph refused. He shall be at his father's castle tomorrow. Perhaps he is there now."

Somewhere in the forest an owl hooted.

the following day

Dawn came to Wolfgang Muller with a clap of thunder that seemed to rattle the very stones of his castle. It was accompanied by hammering rain. Wolfgang pushed open the shutters. Rain spattered over his face. He watched as the deluge pelted the ripening wheat that lined the River Eisen.

"Another summer storm?" asked the miller's wife.

"Curse the bewitchment that's befallen us," replied Wolfgang.

The peasants had sharpened their scythes and sickles. But the water had turned the fields to mud and the grain was infested with rot. Wolfgang would have to work in the rain. The granaries must be opened and grain stored. The bakers had to have their flour.

"It's that girl who's to blame," said Frau Muller.

"The girl is a great beauty," said Wolfgang.

"The girl," said Frau Muller, "is a Jewess. Where is our first-born son, Wolfgang? It is the curse of the Jews."

"Joseph liked to visit the shepherds in the Hills," said Wolfgang. "I'm sure he will return safe and sound."

Frau Muller snorted dismissively, "The only time Joseph takes an interest in sheep is when he eats them. He spends his days talking and singing with heathens. He is a godless lad. And we will pay the price."

There was a knock on the door. "Master and mistress," called a voice.

"Come in girl," said Frau Muller.

The milkmaid entered. Her clothes drenched from the rain. She curtseyed to Frau Muller and then addressed Wolfgang. "If you please, master, you had best come right away."

Heinrich, weary from the long walk home, breakfasted with his family, Baba his mother, and Basha his daughter. Breakfast was a Baba speciality, baked eggs, course greens, dark bread, water and redcurrants. As a wealthy merchant Heinrich employed a maidservant to wait on them. But Baba would not hear of anyone else meddling in her kitchen and always prepared the food.

"Glucke paid me a visit last night," said Baba.

"What did that old witch have to say?" Heinrich savoured his goblet of clean rainwater.

"Glucke told me that Johann, that Christian pig who calls himself captain of the guard has been persecuting us. He gave Benjamin a whipping for going out without his cloak and hat and flogged the broom maker's son half to death for leaving his house on the Christian Sabbath. Something really should be done about that man."

Heinrich nodded.

"And," continued Baba as she looked over at her lovesick granddaughter "Glucke, gave me this to give to you." Baba pulled a delicate silver star from her pocket and slid it across the table to Basha who had sat miserably poking at her greens. "It's from Glucke's grandson Soloman. Now I really think its time we told everybody about you're marriage. I can't keep fending off your suitors all day long."

Basha looked up from her bowl and glared at her grandmother.

"Smile, child," said Baba, "a frown will make the fairest face ugly and if the wind changes you'll be stuck with it."

"Grandmother," Basha slammed her spoon down on the table, "You know it's not that simple. Once everybody knows we're married they'll expect us to live together. Joseph would be happy to come and live with us, but it's not the Christian way. But none of this matters anymore. What if he's lost or dead? I need to know where he is and that he's not in some kind of trouble. Father, what did the travellers say?"

Heinrich broke off a hunk of bread. "They said that Joseph would be returning to his family today."

Basha's face broke into a smile. "Thank you father." She rose, and leaving her meal virtually untouched, walked over to him and kissed him on the forehead. "I don't know what I would do if something happened to him or that he stopped to love me. He's not like other Christians, papa. He's so kind and warm." Basha went very pale. "Oh Yahweh," she said and ran from the room.

Heinrich looked over at Baba who had finished her food and was mending one of Basha's dresses. The old woman's eyes connected with her son's.

Heinrich shrugged. "Love makes people act strangely."

"You are an idiot, Heinrich son of Mendel," said Baba, "Basha left the room because she was sick."

"Sick?" replied Heinrich, "sick with what?"

Baba sighed. "How did I raise such an ignorant boy? Your daughter, Heinrich, is with child."

"But," said Heinrich, "They've only just been married."

Baba rolled her eyes. "It has been known for unmarried girls to have children. What did you think all the rush concerning the marriage was all about, a flight of fancy?" Baba tapped her finger against her head and pointed with her other hand at Heinrich. "God help me that I gave birth to such a stupid child. Give thanks to Yahweh that the miller's son, is a decent boy."

Dressed in a long coat of oiled leather, that kept out much of the beating rain, Wolfgang Muller followed the milkmaid to the swampy margins of the river where the milking cows with calf grazed the green grass among the weeping willows.

He saw Joseph, his son, Joseph beloved by all, a boy who had shown no desire for work yet never seemed to go hungry, a boy who spent his days wandering the fields or playing on reed pipes. His broad handsome head, topped with curly brown hair was separated from his body and impaled on a wooden stake. The rest of him lay beneath a willow beside the churning stream.

Peter, count of Eisenberg, led his guest Krum von Gratz up the ladder on to the watchtower's platform. It was built from fresh pine logs and rose above the seemingly endless swampy plain of Hungaria. A fresh breeze carried summer rain from the south, but this did nothing to ward off the mosquitos.

Peter uncorked a jar of wine, took a swig and handed it to his guest, "There it is" said Peter, "the frontier of Christendom."

Krum slapped a mosquito and took a swig of wine. "It's flat as my daughter's chest and as wet as a whore's dingle. Small wonder the Turks don't seem to want it."

Peter laughed. "But Hungaria's the richest kingdom east of France."

"Doesn't stop it from being a glorified swamp," said Krum. "Come and join us on the road to Rome. Frundsberg is rallying the landsknecht and he's promising the emperor's soft Spanish gold."

Peter was silent looking south across the plain. He was a count, and the king of Hungaria was his liege lord, but he was no knight. He was the paymaster and commander of a troop of landsknecht mercenaries, swordsmen and musketeers, brightly clothed soldiers of fortune. He had long ago eschewed fighting from horseback and led his men on foot with sword and pistol. Krum was an agent of the emperor and he was urging Peter to break his oath of fealty.

"Come, Peter, how much is the king paying you to guard this stagnant marsh? Tell me you aren't tired of eating turnips and poaching the king's deer. I don't imagine there are many women to speak of in this wilderness. Aren't you sick of keeping yourself company with your hand while cultivating sinful thoughts about your pageboy? Come with us to Rome. You'll be eating nothing but honeyed lamb and lying between the thighs of the finest whores in Christendom. You can trust me, as a man who's done his pilgrimage to the Holy City I can swear that there are no daughters of joy finer than those employed by the Holy Father."

Peter laughed as he took another swig of wine. "I've missed you, Krum, you old sinner. Do you remember Pavia?"

"I remember we showed those French knights what swords and muskets could do."

"It was Hell," said Peter. "Smoke everywhere, dead horses, dead people, blood, shit, the very worst of which man is capable."

Krum knocked back another cup of wine in a single gulp. "But you were good at it. I've never seen a man use a short sword to that effect. I know what you felt. And when the passion was gone and you were left shaking with blood on your hands you were showered with gold, clothes, women and wine and the priest forgave your sins. The truth is if you really didn't like the blood you would be home with your wife. What's really keeping you here?"

Peter glanced at the ground. He felt a little embarrassed admitting to Krum the true reason he was here. "The priest in Milan I made the confession to after Pavia, I told him, I felt as you said. But I was haunted by the ghosts of all those Christians I had killed. The priest told me I could do good with my killing, that Christendom itself was under threat and I could gain penance for my guilt by fighting a true enemy of God. Do you see that light in the distance? It's naught but an orange flicker."

"I see it."

"That's Belgrade Castle. It sits on a fork between two rivers. It overlooks the endless plain. Once it was an unassailable fastness. From it the lords of Hungaria ruled in God's name. The Muslims rule there now. The church has been made into a temple for demons, and many Christians have been taken to the slave markets of Istanbul. Their soldiers are baptised Christians taken as babes, and trained to fight the enemy of their new God."

Krum spat out his mouthful of wine. "Christ the redeemer. I never took you for a holy fool. You mean you're hanging around here for the good of your damned immortal soul? I'll find a priest in Rome to absolve everything for a very reasonable fee. Hungaria has stood for five hundred years. It'll last a couple more. Come with me Peter. Come with me to wealth and glory."

After taking a long draft of wine Peter handed the jar back to Krum. "You've come a day too late. A herald from the king arrived this morning. The Turks are marching. We must prepare to fight them." The two men fell silent listening to the yelps of jackals, and the cries of swamp birds.

Ibrahim Pasha gasped as he fixed the image of the full moon with his camera obscura. Moons such as this with such brightness, clarity and contour were rare, fleeting, and precious. Ibrahim set to work tracing the moon's outline onto the paper pinned to the wall. Some might find the work tiresome and finicky, but to Ibrahim it was a passion. As Ibrahim worked filling in the shadow of a crater, he thought about how the surface of the moon seemed so close. It truly was a landscape of bleak, battered rock, a distant world circling Earth. Did it have life?

The cough of Addisu, the black eunuch, interrupted his thoughts.

"What is it?" Ibrahim asked.

"The Lady Nuray would like to know if you are to attend her?"

The Lady Nuray, Ibrahim's new highborn wife, had travelled from Konya to join him on the frontier. Perhaps it was the political nature of the marriage that caused Ibrahim to feel estranged from her. Perhaps it was that she was from the arrogant Mirza family who disliked Ibrahim's origins, perhaps it was that he preferred the embrace of his favourite concubine, that surveying the troops with the sultan had made him tired, perhaps he simply wanted to draw the moon. He would not in any case be rushed to bed by the impatience of his wife. "Addisu," said Ibrahim, "have you seen the moon?"

"Yes I can see it from the harem gardens. It is very beautiful, Great Pasha."

"No," Ibrahim became animated pacing around the room, "have you really seen the moon? Do you know what the moon is?"

Addisu sighed, "What should I tell Nuray?"

"Tell her," said Ibrahim, "that it is the holy day of the prophet Isaac. It is surely best that men and women do not lie together on such a day."

some weeks later

Bishop Lock met with Felix the Dominican, known to the townsfolk as the black monk, in his parlour. Lock had given the meeting room atmosphere by decorating it with his collection of prints and painting, most were classically themed with nymphs and goddesses in various states of undress.

The black monk observed the artworks with an expression of disdain. He was an inquisitor who had been sent to Lock with a letter of introduction from his Holiness. Skilled in languages, he had shown himself to be a useful if unpleasant man. He had built a network of children throughout the city and provided him with a stream of information mostly market place gossip.

"Tell me more about the preacher," said Lock.

"He is brazen and shameless," replied Felix. "He preaches to the simple folk in the Square of Flower Sellers as if he has no fear of our wrath. His voice is as sweet as it is poisonous, and he has a comely look to him."

"What does he say?" Lock poured himself a goblet of wine and proffered the jug to Felix, who shook his head in refusal.

"He says that God cares for all and the only way to his mercy is through their own hearts, that men should read the scripture for themselves."

"A noble sentiment." Lock quaffed his wine.

"Jest not," replied the black monk. "He has denounced you by name, and he has described God's Church as 'pagan hubris, materially corrupt and morally degenerate, interested only in money and whoring.'"

Pagan hubris, thought lock, *what a fantastic turn of phrase.*

"The heretic," continued Felix, "is under the protection of the Countess von Eisenberg. He retreats to her schloss in the mountains and the lady's guardsmen will not let me have him."

"The Countess von Eisenberg is offering protection to an itinerant heretic preacher? Do you think she's sharing her bed with him?"

"We are weak," said the black monk, "We need soldiers."

Lock sighed as he thought of the expense, "I suppose we can hire a few more men."

The copper bell clanged as the door to Heinrich's warehouse swung open. Heinrich was a merchant of luxury goods. He stocked an array of various exotic oddments for the wealthy families of the province – bolts of Chinese silk, dowels of Indian sandalwood, nutmeg, French wines, Italian dyes, and sacks of Greek saffron to turn the bishop's goulashes a rich yellow.

The soldiers entered the warehouse. They made no effort to wipe their feet on the mat. Instead, Johann, commander of the City Guard, paused to gaze at Basha who was ascending a ladder to wipe the dust off some jars of Baltic amber. She was dressed in black, but there was something about her, even in the way she wore her mourning clothes, that drew the male eye – her apron pulled tight around her waist, her ankle reaching out from the bottom of her skirts, her arching feet filling the satin topped slippers. From under her pointed black hat, made from stiffened silk, her black hair cascaded over her shoulders and exposed the skin of her neck.

Bahsa turned and gave Johann a sad look.

Johann leered at her before turning away to face Heinrich.

Heinrich bowed. "How may I be of service?"

"Heinrich son of Mendel." It was not a question.

"At your service," replied Heinrich.

"Heinrich son of Mendel," Johann continued as if he had been rudely interrupted, "You are under arrest for the murder of Joseph Muller. You are to come with us to the city keep where you will await trail."

Peter surveyed his troop as they stood to attention, on the grassy plain, awaiting the arrival of the king. Peter commanded four hundred men – two hundred arquebusiers, armed with matchlocks and short swords, a hundred pikemen, and a hundred long-swordsmen. To a landsknecht his clothes were everything, a symbol of his wealth and success. Each soldier was dressed in the most expensive cloth he could afford – floppy blue hats, silver sashes, velvet doublets, knee-high calfskin boots, hose of many colours, emerald green capes and slashed pantaloons. They boasted codpieces of various lengths, widths and colours. Feathers were a prized accessory, and Peter's lieutenant Sokol, champion swordsman, wore five parrot feathers arranged with an opal on his red cap. The warm south wind blew across the fields, a gang of crows alighted on the grass. Peter, Krum and the landsknecht waited.

"Can't he hurry," said Krum to Peter. "The light is ailing and I want to look upon the king before I start for Pest tonight."

"You should stay," said Peter.

Krum shook his head. "Sorry Peter. It's not my war. I fight for Frundsberg and I like my battles followed by fine wine and loose women. And I see neither of those things around here. I've hardly seen a peasant girl. I like cities, with taverns and brothels and there ain't one of them within a hundred leagues of Mohacs."

"Did I not," said Peter, "agree to your terms and to come with all my men to Rome with you, despite the voice of my conscience? You must accompany me to this battle then we shall leave together. I swear that with the gold that the king gives me, I'll get you so drunk at the first town we come to that you won't be able to get pleasure from the maids I provide."

Krum smiled, "I'm sure you would arrange it like that on purpose you stingy bastard son of priest. But when I fight I like to know who it is I'm fighting against and I like to know that I'm going to win."

"Are you admitting to cowardice?"

Krum gritted his teeth. "I am no coward."

The blare of trumpets frightened the flock of crows, and King Lajos of Hungaria rode into view followed by a throng of standard bearers, trumpeters, and heavy knights. He was dressed in plate armour, crisscrossed with gold trim and emblazoned with gold flowers. The king was young and handsome his thick brown hair rolled onto his shoulders. Behind the king rode the lords of Hungaria and Bohemia, encased in burnished plate, emblazoned with the sigils of their houses and holding steal lances topped with fluttering pendents.

"King of Croatia, King of Hungaria, King elector of Bohemia," cried a herald.

First Peter and Krum knelt, then the landsknecht followed.

"Welcome Count Peter von Eisenberg," said the king, his voice a little weaker than Peter had expected. "You may rise."

Ibrahim Pasha unravelled the linen wrapping of the package and drew out the book. He ran his fingers over its leather cover, before carefully opening its yellowing pages. And there they were, carefully written in flawless calligraphy, illustrated with exquisite miniatures, the rubayart of Omar Khayyam. The possession of the book sent a shiver of delight through Ibrahim Pasha. He opened the book and read:

On the soft green grass I lie
Between the desert and the ripening rye
Where name of slave and sultan is unknown
I pity the emperor on his throne

There was something defiant, even blasphemous about the poetry and yet it reminding Ibrahim of a time and place where there were no duties, but there was a freedom. He read another.

Oh fill the cup, with heady wine
Oh time is ever flowing on
Yesterday unborn and dead tomorrow
Savour today for it is sweet

A shadow fell over his book. He turned to see who had disturbed him. Adisu stood in the doorway.

"Great Pasha," he said, "the fires in your room have been lit. Your wife awaits your company."

Guilt racked Ibrahim. He had spent all day listening to petitions in the muggy heat and arbitrating on petty matters like where one peasant's field ended and another's began. He had listened for hours to Emre's diatribe about Christians dodging their specific dues, and then to the allocation of houses to Muslim migrants from the east. By the time he had finished listening to and then signing off a long report on the province's taxes, he was exhausted and all he wanted to do was eat Iranian dates, drink an impious glass of wine and read Khayyam. *Was that too much to ask?* He did not know why he considered spending the evening with his wife to be more work but somehow it felt like it. "Tell her," said Ibrahim, "that it is the holy night of the prophet Jesus. Men and women must surely not lie together on such a night."

The Battle of Mohacs and the Day of Love,
The 29th of August, the middle of the week,
Year of the Lord 1526

Heinrich ran his finger along the iron manacle that chained his leg to an iron ball. The dungeon in the city keep had one window, a slit in the rock that gave just enough light to discern the contours of the stone walls. The cell was filled with damp hay and a gutter ran along its edge into which the prisoners could relieve themselves, yet the jailor's bucket never seemed to contain enough water to wash away the muck. The dungeon therefore had a stench that Heinrich found difficult to endure. The jailor fed the prisoners cabbage and turnip gruel once a day, poured from a jug into shallow iron bowls.

Hans the cutpurse, manacled to the wall, rattled his chains as he gabbled. "They'll hang you. Sometimes your neck breaks and you die easy, but sometimes you'll be strangled, then you die slow. Either way you'll kick your heals in the Dance of Lord Death and sometimes it takes awful long. But I don't imagine my neck would be that strong. How about you, Jew? The captain said I'd be headed to the stocks again, but you, you'll be straight for the hanging tree, dangle, dangle, dangle." He grinned.

"I'm going to trial," said Heinrich, "I'll be found innocent."

"Innocent, innocent," Hans laughed, spitting and coughing as he tried to keep talking between his sobs of mirth. "Trial? An innocent Jew? Old Captain Johann he'll come down with a pair barber's clamps to pull a few of your teeth and you'll spit out a confession along with your blood. Innocent is no good to him. If it's not your head impaled on North Gate, then he'll have to find another to take its place and that won't suit him. The townsfolk need their sport, one to throw the pig slops at, and another to hang. Everybody likes to see a Jew swing. Because they eat the flesh of Christian babes. People like to know that something is being done. The folk know there is nothing like a dead Jew to bring them a few weeks of hot dry weather. I've heard it said by a gentleman that you folk will eat a Christian babe when the the fancy takes you."

The wooden door squeaked like a rat as it was shoved open.

Captain Johann the jailor, and a guardsman, entered. "Let's get this over with," said Johann, "I wouldn't want to be late for the countess's feast." They unlocked Hans' manacles and then marched him out of the keep.

The Captain turned to look at Heinrich before he closed the door. His look reminded Heinrich of a mural painted on a merchant's house, cats chasing mice; one of the cats had had a particularly greedy and savage expression.

In the long silence that followed, Heinrich's thoughts changed from relief that the irritating and unnerving rants of the cutpurse were over for good to an odd nostalgia for the time when there was at least some conversation in the dungeon. Just as he was about to say something the other prisoner spoke.

"Hey, Jew, Rat-Face is right. Innocent is no good to Sir Codpiece. He'll see you hang. Now I've seen that silver you gave to Sag-Belly the Jailer to keep you comfortable so you can lay down and stretch properly, and the manacle not so tight as to chafe your ankle. What say you drop a few groats for old Harold here and get them to loosen my manacle, just a fingers breadth. That's all I'm asking."

Sonia Muller, studying the ways of God under the good Bishop Lock until her comfortably distant wedding day, sat in the kitchen eating a slab of bread and butter, and thanked her good fortune that she had escaped the tower in which her mother had kept her for so many years. The cook, a sturdy old woman, leaned over a large cauldron filled with beefy broth.

The part of Sonia's body that she thought of as Hell ached with a constant, yet oddly pleasant pain. Hell was a much larger part of her than she had at first imagined and the gates of Hell had been so engorged by ritual practice that the Devil could no longer easily enter. But the bishop had showed her that the administration of sacred oil used for baptism and unction could be used to smooth his passage.

The practice of helling, as she called it, had changed her life. She felt the ecstasy of God several times a days, and even more often at night. The bishop had shown her that he didn't even need to be there, and she could experience ecstasy on her own by arousing the fires of Hell. It was all she seemed to be doing, helling. She would start to memorise a new prayer, forget what she was memorizing a few minutes later, then start to think of helling. She would feel the prickle of Hell and then her hand would slip under her skirts and she would begin to feel the grace of God enter her body. How did people who did not know about this ritual exist?

Sonia was thinking about helling while she reached for a small bowl of fresh milk that the cook had left by the fire. But before Sonia could get her hand close to the bowl, Cook bought her stirring spoon down with a crack on her knuckles.

"Ouch," said Sonia, "what was that for?"

"Are you trying to ruin us you worn down millstone?" Cook always talked like that. Even though Sonia's parents were rich, Cook knew that she wasn't really a lady. Sonia had noticed that since the helling had begun Cook's language had got more colourful. But every time Sonia asked, *what's a hussy?* or *what do you mean by a well-worn-shoe?* Cook would throw up her hands and say, Christ, never you mind, child. Sonia had stopped asking.

"What do you mean? I just fancied a bit of milk?"

"You did? Well that milk is not for you, so keep those sinful little hands of yours off it."

"Well who's it for then?"

"Who's it for? You really know nothing do you, you little sword sheath."

"You know Cook, my mother kept me in a tower to keep me pure."

"Well a fine job she's done," said Cook, "that milk is for the heinzelman."

"Heinzelman?"

"The house elf," said Cook, "a glass of warm milk placed by the fire is all he needs and he'll chase away mice, rats and other vermin and if I've forgotten anything he'll take care of it. But if somebody else drinks his milk or he gets none, or thinks I'm paying him, he'll cause a terrible disturbance. The milk will go sour, the goulash will burn and we will become infested by fleas."

"Really," said Sonia, "and he lives in the house? What does he look like?"

"About a foot high, knobbly as an old tree, skinny as a hungry cat, and ugly as a leper."

"Gosh," said Sonia, "so…"

Sonia's question was interrupted by a knock on the kitchen door. "Come in,"

The kitchen maid curtseyed as she entered. "A visitor," she said, "for Lady Sonia."

"For me?" asked Sonia, "but who would want to visit me?"

Countess Greta von Eisenberg was bored. The feast, held on the terraced cherry orchard behind the schloss, had been her idea. But now that it had come to fruition it seemed dull. The noblemen and women and their households had arrived on horseback or in carriages.

They were for most part village landlords and their ladies. One or two them controlled an old castle, but most could afford a few horses cattle and servants. Under the king's law they were Greta's vassals and owed her rents and allegiance, which she in turn owed to the king. They were bound to bare arms, trained to fight on horseback with lance and sword, though not all could afford full plate armour. These men and their ladies were the basis of the provinces law and order and it was important that they respected Greta's authority.

Fortunately Greta knew how to keep them onside. Everybody loved a feast and she had the best feasts – swans stuffed with prunes, herbs and honey, saffroned pigeon eggs, peppered eels, and live finches encased in pies, ready to fly free on it being sliced. This was all washed down with foreign wine and local ale.

The first round had finished. And some guests had left the table to relieve themselves in the freshly dug effluent trench, or wander drunk beneath the cherry trees. Others pushed back their seats, belched or snoozed. A group of women gossiped amongst themselves, eating honeyed hazel nuts while getting steadily drunker. One of Greta's serving maids had to dodge the groping hands of a drunk guest. It was the time of relaxation and digestion before the dancing. And the Travellers, dressed in their exotic silks and baring their Turkish fiddles, had just arrived to provide the music. Greta meanwhile was entertaining the attentions of two men neither of which she liked.

"We should be sniffing out the lair of these brigands from the east that have made a home in our woods, sending our men in and bringing them to justice," said, Friedrich. He was Peter's twenty-four year old brother, and following his father's death and Peter's absence, the senior male of the local nobles. His interests were hunting, drinking and reading French courtly love dramas, which might have had something to do with his decision to treat Greta as an object of his undying love. She felt a little ashamed that she had at one time encouraged him, for now she had a real secret lover Luke, the Lutheran preacher.

"You're an idiot and you should stick to hunting boar," said Johann. Johann was the captain of the city guard and Peter's cousin, coming from a line of younger sons, he was ill favoured by Fortune, had lost out on inheritance and lived off his military salary. Where Friedrich's attentions were irritating, Johann's were unnerving. He was cruel, desperate and yet seemingly afraid of women.

Greta drifted off, her mind wandering to her lover, the way he held her firm against the wall and kissed her neck. It was, of course, an illicit coupling and only the loyal Magda who served the preacher his bread and milk and lit his nightly candle knew of the servant's passage through which he passed to her bedroom.

Frederic shifted in his chair, "Oh look. Here he comes."

Greta looked over to see whom Friedrich had referred. A man approached the table. He was dressed in a black cowl with the hood thrown back. He had dark tonsured hair, a silver medallion around his neck and an expressionless face. He looked relatively old, and Greta guessed him to be past his fortieth year. *Who comes to a party dressed like Lord Death?*

Frederick waved cheerfully, "Brother Felix, welcome. " He turned to Greta. "Do you know Brother Felix the Dominican? He's fantastic. He's been everywhere and speaks every language under the sun."

"You mean the bishop's foreign necromancer," cut in Johann.

"The black monk," murmured Greta.

"I hope you don't mind me inviting him," said Friedrich, "he seemed most desirous of coming."

"Hush," said Greta, "he arrives."

Frederick rose to greet the monk, which he did warmly, then introduced him to Greta who reluctantly allowed him to kiss her ring.

"I have heard so much of your magnanimity, virtue and beauty I had to acquaint myself with you." The monk's Germanic was stiff but his allocution and polite manner clearly impressed Friedreich who beamed at them both.

Johann glared. His obvious irritation at the monk's presence made Greta warm a little to Felix and she invited him to sit.

"Frederic tells me you are something of a world traveller. Perhaps you could tell us something of your travels."

"I suppose I could," replied the monk. As he seated himself, Greta noted the medallion. It was large and valuable, depicting a leafy branch, a crucifix, and a sword. His face was carefully shaven. It was odd, thought Greta, to see a man without the framing of his beard.

"Yes," said Friedrich, "regale us with a story of your voyages. Do e wine? Here take this goblet."

Sonia's visitor, Basha, was a Jew. Even Sonia could see that. Her black robes and pointed hat marked her as one. Her wrists and ankles were delicate, her face was smooth and pale and her eyes large and dark. They sat in a corner of the kitchen and whispered.

"I'm sorry," the visitor wiped her teary eyes on her cloak, "to be the barer of such ill news."

"Be not sorry," Sonia reached out to touch her visitor's hand and comfort her, "I am grateful. I have lost a brother but have gained a sister. And my mother saw fit to tell me nothing of it."

"Tell me," said Basha, "I am surprised at your indifference. Did you not know, Joseph, your brother, well?"

"In truth, sister, though I loved him, I knew him only by memories. I was allowed no visitors in the tower."

"I find that sad," said Basha. "he was most gentle. Tears formed again in the corners of her eyes and she choked on her words as she spoke. "Will you help me?"

"Of what help can I be?" asked Sonia, "I am of little consequence and less wisdom, all I know is books, prayers and needle work."

"You have the ear of the bishop. He has power. Tell him they have pinned the murder on my father Heinrich son of Mendel. Plead with him to intervene. I believe the bishop knew my father. He is our only hope."

"Oh, sister, I shall try."

"Many thanks," Basha rose from the stool and adjusted her hat, "I must depart and attend to my duties. My kinsman waits for me."

"Before you go," said Sonia low and urgent.

"Yes."

"Will you come and visit me again?"

Basha smiled. "I should like that. I shall come whenever I am able. I am at your service."

Felix refused the wine and began his story. "I am the bastard son of an Iberian lord, and having nothing to inherit, I joined the ancient order of Saint Dominic. But in the monastery I was tempted by youthful sin and was seduced by a woman, so caught up were we in our sin, that the abbot caught us. I expected punishment but none so great as that which was given to me."

Felix paused. "I was sent to sea on a ship bound for India. There are men who are willing to risk dangers barely imaginable to bring back a ship of spice, wealth assured for all time. That was my punishment, a journey to take God to distant lands. South, south went the ship to kingdoms where there is no winter. There is no dawn and no dusk for the sun seems to disappear and appear at the edge of the horizon in an instant. The men there are black as pitch and inhabit great festering jungles filled with birds and beasts most strange. I know not how many days I spent on that ship lulled to sleep each night by the waves and woken each morning to the ringing of the quartermaster's bell, eating nothing but salted fish, and yams bought from feathered kings. Foul winds and icy nights did we endure in the vast southern ocean. Whales and sea serpents writhed around our ship, singing and diving. It seemed to me a miracle that we at length came India, to the fortress of my countrymen at Cannanore.

"No sooner though had we arrived than our fortress was put under siege. The old king, friendly to our traders, had died and the new ruler desired to expel us. As Fortune would have it the fortress was strong and well stocked with muskets, powder and shot, and protected with heavy cannon. Again and again the Indians attacked, and I saw the mighty war elephants that are talked of in antiquity, but they could not penetrate our walls. The dead filled the trenches and the siege went on. Food ran scarce. Men dropped from sickness and starvation. All would have perished had God not saved us with a storm so fierce that many lobsters were washed ashore and even within the fort. Thus we ate the flesh of lobsters and survived until the king's fleet relieved us. So ends the tale of my first voyage, and I hope your ladyship will judge it with favour. But more wonderful and terrible things befell me before I returned home."

"You tales are wonderful." Greta clapped. "I insist that you remain here as my guest until I have satisfied my curiosity about all the lands you have visited."

It was lightly raining as the grey day turned to a colourless evening. The constant rolling crash of the Turkish cannons and the crack of their heavy muskets covered the wet flat ground with a mist of alchemical smoke.

Everybody seemed to be dead. Krum was dead. Three of every four men he had known were dead or dying. There were piles of them and the sound of their agony filled the silences between the shots. Peter stood above the body of Krum. He had been shot through the neck in the first enemy volley and had slumped to the ground beside Peter as blood poured out of him on to his ermine cloak. If the bullet had flown two spans to the right it would have been Peter. A boy lay bleeding to death, propped up against two corpses, slashed by a scimitar. He groped his open belly. Peter knew him. He was one of his men, a candle maker's son from Eisenberg. Peter cut his throat with a quick, piteous slash of his sword.

"The king has fled." It was the rasping voice of Captain Sokol, the champion swordsman. His face, hands and sword were covered with blood. "Do you hear that?"

Beneath the moans of the dying another sound emerged, a gentle rumbling which seemed to rise up from the earth beneath them. And as the rising wind cleared the hanging wafts of smoke in the darkening sky Peter saw a mass of advancing horsemen.

"The sipahi," said Sokol, "faster than a Christian knight, they will skewer us, slice us, they will fill us with arrows, and any who live will be enslaved."

Peter felt fear, fear that he would die. He felt grief for slain friends, and relief, relief that it would soon be over. But beneath the turmoil he felt something else, wonder. The mighty kingdom of Hungaria, bulwark of his world, was no more. The great plain now belonged to the Muslims, all the way to the mountains of Germania.

"We must run," said Sokol, "run or die."

Greta opened the secret door to her bedroom and ushered Luke inside.

"How went the feast?" asked Luke.

"Dull for the most part," replied, Greta, "but things heated up at the end. Friedrich drank too much wine and vomited halfway through professing his love for me. Johann started to beat one of my maids with his horsewhip, so I had to send him home. Herr Bergman was caught trying to sneak a barrel of wine off to his carriage. Herr Schwazborg left his wife at home and took Frualine Messer into the bushes. Frau Sudstern took her shoes off and danced on the table and her husband fell off his horse."

"It sounds like mayhem," said Luke. "I pray that you are not too worn out to receive me."

"No," said Greta, "I have been burning to see you all night."

"Well then I am happy," said the preacher, "and look what I have brought us." Luke reached into his sack and pulled out two large red apples. "The first of the season."

Greta sat on edge of her bed. It was turned from white hazel, laid with goose down, and covered with satin sheets and woollen blankets.

She began by biting off some of the apple to expose its flesh. She then loosened the laces of her gown so that she could slide the love apple into her bosom. She used the apple to wipe up the sweat from under her breasts, then rubbed it under armpits. At length she manouvered the apple between her legs and infused it with her full flavour.

They exchanged apples. Greta bit into hers and savoured the taste of her lover's fresh sweat.

Bishop Lock released the Devil from Hell and let out a sigh as the Devil shuddered and released his load of angel-blood.

"Why do angels have white blood," asked Sonia as she rolled on to her back, and began to rub the angel-blood onto her thighs and belly.

"Because their souls are pure," said Lock as he pulled on his dark blue tights.

"Tell me about the rivers of Hell," said Sonia, "I have always imagined Hell to be quite a dry place but I have discovered through the rituals you have taught me that, though it has fire, it is quite wet."

"A common misconception," said Lock, "the rivers of Hell..."

Sonia started to cry as she raised herself up on the side of the bed.

"Oh child, what's wrong?"

"I'm sorry," Sonia dried her eyes on the edge of the bed sheet. "It's just been so amazing and I couldn't help but wonder. Have you, have you performed the ritual of Hell on, on other girls?"

"Oh no," said Lock. "I have always performed the ritual of the Devil alone. I have known of this ritual only in theory. I give thanks to God that I have been allowed to teach it to you."

Sonia began to sob again but she could not suppress the smile that spread across her face "I give thanks to God for that as well. Lord Bishop?"

Countess Greta von Eisenberg lay on her back, her knees pressed to her breasts, and the soles of her feet pushed against his chest, while he loved her. She had no desire to bare a child to anyone other than her absent lord and husband. A pregnancy would create a scandal that would ruin her, and witches' remedies for the swelling belly were dangerous. Thus to protect herself during the nightly visits from her lover, Greta employed a special trick taught to her by her family's old nurse, a piece of pigs bladder stretched around a loop of willow, inserted into her womanly flesh, would capture men's seed, and it could be removed with a weaving hook.

She felt the ecstasy building inside her constricted body. She cried out as she shuddered and released.

"I think," Luke whispered, "that I am the happiest man alive. For I feel that I love you more than I love myself."

Greta laughed softly. "You sound like one of the characters in one of Friedrich's French romances."

"but I truly feel it," said Luke, "since I have found you, everyday feels like a blessing from God."

"I love you too," said Greta and she bit his ear. "The black monk arrived at my house today. He was most interesting."

She felt him pull away from her. He withdrew from the embrace and sat on the edge of the bed. "What did he want?"

"Only to make my acquaintance. He has been to India and further. I insisted he stay here as my guest."

Luke glanced quickly around the room as if he expected the inquisitor to jump out from any corner.

Greta laughed and sat up in the bed pulling herself over to her lover, kissing his neck. "Do you trust me so little that you think I would have you ambushed while in my arms? Have you forgotten everything that I have told you about my family, about my prayers and wishes? We will expel Lock and take the Church lands. We will print bibles and reform the beliefs of the people. I invited the inquisitor to stay because I do not want him to leave."

Luke turned to kiss her on the lips then whispered in her ear. "Eisenberg will be the spark, which starts a wildfire that will engulf Christendom. And God will reward the righteous and you shall be a just and saintly queen."

"Stop it," Greta withdrew her face from Luke's searching lips, and playfully slapped his face. "I'm just the ruler of a wealthy little county, I'll settle for incorporating the Church lands into mine."

She felt Luke's hands slide up her thighs, "We should act now. I have many followers among the townsfolk. Some are ready to revolt."

Greta allowed herself to tumble onto her back. "We must wait, the nobles are not yet certain."

Sonia lay on her back, watching the candlelight play on the patterns that adorned the bed canopy when she broke into tears again.

"What is it now, my sparrow?" asked Lock.

"Today, I learned that I have gained a sister and that I have lost a brother." Sonia began to wipe her eyes on the bed sheet. "He was murdered and cut into pieces." Sonia began to sob. When I heard the news I didn't really think it hurt me, but the more I think about it the more it does. And I feel so sorry for my poor sister to have her husband taken from her and her father, wrongly accused, is to hang for it. It is all so terrible. I promised her I would ask you for help."

Lock sat up beside Sonia and put a comforting arm around her. "I shall do all that is in power to remedy the wrong. Tell me of the accused."

"His name is Heinrich son of Mendel."

"What!" Lock failed to hide his surprise, "Heinrich son of Mendel is to be hung for murder?"

"You know him?"

"Yes." Heinrich was the exarlarch of the Jews of Eisenberg, he was their leader and a successful merchant. Lock had sought out Heinrich on a tip from Archbishop of Buda. Lock had expressed his intentions to protect the Jews from persecution and had proposed an arrangement. God's law prevented the Church from lending money but the emperors law allowed it of the Jews. Lock could make interest from his treasury if he secretly used Jewish agents. Lock had found Heinrich to be learned, and cautious if a little superstitious. He had enjoyed the exalarch's company and had been looking forward to their next meeting. "You may sleep with peace," said Lock, "knowing that I shall not let this injustice go unchallenged."

"And will you find the truth about who killed my brother?" asked Sonia.

"I promise I shall find out the truth, my sparrow, I shall leave no stone unturned." Lock's fingers strayed to cross that hung around his neck. "I swear it."

two weeks after the battle

Bishop Lock sat at his oiled oak desk in his personal library. It consisted mostly of printed books, Anselm of Aosta's *The Monology, Being and Essence*, a Florentine print edition of Lucretius's *On the Nature of Things*, and a 1492 Venetian printing of *the Decameron*, among others. But he also had a beautiful and valuable collection of hand written, illuminated, vellum manuscripts some hundreds of years old. On the bishop's desk lay an assortment of articles – a silver candle holder, a lacquer tinder box, a sheaf of stiff Nuremberg paper, a glass ink pot, a raven feather quill, a lump of black sealing wax, a gold signet ring, a sliver letter opener, a pair of Turkish spectacles, and three unopened letters.

The bishop held up the first letter to the candlelight. It was adorned with the seal of Pope, Clement VII. Lock carefully levered the seal off the paper keeping it undamaged to add to his collection. Lock considered his Holiness, as he unfolded the letter. He liked Clement. The pope had little interest in theology, but was something of a humanist with an obsession for power, and an eye for fine women. He had a ridiculously long strait nose that gave his Holiness the appearance of some kind of goblin. Lock read. *I have heard disturbing reports that the Lutheran heresy has taken root among the nobles of Eisenberg. So that you may be most effective in stamping out this rot I have made arrangements for a troop of Swiss Guard to be sent to your service, fifty pike, and fifty musket. See that they are appropriately paid and garrisoned. Brother Felix the Dominican is to command.*

Lock tapped his fingers on the table. So Felix had been reporting directly to Clement and was asking for experienced mercenaries, all no doubt to Lock's cost. In a way Lock was happy that papal soldiers were on their way, he supposed he needed them, but he felt uncomfortable with the way things were escalating. *What was Greta thinking, taking an interest in criminal heresies?*

The second letter was from the Archbishop of Buda. *The gates of our great city have been thrown open to the infidel Turks, who paraded through the streets before lodging themselves in the houses of the noblemen. I am grateful to God that the Turks have not sacked the city or defiled our places of worship. But my heart is heavy with a great looming fear. As I write these hurried words in the darkness of my house Janos Zapolya bends the knee to Suleiman. Hungaria becomes a vassal of Istanbul. The black shadow of the Devil has fallen across Christendom.*

No more will the true Church collect tithes from the faithful nobles instead they will pay homage in gold and blood to the sultan. I urge you on behalf of all Christians prepare yourself, for the oldest enemy himself will soon be banging on the doors of your own city...

"Your Excellency," Sonia rushed into the room, interrupting his reading, "It is time for our afternoon ritual."

Lock folded the letter in front of him, and pushed out of his mind the vision of shrieking infidel warriors. "So it is."

"Have you," asked Sonia, "come across any of the other holy rituals associated with helling?"

"Yes," replied Lock after a short hesitation, "I once read a most secret holy manuscript, written by Saint Jared the Black in the time of Charlemagne. He describes that holy ecstasy, with God entering both man and woman, may be attained orally."

"Really," said Sonia.

"Yes indeed," continued the bishop "The details were passed to saint Jared in a dream in which he was visited by the angel, Laliel, who described to him its particulars."

"Have you found the killer of my brother yet?" asked Sonia.

"Not yet my sparrow, not yet."

Countess Greta Von Eisenberg, cut open the seal of Ferdinand Hapsburg, duke of Vienna, and read the Letter. *My dear Greta it is my solemn duty to inform you of the catastrophe that has occurred. The Lajos king of Hungaria has been slain and Turks are overrunning his kingdom. To all accounts Peter your husband did not survive the battle but died bravely in defence of the kingdom. The county of Eisenberg now passes to you. I have claimed the Kingdom of Bohemia for the emperor and hope that you will offer your allegiance to us so the we may offer you protection against the Turks...*

The letter went on, but Greta placed it on her desk and taking a handkerchief from draw dried the tears that had begun to well in her eyes. Peter was dead.

Peter stared at the peasant men that faced him. They were sallow, coughing and watching the landsknecht with weary, starving eyes. Soldiers on either side of the group stood with swords drawn and muskets shouldered.

"Two more stringy chickens and two more sacks of turnips. That's all we could find. It won't go far but it will fill the men's bellies tonight," said Captain Sokol, as two men threw the looted vegetables and slaughtered birds on top of the small heap that was growing in the village square.

Peter felt pity for the peasants. But what was a troop of fleeing mercenaries to do? His men had searched the village stripping it of any hidden food, or scraps of silver. They had separated the men from the women. The men were here in the open square in front of him. The women were held in the communal village chicken coop.

"You may as well kill this lot and be done with it," said Sokol, Peter's Leutenent. "Hearing the screams of your women folk while they're ravaged will drive a man mad, and hunger is a terribly painful way to die. You'd be doing the right thing by them and saving yourself much trouble if you just cut all their throats, three by three."

"I've seen enough blood in the last few days. There will be no rape and there will be no executions."

"Don't ask me to stop it. I value virtue, my lord, but I value my skin more."

Peter shuddered for a moment, then turned to face his sullen looking men. "I am your lord and paymaster. Anyone of you who rapes or kills any of these Christian folk will hang from the village oak. If you see a girl to your liking than you may ask to marry her." Peter turned back to address the peasants in broken Hungarian. "I am Peter, Count von Eisenberg and I am merciful. You shall surrender to us your stores and valuables but we shall leave you with your lives and your honour."

Basha sat with her grandmother, Baba, in the kitchen while they ate chicken and turnip soup.

"Did I ever tell you the story of Little Jan Tovich?" Baba asked as she sucked some of the soup from her wooden bowl.

"I don't think so," said Basha as she looked sadly into her own bowl. Usually she loved Baba's chicken soup but on that night she missed her father, and she grieved for Joseph and her appetite had gone.

"If you want that baby in your tummy to keep growing, you'd better eat something," said Baba. "Little Jan's family, they wouldn't have said no to a bowl of chicken soup. Do you know the story of Little Jan?"

Basha shook her head.

"It was a year like this one. It had been a wet summer, a lean winter and a hungry spring. Jan had a sister and mother and a father. And his father he went hunting and caught a hare. He took it home to his wife and asked her to cook it for him. So his wife put the hare into the pot. She had a few things saved away, a pinch of Russian salt, a cut of wild parsley, some leaves of spring garlic, and even one droopy little turnip. Into the pot it all went.

"Now as the soup began to boil and then to simmer, its aroma filled the good woman's nostrils and she thought to herself, it is very near ready, and I had better just taste the hare to make certain sure it is soft. And soft it was. She was very hungry and she thought she had better taste more to make sure it was soft all over and before long she had tasted it all away. All of a sudden she realised what she had done. There would be no food for her husband or her children, and she was sure that her husband would give her a terrible beating. So she called out to little Jan, and when the boy came into the kitchen, she cut his throat, skinned him, gutted him and threw him into the pot. The good man enjoyed his super very much and so little Jan was eaten by his father and that was the end of him."

"Grandmother," said Basha, "that's a horrible story. Is that supposed to give me my appetite back?"

"It's supposed to warn you," said Baba, "about what people are capable of when they're hungry enough. Now something is on your mind that you're not telling me. Now, spit it out and eat your soup."

"Captain Johan..."

Baba chewed back a mushy turnip with her toothless gums. "That man is a steaming pile of pig shit," she said.

"Grandmother, maybe he can be reasoned with. Maybe there is something he wants."

"What he wants," said Baba, pointing a chicken bone at her granddaughter, "is to get inside your cunny. And once he's used you foully he'll have your father dance the gibbet just the same. I know his type. Don't think about visiting that pig eating brute."

"But, grandmother, could he not be tempted by some of Papa's gold."

"You listen to me, child," said the old woman. "I was once a pretty wee slip of a thing like you. One year the harvest was bad, the folk were hungry, and then there was a pox. It was a bad year. And I tell you when the times are good the Christians are filled with smiles and silver for your wares. But when the times are hard something changes in them. They look at you like it was you to blame, even though you may be hungry too. They become like animals, beasts, and he who once would smile at you on the street will spit at you and call you a witch and a Christ killer. He'll take from you everything he can and he'll give nothing back. Now eat up your soup, child, and for the love Yahweh don't look at it like that. There are no bits of babies floating around in it. I have no mind to prove Christian nonsense true."

Peter was cleaning his teeth with a stick, when Sokol entered his tent accompanied by a dirty weaselally looking villager.

"He insisted on coming to see you," said Sokol, "says he has something for your ears alone."

"Very good," said Peter, "what have you to tell me?"

The peasant fell on to his knees. "I wanted to thank you my lord, for the mercy you showed to our village. In exchange I bring tidings of interest."

"I'm listening," said Peter.

"I was wandering in the woods this morning. I poach rabbits on the king's land. Now the forest, lakes and hunting grounds there belong to the Turks."

"Go on," said Peter.

"When I went up to the forest this morning, I saw a pavilion. It was like something from a dream, cloth so light, and so bright a colour I've never seen. And there was a Turkish lord, richer than any Christian I've laid eyes upon. It was like his body was covered in gold and gemstone. He was hunting. He had men with him, but not so many. I would think, if a noble, Christian warrior like you were to ambush him you would win enough wealth to buy your heart's desire. I can lead you there. I know the path."

As the man fell silent the late summer rain blew from the north, and the sound of a hungry, crying baby carried through the rickety village.

Ibrahim Pasha sat in his tent, enjoying the warmth of the night. What a fantastic idea to survey the newly won lands, hunt in its plentiful forests, and dispense charity to its suffering poor. A slave entered and prostrated himself before Ibrahim

"Here it is master," the slave pushed forward a black lacquer box, "the finest Persian hashish, infused with sugar and rosewater."

The heady aroma of the intoxicating resin filled Ibrahim's nose. A quiver of excitement ran through him. He took one of the dark round balls and put it into his mouth. The sugar and rosewater did little to mask the oily, dirty flavour of the hash but Ibrahim quickly swallowed.

The slave poured him tea. He watched as the red liquid swirled in the glass cup.

Ibrahim had lost track of time. He was walking in the forest when he realised that the hashish had been fully digested. This realisation came simultaneously with the revelation that he needed to write more. There were so many things in the world that needed to be illuminated – Ibrahim's own journeys and discoveries, the battle against the Christians, his observations of the moon. Future generations might read what he had written. What greater legacy could he have than that? With this firmly in his mind Ibrahim set off back toward his tent.

He did not at first see the slight, elegant figure that hastened to intercept him.

"Where, Great Pasha, do you go with such urgency?"

Ibrahim looked at her in the moonlight through hashish-glazed eyes. She was indeed beautiful, this long dark haired princess of the distant Anatolian steppe, Nuray, Bright Moon.

"My prince." She held out her hand to stroke his face. "I have waited many nights for you. Will you not come to me now."

Ibrahim wished he could say yes, but the hashish had quelled his manly spirit and sent a thousand voices of devilish doubt into his mind. "Nuray," he whispered, "Tonight is the holy night of Fatima the wife of the prophet. Tonight I can not come to you, but by the Beard of Mohamed, tomorrow I shall come to you, I swear it, by all that is holy."

the next day

Bishop Lock, accompanied by his thuggish chief retainer, Steffen, walked past the prison tower, the city guard barracks and to the doors of Johann's house. The steward admitted them to the parlour, a tasteless room filled with hunting trophies, where the captain was sharpening an Italian style rapier. Lock took a chair opposite Johann. Steffen remained standing.

"Of what service can I be to you, Lord Bishop?" Johann asked sullenly.

Steffen's hand closed around the pommel of his own sword.

"You have not complied with my orders to release Heinrich the Jew," replied Lock. "I have come to collect him."

Johann placed the whetstone on the stool beside him and began to inspect the blade. "The Jew is sentenced to death for the murder of the miller's son. I cannot simply let him go free. It is my duty to keep order in the city. I can not let confessed murderers loose."

Lock caught a whiff of stale sweat. By the wood of the true cross, Johann stank. *Did the man never wash?* "I believe Heinrich to be innocent. By the grace of my rank I command you to realise him."

Johann slammed his sword between the flagstones of the floor. "No. I am sworn to the counts of Eisenberg and to the king. Not the bishop. If you want the Jew released take it up with the countess."

Lock was taken aback. He had not expected that Johann would openly defy him. He was shocked by the sudden challenge to his power, and acutely aware that the neighbouring barracks housed soldiers that answered to Johann. "Forgive my presumption captain, but allow me to ask for your account of the murder?"

Johann got up from his seat and began to pace the room. "The Jew's daughter was to be married to Joseph the miller's son. The Jew disapproved of the marriage and killed the boy to prevent it in the evil manner of his people. He was seen on the morning of the night of the murder leaving the city in the direction of Muhlborg and the forest road leading a donkey. His daughter arranged a meeting with the miller's son, but instead of his whore he met his death. The Jew then beheaded him loaded him onto the donkey and left the boy's remains by his father's house."

"Why would Heinrich risk discovery by carrying the remains to Herr Muller's house?"

Johann shrugged "I know not, and care not to understand, the motives of evil wizards."

"I shall talk to the countess," said Lock, "and while I am about that see that no harm comes to Heinrich or I shall make you pay."

Peter with a dozen handpicked men followed the Hungarian poacher deeper into the forest. It was a good afternoon for a hunt, clear and cool. They travelled through mixed forest, oak, birch, and chestnut with a scattering of mossy glades. Crickets sang while finches, doves and black birds flitted between the trees. More than once Peter caught sight of skittish groups of roe deer, saw the signs of wallowing boar, and heard in the distance the barking of a stag.

"There it is," the poacher pointed forward into distance between the trunks of the trees, "I've been as good as my word."

The group moved quietly forward, creeping from tree to tree, and there beside a bend in a sluggish stream was a grassy clearing bordered by willows. In its centre stood a red, white and green pavilion. The silk flaps of its entrance billowed in the gentle breeze. Posted around the pavilion were several Turkish guards. They wore baggy white pants stuffed into high black riding boots, above which their long shirts reached nearly to their knees. Their hair was hidden, wrapped in their colourful turbans. Muskets were slung on their shoulders and scimitars, strapped to their waists. They were seated on the ground drinking reddish liquid from small glass cups. They spoke in hushed voices.

Keeping behind the trunks of the trees Peter and his men, tamped black powder into the muzzles of their weapons, inserted the iron balls, then, with the aid of a tinderbox, lit the wicks of their matchlocks. They positioned themselves to fire. A black and white heron spotted them. It let out a warning screech and took wing. The guards saw the smoke from the matchlocks. They shouted, drew their scimitars and scrambled for cover, but were too late. The mercenaries fired, the matchlocks belched smoke and a ringing crack echoed through the forest that put all the birds to flight.

Peter plunged into the stream. The murky warm water went up to his knees. He leapt up on to the grassy bank, killed an injured guard with a sword jab to the throat, wiped his sword on the dead man's shirt and pushed into the pavilion.

Inside were two women. One, a servant, wore a blue silk headscarf and a purple gown that reached from her wrist to her ankle. The other, a lady, wore baggy orange trousers tied tight around her ankles, where her feet fitted into pointed slippers. Over that she wore a blue knee length gown embroidered with gold lace and a necklace of polished moonstone. She held a Turkish dagger, pressed against her own throat. She let forth a stream of impassioned words in a language that Peter could not understand.

"Come no closer," said servant woman in Latin, "Her Ladyship Nuray will kill herself rather than be violated by the brutish touch of a pig eating foreigner."

Greta von Eisenberg walked beside Felix the black monk as they descended a stone pathway lined with fruiting rowans.

"In those strange foetid, winterless jungles of the East I saw many wonders." The Dominican paused in his telling to tighten the belt of his habit and look around at the forest, which clawed at the edge of Greta's park. "There are birds of a thousand shapes and hues, whose strange cries fill the understories of that forest where they dwell in endless night. There are flesh-eating plants that will grab the careless wayfarer. There are spiders larger than rats, while elephants, tigers and true unicorns move through meadows of grass that are higher than a man's head. I have seen grey armoured, venom spitting dragons. And tribes of cannibals whose skin is as black as basalt. Despite all these dangers it was the steaming foreign vapours that were most deadly to our people and men dropped daily from the fever. So it was with great relief that we arrived in the lands of a king who made us welcome as his guests. His gardens were filled with spices and fruits of myriad shape and flavour and the men of that kingdom lived in perfect ease."

"And what of the women?" asked Greta.

"Oh, the women! Owing to the ease of their lives they were beautiful as nymphs and each greatly accomplished in the arts of music, dance and serving."

"I'm surprised," said Greta, "that having found such an earthly paradise you would ever leave."

"It was with a heavy heart that we left, for the kingdom became afflicted with a terrible curse and so it was that the children began to disappear. The king believed the words of his evil advisors, that we had brought this curse upon them, and so he banished us from that paradise."

"Incredible," said Greta. They had reached a walkway that wound under a row of willows beside a flowing mountain stream. "Here, I promise you, you will see nothing more exotic then a flock of storks. They transform themselves into human folk in the winter it is said. But forgive me I diverge. There was something I wanted to ask you. Was it on your return that you met with his Holiness and was offered the position of inquisitor?"

Felix stopped walking and stared at Greta.

Greta laughed. "You are surprised at a lady having such astuteness. Fear not.. It is not from magic that I have discerned that part of your story but from your medallion. A branch, a cross, and a sword, is that not the mark of the inquisition?"

"Yes," said Felix quietly, "It is. Fortune has endowed your ladyship with superior intelligence."

"Has she really?" Greta resumed walking, looking over her shoulder to make sure that Felix was following her. "I am afraid you flatter me without due cause. I am a frail woman. My knowledge of such things is a matter of ordinary coincidence. I am only an Eisenberger by marriage. My maiden name is von Tachov. My family were Bohemian Hussites. The symbol of the inquisition is easily recognisable to those who were brought up to fear it. But tell me. I should like to have your wise opinion. As an expert in the ways of evil who is worse, the idolatrous Turk, who crushes good Christian nations under his boot, or is it the Lutheran whose belief in Christ and God is sincerely held?"

Felix answered without hesitation. "The heretic is worse, far more dangerous than the Turk. The Turk is an external enemy and thus can never truly mar the light of God. But the heretic twists scripture to his own whims. He is by far the greater devil. There is no evil in this world more pernicious than the rot of heresy."

" I see," said Greta, "I thank you for your wisdom and candour. Come there is something I wish to show you. My father in law built this most beautiful and secret little shrine. It goes by this little door and under a mound. Come, you must see it."

Felix followed Greta along the edge of the stream, past a group of ducks, around a corner and onto a path, thick with fruiting brambles, nettles, willow herb and wild roses. The path descended into a little dell, on one side of which was a stone wall and a small arched door was set into the side of the mound.

Greta took a key from her purse and fitted it into the door.

It was cool and dark inside the mound. The only light came from a circular opening at the top of the domed structure. Around the edge of the dome was a circle of columns.

"Isn't it beautiful?" Greta's voice echoed, dancing back and forth among the columns.

"It is," said Felix.

"And I?" said Greta as she walked to the middle of the shrine so that the light flowing through the circular opening illuminated her, "do you find me beautiful? You may speak in confidence for no one know our whereabouts."

The monk hesitated before he spoke from the shadows. "Yes, Countess, I find you beautiful."

"And what if I were to tell you that I was a believer in the way of Luther, well what then? Would you still find me beautiful?"

Felix was silent.

"Well," she pressed, "what then?"

"Then I would have you put into a barrel filled with iron nails and roll you down the hill."

"I do not doubt it," said Greta, "It would not bother you. I'm sure you love the sound of shrieking innocents."

"I derive no pleasure from my duties."

"Do you not?" Greta moved between the columns her heart raced with fear but she did her best to keep her voice calm and even. "Your story of the east was so wondrous, and I believe it. But I could by the flick of your eyes, by the hesitation in your voice, tell that there were some things you did not tell me. Tell me now, why did the king of that earthly paradise eject you from his kingdom?"

She watched in the dim light as Felix drew his dagger from his belt. "He ignored the word of God so we enslaved the children of his kingdom to work on our new domains."

Greta circled back around keeping to the shadows between the columns. "And when you first arrived in India what was the cause of the conflict with that kingdom."

Felix walked into the middle of the shrine so that the light struck his dagger. "The Indian workers would not obey our orders, they would not accept Christ as their savour so we sewed them alive to the sails."

Greta had made her way back to the door and as it creaked open Felix moved swiftly toward her brandishing his dagger, but he was too late. She closed and locked the door behind her.

The streets were covered in mud, the contents of chamber pots, and the excrement of animals, so Basha walked with wooden platform shoes to keep her feet above the filth. The night was dark so she saw her way by looking up at the starlit sky. A street cat paused to watch her pass, then fled. A pig grunted from a neighbour's yard, and a bat flitted between the eves of the houses. She slipped into the shadow of an overhanging house to let a group of men pass, singing in discordant, drunken voices. She passed the looming shadow of the church and at length came to the area around the barracks by the inner-city wall. She passed the tower, where her father was imprisoned, and the stone barracks beside it, and came to the house of Johann captain of the city guard. It was built with wooden frames filled with layers of straw and plaster, and topped with a steep slate roof.

She took the heavy iron knocker, fixed into the oak door, and knocked.

There was no answer.

She waited.

Drizzling rain blew from the north, dampening her hat, cloak and shawl.

She felt alone, as the raindrops collected in her hair.

She was about to depart when the door creaked open. An old servant answered. His hair was white and wiry, his face cadaverous. He led Basha along a corridor into a parlour where a fire crackled in an open hearth. The room was adorned with hunting trophies. The heads of hulking boars thrust themselves from the walls, between the busts of stags and bison. In the middle of the flagstone floor was a large bearskin rug. Beside the fire sat Captain Johann, and beside him, a huge hunting hound. Basha's heart leapt into her throat, but then she noticed the strange contortion in the beast's face and body. It was as dead as the other animals.

"Show the Jewess where she may sit," said Johann.

Basha followed the old servant who indicated a stool placed beside the fire. The hairy animal skins tickled her feet as she crossed the room. Basha sat and mentally ran through what she must say for the hundredth time. *My Lord Johann, you must understand that my father is innocent. The horrible murder of my betrothed hurts us both. But I understand that your job is a difficult one and thus I thought that if it pleased your lordship to free my father I could give you fifty pieces of Spanish gold. It is all my family has.*

As the greedy eyes of Captain Johann drilled over her, the order of her words flew from her mind like ducks scattering from a hunter's bow.

Basha's lip quivered, she toyed nervously with the red woollen charm around her wrist "My... my..."

"You are here because of your father," said Johann. "You have come to beg to free him."

"Yes," Basha looked at the ground. "He's innocent."

"Well go on then, beg."

Basha was silent not knowing what to do or say.

"Get down on your knees," said Johann, "kiss my feet and beg."

Basha felt the tears come streaming out of her eyes she fell off the stool and crawled toward Johann, burying her face in his boots, she cried as she kissed the leather. "Let him free," she whispered, "Let him free."

Basha screamed as Johann kicked her in the ribs.

"Get up," he said.

Wiping the tears on her shawl Basha rose.

"Strip," demanded Captain Johann.

Basha was frozen, shamed, humiliated.

Johann rose from his seat and Basha saw that he gripped a riding whip. His face was red and shaking. "Strip for me, you whore," he shouted, "or by the Devil I'll whip you half to death."

As her outer gown slid to the floor, the gold stitched into its seems clinked as it landed on the wooden boards and a feeling of dark despair fell upon her as she detached her mind from the horror of her predicament.

but a few days later, the Day of Spells, The 17th of September, Day of the Moon, Year of the Lord 1526

As Asra walked through the harem gate, escorted by the black eunuch, she gave thanks to Allah that she was no longer held captive within its walls. She walked past the eunuch dormitories and a royal bathroom, then along the Court Yard of slaves girls. Each of these places held memories, memories of waiting, years of waiting. It was the harem that had made her what she was. Time was one thing that a harem girl had in abundance, and Asra had used it to master the myriad tongues. The slaves of the harem came from all across the world, and of their old lives they carried with them their languages and Asra had learned them and hoarded them.

At length she came to the Harem Garden. And to the presence of Sultan Suleiman the Lawgiver, Emperor of the Turks, Caliph of Islam, most powerful man in the world and Asra's occasional lover. He sat on a cushioned rug, listening to the flutes of the harem girls. He drank Chinese black tea from an Arab-glass teacup, sweetened with a spoon of Indian cane sugar. When Asra had first been called on to attend the sultan, it had been nothing more than a lucky chance. Asra had known that her chance for freedom would not come again. So she had challenged the sultan to a wager, if she could outperform him in the number of languages in which she could say the name of God he would grant her a boon, if she lost she would kill herself. Asra was not fool enough to allow herself to win, but she had sufficiently impressed the emperor to ask her boon, freedom.

Asra prostrated herself before the sultan, kissing the carpet at his feet.

"Rise," said Suleiman.

"How may I serve you, Prince of the Faithful?" When she had left the harem she had been employed as a spy, where she had put to use her skill in languages, and trained in weapon craft and disguise. She had become the mastermind of a network of female informants, among brothels and slaves girls across Rumalia and had earned the ear of the sultan. She had risen high indeed for a slave girl orphaned at the sack Durres.

Suleiman indicated that she should eat from a bowl of Persian dates. "What can you tell me about Nuray, Bright Moon?"

"Ibrahim Pasha's disappearing wife? I doubtless know nothing that your majesty does not already know, that she has been kidnapped. By who I know not. Other than that, I have only women's gossip that she was wishing herself to be captured out of boredom. *The Nine Holy Nights during which men and women must not lie together*, Ibrahim barely took the time to look at her."

"Nuray is my kinswoman," said Suleiman. "She must be brought back, willing or not. My scouts report that the kidnapper is a German mercenary, from the northern frontier. You can speak the Germanic tongue?"

Asra nodded.

"I'm sending you to the northern frontier. I want you to bring me back Nuray and find out what you can about those mountainous borderlands. I'll give you a thousand silver akce and an escort of soldiers led by Mustafa Khan."

"Mustafa," asked Asra, "Mustafa the Tartar lord?"

"Yes."

"Mustafa treats women like they're goats, to he herded around with shouts and sticks, and locked inside at night so they don't runaway. How can I work with a man like that?"

Suleyman held up his hand, "He's a great warrior, horseman and tracker. His people have been raiding deep into the Christian lands for many years. There is no one I trust more to take you swiftly and safely on your errand. And I trust you shall not fail me."

Asra bowed and kissed his feet. "I shall not, Prince of the Faithful."

Peter watched Nuray as she rode in the supply wagon sitting on top of the bales of straw, sacking and booty. Nuray struggled to keep her composure with every bump and swing of the wagon as it rolled along the forest road. Her eyes and cheeks were red from weeping. But the way she held her head, the way she washed her hands and feet and prayed at every stop, spoke of a woman whose spirit was unbroken.

Peter was not a man overly given to lust, or to love. He had like every soldier milled his grain in a brothel, but he did not live for it the way that Krum had. The truth was he felt for his wife Greta and guilt plagued him when he took another woman. But Nuray had kindled something different in him, something he had not felt in a long time, if ever. He found he could think of little else and his heart smouldered with constant yearning. She was so beautiful, so proud, so different. She was like a wild falcon caught on a leather thong, elegant like a young doe in flight, yet fierce like a jackal.

Nuray became aware that Peter was staring at her. She began to scream and curse him in her own language. She spat at him and strained against the knots that tied her to the wagon. She had tried to run away but having thrice been brought back wet, miserable and hungry, she no longer bothered, settling instead on vocal grieving and cursing. She had tried to kill herself but did not seem to have the stomach to cut deeply enough. In all, it had seemed prudent to keep her bound.

Captian Sokol drew up beside Peter. "If you take her," he said, "it'll drop her ransom value, drop it by a lot."

Peter winced. Were his thoughts that obvious?

Sokol pointed north along the flat road toward the horizon, where billowing black clouds were forming. "Rain is coming and thunder too by the look of it. No man is that keen to spend another night outside. The scout says there is manor house only an hour or so march from here. Should we billet ourselves there? There are now no lords of Hungaria and we might find victuals and warm beds."

"You've been most kind to a poor, destitute prisoner," spoke Harold as he stretched himself out on the floor, "Thanks be, that Sag Belly is a greedy man."

Heinrich shrugged. From where he sat leaning against the wall, the dampness seemed to have seeped into every bone of his hungry body. The straw was mouldy. Moss grew from parts of the stonework and the urine and diarrhoea of the prisoners had pooled at one corner of the dungeon. "It is as you said," Heinrich sneezed, "if I'm going hang either way no harm in helping a fellow man."

"May Lady Fortune bless you," Harold stood up and even in the dim light of the dungeon Heinrich could see that beneath his dirty rags Harold's rib bones visibly protruded. "I never told you what I'm in for, did I."

"No," Heinrich touched the fragment of the tora he kept around his neck.

"I'm in for me debts," said Harold.

"For your debts?"

"You heard me. I fell behind in my rents. Hard year and truth be told I wanted a new gown for the wife, boots for the son, and a hat for myself. Is that not reasonable?"

"Very reasonable," said Heinrich as he wiped his runny nose on the hem of his robe.

"I couldn't make my rents and old Long Chin the landlord he had me taken off to the keep until my family paid what's owed. I figure I'll be here till Lord Death takes me, for there's little enough chance that my poor wife, nor my little son, bless their souls, will scrape together enough groats to feed themselves let alone free me."

"It's a cruel world," said Heinrich

"That it is," Harold scratched his head, "us both have been ill used by Fortune. But I've been thinking there might be a way to save you."

"Go on," said Heinrich.

"Those big hats, you Jews wear, they give much shade to your face, and that cloak of yours, covers you well does it not? So if another man were put in your place now, well it would take a man with a keener eye than me to tell the difference. Now, Sag Belly's a greedy swine, and no one cares much about me. If we were to bribe him to let us change places and then you could pay him off and escape. Then more then likely I'll hang in your place."

"But what good do you get from such an arrangement," said Heinrich.

Harold grinned, "I get to go to the land of glass and gold and bow before the All Father, so that my immortal soul will dwell forever in bliss, then I would welcome the scaffold. The bishop sells indulgences and that's what I want. You buy me to heaven and I'll get you out of here." The debtor spat on his hand.

For the first time in weeks Heinrich felt his spirit lift. Perhaps he could take his family, go south with the Travellers and flee Eisenberg.

"There's just one problem isn't there," Harold continued, There's no way I can trust you to keep your word."

"I can swear an oath, an oath on this tora scroll I have around my neck."

"That won't do," said Harold. "You folk killed the Lamb of God. The oath of a Jew can't be trusted."

The evening rain spattered off the hats and cloaks of the mercenaries as they marched through the rows of dripping grape vines heavy with the new seasons fruit.

"This Lord will have a rich cellar," said Sokal as they drew up to the high, arched oak doors of the noble house. The mercenaries kept their hands on their weapons as they crowded around the threshold.

Peter lifted the iron knocker and slammed it three times against the wood. The cold northerly sent sheets of rain hammering into them and peter was about to suggest breaking the door down. When he heard the sound of a latch moving.

Standing to greet them was a portly man with receding grey hair, dressed in wealthy yet old-fashioned hose and tunic. He looked at the assembled soldiers and Peter could see his eyes moving over their swords and muskets and lingering on the Turkish princess. "Welcome," he said and bowed, "to the house of His lordship the Marquis Ujlaki."

"We are in need of lodgings," said Peter, "is the lord of the house at liberty?"

The man paused.

"Dead is he?" shouted one Peter's soldiers, "Like all the other idiots, used his blood to oil a scimitar."

"Don't matter even if he is there." Called out another, "the only lords in Hungaria now are those that wear turbans."

"Best stoke the fire, master, and fry up the salted pork," said a third man.

"Send yourself down to the cellar and break open your best casks," said a forth.

"Have the maids and serving girls meet us in the hall," said a fifth.

Peter smiled at the steward. "You'd best let us in quickly. The wetter my men are the less open to persuasion."

"Tell me more about this Jewish Magic," Harold's pale skin appeared slightly luminous as he drew close to Heinrich, as close his manacles would allow.

"I don't know if I can," said Heinrich, "It's dangerous to even speak about it, especially to a Christian."

"Can it summon him," whispered Harold, "the Oldest Enemy?"

"Oh no," Heinrich looked toward the ceiling, "It summons the power of a dybbuk."

"A dybbuk?" asked Harold, "what diabolical thing is this?"

"Shh, do not speak its name so loud. It is the dispossessed soul of a dead man bound to this earth."

"And does it work, this Jewish spell?"

"Oh it works," said Heinrich, "You feel a chill enter the room when the dybbuk is summoned, and if ever an oath made under such a ritual is broken the dybbuk will attach himself to the spirit of the oath breaker, it will torment him day and night and drive him to lunacy."

"Will it?" Harold stared at Heinrich. His eyes had, over his long imprisonment, become like hollows in his thin bony face. "Will it harm my soul to be present for such a ritual?"

"I believe not," said Heinrich, "It is after all us Jews who perform such magic, and there is little hope for our eternal souls in any case as we are forever damned by the murder of Christ."

This answer seemed to satisfy Harold and he grinned excitedly. "Let's do it. Let's do it and then tomorrow we'll bribe old Sag Belly to let us change places. You can walk and I shall go to heaven."

"First," Heinrich cleared away the mouldy straw. "We draw on the ground the six pointed star of David." Using the iron case that held his scroll, Heinrich scraped the sign into the damp rock. Around the star he drew concentric circles. Then scratched beside them the Hebrew letters B and J.

"What now?" Harold whispered.

Heinrich began to chant prayers in Hebrew.

The sound of his secret language excited Harold even more who from his squatting position on the ground rocked back and forward.

"Dybbuk, dybbuk," Heinrich cut his finger on the sharp edge of his manacle and dropped his blood into the star. "Dybbuk, hear me. It is Heinrich son of Mendel. I call you. Come, you are bound to me. Come I have an oath to make before you." As Heinrich spoke he felt a chill in the air and his heart began to beet. In that dim, cold dungeon, his blood dripping onto the stone, Heinrich could easily imagine that he had actually summoned an evil presence. "Yahweh forgive me," he murmured under his breath. "Dybbuk," he spoke, "I feel that you are here and I ask you to hear my oath and if I should break it then…" he paused unwilling to say the words.

Harold looked on in horrified satisfaction.

"If I should break my oath, then my soul belongs to you, may you haunt me till Death take me."

A fire raged in the grand hall behind the open hearth, fed by two soldiers with chopped beech and vine. The trestle tables were dressed in brown cloth, and the servants placed upon them dishes of bronze and silver, legs of roasted pork, boiled chickens, baked apples, and dense hot bread, to placate their unwelcome guests. Out in the gathering darkness came the rolling crash of thunder.

Peter sat in the high backed wooden throne, and drank red wine from a jewelled goblet. On his left sat Nuray. Her wet cloak hung by the fire, and Peter had wrapped her in his own, woven from red Flemish wool. Her hunger had overtaken her anger and she greedily sucked the flesh from the chicken bones. On Peter's right stood the steward of the house who kept Peter's goblet filled, pouring the sweet aromatic wine from a clay jug.

"This is," said Peter as he raised his cup "the finest thing I have ever drank!"

"Your lordship has fine taste," replied the steward, "for this is a well aged barrel and here we make the finest wines in the world. It is said, that it was Markus Aurelius himself who planted the first grape of this vineyard. And when the tartars came and savaged all the land before them, like devils out of Hell, they loved the wine of this vineyard so well that this very house was protected when all else around was raised to the ground. Princes, we say, come and go but the wine of Borfold is eternal"

Peter watched as a serving woman walked beside the table filling the cups of his men whose voices rose in an excited intoxicated hubbub. "And what is your oldest vintage?"

"The Black Vintage," replied the steward. "It was bottled in reign of Zoltan, and it was made by Stefen the Black, a powerful magician. His wine is infused with elder berries, and leaves of hawthorn. It is known as the giver of dreams."

"Bring it out," Peter ran his fingers through Nuray's long wavy hair, "My lady and I shall drink it."

Nuray stiffened at his touch.

"As you wish," said the steward, "but I warn you, it is no wine to be drunk with gluttony."

"Bring it forth," said Peter.

When the jugs were brought and the wine was poured, he drank. The liquid was cool in his mouth. It was sweet and smooth and did not burn his throat.

"Drink," Peter slid the goblet of wine toward Nuray. She looked at him with anger and disgust as she picked up the goblet and he thought she would throw it at his head. But she too drank, drank with a sudden abandon, the wine splashed over her cheeks and chin.

Basha found her way around the darkness of the cellar by touch. Save for the moulding hay it was empty, but the stone was rough-cut and she could feel out its stories, tracing the gaps between the slabs, probing them for a secret, perhaps a message, a needle or some other small forgotten treasure. It was so unlike her cellar at home, where Baba kept flour, butter and apples and where there were also some of Basha's old toys, a doll, a rocking horse and a cradle. She stroked her belly. Her child was still alive and growing.

Her back and breasts stung from lacerated welts where Johann had whipped her, and it seemed no part of her had been spared the prodding, lash. He had bound her by her wrists to one of cellar's wooden beams. And there she had dangled, the rope burning her wrists, while he examined her with whip and dagger.

"Soon," he had whispered to her, "soon I shall do with you what I want."

Then he had left her to dangle in pain, in the dark, and in silence. Mercifully the old servant had come, cut the rope, and let her fall upon the floor. She had lost sense of time in the smothering darkness. Sometimes the servant would come with a hunk of bread and a jug of water and he would empty the wooden bucket that served as her chamber pot. Sometimes Johann would visit and always it ended in pain, a lash across the face, hot wax poured on her legs, her fingers held till she screamed in the guttering flame. He would whisper than shout, *slut, witch, whore, succubus*, yet he never violated her though Basha could sense his yearning.

In the spaces between the visits, in the blackness, in the silence, Basha would return to her rituals. She made a circle around her with breadcrumbs. She had woven the Hebrew letters "B" and "J" out of straw and placed those around the circle. She took off the little piece of the torah that she wore cased in iron around her neck and put into the centre of the circle. And began to pray.

"Oh Prince of the Torah, hear me your humble servant. I have created your holy circle. I have fasted for many days, kept clean my hands and feet. Come in my moment of need and hear my plea. Though it must be difficult for you to fly from your eternal paradise, from the world of light to this dark cell. I compel you with the words of prophets to come to me and to guide me."

This was the ritual that Baba had taught her but she knew that it was no easy thing to summon an angel and that the greatest rabbis had tried and failed. It took patience and days. But it seemed to her that in that moment her spirit lifted. The pain in her body felt less and without any tangible reason she felt hope. She then heard the key in the door.

Johann pushed it open. He carried a whip in one hand and a

lantern in the other. A cloaked and hooded man followed him into the room.

Basha quickly swept away the evidence of her ritual.

"Stand up," Johann ordered.

Basha rose to her feet and straitened her gown.

"So this," said the hooded man, "is Basha the beautiful. How wonderful. May I touch her."

"As you wish," Johann tapped his whip against the palm of his hand. "She's learned to fear the whip. She'll comply."

The hooded man stepped next to Basha and ran his hands over her belly. The way his fingers probed her womb were almost harder to bare than Johann's lash

"Ah there he is," whispered the hooded man, "Alive."

"How soon can you dispel her Jewish magic," cut in Johann.

"Have patience," said the hooded man as he stepped away from Basha. "You have done your utmost to put this evil temptress in her place. You have given her what she deserves. But the Jewess is with child and her evil magic is only growing stronger. If you want to avoid the evil of her spells you must ensure that the child survives. I promise you that I will lift her evil magic and you may do with her as you will, but I can not act yet, the stars are not correctly aligned. But for now you must have fear for the child's life. Feed her well and house her better."

The musicians among the servants and mercenaries played upon their pipes, drums, psalters and fiddles. Some men cried for more wine, others seized the serving girls and whirled them around in a wild, leaping jig. Each man danced the dance of his village, and into the fire-lit hall, crept to each man, scarred by war, the fondest of his memories, the smile of his sweetheart on a warm spring day, the raising of the maypole and the gathering of birch to make the crowning wreaths.

Peter felt it too, memories that were once so joyous and yet melancholic in their remembering. He thought of Greta and their wedding day. She had been so beautiful clothed in white and she had looked at him with innocent love while they were pelted with handfuls of grain.

The mood in the hall changed. The memories crept back from whence they came and were replaced by elation and exuberance. Nuray climbed upon the table and taking the wine jug in her hand she drank long to the soldiers' whoops. She began to dance, sending plates and goblets crashing. Faster and faster she danced whirling and wriggling to the music.

Peter climbed onto the table after her. The men began to clap and he too began to dance as if his legs had a will of their own. His eyes fixed on the lean bearded face of Sokol, he was laughing and his laughter echoed strangely in Peter's head. He watched as Sokol began to transform. His hair grew longer, his beard richer and goat horns sprouted from his head. The wind rattled at the door and the thunder rolled.

He turned to face Nuray who danced before him and saw instead a monstrous cat with wide green eyes standing upright on her hind legs. "You will die with a sword in your hand," said the cat.

Book Two

The Bishop's Gambit

Thirty-four years earlier
The Journeys of Brother William 1492

I became most curious when I discovered that the province of Esienberg is home to the famed Abbey of Saint Hildegard the Virgin. The abbey had been built before Germanic settlement and had been carved into the rock face by the ancient folk of that valley.

It is said that it was Hildegard, a woman, who first brought the word of God to the savage pagans then living in the valley. The local chief said he would be baptised if Hildegard would marry him, but the saint told the chief that she had promised herself to God. The chief became so enraged with her answer that he locked her in a tower. But God heard the saint's prayers and changed her into a wild goose so she could flee. A feather of this wondrous goose is said to be held by the sisters of the Abbey.

Wishing to inquire further I took leave of the count and took the South Road into the mountains. On arrival, however, I was refused entry on account of being a man. Not being turned easily off something once I have set my mind upon it, I took lodging in a nearby village and waited for Fortune to put something in my path. And blessed I was in that I did not have to wait too long.

Though the good nuns of the Abby include among their number bullish specimens of the weak sex and are for the most part not in need of the strength of men, there are some tasks for which the nuns do allow in small numbers of men. Yet so that these men may not threaten the honour of the nuns or be tempted by the youthful girls among their number, only those who suffer from blindness are given work. I therefore endeavoured to disguise myself as a blind pilgrim and seek access to the abbey through trickery.

I must confess that as a blind man I did not make a very able labourer. I therefore covered my eyes with gauze through which

I could observe some of my surroundings and yet have my eyes remain unseen. It was in this fashion that I both acquitted myself as an able labourer, and made the observation that the sisters were quite unconstrained in their interest in the blind men. I also became quite aware of the comeliness of some of those good women who were both well fed and in the flower of their youth.

My usefulness caused me to be used for more particular work than the chopping of firewood. And the lifting of ale barrels. I began to be employed in carrying candleholders. It was when bringing one such holder for a certain chaste sister, who enjoyed writing at night, that my lips first touched the lips of one of those earthly angels. In the weeks that followed I became the happiest man on earth. As rumour of my dalliance spread so more ladies sought my assistance. I stopped being employed as a candle carrier and began work as a Gardner. I was given lodgings in a small cottage in a wild part of the abbey grounds. My duties were to keep this garden as wild as possible, with a number of very pleasant alcoves among the soft heather and long grass. The sisters would visit me at various times of the day and night. They brought with them dainties from the kitchen and mugs of warm spiced ale. I do not know how it was done but their visits were so timed that they were never interrupted. And so months passed in the most perfect contentment imaginable. For a year I lived in the garden and never once did I tire of the sisters' company.

It was in spring, when I met the abbess. She confronted me, alone, when I was watching a wild falcon. *Beautiful is it not?* spake she. *Beyond compare,* I responded. *You have quite the eye for a blind man,* were her words and I realised I was speaking with the ruler of this Godly domain. Though the bloom of her youth was behind her the abbess was still a beauty, with as finer intellect as many a theologian of Paris. The abbess took me into the heart of the abbey, carved out of the very mountain itself. Here was their treasury. There were books and scrolls in their hundreds, holy relics which any prince or bishop would have coveted. There was silver and gold stamped with the head of an emperor of antiquity. There was wine, spices and dates. But sadly, though, I did not then know it, my life in that house of God was drawing to an end.

Day of the Witch
Morning of the 30th of September, the Holy Sabbath, Year of the Lord 1526

Bishop Lock was finishing his breakfast in the office – bread, butter, and eggs boiled with saffron, giving them a yellow muddy colour. After he'd swallowed the last bit of bread, he pushed aside his plate and rewound his clock. He took a moment to contemplate with disgust the brute mentality of his fellow man – their filth, their lack of hygiene and their lack of higher mental faculty. If only Lock had lived in an earlier age, late antiquity perhaps, an age where all men were educated, spoke Greek and Latin, conversed in philosophy and visited the baths daily. History was a kind of backward slide into beastly regression, both moral and aesthetic. He himself, Lock mused, was a stray gem. He turned his attention to the two pieces of paper before him.

The first was a heretical pamphlet, that had been circulating in the markets and alehouses. The pamphlet proclaimed that the Church had become corrupt, debauched even, and that he, Bishop Lock, had been stockpiling grain and that he took joy in the *Devil's succour*, summoning demons with which he satisfied his *carnal appetites*. He had, according to the pamphlet, been seen in the company of a cat and a goat at the full moon, with both animals walking on their hind legs. Lock felt a creeping fear. The pamphlet may seem ridiculous to him, but many of the town's folk had grown up in villages. They were credulous and if the pamphlets were read aloud and such rumours were not controlled then Lock faced a fate that he did not like to contemplate. He had not taken the heretical preacher seriously enough. Letters from colleagues in Nuremberg, Kassel, and Amsterdam had told him that the Luther heresy was sweeping through Christendom, but he hadn't expected it to confront him in such a personally way.

The second piece of paper was unusual. It was a kind of proclamation. It declared that, *there were most foul and evil witches among us*. These women could be ordinary women, the paper explained, *they could be our wives, daughters, even our mothers.* Signs of witchcraft had been detected in the province. A serpent had been discovered with two heads and a pig had been born with a third open eye on its forehead. The unseasonable rain that had ruined so many crops was the fault of witches. But a professional witch hunter had arrived, William from Munich. Anyone with any information regarding the activity of witches was to report to William at his board at the Golden Antlers, an alehouse close to the North Gate.

Bishop Lock considered the two pieces of paper. They had obviously been printed by the same printer, the matching discrepancies of the letters was clear to see, and clearly not produced by Lock's own print set that he had commissioned from the iron guild. Somebody was running a heretical print shop. Lock held up the two pieces of paper to the light. Paper sometimes contained the mark of its producer, and there it was, a faint watermark emerging through the glow of the paper – Munich.

Lock took a fresh sheet of paper from his shelf he ran a finger down its edge, sharp as a dagger, and with a faint chemical perfume, Venetian, Lock only used the best. He retuned to his desk and dipped his goose feather quill in his glass of ink.

"Cook," asked Sonia, "What's a well-ridden-saddle?"

"It's what you are, child," replied the cook as she stuffed prunes into a pheasant.

"Yes, so you keep saying," said Sonia, "but what does it mean?" Sonia began reaching for the prunes.

Cook, who seemed to be in a grumpy mood, slammed down the wooden spoon, just missing Sonia's fingers. "Get your hands off those prunes or I'll redden your arse whether or not the pope himself gets to take you to holy ecstasy."

"Cook?" asked Sonia

"What is it child?"

"How was the market place today?"

"It's no place for a you. There's all manner of no good folk around these days, young men who'll wave their cod pieces at any girl or woman who walks past. And you can't trust the peddlers. They'll sell sheep dropping as cures for wrinkles if they think they can get a groat from you. I'd hate to think what would happen to you out there. You'd be robbed before you could say Holy Mary, and wind up working in a bathhouse." Cook poured Sonia a cup of broth.

"What's wrong with working in a bathhouse," asked Sonia as she blew on the steaming cup.

"Never mind, child. Here, leave that to cool and help me with the bellows. That's it. You need a hot fire to roast a pheasant." Cook now lowered her voice as she moved closer to Sonia and began to stuff the prunes into the pheasant. "In truth there are things I've heard in the market which worry me greatly. It's always been a place where you see the more wretched folk, beggars and the like, and some foreign folk too. Now there seems to be a good deal more of both and no good can come of that. Now people are saying that the bishop's a bad man and the Church doesn't speak for God. I used to be proud, being cook to his Excellency, now I keep it quiet. Even some folk who used to slip me some copper and ask me to say their prayers in the bishop's house, now they don't meet my eye.

"If that weren't bad enough, I've never seen a summer with so much rain. The grain is rotting and it'll be a hungry winter. The cheese maker's wife has been saying it's God's punishment and the bishop is to blame. But I said to her, 'that's foolishness.' You can stop with the bellows now. We don't want to char the pheasant. Start chopping that bag of apples... No not like that. Like this. Sweet love of the Savour, Child, did your mother teach you nothing? Everybody should know that the reason we have so much rain is because somebody has offended the oak spirits. They're very powerful and very old and they have the power over the rain. You can wager your prettiest gown that somebody's chopped down an old oak tree and that's the root of trouble."

"Really?" said Sonia.

"Certainly," said Cook, " now careful with that knife. I don't want to have to explain to his Excellency how your finger ended up in his dinner. The rain is bad, but there is worse to come. There's a witch hunter in town, and Werner, the turner's son, loved Anna the broom maker's daughter, but she didn't love him even though he was richer than her and she went off with the baker's boy. Werner got jealous and told the witch hunter that Anna was a witch. Everybody's terrified that she'll be burned. Ever seen a woman burn, child?"

"No," said Sonia.

"Well I haven't either," said Cook, "but I seen a plenty a pig roast on a spit."

The Golden Antlers was a crooked, lopsided wooden frame tavern that leaned out onto the street. Lock watched with satisfaction, as

Steffen, his brutish retainer, pushed open the doors. Lock had with him a band of retainers, armed in the Italian fashion with sword and dagger. He stepped into the grimy barroom. Inside a brown haired young woman was hanging naked by her wrists from a ceiling beam. She had been whipped till her back was raw and covered with open wounds. The floor was slick with blood. She was dead.

Lock tried to hold back his stomach but failed. He knelt down on the floor and vomited.

Peals of laughter rang across the room.

"Shall I fetch you a bucket, my good man?"

Lock lifted his gaze from the floor to look at who had spoken.

Standing in a group around a barrel of ale were half a dozen men and in the middle was a man wearing a sausage shaped red hat, yellow hose, a slashed velvet doublet, and an immodestly sized white codpiece. Sword and dagger hung on either side of his waist and he held a loaded matchlock pistol with a smoking wick.

"William von Munich, I presume?" said Lock.

The dandy eyed the bishop's men with a calculating eye. "Are you here to report a witch or help hunt one?"

Lock's retainers poured through the door, drawing their weapons. "It looks like you already have your witch," said Lock as Steffen helped him to his feet.

"She was innocent," replied William, "A witch would have survived the cutting."

"You are under arrest," said Lock after he had wiped his mouth on his handkerchief, "for heresy and murder. Steffen relieve these men of their weapons."

"Stay, right where you are. I am under the protection of Captain Johann of the City Guard, and I do God's work. I have a written warrant to hunt witches signed with seal of the countess." As the witch hunter was talking he moved his finger to the trigger of his pistol and fired. The smoking wick of the pistol connected with the touchhole. The crack of the pistol deafened the men and gunpowder smoke filled the alehouse. One of Lock's retainers fell, clutching his chest.

Steffen shouted a war cry and bounded forward, grabbing the first man in his way and smashing his dagger hilt into his face.

Lock's retainers surged forward.

The witch hunter and his men fled.

Lock and his men pursued.

They chased the witch hunter's men through the steamy kitchen and out into a muddy yard filled with swine, leaping and dodging the squealing pigs their pursuit. The witch hunter's men pushed open the cart gate. Women watched from the windows of the over hanging houses as men and pigs streamed on to the street. Lock's retainers tackled the witch hunter's men to the ground and kicked them into submission. But the colourfully dressed dandy himself escaped into the maze of streets and allies around the square of Flower Sellers.

Basha sat cross-legged on the pile of straw that was her bed, and told her unborn child stories to while away the time. It was dryer and lighter here in the upper rooms then it had been in the cellar, and the servant came more often with bowls of steaming pottage. The angel had answered her prayers, yet she was still a prisoner. And Johann took care to lock the door after each visit and the window was fixed with iron bars.

"What will become of us?" said Basha as she touched her belly and felt a muffled kick in reply. "I don't know what these men mean to do to us. But I am sure it is nothing good."

Basha walked to the window and peered through the bars. It helped that she had the window and she would spend much of the day with her faced pressed to it, watching the street. She might see guardsmen in their bright clothes, carrying shiny halberds and going to and from the barracks on their patrols. She might see a prisoner being led to the keep, or a soldier's sweetheart bringing him bread and salted pork. She might see carters and porters arriving in the early morning to deliver wares. She might occasionally see a burgher's lady, dressed in silk and chaperoned by her man.

Close to Basha's window was the hanging tree, an old pruned ash with a low horizontal bow. She liked to watch its leaves tug at its branches in the wind, but averted her eyes to the scaffold built bellow it. Three times now she had heard the sound of wild geese as they flew south and she thought of the story the Christians told of Saint Hildegard who transformed herself into a goose to escape her captor. It was a beautiful story for there was something so free about the geese. At this moment it was raining, soft light rain. She didn't recoil from the rain. It reminded her of what it was like to be free.

"You know," she said to her belly, "I have an idea. We'll take my black kerchief," and as she spoke she unwound the cloth from her hair, "and we'll tie it to the bar right at the edge of the window. And you never know, my little darling, perhaps a friend will see it."

As she tied the knot she heard the key turn in the keyhole and the door to the room swing open. She turned to face the door. The Captain's face was a concoction of lust, fear and rage. And as always when she felt his violence about to be visited on her she froze.

Johann crossed the space between the door and the window in four strides, and pushed his face close to hers. She could see his desire to strike her tempered by his fear of her. "Soon I'll have you cleansed of Jewish magic but for now I have something that I would like you to see."

Johann pushed open the shutters and beckoned Basha to the window.

Basha's heart raced, Johann would see her kerchief, and that shred of hope would be taken from her. She walked mutely to join him by the window. To her surprise Johann was too concentrated on what was going on in the street to register the black cloth tied to the bar.

Basha followed Johann's gaze. A prisoner, led by four guards, and followed by a group of onlookers walked toward the hanging tree. She instantly recognised her father's robes and hat. Her heart leapt to her throat. Her father was about to die. Johann turned to look at her, taking evident pleasure in the suffering on her face. But as the prisoner drew closer and ascended the scaffold, she began to hope. It was something about way the man moved, the way he seemed to go so willingly to his death. Something was wrong. She watched as the executioner took off his hat, fixed the noose to his neck and kicked out the trapdoor from underneath him. As the man swung on the rope, Basha caught a look at his face. It was not her father.

Johann turned to look intently at her, and Basha had no trouble in making herself cry. Johann turned back to the window, saw the black kerchief, untied it from the bar, and eyed Basha with a rageful stare.

There was a gentle tap at the door.

"What is it?" Johann shouted.

"A message from the countess," said the raspy voice of Johann's servant.

Sonia and Lock ate supper together in the library.

"You look troubled my lord, and you have been gone all day."

"Troubled barely begins to describe it," Lock chewed miserably on the roast pheasant stuffed with prunes, and glazed with honey. Cook had really outdone herself, but it did nothing to lift Lock's mood.

"Is it something to do with the witch hunter?"

Lock choked on a piece of pheasant. "How do you know about that?"

"Oh I know a few things," said Sonia breezily, "are you going to tell me what's making you grim?"

"I wouldn't want to burden your innocent head with my terrible worries." Lock washed down his mouthful with a goblet of wine."

"Oh please do," said Sonia. "It always helps to share your worries, I'm certain I shan't understand it anyway. So little harm will be done."

"Very well," said Lock, and just having made the decision to share, did indeed make him feel better. "Heresy is spreading in the city, the countess is somehow involved in it, and I feel the nobility are turning against me. But I have no information because Felix the black monk has disappeared and I have heard no word from him or his spies. There is a secret printing press that is spreading lies about me and this is somehow connected to a witch hunter from Munich. The captain of the city guard has gone rogue, and I would have believed him to have executed Heinrich the Jew, had I not seen the man alive with my own eyes. He came to me in disguise insisting that he pay for indulges for the man hanging in his place because of an oath he made to a demon. And as if all of that wasn't bad enough, the countess has invited me to attend her at the schloss tomorrow. And I cannot workout whether or not I should go. If I go not it will show weakness and the hounds will pounce. But if I go I could be walking into a wolf's lair."

Sonia nodded seriously. "Do you know the countess well?"

"Certainly I know her. I always felt she disliked me, though I know not why."

"Is she a good person?"

A good person? Lock paused to consider what that might really mean. He had read Plato and Aristotle, but had never been convinced on the merits of virtue, tending instead to predict people's actions based on their baser nature. "I'm not sure I know what good means?"

"Does she want the best for her people? Does she make certain to make offerings to the spirits of house, field and forest?"

"Make offerings to the spirits of house, field and forest? By the nails of Christ, child, I must forbid you to spend any more time with the cook. I hate to think what your mother will say when you come home recalling pagan customs."

"You are only being cruel because you are worried. I understand. All I am saying is that if the countess has at least some good in her, she will not want a war in which many people will suffer. Remonstrate with her. You say you may risk your life by going. But isn't that what a good person would do? Risk their life to bring peace?"

Lock was struck momentarily speechless. Her logic was flawless. And yet... "I'm afraid I suffer from cowardice."

"The greater the fear, the greater the courage." Sonia smiled warmly. "Have you come any closer to solving the mystery of my brother's death?"

"No," said Lock flatly.

the next day
the 31st of September, Day of the Moon, Year of the Lord 1526

Greta sat staring out of the high mullioned glass windows that faced the park though she could see little but a blur of green beyond the lashing rain. Greta sat on a cushioned throne, drank wine from a silver chalice and smiled to herself. Lock had taken the bait, and with the storm it seemed that God Himself had aided her. "Do you think," she asked, "that they will ever invent glass that is in big pieces, so we don't always have to look through an iron mesh?"

Bishop Lock, ignoring the question, as well as his chair, paced the room.

Greta observed that Lock was extremely agitated. He was sweating. Greta found that she was enjoying his discomfort. She had always found Lock to be haughty and arrogant, he thought he knew everything though he was four years younger than she. Having him where she wanted him put her in good humour. "It's several hours ride from Eisenberg to the schloss," said Greta, "You were lucky to have made it here before the storm, but did you enjoy the ride?"

"I try and avoid the unpleasantries of exercise," replied Lock, "and horses don't agree with me. I came by carriage."

"I love riding," said Greta. "Though I do hate for the sun to ruin my complexion. Its terrible, your Excellency, the sun is shining and I'm thinking I should love to go riding, but than if I go riding, I'll end up with skin like a peasant. That's why I'm always praying for cloudy days."

"May I," said the bishop as he accepted a cup of wine from Magda, "speak with your ladyship frankly?"

"Naturally." Greta was happy she had chosen to wear her silk ruff. It gave her face a more regal frame. She always felt more authoritative and confident when she wore that ruff.

"Eisenberg is rife with heresy and the pope knows it. He has despatched an elite unit of Swiss Guard, pike and musket, to be under my command. He expects the place to be cleaned up and that includes you. I am well aware that you offer protection to the preaching zealot. He has been whipping up hatred against the Church and now has a following among the townsfolk. Captain Johann defies my authority and allows innocent men and women to be murdered. He does so because he claims your protection, countess, you who are clearly indicated in the spread of heresy. But," the bishop raised his arms heavenward, "I am a practical man, *give unto Caesar what is Caesar's*. I see no reason to turn the province into chaos. I have a proposition."

"Yes?"

Lock paused and gave Greta a searching look.

Greta returned his gaze with sincerity.

"Give me the zealot," said Lock, "a list of a few prominent heretics, and pay your autumnal tithe. An example must be made, and when the papal troops arrive, the heads of the heretics will be put up on stakes. You and the other nobles will attend mass and we shall forget that this ever happened."

Greta considered the bishop's offer. He made it sound so reasonable. But behind it were the things that Greta had come more and more to resent, the arrogance, the tithes and the indebtedness. Lutheranism had made her feel free, free from Lock and the chains of his Church of dues and duties. Luke was her lover. *Could she give him up?* Would she not rather have Lock seized, his corruption uncovered, and his lands shared out? Instead of Lock, her lover would stand at the head of a people's Church where folk found God for themselves. And that dream was about to be realised. "My husband always said, never make a decision without sleep. We must obey the wishes of our husbands. Must we not, Lord Bishop? I shall sleep on your offer and give you word in the morning. You of course must allow me to host you for the night here in the schloss. It would be dangerous for you to return in this weather. You know Herr Schwatzborg's carriage was washed into a gully trying to make the road in a thunderstorm?"

Lock felt the trap close around him. "How do I know that I can trust you? Do you give me your word that I shall not be harmed?"

"I swear," said Greta, "that you shall not be harmed, while you are within the walls of my house."

Lock sighed, "I guess I can hope for no better."

"Magda?"

"Yes my lady."

"Arrange to have the guest quarters prepared for his Excellency. I am thinking the sunroom?"

Lock watched the maid leave. The tightness of her bodice accentuated her hips.

"Isn't she lovely," Greta had followed the bishop's eye. "Teach a peasant girl some manners and she will surprise you with her wit, charm and tales of witches, goblins and magic tablecloths. I know a girl, Lord Bishop, who would love to wait upon a man as eminent as you. I promise that you shall enjoy your stay." Greta looked genuinely pleased, and Lock felt a moment's nostalgia for a time when they had not been enemies.

"Countess?"

"Yes, Lord Bishop?"

"I have a question to ask?"

"Speak and I shall see if I can answer it."

"Johann has executed Heinrich the Jew for the murder of Joseph the miller's son. He was innocent. The dead boy's sister is my ward and I promised her I would look into the matter." Lock observed the countess. There was something about the way the she looked at Lock, an odd expression of familiarity. Lock shook his head in feigned sadness. "He was such a fine and gentle lad."

"Yes," said Greta, "He was."

Peter was a rich man. The wagons of his troop were stuffed with loot much of it coming from the Manor of Ujlaki and the ponies groaned under the weight of sacks of treasure, barrels of wine and bolts of cloth. Yet he was not sad to be leaving Hungaria behind. Gone were the endless flat land, the mosquito infested swamps, muddy fields, terrified villages, and tangled forests. Some of his men had become feverish and Peter hoped that the mountain air might do them good. Since morning they had climbed and as the late afternoon sun left the alpine meadows, they made camp in the ruins of a stone tower under the watchful eyes of a herd of chamois.

Peter knew where they were. They were nearing home. The road continued through the mountains to the Pass of Eagles and from there down into the valley of the River Eisen, to Esienberg, and to his wife, Greta. For years he had thought of seeing her upon his homecoming, but now that that moment drew near he was consumed by his desire for Nuray, the Turkish princess. Now that she had yielded to him, and spent her nights in his sheepskin bed. She intoxicated him more than the looted red wine that he drank daily. Krum had once told Peter that love was all in the chase. That once he had tamed a horse all he wanted was a new one to break in. Krum had been wrong. The more time he spent with Nuray the deeper he fell for her.

He felt her eyes on him now as he hammered the peg of his tent into the stony ground.

Nuray cursed him loudly in her own tongue.

Peter rose to his feet as the men approached. He knew them by name, Hans, Erhart, Rolf, and Jan. They were Eisenbergers. They were survivors. Their short swords hung by their wastes, their satin clothes were battered and dirty, and Peter saw that they had a mutinous look, for they approached hesitantly afraid to meet his eye. Peter stared them down. He had hung men before and he would do so again. "Speak your mind," he said as the men drew close. "There is much to do before nightfall."

Jan prodded a stone with his boot. "You're taking us over the Pass of Eagles, my lord?"

"That's right," replied Peter, "we're going home."

"The Pass of Eagles is a road of ill repute my lord," said Hans.

"It is guarded by the dragon Steinbauch," said Rolf

"A ferocious man eating monster," said Erhart. "He will not let us pass."

"Steinbauch is but a story to scare children," said Peter. "Are you children or are you men? There is a real enemy." Peter pointed back along the road they had come. "They are coming for us from the plains. You have seen the plumes of dust thrown up by riders. They are Turkish slavers come to take you to Istanbul in chains. If they ride hard they will be upon us before nightfall. Have you sharpened your swords and oiled your muskets?"

"Steinbauch is no child's tale," said Rolph, "he's as real as you and I. My father was a shepherd and he has seen the beast. He has a body like a huge lizard and the head of a bloodthirsty dog. You may have ridden the pass my lord and were lucky. But can you assure us of the same luck this time?"

The other men nodded and murmured their agreement.

"There may be a way to appease the dragon," said Rolph, "It is said that the monster has a particular love of fair women. If we leave the foreign woman as a sacrifice I'm sure he would let us pass."

Peter drew his sword. "The next man to suggest that again gets his throat cut now and his body left for the vultures."

Peter lit the match of his musket, and stood behind the barricade of baggage and wagons. The thick mountain fog had seemed to arrive from nowhere, blotting out the view of the southern road, the shepherds huts, the stands of pine and mountain oak and the riders whose hooves sounded in the distance. The fog could mean their death. If they could not see the enemy to shoot them they would have little chance when the cavalry were among them.

"It is Steinbauch," Peter heard Hans say. "He controls the fog in the mountains and he wants the Turkish princess."

Peter did not rebuke the mutinous soldier. Instead he kept a tight grip on his musket the sulphurous smell of the smoking wick filling his nostrils. The clop of hooves and the tinkle of bridle bells drew closer.

Beside him Peter could see his arqubusiers kneeling aiming their muskets into the grey blur. "Halt," said Peter in Latin at the invisible enemy, "halt or be fired upon."

The sound of advancing hooves ceased.

A wind blew from the mountains and slowly the fog began to pass, revealing a troop of horsemen, red pendants, fluttering in the ailing light. At first Peter took the horsemen to be Turks but as he looked closer he became less certain. They were not like the knights in their heavy burnished armour that had been broken and massacred at Mohacs, but nor were they Turks. Like the Turks, they were lightly armoured and slashing scimitars hung at their waists but they carried the lances and shields of Christian knights and wore high pointed metal helms, decorated with horsehair plumes. And rising from each saddle was a curved wooden pole, lined with long feathers, giving the warriors the appearance being winged.

"You are Peter Von Eisenberg," said the leader of the riders in Latin, "I am Stanislaw from Krakow and I am fighting Turks not Germans. Tell your men to put away their muskets. We come as allies."

Lock washed his hands and face in a basin of steaming water filled with crushed comfrey. He unbuttoned the front of his shirt so that he could rub the soaked plants into his neck and chest. Though it was not as good as emersion in a full barrel of hot water, filled with rose petals, the hot water on his face and chest had a calming effect. The pretty maid, Zuza, was quietly watching him rather oddly. *Who was she?* Lock didn't trust her. The way she was watching him now, it reeked of treachery and heresy. The countess had planted her there to watch him, to spy on him. He was sure of it.

"Your highness," she asked, "Is it true that you have been to the Holy City, that you have been to Rome?"

Perhaps, thought Lock, he had been wrong about the girl, and that here amidst all this uncertainty, heresy and witch hunting the simple shepherd's girl had never wavered in her devotion to the true Church. What mattered it to her that Rome was a diseased hole, infested with thieves and plagues of starlings? To her it would always be the shining, Holy City. What mattered it to her that the Pope, the Little Father, was a power-crazed maniac and a womaniser, with a peculiar penchant for pagan classics? To her he would always be a living saint, the heavenly voice of the Creator on Earth. "Your Excellency," said Lock after he had dried his face on the hand towel, "you may address me as your Excellency."

The maid looked perplexed, then remembered her training. She blushed then curtseyed. "Yes, your Excellency, forgive me for forgetting my place. I just couldn't help but wonder about God's city."

"You are right to wonder my child," said Lock, in a tone that was suitably resonant, "It is a place like nothing else on this green Earth. The towering illuminated frescoes of Saint Peter's Basilica is like a shard of Heaven, that land of glass and gold, that has fallen upon this Earth, and out stream fountains that rush up like glittering trees of water, and the sick, the lame and the blind are cured as they are doused in them." What mattered it to her that Saint Peter's had been knocked down twenty years ago and never been rebuilt.

The maid let out a long sigh, "Oh it sounds so marvellous. Do you think we will see such things when we are in Heaven?"

"Oh," said the bishop, "you will see far more majestic things than that in Heaven, where the singing of a thousand angels keeps the spirit in a state of constant bliss."

Zuza began to sob. "Oh your excellency, I must make your confession."

Lock generally found confession to be a tedious job, but he felt he could hardly now refuse. "Very well, kneel before me."

Zuza prostrated herself on the floor.

"Are you," intoned Lock, "guilty of the sin of Gluttony?"

"Oh yes," replied the girl, "I like to eat, and the countess feeds us all very well. We even eat chicken on Sundays?"

"God forgives you," replied Lock, "what of the sin of lust?"

"I sleep out of wedlock with the stable hand. But its not that that bothers me your excellency."

"Go on," said Lock.

"Some of the lords and ladies and the servants have started to give their own mass, and though I knew it was sinful I ate bread and drank wine in a ritual not presided over by a priest." Zuza began to cry. "Now I am sure my soul is going to Hell and not to Heaven, and I don't care what the others say"

"There now," said Lock, "dry your eyes. God's Kingdom is never closed to those, who with a willing heart, renounce their sins. What else as been happening in the house?"

"They," Zuza sat upright her eyes brimming with tears of relief. "They have captured a monk, a good man of God, and hold him captive in his lordship's chapel. I have been sent to give him water and bread."

"Felix the black monk," whispered Lock.

"And I fear for you too my lord. There are two men servants guarding your door. They are under orders to prevent you from leaving your room."

"Zuza," said Lock, "God forgives you for your sins, and if you help me I can assure you a place in Heaven among the angles."

"I'll do anything I can."

Peter's tent was made from tanned hides with a willow frame and a linen lining. The two men sat on stools, in the candlelight, beside a barrel of Hungarian wine, which they drank by dipping their vessels into it, Peter from a looted silver goblet, Stanislaw from an ancestral aurochs horn.

The wine was dark, grainy and filled with stirred up sediment. Peter felt the world become unsteady around him and the face of Stanislaw blurred. The prince was strong and handsome with a well-oiled moustache and beard. He was much younger than Peter, perhaps no older than twenty, yet Peter recognised something in that face he knew in himself, the horror of war, the gallons of blood that never washed off. It drove a man to drink.

Stanislaw refilled his horn. "You escaped Mohacs?"

"I guess I'm lucky."

"What happened? One day there was the glorious Kingdom of Hungaria, the next Turkish infidel soldiers were threatening our marches."

"Ten thousand Christian knights, each a lord of the land, charged at a column of janissaries. The janissaries fired mass volleys of muskets. I think a handful of knights made it back alive. Then they attacked." Peter paused as he remembered, the slashing swords of the Turks against skewering long swords of the landsknecht. "We repulsed them," said Peter as he downed his wine, "and then we fled."

Stanislaw leaned forward grinning at Peter, "And what did you flee from?" but his twisted smile said that he already knew the answer.

"The Turkish horse."

"Aren't they beautiful," said Stanislaw.

"I wouldn't know," said Peter, "I didn't wait to find out."

Stanislaw laughed and slapped Peter on the arm. "You missed out on a beautiful sight. For weeks they harried us across the plain. But we," the lancer's face glowed with pride, "but we have faster steads and longer spears. You Germans think you can fight the Turks without proper horsemen? You are fighting blind. Germania is but a collection of pretentious princelings. The Turks will knock you over one at time and their armies will move faster than the news of them."

Peter felt in his pouch for some cheese wrapped in linen. He sliced off a piece with his dagger, and proffered the remainder to his guest. "Where are you headed?" asked Peter, trying to change the subject from marauding enemy armies laying waste to Christendom.

"East, to Vienna. If the Turks are to be defeated then Christians must unite. Only if the Commonwealth and the Empire work together can we contain the threat." Stanislaw slapped his satchel; "I have diplomatic letters from the King of Krakow to the Emperor of the Germans."

Peter refilled his cup. "Last I heard of the emperor was that he was recruiting men for an invasion of Rome. He was offering excellent pay."

"What!?" Stanislaw, spat out the wine, spraying it on the walls of the tent. "Christendom is under threat and he's planning an invasion of the Holy City. *Kurva mac.*"

Nuray threw open the flaps of the tent and walked in. "*Seni alman domuzu,*" she walked over to Peter picked up his goblet of wine and threw it in his face and spat at Peter's feet.

Stanislaw laughed. "What a spirited vixen! How much would you sell her for?"

Peter drew his dagger and slammed it into the barrel. "She's not for sale."

Lock listened through the keyhole, while Zuza spoke to the guards.

"Her lady has finished feasting with her guests. But it seems as if the party had little hunger, for there are plates of leftovers, even saffroned lamb, and plenty of wine. It has all been taken to the kitchens. But you must make haste. I don't imagine that there will be much left after a turn of the clock."

A few moments later after the sound of their footsteps had receded. Zuza pushed open the door. "Come your highness we must make haste before we are discovered.

The Pink Room had been built to accommodate Greta's late father-in-law's collection of antique arms and armour, the prize being five suits used in the crusades, each covered in a white surcoat emblazoned with an iron cross. The walls were coated in pink plaster for its vibrant manliness, and the room was lit with an open fire. It was here that Greta brought together the meeting of conspirators, two dozen of the most prominent nobles, burgers and guildsmen, invited for their commitment to the cause. Among them were Friedrich, Johann, and the richest engineers of the Iron Guild.

The anticipation in the room was palpable and when the last guest had arrived, Greta clapped her hands, to silence the murmuring crowd. "I am grateful that you have come to attend us here. Now that we are all assembled, I see no reason why we should not begin forthwith."

Luke spoke from where he stood beside the fireplace, its light playing off his handsome face and warm smile. "We are here because we believe, nay we know, that the only way to God is through Him. Only through prayer and our own reading of the scripture can we attain that, and the only place the corrupt Church leads you is into the arms of the Devil. Brethren, we are at the dawn of a new era in which we will create God's Kingdom on Earth and it is His will that we shall be rebaptised for only as an act of conscious will can one be invited into His Kingdom. In the barrel you see beside the fire is the purest water from a mountain spring. Who would like to be first?"

Greta rose to her feet. "I shall."

She gasped as she immersed herself in the cold water and she felt it seep through her layers of clothes.

"He that is baptised and believes shall be saved," whispered Luke.

Zuza led Lock through the shadows of the trees, Hazel, birch and fruiting Elder. Lock stared into the darkness beneath the trees. An owl hooted in the forest. Lock Shuddered. He had always been a little afraid of the dark. "Is it far to Go?"

"Not far, your Excellency," whispered Zuza. "We are nearly there."

Lock followed the girl down into the ditch. Wild roses clawed at his cloak and nettles brushed against his leg. He followed her up a grassy mound. At the top of the mound was a black hole.

"There," whispered Zuza, "He's down there. Inside the chapel mound."

"Brother Felix," Lock called into the hole and heard his voice echo in the space beyond, "are you in there?" As he stared into the darkness Lock felt fear grip him. Maybe the girl had tricked him and would push him in.

"Your Excellency," the voice of the black monk echoed back, "can that really be you?"

"Yes," said Lock, "it is I. How do we get you out of there?"

"A rope," replied the monk, " throw me a rope and pull me through the hole?"

"A rope," Lock turned to Zuza, "do we have a rope?"

"I don't have any rope your excellency."

Lock began to pace backward and forward. Somewhere nearby a nightingale called.

"Your Excellency," began Zuza, "forgive me for asking, but if we tie our cloaks together, and I could even remove my gown, then perhaps we could make a rope long enough to reach the monk."

"That's it," said Lock, "bless you child."

"Of course," said Greta conversationally to a dripping Herr Fluss, "now that we are Lutherans we are freed from all our debts to the false Church."

"Not to mention," said Friedrich, who was wringing out his sleeves, "our annual tithes. I don't know about you, but I can't spare any of my harvest this year to pay for Lock to bathe in milk and sup on boiled swallows."

Water pooled at Captain Johann's feet as he sat on the edge of his stool. "Oh why don't you just speak to the point. We're Lutherans now. That means Lock is gone. The question is how to divide his property?"

A brief and awkward silence followed, that Greta felt compelled to fill. "The villages in the northern part of the river valley pay Lock for tenancy. It would make sense if they came under the protection of the von Eisenberg domain. If we are to begin spreading the word of Luther then the common people must be persuaded to follow."

"I suppose the bishop's departure would leave empty his town house," observed Herr Ebes, a wealthy Burgher.

"Hold on to your clock," said Johann, "The town properties of the Church must surely pass to the city guard."

"What," said William, the foreign witch hunter, "of the abbey of

Saint Hildegard the Virgin? I will give my men and my pistols for the first of their treasures."

Greta felt discomfort creep over her. The abbey was part of her emotional landscape and she visited it to give alms. Ivy covered its walls, shading the neat gardens tended by the dark robed sisters, at the foot of the cave filled cliffs. They made excellent cakes, and omelettes and even brewed their own ale. It was a haven for women and girls from across the kingdom "Are abbeys," asked Greta, "disallowed by Luther?"

"A monastic life," said Luke the only dry person in the room, "has no basis in scripture, either for men or women. But I am not here for material gain. I am here to spread the new creed. The question then is how do we destroy the power of Bishop Lock?"

"Exactly," said the Widow Messer, "If we kill Lock, seize his lands and reject the Pope, then won't that put us at war with the Empire?"

Greta smiled. She'd hoped somebody would ask that question. It was the one she had long dwelt on herself. "Do not worry about the emperor. He himself is at war with Rome. I have been writing with Duke Ferdinand of Vienna. He wants our support against the Turks. Other princes have embraced Luther. Ferdinand considers faith to be a matter of a noble's conscience."

"What about Peter?" asked Herr Fluss. "The count was always on good terms with the Bishop."

Greta thought about her husband. He had been obsessed with fighting and spent most of his hours with his soldiers, yet he had lavished every favour upon his wife, and Greta's memories of him were fond. He had been fair, and at times gentle, and she had loved him but that was long ago. "The Count von Eisenberg," said Greta, "is dead, slain by the Turks on the field of Mohacs."

The group began to talk in a low hubbub.

"My condolences," said Herr Fluss, "Peter was a good man."

"I suppose," said Friedrich with a grin, "that makes you the Widow von Eisenberg?"

"That solves it," said Johann. "I will have Lock seized tomorrow."

"There will be no need for that," said Greta and here she let the fox out of the sack, "I have him and that cursed inquisitor under guard in this very house. There will be no need to spill any blood."

At that moment there was a knock on the Pink Room door, and an armed servant entered, a glum expression on his face.

Lock and Zuza, heaved as they pulled Felix, span by span toward the hole. Lock felt distinctly vulnerable without his regal cloak and tunic and distinctly aware that the young woman, pulling behind him, was at least as strong as he and that his fatness was clearly visible in his white under shirt. He glanced over his shoulder and saw that the girl, stripped to her under gown, was the very picture of physical fitness.

"One, two, three, pull," said the girl.

They both pulled. There was bang and a curse from inside the hole.

"I think he's at the top," said Zuza.

The two of them watched as Felix pulled himself out of the hole and stood on the mound, his silhouette illuminated by the rising moon. His monk's habit flapped in the wind. He turned his face heavenward. His face looked gaunt and his beard covered his mouth. The storm had moved on and the wind had whipped the sky clean of clouds. "There is a bright moon tonight," said the black monk, "and enough light to ride by. Horses, we must have horses."

"You'll find them in the stables. Only the stable boy will be watching them. He's a good lad."

Felix turned his attention to the girl. "Who," he asked Lock, "is she?"

"She is something of a saint among this den of heretics," said Lock.

"I see," said Felix. "You shall be returning with us to the city?"

"Oh no, I couldn't do that," she said, "I have my duties to attend to." Dressed only in her underclothes the girl shivered.

The black monk shrugged.

Lock opened his mouth to speak, but before he had chance Felix drew a long dagger from his robe and slit Zuza's throat in one swift movement.

She collapsed on the ground blood flowing over her white undergarments.

"Why?" shouted Lock, anger rising in his voice.

"Quiet," said Felix, "we are in the midst of a war between God and the Devil. She has served her purpose. Shed your tears over the peasant later. Come with me if you want to live and win."

Basha was thirsty. It had been a long time since the servant had brought victuals. Her chamber pot was full and her body ached. The baby inside her needed water. She tossed and turned in her bed, unable to sleep. Tears began to flow from her eyes."

"Basha, Basha, Babushki?"

Was she going mad? Somebody was calling her name. It sounded like it was coming from the pile of straw. Was it a Dybbuk, a ghost or a daemon?

"Babushki it is I, Soloman son of Abraham."

Basha knew now that the voice speaking must be that of a spiteful Dybbuk. "Go away you evil spirit," she shouted, "Leave me in misery. No friend could find me here."

"No, Basha," said the voice. "It's I, Soloman. You do not really think that your grandmother will let anybody have any peace until you've been brought back? I'm on the other side of the wall, in the neighbouring room. I climbed up the hanging tree and through the windows. Jango the traveller, son of Zafir, saw your black kerchief when he went to see the hanging. The word spread that you were here. I have brought a saw and an axe and I shall rescue you."

Despite the pain Basha leapt to her feet. "Solomon," she shouted, "you don't know how much I love you."

When Lock and Felix arrived at the Forest Gate, Lock fell of his horse while trying to dismount. He wasn't sure what felt worse, his arse from the long dangerous ride, or his heart from the pointless slaughter of Zuza and the stable boy. Lock had always thought of Sonia as innocent and chuckled to himself at her gullibleness, but in that moment as he lay in the mud outside the city gate, he realised that he was scarcely less innocent then she. In one day he had seen a women hung by her wrists and whipped to death and had had a friend slaughtered in front of his eyes by a man he had considered his ally. *Were the lives of women so cheap that men could slaughter them for sport? What kind of god approved of such barbarity?*

Felix pounded on the door with his fist. "Open in the name of God," he shouted. "I escort his Excellency the Lord Bishop Manfred Lock."

The oak doors swung open. Three men stood between Lock and the city. One man held a lit torch. And Lock could see the blue and yellow of their slashed satin doublets. They wore steal breastplates and black helmets, in the Italian fashion, adorned with red feathers. They carried swords and daggers. "Bene est, qui venit in nomine Domini Dei vestri," said the middle of the two men, "For I am Aldo captain of the Swiss Guard sent by his Holiness. I have secured the city."

the next morning
the 29th of September, Day of the Archangels,
Year of the Lord 1526

Bishop Lock stood at the altar in the gothic church. Ranks of smoking candles lit the faces of the crowd with a gloomy light. The size of the crowd surprised Lock. It seemed that much of the town was there. Lock did not have a reputation for exciting sermons but now it seemed he was the man of the hour.

There were few nobility present, but the townsfolk had crowded into the church to hear him speak. There were innkeepers, tanners, shopkeepers, smiths, breeders, brewers, masons and broom makers. There were cobblers, tailors, butchers, cooks, turners, weavers, painters, wheelwrights, carters, chandlers and cheese makers. There were devout country folk - peasant women wrapped from head to foot in thick layers of colourful cloth, sitting beside men in sheepskin coats and wooden shoes, all with dark tans and emanating the irrepressible stench of sheep.

And hanging by the door and spilling out into the courtyard were people that usually avoided the church – Leopold the alchemist, dressed in a peculiar blue robe decorated with crystals that dangled from strings. There were whores and pickpockets, known usurers and counterfeiters, pimps and beggars. And beyond them were the most unexpected of all, black-cloaked Jews and a handful of bejewelled Travellers.

Lock read off the paper. It was not the kind sermon that he would have given. The document had been hammered out during the night with Felix and Aldo of the papal guard. They allowed him to have moments of creative flourish but they had insisted on the inclusion of sections that Lock considered too incendiary. Lock's shaky voice was carried by the ingenious acoustics of the building to its furthest corners.

"This is the day of the Archangels, the seraphim, the highest of the Lord's servants. And on this day I am moved to think of one angel in particular, Michael, for he is the wielder of the sword, the holy avenger of the heavenly Father who drove the traitor Satan into the frozen depths of Hell. He is the commander of the heavenly hosts and most feared by the demons and the enemies of God. Today we must pray to Michael and his shining sword for we face here in Eisenberg our own day of reckoning.

"There are men and women among us who have fallen from God's grace and embraced the heresy of Luther. Know that thenceforth they are excommunicated from the true Church. It is no sin to kill a heretic nor to seize or destroy his property. This city is now in the hands of the servants of God and no heretic either noble or baseborn shall be shown mercy."

Book Three

Pike and Powder

the 16th of October, the eve of the battle
Year of the Lord 1526

They rode through the city in the warmth of the midday sun – proud men and boys on fine horses and ponies, dressed in silks with long black hair. The women and girls, their faces pierced with silver and gold rode in the wagons. And as the wheels rolled they sang the song of wanderers, and its strange melancholy touched hearts of the townsfolk that had gathered to watch the Travellers pass.

Basha stood and watched beside her father Heinrich. Both had escaped captivity, and the Church, that now held the city in an iron grip, had pardoned them. They had reason to be happy, but the threat of war and violence hung over the slate roofed city like a flock of gathering crows. The black monk was said to spare no one accused of heresy and townsfolk disappeared in the night while disfigured corpses multiplied on the city walls. The nobility had fled the town and Heinrich's commerce had slowed to a trickle.

"Where do the Travellers go?" Basha asked her father.

"They go where the sun shines, the days are never short, and the swallows flock in the winter."

One of the horsemen slowed as he passed. He was dressed in silk pants and an open sheepskin coat. It was Jango, son of Zafir. Basha caught his eye and smiled at him.

He nudged his horse toward her and slid elegantly off its back. He took her hand in his and kissed it.

Basha laughed and kissed him on the cheek. "Jango, I do not know how to thank you. If it were not for you recognizing my kerchief I should still be a captive in Captain Johann's house."

"Come with us, Basha the Beautiful" said Jango. "My father's wives have read the oracle. An ill fate hangs over these mountain valleys.

War is coming. Come with us. You will fear no evil captain. You will see realms, strange and wondrous, and I shall protect you."

Basha reached her hand to her belly. "I am with child. Strange though it may sound, I know that it is his destiny to be born here. It is what Joseph would have wished. And I belong here with my father and my folk."

Jango looked back at the procession. The last wagon was passing. He turned his attention back to Basha and pulled open his coat to reveal his two daggers and pistol that rested in his orange sash. "But Basha I know of no woman in any land Christian, Muslim, traveler, or Jew who is as beautiful as you. I love you. Come away with me and I will be a father to your child. And when the summer comes we will return to the green grass and fields of your home. "

"Dearest Jango," replied Basha, "I cannot come, and I cannot yet love you except as a brother. Would you stay and be a brother to me?"

Jango's eyes moved from Basha's face to the walls of the inner city behind her, where dozens of men were hung, dead and flayed accused of heresy. He brought his eyes back to rest on Basha's face.

"Must we meet here?" asked Lord Bishop Lock.

The troop of papal guard had set themselves up in the barracks and tower of the inner city North Gate, while Felix, the black monk, had appropriated Johann's house. From here they instigated a reign of terror. The soldiers of the old city guard had either been executed for disloyalty or absorbed into the Swiss Guard. Everyday the papal troops dragged a handful of townsfolk before the black monk who invariably tortured them to death. His favorite tool was a pair of iron pincers, which he kept red hot in the fire. Lock had tried to tell Felix that the maiming and killing was not increasing the Church's popularity. But the inquisitor was impervious to reason.

"Your Excellency must forgive me for not visiting you in your house. I am a busy man. I have been informed that the countess plans to attack on the morrow. Her forces have mustered at the schloss. We're abandoning the outer city."

"Is that wise?" said Lock, "surely it demonstrates a loss of authority? We have already been unable to secure the iron foundries"

Felix gave Lock a cold look. The loss of iron foundries infuriated him. No one had expected the Iron guild to declare for the Lutherans. But they had and they had fortified the foundries outside the city walls on the east bank of the river, where they were protected by cannon. "He who defends everything defends nothing," said Felix, his eyes locked on the plans of the cities defense held down with iron weights on the wooden table. We are only beginning to understand the depth of the evil we are facing. The heretics will come and I cannot defend five miles of wall with three hundred men."

"Three hundred and fifty men," said Lock.

"Oh yes," said Felix his voice heavy with sarcasm, "the Bishop's Guard? Have they ever been in a battle or are they just trained in extracting payments from soft fingered merchants?"

"They know their stuff," said Lock defensively.

"I'm sure," said Felix. "Now, once we have abandoned the Outer City we weaken the north gate of the inner-city to invite an attack. Here," he tapped the map with his poker, "we will create a killing ground."

Sounds lovely, thought Lock. He was hungry for something well sugared and in need of distraction. The inquisitor, who he had always considered to be worldly and well educated, had become a bloodthirsty tyrant. With the power of the Swiss Guard behind him he paid only lip service to Lock's seniority and did as he pleased treating Lock like a meddling grandmother. He was actually surprised that the monk was sharing his battle plans, but the more Lock heard, the less he cared for it.

"You," the black monk directed his poker in the direction of Lock, "will remain in your house protected by your guard. We cannot risk you being killed or captured, and allow the Lutherans to claim victory."

"There you can depend on me," said Lock, "I have no interest in being killed or captured."

A guard entered the meeting room. He was armed with sword and dagger. It was Steffen, Lock's own man. "Heinrich the Jew is here to see you your Excellency," he reported, "shall I send him away?"

"No," said Lock, "send the good man in."

Felix gave Lock a scathing look, stood, took his cloak and threw it over the battle plans.

Greta watched from her wooden throne that had been moved down to the parade ground as the mounted nobles charged toward the straw men. They were an impressive sight nearly three hundred mounted Lutheran knights, the male members of the noble families of the province.

Greta watched as Friedrich, dressed in full plate armour, collided with a straw man driving his sword into the scarecrow's head. Greta wondered what it would be like to watch if it was a real man of flesh and blood. She felt a surge of fear and anticipation at what was about to happen. Lock and the black monk would pay. She had tried to do things without spilling blood, but it had already been spilled. She felt cold just thinking about the stiff lifeless body of Zuza the maid, and the gutted stable boy. She had not seen the bodies that decorated the inner city wall, but she had heard of them. Her people were suffering and she was determined to end it. Tomorow the iron guild would train their cannons on the River Gate, and bombard the city through out the following day, drawing the Church forces to the east. Meanwhile her forces would arrive at the Forest Gate in the west. Loyal townsfolk within the city would then open the gate. The arrival of the nobility was to be the spark that would set off an uprising against the bishop's tyranny, from which she hoped to extract a quick surrender.

Frederick wheeled his horse, cantered over to Greta, and dismounted from his white charger. A pageboy came forward to take the reigns. Friedrich removed his helmet "Fear not, my lady," he said, "we shall give them hell on the morrow. And bring you the heads of Bishop Lock and the black monk the following day."

"What do you mean bring me the following day? I shall be commanding the assault."

Friedrich laughed, "Absolutely not, a battle is no place for a woman."

"But what about Joan of Ark?" said Greta?

"You are not Joan of Ark," said Friedrich his tone becoming haughty and frustrated. "There will be blood and horrible things happening in the battle. You will most likely faint and then we will have to spare men to carry you out. Something could happen to you. You could get shot. And then who would I have to marry after this bloody thing is over?"

"Uh," Greta put her shoulders back and expelled air through her mouth in a sound that suggested her indignation on multiple levels. "I hope, Lord Friedrich, that your concern for me is not simply in the manner of a future marital investment because I tell you now that you are not going to marry me."

"We'll see about that," said Friedrich, "An unmarried woman is an abomination unto God."

"Shall I tell that to the bastard son that you fathered of my kitchen maid?"

Friedrich was about to reply when Luke, the Lutheran preacher, also rode up and dismounted. He was dressed in the clothes Greta had given him on the night on which he had appeared and was armed with a sword and pistol. He bowed to Greta, feigning a lack of familiarity. He also inclined his head toward Friedrich. "Are you ready," he asked her, "to lead the forces of goodness to victory?"

Greta smiled warmly.

"The countess," said Friedrich through gritted teeth, "Is not going into the city even if that means I have to tie her to a tree."

"I'm sure you would love that," said Greta, "tying to me to a tree while I scream at you. Is this the kind of treatment that I have to look forward to in your marital fantasies."

A third man then rode up but did not dismount. It was Johann, formally captain of the city guard. He was loathsome but at least he knew how to fight. "I have a boon to ask." He said almost rudely. "I do not wish to join the main assault."

Heinrich stroked the piece of the torah he kept around his neck for luck as he entered the house in which the evil Captain Johann had once imprisoned his daughter. Now it was the headquarters of the black monk. He was accompanied by his new sworn son, Jango, armed with sword and pistol, and by Isaac son of Isaac, who was known for his strength and bravery. A musketeer led them into the square stone room that was the parlor. Iron pincers and an iron poker glowed red in a bed of hot embers in the fireplace. A table stood in the middle of the room, covered with a black cloak. The lord bishop and the black monk each sat on a chair. A further chair was placed for Heinrich to sit.

Heinrich bowed, sweeping off his black pointed hat. "Heinrich son of Mendel at your service."

"Heinrich, you old wizard," said Lock, "I shall make use of your service forthwith. I have a metaphysical problem. Brother Felix claims that Jewish folk are evil. Brother Felix is in a foul mood. " Lock held Heinrich's gaze, "He has not killed anyone since breakfast. Our problem is this: if the way to God is through Christ why should Brother Felix suffer a Jew to live."

Felix sat immobile, silent and expressionless.

Heinrich inwardly smiled, while keeping his outward appearance of fear and difference, " I can answer your question my lords. There was once a great prince. According to tradition he would bestow upon his favorite son the ring of his forefathers. Now it so happened that the prince had three sons. He did not want the others to know which was his favorite so he made two identical rings and after his funeral rites had been committed, no son could tell who had the true ring. This is the same as the three great religions of the world Christianity, Mohamedism, and Kabbalism. We all consider ourselves to be the heirs of God's truth but only the Father knows, and no man can claim they know more than God."

Lock clapped his hands "And there you have it, Felix. How could we relieve the man of his life when such weighty matters remain unresolved? Now, put that cursed poker away. Heinrich, we would be grateful for your aide."

Heinrich inclined his head. "Last night the council of the exiled met. It is not our custom to involve ourselves in the conflicts of Christians. But we cannot risk Johann reclaiming power in Eisenberg. You have shown yourself a friend of the exiles. And we are willing to bare arms with you. I tell you now and in earnest, you have not made yourself loved among your fellow Christians and you shall need us if you are to win. In exchange we ask that you lighten the rules of the kingdom that bind us, and that our lands and houses may belong to our children ad infinitum."

With one hand Jango stroked his beard, the other hand rested on the butt of his pistol.

"How many fighting men do you have?" Felix drew his cloak from the table revealing the plans of the city.

Lock breathed an audible sigh of relief. The black monk was not so blinded with hate as to recognize help when he saw it.

the Day of the Battle, 17th of October
Year of the Lord 1526

"It was the best I could do," said Lock. The war gear was several generations old yet still formidable, the legacy of Bishop Shultz, one of Lock's military minded predecessors from a time when the Church was the undisputed power of Eisenberg.

The Jews worked loading the leather tunics, brimmed iron helmets, swords, bucklers and crossbows onto donkeys and carts.

"May God favor us," said Heinrich after fitting a leather tunic over his robes.

"Tell me," said Lock "it must feel good to have escaped from a sentence for murder."

Heinrich watched as a tailor counted out a collection of cross bow bolts. "I am innocent of that ghastly crime."

"So I believe," said Lock. "But I have sworn an oath to the boy's sister that I shall find out the truth of his death. Who did kill Joseph Muller, and why? Was there any man who wished the boy ill, perhaps jealous of the love of Basha the Beautiful?"

Heinrich shook his head "I can think of no man who would have done such a thing."

"Can you not?"

"No."

"But there's something that bothers you isn't there? What is it?"

"Zafir, Prince of the Travellers, his first wife," said Heinrich, "She is a reader of oracles. She knew. She said Joseph would be at his farm the next morning and so he was."

"He had been missing?" said Lock.

"Yes for several days and he had sent no word to Basha. It was unlike him. Zafir's wife said he had been made an offer by a man and it was an offer that he had refused."

Countess Greta Von Eisenberg rode beside Friedrich, who was the younger brother of her husband, Peter, dead at the hands of the

Turks. The overhanging bows of the ancient beech trees, their leaves tinged with yellow, created a tunnel above the mud-rutted track that was the Forest Road. The road was ploughed into thick mud by the hooves of myriad horses and torn up by the tusks of wild boars. The mounted nobles rode two by two, their velvet doublets and vellum boots flecked with mud, swords and daggers clanging against their armour in time to the motion of their horses.

It was late afternoon when Greta saw the walls of Eisenberg. The slanting sun gave the grey stonewalls an orange glow. The shadows of the trees loomed over the single sodden field that separated the army of nobles from the city gate. There were no signs of any guards or watchers. Two flags, baring the hammers of Eisenberg and the cross of the church hung limp in the still air from the slate roofed gate turrets. Seven iron cages dangled from the gate's parapet, filled with the dismembered bodies of townsfolk. Crows, ravens and hawks clung to the cages or circled above them.

Greta instinctively crossed herself. *What further proof was needed that she was on the side of right?*

All was silent. The Iron portcullis was lowered, and the gate unmanned and yet it appeared as impregnable as if it had been crowded with enemies.

Greta felt a churning in the pit of her stomach. She glanced at the men around her. She knew them all and she saw in their faces that they felt as she did. They were men of peace who had lived their lives hunting, dancing and feasting. They were little more than wealthy peasants. Herr Schwazborg had brought his hunting dogs and they scratched themselves happily in the mud while their master looked pale.

Friedrich glared at Luke who nudged his horse forward so that he sat beside Greta.

Friedrich leaned forward in his saddle. "You had men on the inside to open the gate. Where are they?"

"They are waiting," said Luke, "ride to the gate and sound your hunting horns and we shall see if God will answer."

Friedrich wheeled his horse to face the assembled army. "Advance to the gate and sound the horns," he shouted.

Schwazborg's dogs barked as the nobles spurred their horses and blew their horns. They galloped forward churning the mud of the field.

Greta had passed through the Forest Gate many times before but now it seemed to tower above her. The sound of the horns ceased as the mass of nobles drew up to the gate. The dogs kept barking.

Nothing happened.

Some blew more blasts on their horns but still the portcullis did not move.

The sun slid behind the hills throwing the walls into shadow.

"Where are your men?" shouted Friedrich angrily. "We are waiting like fools on the door step."

A blast of horns, drums and trumpets sounded from within. Men began to appear on the walls. Brandishing scathes spears and pitchforks. "For God," they shouted, "for God."

Greta suppressed an involuntary shudder. She knew that the townsfolk greeted her as a savior and ally. But there was something about an armed rabble of common folk that twisted in her noble gut.

Guild Master, Albrecht Schmitt, lovingly surveyed his small army. He may only have fifty men but they were armed with the new creations of his workshops, creations that would make him richer than many a king. They were armed with wheellock muskets, faster and easier to fire then matchlocks, their spinning iron wheels would rub against cylinders of brimstone which would send sparks into the flash pan. His men were armoured with black-iron breastplates and full metal helmets. They carried satchels filled with bombs, iron cases stuffed with black powder and set with fast burning fuses. He also had his secret weapon – two mobile cannon. Fresh off the furnace, each gun was pulled by two mules and crewed by five men.

Albrecht was the man of the hour. He would storm into the city before the nobles could get through the gate, take out the papal mercenaries and claim the spoils of the victor. There would be a new lord of Eisenberg, and it would be the baseborn son of a blacksmith.

The first cannon ball left the muzzle of the weapon with a resounding boom. It crashed into the seasoned oak of the River Gate. The structure shuddered and held.

It took eight rounds to reduce the doors of the River Gate to a pile of splinters and twisted iron. The soldiers of the Iron guild marched across the bridge. The mules pulled and the cannon rolled forward. The river, dark and swollen with rain, roared beneath them.

There were no enemy to meet them on the other side of the gate, where the merchant houses, of the southeast quarter lined the street that wound toward the inner city.

"Load the cannon with grapeshot," Albrecht ordered as the troop paused at the breech.

Greta rode under the stone arch of the Forest Gate, Luke on one side, and Friedrich on the other. The smell of the rotting bodies in the cages filled her nose.

"If I bring you the head of the Inquisitor will you marry me?" asked Friedrich.

"Women usually prefer bunches of flowers to severed heads. If you're to have any chance at all, you will have to master the basics." Greta realized that the banter was a way of calming her nerves and her voice hadn't carried the genuine rage and disgust she felt earlier at the proposition.

Three by three the Nobles filed into the Square of flower sellers. The square was normally the sight of various entertainments, traveling tumblers and players, criminals in stocks, or exhibitions of the bizarre. The edges of the square were usually filled with flower sellers, peddlers, beggars, buskers, and food sellers. But on that night dead men and women hung from the gate and the square was filled with grim determined townsfolk, men and women, who parted to let the column of cavalry pass. They carried carving knives, pokers, axes, cudgels, hammers, sickles, lanterns, torches and cobblestones. The hill of the inner city loomed up before them, a maze of narrow streets and slate roofs. Perched on the highest rock was the bishop's house, candlelight glowing in its tower. No lights illuminated the windows of the wood and thatch houses that clustered together overhanging the square.

As she passed the townsfolk Greta felt unsure of what to do next. Should she smile at them, say something to inspire them, tell them to fall inline beside her. Greta wavered. She felt herself wishing that Peter were there. He was a soldier. He would have known what to do. But Peter was dead.

Somewhere in the evening a boom shattered the oppressive silence and reverberated through the city.

Greta's horse reared and clapped his hooves of the cobbled ground.

The assembled townsfolk looked around them frightened and unsure. They began to speak in low murmur of voices.

"I shall speak to the people," she heard Luke, the preacher say.

He spurred his horse back toward the city gate, dismounted and climbed the stairs on to the city wall. "Folk of Eisenberg," his deep resonant voice carried through the square and into the streets. "Your countess has come to you in your hour of need to deliver you from the evil that grips this city. Now she has need of you. The granaries and the treasures of the Church shall be opened, for the Church should be poor and its wealth will be distributed. We will need you to risk your lives for what is right and holy but know that your nobles are not afraid to ride first into the swords of the enemy. The cavalry shall lead the way. The enemy will fly before them, and you shall follow in the breach, to gold, glory and the Kingdom of Heaven, for good shall always triumph over evil."

The townsfolk cheered and raised their weapons.

Bishop Lock had no stomach for pacing the battlements and instead opted for a quiet dinner with his lover Sonia in the calm of his town house. He began to relax, surrounded by his books, his collection of seals, and his paintings of helpfully nude pagan goddesses. But sadly he had no appetite for the duck stuffed with apples and plums and he chewed listlessly on the same piece of flesh while contemplating the pale supple breasts, and glossy cascade of blond hair attributed to one of his Aphrodites.

"What's wrong my lovely Devil?" asked Sonia moving her hand over to touch his.

Lock turned to survey his innocent lover. *Would the Lutherans spare her, or, as Lock's consort, would she swing decapitated from the city walls with her head impaled on a stake?* Would Lock's own life soon be forfeit? If anybody must die, surely it must be him? He was after all the very symbol of papal avarice. And it was his wealth that they wanted. *How would they do it*, he wondered, *hanging?* That was much too tame. Quartering? Burning?

"You're afraid aren't you?" said Sonia, "You're afraid the heretics will come into the inner city and they'll take us all and boil us to death."

Boiling? Surely that was the worst.

The crash of cannon sounded in the city.

Evening came and the room grew dim.

William von Munich the witch hunter leaned against the rock of the cliff that made the south wall of Eisenberg more or less impregnable. He was dressed for battle in his slashed silks. Sword and dagger hung from his waist while each of his two pistols sat in a holster.

"Those fancy silks of yours, they'll be ruined before the night's out," said Captain Johann.

"One never knows when he shall meet a lady," replied William, "or for that matter a witch. I always like the young witches to admire my taste, wealth and physique before I begin to extract their confession."

Johann gritted his teeth. He hated the arrogance of the witch hunter and his tales of dealing with wicked young witches and hungry succubae had poisoned Johann's heart with jealousy. But he had to be patient. His guardsmen had been executed or dispersed and William was the only person who had listened to his plan and agreed to accompany him. If he got to Lock's house first and held the bishop captive then he could claim the victory and he alone. Johann fitted an iron key into the tiny wooden door built into the south wall.

"And you believe this passage leads up under the hill to the bishop's house?" asked William.

"I'm from Eisenberg," replied Johann, "my father was from Eisenberg and so was his father before him. The tunnels of the old iron mines lead through the berg to the bishop's house."

The door creaked and shuddered as Johann pulled it open to reveal a rough cut stone staircase winding down into the earth. A musky damp smell rose from the passage and the cool breeze caressed the faces of the two men.

"Aren't we supposed to be going up?" asked William.

"You'd better set to work on that tinderbox," Johann ignored the witch hunter's question, "And get those candles lit."

The army of the Iron Guild marched slowly along the winding street. They made no secret of their passage, the men grunting and swearing, the mules braying and complaining, and the guns rattling and creaking. It was twilight when their path led them into the tightly packed and overhanging houses of the Jewish quarter. No candlelight seeped from the shuttered windows. There was no person to be seen. It seemed the Jewish folk were wisely huddling in the darkness behind their locked doors. If Albrecht had been a Jew, he would be doing the same. He would not want to be seen on the street while a troop of battle ready smiths armed with the greatest weapons in Christendom patrolled their streets. Albrecht stroked the butt of his wheellock pistol. With a pull of the trigger the flint wheel would spin against a piece of brimstone firing the weapon, so much more elegant than bothering with a burning wick. Albrecht found himself hoping that he would find a Jew wondering about outside. He wanted to see the pistol in action.

They were marching through a crossroads when a set of shutters was thrown open, a man stepped toward the open window with a crossbow and fired. The bolt hit Albrecht's breastplate at an angle and glanced off, clattering on the cobblestones. "Son of a whore," he swore. His armour had turned away the bolt but the force of it had stung like the Devil.

There was a clatter as the shutters along the street were thrown open and the barrage began.

Basha handed the next loaded crossbow to Jango. She took a moment to glance out the window and listen to the twang and hiss of the crossbows. The Christians were pinned around their cannon. Many bolts missed their mark smashing harmlessly on the ground. Many were turned away by armour, but some bit home. Basha watched as a bolt sank into a man's neck. He gargled as he fell choking on blood. A mule screamed as it was hit in the flank. A man fell onto his knees as a bolt cut into his thigh. She felt no pity for them. Her time as a captive had changed her and she wanted only to see them suffer.

She heard their leader shout an order. The Christians stood and aimed their muskets at the windows and fired. Sparks flashed. The muskets let off a rippling crash followed by a cloud of thick, stinking smoke. A bullet smashed through the wood of the shutters.

"Bombs," she heard their leader shout.

Albrecht watched as the men lit the bomb fuses from the nearest lantern, and then hurled them at the houses or into the side streets and courtyards. There was a moment's silence and then a series of fantastic explosions that made Albrecht's heart soar with pride. The top of a house was blown open in a shattering crash of slate. Another house had caught fire. People were screaming.

Albrecht watched as another bomb soared through the night and through the open window of a house. But no sooner had it entered the window than it was caught by an enemy and thrown back, landing among a cluster of Albrecht's own men.

As the bomb exploded it ignited more bombs setting off a terrible blast of black powder that knocked Albrecht to the ground.

Albrecht picked himself up and looked around. Many of his men had been torn apart. He felt sick. He heard the shouts and war cries of the attackers. They surged from the doorways of their burning houses, dressed in black cloaks and wielding swords and shields. His dreams of becoming the ruler of Eisenberg were over and he hadn't even made it to the North Gate

Greta rode through the streets of the outer city, leading the column of nobles steadily toward the North Gate of the inner city. They progressed slowly, blowing their horns and trumpets. As they marched the crowd behind them swelled to the sound of spoons beating on iron pots, until it felt as if the whole town was behind her and Greta felt elated and invincible. Surely with such a show of popular support Lock could be persuaded to surrender. She would reward him with a quick and painless death.

An explosion to the north rocked the city, momentarily drowning out the sound of pots and horns.

The procession halted

"That must be Albrecht and the iron guild," shouted Friedrich. "He must have encountered trouble on the way."

Greta thought quickly. *What should she do, what would Peter do?* "Send a man to them. Bring back word of what has happened."

Friedrich nodded and gave the order.

Greta had expected to find North Gate closed against them with papal gunners manning the wall. She had expected to need the help of Albrecht and the cannons of the iron guild to blast through it, but to her surprise the doors were open and the portcullis raised. Torches smoked somewhere in the space beyond. Perhaps the bishop was indeed ready to surrender. She was about to spur her horse onward through the gate, when Friedrich grabbed her shoulder. "You should not go first Lady Greta. This is our moment. I will lead the charge and if I survive then I will marry you."

"No number of pronouncements on your part will cajole me into polishing your sword," replied Greta. She was feeling flushed, confident. The gates were open and there was throng of people behind her.

"He's right," Luke rode forward and drew level with them to survey the gate. "Don't ride first, you are too precious. Stay with me. We shall ride at the back of the charge, my love." The last words he added in a barely audible whisper.

Lock and Sonia looked out of the windows of Lock's house. From there they could see the town spread out around them. To the north east in the Jewish quarter a fire blazed, spreading through the houses, and Lock, wondering how Heinrich was faring, said a short prayer for his friend.

"Look," said Sonia, "There."

At the north gate of the inner city, was a press of bodies, visible by their torches and candles. The mob was shouting. Lock could not make out the words, but he was sure that they were calling for his blood.

"What if we don't win?" asked Sonia.

"Then they will kill me. I hope that you will be spared."

Sonia turned and hugged Lock, "Oh God, let us hope it will not come to that. I have an idea."

"What is it?" said Lock.

"Oh no its nothing."

"Come, speak to me, dear child. I swear that I shall not laugh no matter how foolish it may seem."

"And do you swear you will not be angry at me."

"I swear it."

You know," said Sonia, "sometimes I like to help Cook in the kitchens, and one time the serving maid was busy and Cook asked me to get some salt from the cellar. So off I went, down into the cellar. I had some trouble looking for the salt. And I was looking up and down the cellar when I discovered the trapdoor. I thought it very odd that down bellow the earth there should be something lower still. Perhaps I thought the salt was in there. So I placed the candle on a wine barrel, and seeing that the trapdoor was not locked I pulled it up. It was very dark and cold beyond but I could make out the outline of stone steps. My curiosity, I must confess Lord Bishop, was most shamefully enflamed and I had by this point quite forgotten about the salt. Perhaps there was some terrible secret that I was about to discover. Yet when I moved closer to investigate, a gust of cruel wind blew up from the passage bellow, snuffing out my candle and giving me such a horrible fright that I screamed.

"Fortunately I was not left long to anguish in the cellar as the serving maid had returned and promptly arrived to find what had happened to the salt. When I asked Cook about the trapdoor she waved her carving knife at me and told me that I was 'a silly tramp,' and, not to go poking my nose in where it wasn't asked for. 'You know what happened to the over curious girl?' She asked me. I didn't but at that stage I was too frightened to ask. It seemed to me that the passage went deep, if it is not a means of escape then perhaps it is at least a place to hide. Do you know where the passage leads?"

Lock turned his eyes from the horsemen that were pouring in the gate to sadly survey his young ward. "Alas I know very little of this house or even of this city. I'm not from here. My father was a knight of the Palatine. I was, as was the custom, educated in the clergy. I went to university in Cologne where I acquired a reputation for my eloquent commentary on Saint Augustine. University is all about connections you see and when the bishopric of Eisenberg became available I was encouraged to apply for the position. A number of churchman spoke well on my behalf and at the diet of bishops I was duly elected. The place was far to the east but I was assured by all that the people were pious and church lands rich. I know nothing of this cursed house, or the ancient secrets it conceals. And now look what has become of me. He alone in Heaven knows what these fiends will do." As Lock had been talking his voice broke and tears welled at the corner of his eyes.

Sonia held her arm tight around Lock. "Cry not your Excellency. We will find a way. But do you mean that your father was not the bishop before you?"

Lock blew his nose on his robe and smiled. "You are a dear precious thing, Sonia."

The night was black before the rise of the moon and Felix the Jesuit toyed with his silver crucifix while he watched them come, come like lambs to the slaughter. He had burned and demolished all the buildings around North Gate so that his fifty musketeers could fire unimpeded in a double rank. The line of musketeers was broken at intervals and protected at the edges by clumps of pikemen who would skewer any attacker that got through the wall of fire.

The mass of cavalry, urged on by the cheering mob, filled the open space just beyond the gate. Felix watched as the cavalry formed into a classic tight line formation. He felt no compassion for the godless heretics, no more compassion than he had felt for the dark skinned pagans of India that he had helped sew to the ship's sails. They were fools and he was the hammer of God.

"*Ordeneum Severte*" Felix gave his orders in Latin. The well-drilled Swiss mercenaries remained frozen.

"*Ordenum*," ordered Felix as the cavalry broke from a walk into canter and the angry mob poured through the gate behind them.

"*Unos fenis Impetus*," ordered Felix as the cavalry began gallop.

The smoking wicks of the matchlocks ignited with the powder in the flash pans. There was a ripple of bright red bursts of fire. The smell of black powder filled Felix's nostrils and he remembered how much he loved the smell. The sound of the guns was deafening, and through the wafts of smoke, Felix saw the line of cavalry falter.

Bullets ripped through cloth, flesh and metal. Men screamed as they fell from their horses and the horses screamed as they were shot from under their riders.

"*Duo fenis impetus*," ordered Felix.

A second rippling crack rolled like thunder crossed the square. And those nobles that had survived the first volley and had continued to charge on, hunting dogs yapping at the hooves of their horses, now fell dead or spurred their horses around and fled.

Felix watched as the leader of the nobles, a long glittering sword held outstretched in his hand, took three bullets to his chest and fell with a clash onto the cobbled ground. His black charger reared, snorted, and screamed with terror. Two dogs howled with grief before their fallen master. One cavalryman had made it close enough to be killed with a pike. He died on his knees clutching his bleeding stomach. So died a great number of the noble households of Eisenberg. They died for their beliefs and for the countess, for their oaths and for the lure of the Church's wealth.

"First rank load," ordered Felix.

Basha felt her heart swell with pride as she watched her menfolk rush the surviving soldiers of the iron guild. This city had once belonged to the Exiles before the Christians came and it would be so once again. The Christians who liked to spit on them and curse them, as Christ's killers would be killed themselves. Basha never thought she would enjoy violence but those weeks in Johann's captivity, chained, whipped and prodded, had changed her. She watched the Christians die with satisfaction. Those Christians that had stared wantonly at her could lick their own blood off her fingers. Baba was right, Christian men could never be trusted. They wanted only to beat her, use her. Joseph had been good and look how his own people had rewarded him, his head cut from his shoulders.

Baba stood beside her now. The old woman licked her lips while holding a carving knife in her hand.

Basha recognized in her grandmother what she felt in herself, pleasure in the destruction of their enemies. "We will never be slaves," Baba said to her daughter, "never."

The Christians had retreated into a cluster around their one remaining cannon that they were struggling to turn. Most of them had been cut down, too slow to react to the lightly armed Jewish militia. Basha watched as Jango fired his pistol into the chest of a Christian and slid his sword into the throat of another. She smiled.

Perhaps she would marry him after all.

"Fire."

Basha heard the desperate command of the guild leader.

Another Christian fell clutching his groin where a thin sword had slid through a gap in his armour.

The sound of the cannon was louder than anything Basha had ever heard. The grapeshot spewed from the weapon's muzzle. Fragments of rock and iron cut through the Jewish militia. Basha watched Jango disappear beneath the hail of shrapnel, his body a bloody mass on the dirty mud rutted street.

Basha felt adrenaline rush through her, terror, grief, denial, disgust, and fear all mixed together.

The remaining dozen guild soldiers fired a volley of muskets and pistols, their bullets smashed into Basha's kinsmen. She watched as Heinrich her father fell onto his knees.

Basha froze. She couldn't turn away.

"Come." Baba gripped her arm. "We have to run."

"Unos fenis Impetus," said Felix.

The balls of lead poured into the flesh of the townsfolk and the sound of their agony filled the square. Felix stepped forward careful not to slip on the ground slick with the blood of the heretic noblemen and their horses.

"Moveo," said Felix.

The pikemen and musketeers tramped forward stepping over the bodies of the horses and crushing slain men beneath boots.

The cries of anger turned to screams of terror as the mob turned, trying to force their way back through the gate. More were shot down, others stabbed, as the troops of Pope Clement VII mascaraed the townspeople.

Bishop Lock removed his hand from covering Sonia's eyes, as he turned his own face away from the slaughter. He had under estimated Brother Felix.

"Oh sweet child," he murmured speaking more to himself than to Sonia, "It is an unseemly massacre of folk who know naught of pike and black powder. Oh unhappy day that I should see so much blood and on my own hands. Oh God that is greater than all things, My thoughts have seldom lingered on the offer of your paradise, and yet by the blood of innocents I will never rise to see your heavenly land of glass and gold, but shall be cast down to the world of devils, for surely it is the place that I belong."

Lock felt Sonia's hand search out his and clutch it.

"It's not you who is to blame," she said, "and God surely knows that. But I have a terrible feeling, Lord Bishop, that worse is yet to come. Pray let us escape the city together."

Countess Greta von Eisenberg vomited on the side of the street. The smell of blood and shit was overwhelming. Death was all around her, in the pale stricken faces of the fleeing townsfolk, in the screaming broken legged horse, in the howling of the dogs, in stench of gore and the fumes muskets.

In the press of bodies Greta fell, slipping on the blood slick ground. She was, she realized, no queen destined for greatness but just another woman close to the touch of Lord Death, just another woman who had shat herself in a moment of terror. *Is this how Peter died?* She wondered, his pants full of shit, his mouth smeared with vomit? Friedrich had been right. She should never have come. A man swore as he stumbled over her. The crowd was thinning. She raised herself up on her hands. She could see the advancing papal soldiers, silhouetted in the dim light of the raising sickle moon. She felt someone touch her shoulder. She turned.

Luke, her lover, the Lutheran preacher, knelt beside her.

Anger flared in her. "This is your doing," she said, "everybody's dead." Then she cried.

"Come," he said.

She allowed herself to be helped to her feet. She allowed him to embrace her. He felt so strong and confident.

He kissed her.

"Come," he said, "no time for weakness. We must run."

Johann felt his way along the tunnels of rough-hewn stone illuminated only by the flickering light of the candle. Whenever he passed an intersecting passage he marked the way he had come with a stick of charcoal.

"You sure you know where you're going?" asked William the Witch Hunter.

"If you don't trust me then perhaps you would like to find your own way out." said Johann.

The two men fell silent as they continued their slow passage through the mountain.

"I often find," said William, "that in dark and tight situations where the pulse is likely to quicken, that it helps to speak of women to move the heart of fear to distraction."

The two men reached a fork in the tunnels and Johann paused, lifting his candle to examine the rock face.

"My pulse," replied Johann, "is perfectly regular, but I see no harm in hearing a tale or two."

"In Munich," began William, as the two set off again, "there was a girl, a great blond beauty, the daughter of a courtier. I happened to have seen her in the market square accompanied by a serving girl. I decided that I would take this beauty to my bed."

"And how did she take that?" asked Johann.

"She resisted my most valiant efforts. It seemed she was determined to protect her honor. Yet as is the way with such things her refusals only served to inflame my desire. As it happened my influence in the city was growing, and I had a servant spy on her and reveal to me any information that might aid in my satisfaction. It was thus that I discovered that the girl was enamored with a young man of noble blood but of little means. My reputation for hunting out the Devil worshipers was becoming established in the city and I promptly had the young man arrested. I extracted his confession regarding his dealings with the Lord of Darkness. I then summoned the girl to me and explained to her the direness of the situation. I told her that I could perhaps do something for the young man, but it would require her to do something for me. She was much distressed but after I showed her various toes and fingers I had removed from her love she relented. I proceeded to enjoy her immensely."

Johann chuckled.

"Let's hear one of yours," said William.

"You may know," said Johann, "that I am a widower, but you may not know how that came to be. My wife became the lover of a baseborn baker. He would come and climb the oak tree at her window at carefully arranged times during which he would grind his wheat at her mill. A beggar wanting to make a few groats alerted me to these goings on. Doubting his word, I hid in my wife's bedroom at the time appointed, and indeed the cries of my wife's pleasure, as she was ploughed by some baseborn filth, filled my ears just as the stench of her sin filled my nose. I wasted no time in taking the sinful pair to my cellar, where I hung them both up on meat hooks and cut them into pieces. I told my wife's family that she had died of a fever and I had her buried in a covered coffin so that her vapors would not affect the humors of the mourners. I fed the baker to my dogs.

William didn't laugh. The two men came into a wide cavern. "Ah," said Johann, "here we are, the hollow heart of the berg."

"Shall we pursue?" asked Aldo, the papal commander.

In the pale moonlight Felix had seen Greta and her heretic flee though the gate, so tauntingly close to striking distance of his own long Spanish dagger. Felix paused to look around. It was great pile of death that pleased God. He kissed the talisman around his neck knowing that his place in Heaven was assured, and yet as long as those two survived his victory was incomplete. She, the heretic whore of Eisenberg, had tricked him and trapped him like a spider. Though Felix neither forgot nor forgave, he was a patient and cautious man, yet here was an opportunity to finish things. Felix disliked the chaotic street fighting that could result from a pursuit but the Lutherans were already broken. The mob would be caught in the narrow streets and killed while they ran. He would personally cut the whore into pieces.

Felix drew his dagger, "*Oppugnare,*"

The papal soldiers, slung their muskets over their shoulders, drew their swords and broke into a run.

Sonia and Lock watched as the papal soldiers poured out of the inner city in pursuit of the townsfolk. Glancing downward Lock observed his own guards. They were loitering like a pack of dogs around his gate. Steffen crouched on the step sharpening his sword on a whetstone.

"There is no need to flee," said Lock, "Terrible though the massacre was to behold, the papal soldiers are nevertheless on our side. We have won and I still have my own guards protecting our house. Let us wait until morning and then we can leave the city like the law-abiding folk that we are, rather than descending into caves that we know not where they will lead. You must see the sense in that."

"My lord," said Sonia, "you are much wiser than my miserable self. You know so much of so many things. And your knowledge of the Lord has brought me untold pleasure. Men are the stronger sex and women it is said are ruled by their emotions being of a more tender and vulnerable disposition. It is only right that we should be led and governed by you. And yet I have heard it said that though God bestowed his greatest gifts on Man, and Woman He punished for her sin, He did bestow on her one gift, the gift of intuition, so the she may bless on some occasion Man with divine insight. Know this my sweet and lovely Devil. I have had a vision. I saw your fine house in ruin. I was holding you tight while a dark shadow crept up from behind you and snatched you from me. I know not where the tunnel leads but come let us leave this place."

"What about my books?" said Lock, "I can't leave without them. They're priceless. I have had many of them carted from Cologne at much expense and danger. I have illuminated manuscript versions of the psalms from the time of the Emperor Barbarossa. And what about my Boccaccio? It's such a well rendered edition."

"I don't know what to do about your collection of books your Excellency. But I believe that we must leave this place. I have a terrible feeling that we if stay something truly horrible will happen to us. Please. Let us take the trapdoor and see if we can find our way out of the city."

"What about my seals?" said Lock. "I have the seals of several popes, kings, dukes, margraves and bishops. I even have the seal of the Emperor Karl and the tughra of the Sultan of Algarve."

"I don't know much about seals and the doing of great people like you do," replied Sonia. "But I do know this. I know that I cannot imagine my life without you and the helling we share. And on account of the love I bare you, I beg you let us make our way out of this house. Take what you must, but I pray you let us go."

Lock shook his head. "This is madness."

Greta thought she would die. A tall heavy mercenary pinned her against the wall of a house, holding by her neck. The city was on fire and the papal guard had pursued the townsfolk into side streets of the outer city.

The mercenary pushed his flat bristly face close to hers, "You're a pretty one." He said. His Germanic was strange but Greta understood him well enough. "You smell nice too." He pulled off his glove with his teeth, reached his hand under her skirts and tore away her undergarments with what seemed to Greta, to be a well practiced motion.

Greta didn't struggle or scream. She wouldn't give him that satisfaction. She stared into the face of her attacker with cold hatred.

"Always time for a quick one," said the mercenary as he removed his hand from Greta's flesh and began to loosen the drawstrings of his codpiece.

Albrecht had met Greta's messenger with grim cheer. The last of the

Jews had fled. But all that remained of his troop were five able bodied men and a single cannon loaded with grape shot and pulled by a pair of terrified mules. It was therefore with trepidation that Albrecht had agreed to precede to North Gate.

His exhausted men marched away from the burning houses with a mechanical tread that reminded Albrecht of the clockwork creations, of the emperor's mechanician in Vienna. Their hair was singed, their armour dented, their eyes watching every house and window, and their hands gripping tightly their primed muskets.

As he approached North Gate it became clear that all was not well. He heard the screams and shouts of battle. He rounded a corner and looked on the wide street that ran from North Gate. A group of townsfolk fled toward Albrecht. They did not stop at the soldiers but only pushed past, glancing at his men with terrified eyes.

Albrecht saw what they were fleeing. Illuminated in the red light of the now distant fires, a mass of papal guard armed with slashing swords, and armoured in burnished breast plates and high steel helmets advanced. Blood was splattered over their faces and weapons and they cut and trampled anyone who was near.

"Fire," shouted Albrecht. This time his men were ready. The crack of the wheellocks halted the charge of the papal guard as several men in the front line fell. The gunners positioned the cannon. A crewman brought the match to the touchhole. For the second time that night the cannon fired a round of grapeshot. When the smoke cleared all that remained of the mighty papal guard was a mass of ruined, mangled bodies.

An explosion sounded nearby. A house collapsed in a pile of timber and thatch. Screams, dust and smoke filled the street. The mercenary loosened his grip on Greta's neck and turned to look at the commotion.

Greta did not hesitate. She pulled the dagger from her attackers sheath and as he turned and tightened his grip on her neck she drove the dagger up underneath his jaw and into his brain.

He gargled blood and stumbled. His hand still locked to Greta's throat, he pulled her down with him.

Greta pried his dying fingers off her bruised neck. She wrenched the dagger out off the man's head, stabbing him again through the face. It was violence that she had not thought herself capable of. But the moment of violation had stripped her of humanity. She felt corrupted, debased, and her heart filled with cold rage.

She pulled herself out from under her attacker, and looked around. Chaos reined. The papal guard had lost their discipline and the townsfolk heartened by the arrival of the cannon, had returned for vengeance. Two men bludgeoned a papal guard to death with rocks. A mercenary fought with a townsman, parrying his carving knife with his dagger while cutting his throat with his sword.

Greta watched as a man in a black robe killed a townsman cutting open his stomach with a dagger and kicking him onto the ground.

The man looked straight at her. It was Brother Felix the Dominican.

Greta gripped her own dagger.

He walked toward her.

Greta let all her rage, anger and grief out in a scream that she hoped would curdle blood. She ran at the black monk. He smiled. And she saw what he saw, an enraged irrational woman who did not know how to fight, a woman whose attack was obvious, a woman who would die. She saw that he was about to parry her high lunge, draw his second small dagger and cut open her belly. At the last minute she changed the direction of her lunge aiming low. The black monk parried too high and missed. She forced the dagger right into his sternum.

Basha and Baba fled the raging fire. Their house, warehouse, and everything they owned had been consumed by it. Now it spread across the Jewish quarter and the north breeze carried it toward the wealthy houses close to the River Gate. A burning beam snapped and broke behind the two women. Basha could feel the warmth of it on her back and the smoke made her cough. No one bothered to fight the fire. It was beyond control.

"To the graveyard," said Baba.

The Jewish graveyard was a maze of tumbled stones each with a symbol of how the deceased had lived. There were geese, roses, books, calves and hexagrams. Baba and Basha ran through the long grass and lichen covered stone till they came to the centre of the graveyard. The stones here were old and had no inscription and an old yew grew. The tips of its dark green leaves were covered with tiny red berries. It was here that the women met wrapped in their long cloaks crowned with their pointed hats. They shared in whispering voices the scale of their loss, the loss of their houses, their husbands and their sons.

"Papa, Papa" Basha whispered and began to cry, "Given back for so short a time only to be so cruelly taken. Papa, Papa, all have gone to paradise." The women held each other's hands and hugged and kissed, and then they cried.   Somewhere in the night the blast of cannon sounded. Nearby a cat hissed.

Lock and Sonia watched as the mob streamed back into the inner city carrying the torches and the pikes of the Swiss Guard on which the mercenaries' heads were impaled. They moved purposefully, slowly at first and then, with increasing confidence, toward Lock's house.

Lock and Sonia watched as the lanky cat-like figure of Steffen armed with his long sword walked to greet the first of the mob to approach. Steffen exchanged words with one of the men but Lock could not hear what was said. Steffen turned and pointed to the window from which Lock looked out. Steffen had betrayed him.

"Do you believe me now?" said Sonia.

Lock imagined his own head being hacked from his body and being impaled on a pike. "Let us make haste," he said.

"Once," said William von Munich, "a man came to see me baring the information that a woman of his village was a witch, claiming that she had taken the form of a succubus and seduced him, and during the period of their unholy union she had used her evil magic to drain some of his life force. I had the girl brought before me and noticed at once the ripeness of her youth and the comeliness of her appearance. I asked her to illuminate the accusations laid against her. She claimed that the man who had testified against her had never taken her to bed in any form, demonic or otherwise, despite his fervent wishes. He, she said, had falsely accused her out of his own jealously.

"The spiritedness of the girl aroused my manly urges and I became determined that I would plough her in any case. I reprimanded the girl for taking accusation of demonic possession lightly and impressed upon her that death by burning, which I was considering giving her as a sentence, was a very painful way to die. The girl instantly fell on her knees and began kissing my feet begging me to spare her life. I gently explained to her that there were ways of purging her of a succubus's possession that I was willing to try rather than let her burn. Once she discovered what I had mind she was most furious and refused to yield. As luck, however, would have it I caught another witch that night that I promptly burned. The girl watched and when I later visited her cell I found her most compliant."

"We're here," said Johann as he led William to the top of a spiral staircase onto a wide landing. "See those boards above our head?"

"Ah ha."

"That's the bishop's cellar."

"Here at last." William placed his lantern on the ground, opened it and lit the wicks of his matchlock pistols. "Thank God we got out of that hole. I was starting to run out of stories."

"Shhh," Johann lifted his dagger to his lips, "I hear boots. Smother the light."

"But…"

Johann took off his cloak, and threw it onto the lantern.

The light went out.

"Two people," said Johann, "one heavy, one light. Voices, a girl's voice, they're escaping downward. Quick get over here don't attack till they are all in the dark."

"I'll go first," said Sonia, "secure the rope, pass the lantern and bags down and to me and then you follow.

"Bless you, child," said Lock, as he glanced behind him. He could hear the sound of a door being kicked open, a pot clanging to the ground, and raised voices. He could even smell the scent of smoking naphtha. "Make haste."

"Look at those legs," William barely breathed his remark as the girl descended the rope into the passage. "I lay first rights on churning her milk."

Sonia landed with a tap of soft leather shoes on the rough stone. She saw neither William nor Johann as she gathered the bags and lantern that were handed down from above.

"And here comes the fat old sinner," said William.

But he spoke the words just a little too loudly, and just before Lock dropped onto the ground, Sonia who was holding the lantern turned and saw the faces of William and Johann staring at her from the alcove in the rock. She screamed and ran.

Johann stepped forward, grabbed Lock around the waste and held his dagger to his neck. "Not so clever with your words now are you, you filthy adulterer. Make any move and I'll cut your throat here and now."

William moved his cloak to reveal the red glow of the pistol wicks.

"Thanks to you, the girl got away," said Johann.

"Uhh," said William, "What use do we have for a bishop's whore? Let her run. She will not survive."

"Were you not at the meeting?" Johann broke the chain that held

Lock's sliver crucifix around his neck and rubbed his thumb over the burnished silver.

The bishop remained quiet and pliant.

"We are going to give this slug a trial," Johann continued, "and the girl, who he's no doubt been fucking, will be the star witness. Now you guard this servant of Satan while I find the girl."

"I see what you're up to." William waved his pistol at Johann. "You're trying to get in on my privilege. I accompanied you on this mission through these horrid caverns. And I called first right on that little piece of meat. And by the Lord, I'll have it. I won't be guarding this maggot while you fill the space between a maid's white thighs with your prick. That pretty little Jewess you had locked away, well isn't she something fine? You're so pure you would only look to spit on a baseborn man. Yet you still like your Jewish cunny. When this business is done I'll track down that Jewish sow then I'll send her to you after I've done with her, and you won't want her then."

Johann had had enough of William. He lashed out, ducking William's shot and drove his dagger into the witch hunter's chest.

Lock took his chance. He grabbed his bag and ran, stumbling and rolling down the stairs, his only thought was to get away.

Greta stood on the battlements of the inner city. Eisenberg was hers. Its steep curved slate roves and cone shaped towers stretched out before her. Fires still blazed in the Jewish quarter and great columns of smoke rose into the sky. Lady Victory had given her relief but not joy. Only yester morning when riding through the forest to the gates of the city it had seemed like a wonderful adventure. And the jovial remarks of the noblemen had made it seem like nothing more than an extended hunting party. Now they were all dead.

The battle had been won by baseborn common folk. At first the idea of raising the common people to her banner had appealed to her and had felt empowering in front of Friedrich's arrogance. But now it made her anxious. They had praised her and chanted her name and she may have inspired them with her words, but she had not commanded them.

Luke joined her on the battlement. He placed his arm around her but she did not turn to kiss him or throw her arms around his neck, but remained staring and thoughtful.

"Victory," said Luke, sensing her mood, "is seldom without sacrifice. Even God Himself sacrificed His Son for the sins of man. Eisenberg will be the spark that will start a fire in the world and you have much to be proud of."

Sonia, taking the lantern with her and thinking only of escape, had run. She had run down the narrow spiral stairs, down one passage and then another. By the time she had caught her breath she realized that she was lost in the caverns beneath the Berg. Fear crept over her. *What if she never found her way out?* The rock seemed to lean in from every angle. Sometimes she had had to duck and even crawl.

She reached a place where four passages met and stress overwhelmed her. She sat down with her back to the stone and caught her breath. She watched the lantern playing on the rock face and remembered the stories Cook had told her. Underneath the ground in caverns like these lived kobolds who would play tricks on people who entered their realm. They would lure unsuspecting visitors into dark holes from which they would never return or into a passage that would collapse trapping the intruder. There were also gnomes who guarded treasures and who could move through the rock like it was air.

Sonia tried to relax. *You are lucky,* she told herself, *that Cook has told you about the kobolds and the gnomes and that you know how to appease them.*

She then took what money she had in her purse, a silver florin, a gold crown, several groats and a pair of guilders, and placed it in a little alcove.

"Oh kobolds," she said aloud. "I know this is your world down here, and you don't like people visiting. But I'm trying to escape people who are trying to kill me. But in doing so I have lost my way and I have lost my dear Bishop Lock. I know that you can help when you wish to. I therefor beg you to show me a way out of your caves, and if you could also please deliver Lock to me, I would never forget the service you have done me. Please take this gold as a gift and a sign of my good will and nothing more."

Sonia made sure to emphasize that the gold was a gift and not a payment as, if the kobolds believed they were being paid, they would become furious. Having made her offering to the Kobolds, Sonia felt better. *There's nothing to be gained from sitting here and feeling sorry for myself,* she said and set off down the passage to her left. She had a good feeling about that passage. It was narrow but high and looked like it had been carved with some care. At length Sonia came to another junction. She saw that one of the tunnels was marked with a charcoal arrow. "Thank you" she said to the kobolds and hurried on her way.

Lock could not remember ever having felt more miserable. He bled from where Johann's dagger had scraped his flesh. Most of all he hated caves and hated darkness and he was stumbling around in both. He had a fear of spiders and couldn't suppress the feeling that in the blackness of the tunnel they were all around him. *What was God thinking when he created such horrifying forms?* Lock was certain he would die down here, and he could only hope that Sonia had enough wits to escape. Only now that the last glimmer of light had disappeared and the shouts and screams of his assailants had become distant echoes, did Lock deem that it was time to rest. He sat, panting, on his bag. And gradually his fear of capture gave way to an oppressive claustrophobia. He could not see his hand waving in front of his face. The darkness seemed to weigh heavy around him. He began to sweat and then to wish that he had been captured and hung rather then to die in this abominable labyrinth.

He called out first to Sonia, and heard his own voice resound deep in the hollows of the earth but no reply came. Then he called out to Johann. "I am here you Heretic bastard," he shouted. "Come and get me. Roast me on a spit for all I care but get me out of this dark hole." Still there was no reply. And Lock began to weep in terror. After sometime he stopped and despite his beating heart he began to rummage in the bag to see what Sonia had packed. There was his collection of seals, and he found the touch of the hard disks of wax comforting. There was some bread. *God bless, the girl* he thought as he broke off some of it and stuffed it onto his mouth. Then he touched it, the stump of a candle and an iron tinderbox.

"Sonia, you angel," he said aloud.

He fumbled in the dark, opening the tinderbox and gripping the loop of fire steal while he struck sparks into the charcloth. He sheltered the fragile flame, and when the candle was lit he dared to look at the yawning passage before him. Briefly his curiosity overtook his terror and he saw that men had cut the passages and he wondered by who and when such work had been done. As he rose to his feet he saw that there was a charcoal arrow pointing down one of the passageways.

Book Four

The Mountain Pass

the 24th of October, the Day of Service,
Year of the Lord 1526

"We're being followed." Stanislaw, free prince of Krakow, vassal to Sigismund the enlightened king of Poland rose up in his stirrups to survey the dusty mountain road behind them. "They can't even hide it anymore. Look at them."

Peter could see them, a small column, like ants slowly winding their way steadily toward them."

"They're traveling faster than us," said Stanislaw, "much faster. My scouts report a band of mounted tartars. Have you ever fought tartars?

Peter shook his head.

Stanislaw gave Peter an irritatingly superior look for a man that was ten years younger. "Pray you never do. They'll have caught up with us by tomorrow if we can't increase our pace."

Shielding his eyes from the glare of the morning sun, Peter stared at the enemy column. "There doesn't seem to be very many of them. Surely with our combined forces we could destroy them."

"Your mind is like a mirror to my own," replied Stanislaw. "My scouts report that as the road approaches the Pass of Eagles, the land widens into a plateau with cliffs dropping on one side and other cliffs rising like a wall on the other."

"That's right," said Peter, "Drachen's plate. What do you have in mind?"

Stainslaw pulled on his long moustache. "A classic ambush. There is a swathe of pines between the road and the cliffs that rise up. It is ample to conceal my lancers. While we remain hidden in the trees your infantry shall hold the road against the Turks. While they are preparing to engage we charge their flank. Before they know it, its all over."

Peter studied the prince of Krakow. He was a handsome twenty-year-old. He wore a looted Turkish scimitar and a fine pointed helm, with a plume of horsehair in the Polish style. He gave the impression of being brave yet not a fool. He treated Peter with a haughty yet respectful deference, and yet as he explained his plan, Peter couldn't help but feel that there was something he was withholding. "Why do you think that the Turks would attack us with such a small force?"

Stanislaw shrugged. "I'll wager my finest stallion that it's got something to do with your princess."

"My lord." Captain Sokol approached the two men. "There's a beggar woman on the road. She demands to speak with you."

"Can't you see," said Peter, "that I have no time to converse with beggar women. Give her some victuals and tell her to be gone."

"The men," said Sokol, "think she is a witch. Her presence makes them uneasy. I promised I would pass on the request."

"There are no such things," said Peter, "as witches."

"I'm just doing my duty," said Sokol.

The company was refreshing themselves by a mountain stream that gushed from a little waterfall shaded by the bows of birch and rowan while the horses grazed freely on the roadside grasses. Asra pretended to be in prayer while listening to Mustafa Khan conferring with his scout.

"There can be no doubt," said Mustafa, "That the Christians know we are coming. And they will by Allah be planning some surprise. It is up to us now to make sure that those who would dupe us are themselves duped. Bring me a shepherd and tell him that we will shower him with gold."

For days Asra had been worrying that Mustafa would ruin the mission by attacking the Christians and eliminating the chances of an easy and peaceful return of Nuray and now she had confirmation of it. She had to act. She cleared her throat.

Mustafa turned to look at Asra. He was built like a bull and his scared face displayed nothing but smouldering anger. "Does the Pasha's whore wish to speak?" said Mustafa in a voice loud enough to draw the attention of the troops, who snickered.

"We are not here to fight the Christians," said Asra as clearly and bravely as she could. "But to deliver our terms for the release of Nuray. We will approach the Christians with white flags and olive branches. I shall be disguised as a captured Christian noblewoman I shall be handed over as part of the ransom. From there I will begin to gather information and you will take Nuray back to her husband."

"Quiet, woman." Mustafa waved his stick at her. "These are conversations for men. It is not the place of women to question or to think about such matters of which they know nothing."

"I," said Asra, "was commanded by the sultan himself to bring back Nuray and you will listen to me or answer to him."

Mustafa walked up to her and pushed his face close to hers. His blue eyes shone in his dark tanned face. "You may open your legs to the sultan, but no woman tells Mustafa Khan how to command. It was I who was first through the breach in the battle of Belgrade and opened the city to the sultan. It was I who fought the Arabs in the deserts of the south and chased the rebellious Cappadocians into the depths of their caves. To think that I should to be told what to do by a woman whose only claim to rank is that she knows who to open her thighs to. It shall not be borne."

Asra willed herself to stand her ground. Surely the threat of Suleiman's wrath would make Mustafa back down. "Speak carefully. I have the ear of the Sultan."

Mustafa struck like a snake. His slap knocked her to the ground. Her head reeled and she felt her face swell with pain. She bit hard on her tongue to stop herself from crying out.

Mustafa turned to face the men who had silently watched the confrontation, chewing on dried horsemeat. He placed his hand on the pommel of his scimitar. "I am Mustafa Khan, prince of the Black Sea. I follow Sultan Suleiman the lawgiver, but I do so free prince. I am not his servant. The Christian soldiers on the mountain road are all that stand between us and the fat provinces beyond. We will crush them and sack their cities."

The band of tartar warriors cheered. They were tribesmen and Mustafa's kin and blood brothers. They were dressed in fur, silk and leather. They carried scimitars, but their most prized possessions were their bows, made with the horns of a prize bull with a shaft of Black Sea maple, strung with tendon, they were lighter and stronger than the bows of the Christians. They were horse archers, the decedents of the Golden Horde, born to the saddle, proud and ferocious.

"Good," said Mustafa. "Salim, bring me a shepherd. Özgur, gag this slut so I do not have to listen to her strident cries."

Peter stared at the hag. She really was extremely ugly. Her face was covered in large warts. Her nose seemed to suffer from some terrible ailment, looking more like a fungal growth than a human appendage. Her hair hung about her in dark greasy knots. She was dressed in a dirty shift and she stank.

"All I'm asking for is gainful employment," said she.

"What could I possibly want from you? Take a handful of groats and a turnip and never let me see you again. And don't trouble yourself to wave any of your chicken bones at me, because you're about as much a witch as I am a saint."

"Call yourself a gentleman?" said the hag. "I'm nothing but a poor old woman on my way to Eisenberg to visit my daughter and wishing for a bit of protection and company on the road. Wolves are out in the mountains. I've heard them howling around in the night. It's also cold. To drive me away now is as good as to let them have me. I don't need your turnip. I have my own crust of bread to suck on. All I'm asking is a place by the fire and a thimble of wine to drive away the cold. It isn't kind and it isn't right, to treat an old woman thus. And it is said by all that to shun a helpless stranger from your fire is sure to incur the ill favour of Saint Christof, who all wise travellers light a candle to."

"She's right," said one of the landsknecht who sat nearby mending his boot with a needle and twine, while his long sword leaned against a blueberry bush. "Saint Christof doesn't like to see travellers turned away."

"Curse it to hell," said Peter, "you can have a corner by the fire but don't let me see you."

The hag gave a wide toothless smile. "God bless you my lord."

Asra watched as Ozgur cut the length of green turban cloth that would serve as her gag. She complied as he held her. She felt the warmth of his breath on her neck. She smelled his scent of sweat, tea, horse, and olive oil.

"You know I have the ear of powerful men," Asra whispered, "when we return to Belgrade I could have you executed."

Ozgur did not reply as he raked his fingers through her well-combed hair, pulling it up to reveal the nape of her neck while he wound the cloth around it.

"I shall," said Asra, "of course remember your kindness."

The cloth tightened in Asra mouth and she said no more.

The sun was setting over the Pass of Eagles. The long shadows of the pines fell like swords across the open meadow of Drachen's Plate. Stanislaw sat on a stool outside his pavilion. The Krakowian lancer encampment was some distance from the landsknecht, under shade of the pines from which they were to launch their ambush. But Stanislaw was not thinking about the ambush.

His thoughts wandered to the same territory they had for the last week, the beautiful Turkish princess that Peter the German had some how managed to acquire as a concubine. The more Stanislaw thought about it, the more consumed he became, both with the intoxicating thought of possessing the woman for himself and with the ways in which he could act on that desire. *What right did Peter have to bed this Turkish nymph?* No more right than he, Stanislaw prince of Krakow, commander of the winged lancers. Did the woman love Peter? Nay, she had turned on him with scorn and hatred. Peter was a beast holding the woman against her will. She needed saving. And Stanislaw was the man to carry her off, and show her what it would be like to be with a real man. She might resist at first but she would soon learn to love him. *What damsel didn't?*

"My Lord Stanislaw. "Michal, his lieutenant, bowed before him. He and his six trusted men, all bearded and moustached looked striking in their looted janissary uniforms. Though tying the turbans had been difficult they were passable Turks. Not, thought Stanislaw, that all this trouble was needed. A few musket shots would be enough to rouse Peter, and they would be gone before they were seen.

"Rise," said Stanislaw. He reached into his saddlebags that were draped over his stool, and drew out a brass clock. The clock was an old model now but it kept the time as well as any other. He handed it over to his lieutenant while his fingers stroked the edge of his own clock. It was so small that he was able to wear it around his neck like a medallion. It was made of glass and gold and crafted by the finest clock maker in Krakow. "Remember," said Stanislaw, "wait until the hand strikes four."

Asra had been ungagged so that she might translate the words of the goatherd. He had been suspicious at first but when he had seen Mustafa's gold his tongue had willingly loosened.

"There is one more thing that you must know," she translated. " He takes only that road when the wind is blowing from the north."

"Why is that?" asked Mustafa. "Ask him why."

"The plateau is the home of the dragon Kamenne Brucho. Only when the north wind is blowing is it safe to bring the flock that high, because when the wind is blowing away from the mountain the dragon can not smell him."

"There are no such thing as dragons," said Mustafa. "Here," Mustafa held out a pouch of gold to the goatherd. "Allah is generous, as is his servant on Earth, Suleiman the Great. Salim, lead him from the camp."

Mustafa turned to address the tartars. "The Christians are laying a trap for us. They will use the open space to take advantage of their greater numbers and give their cavalry space to deliver a charge." Mustafa crouched down and began drawing in the dirt with his dagger. The other warriors drew around to listen.

Asra could see why the men respected him. He treated women with contempt, even hatred, but he treated all men like they were his brothers.

"Here," said Mustafa sweeping his dagger through the dirt, "is a swathe of pine forest. The Christians will conceal their cavalry here. The Christian infantry will block the road here. When we engage them the cavalry will take our flank." Mustafa threw the dagger into the ground. "We lose."

"How do you know this?" asked one of the warriors.

"Because it is the best thing they could do. Always expect the best of your enemy then do one better. If we leave our camp at dawn we would reach the plateau sometime in the afternoon. That is what the Christians expect us to do. So we do what they don't expect. We ride through the night and attack at dawn before the Christians have prepared themselves. We will not follow the road and engage the Christian infantry but make straight toward the pines to eliminate the Christian cavalry. We shall then attack the Christian infantry from the rear. I can see from your faces that you see the same the problem as I do. The Christians sentries will hear the sound of our horse's hooves on the road. In Syria near Antioch we surprised the rebels with a troop of horse. The horse's hooves were tightly bound with cloth, which muffled the sound of their hooves."

"I may not be much to look at," said the hag as she licked chicken fat off her hairy upper lip, "But I know many a pretty maid, and lusty ones too, desperate, desperate girls, just dying to get their hands on a soldier's long sword. And soldiers with such finery as you men, I swear you could have three of those little sword polishers a piece."

The men around the fire laughed and drew nearer, their disgust at the hag giving way to interest. "Tell us more old woman and we'll give you more of that chicken."

"I don't know how you men like your scabbards, but with these girls you got all kinds, light, dark, plump, lean, large, each in the flower of their youth. And," the hag gripped her finger in her fist, "they each have sword sheaths as tight as a kidskin glove, and hot little mouths hungry for stallions' milk."

"Where are these girls?" asked one of the Landsknecht, standing and placing his hand on his codpiece. "My sword is getting rusty and my millpond's overflowing. I'll give these maids as much milk as they can swallow."

"Yeah go on old woman tell us where we can find these maids," said another man.

"That's just the thing," said the hag, "Just a few hours walk on foot and we'll be with them, you'll be able to wash the rust off your swords in the purest mountain streams and be back in time to fight the battle on the morn."

"The old witch is taking us for fools," said one of the men, "we are in the middle of a mountain wilderness. There are no fair maidens for many leagues."

Another man drew his dagger. "Maybe she's trying to lure us out of the camp."

The hag put her hand to her heart. "Saint Kristof's oath, I'm no liar. I'm only here to bring men and women together where is needed, and earn my place at the fire. Now you hear what I have to say before you persecute a defenceless old woman, shame on you."

The men were silent.

"Some of you men are from Eisenberg," said the hag, "and you should know as well as any that close to the Pass of Eagles is the Abbey of Saint Hildegard the Virgin. Come surely some must know that."

Some of the men nodded and murmured their agreement.

"And some of those young sisters, Saint Kristof's oath, are the very same little hussies that I'm been speaking of. Can you imagine, poor little creatures shut up in that big stone abbey without a single man to please and to lead them? I tell you again their fields are fellow, but fertile as a meadow in spring. Tonight is full moon, and I happen to know that at this time these fervid nymphs all, well pardon my frankness, bleed together on this day. And on account of that they travel through the wilderness to Hildegard's spring to bath in it and spend the night beside it. It's but a walk from here."

The hag paused to survey her audience. She had the full attention of every man. "The thing that you must know is that this is best time to visit them. It is when they are bleeding that they are at their most fervid and wanton." The hag bared the stumps of her own blackened teeth. "The blood is like oil to a man's sword."

Peter gazed at Nuray while she combed her long hair. She spoke to him as he watched her. He did not understand her words. But they were spoken conversationally as if she was talking to an old friend about nothing of particular importance. It was a warm and gentle mood and Peter savoured it.

Since she had yielded to him, he had come to know something of her. He had never met a woman who wanted to wash as much as she. She was like a loaded musket, ready to explode at the slightest provocation into screaming and anger or into weeping and grief. Peter had taught her to enjoy the taste of wine and for a moment, in the grip of intoxication, she would dance or sing, even laugh.

She never allowed him to take her without resistance. She would bite him and scratch him, but then she would go limp and then cling to him. Nuray, he loved her. He struggled to keep his mind from her and on the pressing business of his command. *Where would it end?* he wondered as his eyes traced the line of her cheek to her chin. He stood and filled a goblet with wine. He offered it to her.

She placed her comb beside her on the ground and stood, coming over to him, her silk gown clinging to the lines of her body. She took the goblet in both hands and raised it to her lips, filling her mouth with the red potion. With her hand she drew Peter close to her, making as if she wished him to drink from her mouth, but as he drew close she spat it over his face.

25th of August, full moon, the witching hour

"And there it is," said the Hag, "Hildegard's Spring."

They were in an open rocky land of shallow rooted plants. In the moonlight they could see a small stream, which flowed out of a crevice in the rock and into a wide pool before cascading down the mountainside.

"Where are the women?" asked one of Landsknechts.

"Oh, I'm sure they are here, said the hag, they will have heard us coming and gathered somewhere to hide. They are desperate little vixens but they are also naturally a little shy at first, especially with handsome, manly men surprising them. Come let me call them and let us see if they come." The hag addressed herself to the rocks and flowers, "Ladies of the Blessed Virgin, it is I, Helga the crone. I bring with me two score handsome young men, all soldiers and richly dressed they've come to pay you their respects."

To the surprise of the soldiers, who had begun to doubt their mission, three young women appeared from behind the rocks, they wore white cloaks and their hoods were drawn back to reveal long hair and comely faces. The three women hesitated as they surveyed the group of armed men that had come to visit them.

"Wait here," said the hag to the soldiers, "be patient. I believe they want to speak to me first in private. Doubtless," she whispered, "the fervid little sows have some kind of little game in mind. But don't you scare them now. They don't after all know your intentions."

With the aid of her stick the hag ascended to converse with the figures, dressed in white. She exchanged some words, which the soldiers could not hear and then she returned, hunched and hobbling to the waiting Landsknecht.

As she drew near she broke into a smile. "Oh my boys. You're in for a treat. Those damsels watched us come and most of them are hiding in the woods yonder. But before they approach, these virtuous sisters want you to prove your strength and manliness; naturally they don't want to squander themselves on weak cowards. And this thing they would have you do, it will not long postpone your pleasure indeed it may hasten it."

"What would they have us do?" asked one of the soldiers.

"Patience young cock," replied the hag, "I will speak to the matter forthwith"

Some of the men snickered.

"Hildegard's Spring is remarkably cold and the sheep have already been brought down from the high pastures. The beautiful young nymphs ask of you only what they will do themselves. You must strip yourself and then you must bathe in the water but worry you not of the cold for soon you shall be warmed by women's flesh."

"It's been long enough since I bathed," said one soldier, "And I shall gladly do so now." He unbuckled his sword and let it clash to ground, while his fingers sought out the buttons on his tunic.

Thomas was beginning to really feel the cold. He whooped with the other men as he entered the freezing water, eager to display his manliness to the women, but having immersed himself in the icy tarn, a numbness began to creep up his legs and he had to clench his jaws to stop them from chattering. Then he saw them and he could scarce believe his eyes. It was just as the hag had promised. A company of young women was approaching the spring. They were dressed in long white shifts but the skin of their necks and faces were visible in the moonlight. They wore their hair long, combed and thrown back over their shoulders. Thomas caught the eye of one girl. She had a round and pretty face with wavy hair. Thomas smiled at her and she smiled back. Thomas willed his frozen limbs to move as he imagined the heat of her body warming his cold skin.

He ran blue lipped to meet her. They drew close.

She smiled.

He reached out to embrace her.

She drew a long dagger from her cloak and stabbed him through his naked chest.

Stanislaw had dressed himself in black and smeared his face with charcoal, all the better not to be seen. He wore no armour so that he could go unheard. His only weapon was his looted scimitar, strapped to his back. It hadn't taken long for Stanislaw to recognize the superiority of the Turkish cavalry. Their slashing swords were part of their success and everyday Stanislaw drilled his men in their use. His sword was taken from a captain, and was the perfect fit for his hand. The hilt and handle were silver coated. It was light enough to be used with speed but heavy enough to chop.

Keeping low in the long grass Stanislaw made his way toward Peter's camp. He skirted a group of grazing roe deer and arrived at the stroke of half past three. Stanislaw felt an uneasy tension begin to build in his stomach. Something was wrong. *Where were all the sentries? Where were all the men?*

As Stanislaw drew closer he saw that there were some men, perhaps four dozen. Clustered around two fires, a couple of sentries stood facing out into the night. Moving from tent to wagon Stanislaw drew closer until he could position himself behind one of the baggage wagons. The men were engaged in some kind of conference or dispute. *Was it a mutiny?* Stanislaw watched as Peter stood with his arms folded. Beside him, wrapped in fur sat the Turkish princess. Stanislaw allowed himself to breath deeply and study the object of his desire. He would abduct her, and ride by moonlight toward the pass, leaving Peter to face the Tartars alone. He would then ride into Eisenberg with his cavalry, and proclaim it as his territory through right of conquest before returning home a hero.

"We should have all gone. It's all well for your lordship, you have yourself a foreign princess but what about us and splitting the company?" Stanislaw heard a soldier say.

Peter took a step forward and drew his sword. Stanislaw studied the weapon, a famous, cat skin sword, short, double-edged, wide bladed and made for slashing, about two-thirds the length of Stanislaw's scimitar. "Next man to insult the princess won't get a Christian burial. We are not going off in search of fanciful women in a wild mountain pass at night, when expecting an enemy attack, abandoning all our supplies and baggage, for the word of the ugliest woman I've ever seen. Have you all gone mad?"

"His lordship's right," said Hans, a longswordsman, "Just a few nights past I was urging him not to take this road as it passes the lair of Steinbauch the dragon. That woman was no inn hostess. She is the witch Schwatekathe, the wife of Steinbauch. Those men have not been taken to a band of lustful maidens but to a dragon's lair where they shall be cooked and eaten."

There was a murmur of agreement among the men.

Peter considered reprimanding Hans for his belief in fairy tales but didn't after seeing the looks of his men. What mattered was that they were alert. The disappearance of half his troop was uncanny and he had a feeling that something was about to happen. Peter looked at Nuray sitting on a bag of turnips beside the fire. She sensed that something strange was happening and her expression was thoughtful and apprehensive.

One of the sentries gave a sharp whistle. Peter turned. On the edge of the camp, illuminated by a perimeter torch were a group of men. Peter could just make out their turbans. They were Turks.

The Turks shouted and let off a small-uncoordinated musket volley. Fmaliar crack and smell of gunpowder assaulted Peter's senses. The wagon ponies whinnied. But not a single shot hit home.

Peter counted the shots, seven. *An opportunistic scouting party? How did the Turks get here so soon?* He heard the scraping of ramrods in the musket barrels. They were reloading. "Sokol, guard Nuray. The rest of you, follow me."

Peter drew his sword, sprinted past a baggage wagon, jumped over a tent rope and ran onto the flattened grass between the last tent and the attackers. The other landsknechts weaved through the camp, joining in a loose mass behind Peter.

The attackers were struggling to reload, and they seemed to Peter to be poor musketeers. His men would have fired another volley by now.

The Landsknechts closed on the Turks.

They threw down their muskets and fled.

One of the Landsknechts was carrying a musket and he knelt and fired at the retreating attacker. Seconds later they heard a shout of pain.

"Halt," said Peter, as they arrived at the camp perimeter. "Don't pursue. It could be a trap."

"I hit the bastard," said the man with a musket. "He didn't get far."

"Something's not right about those Mohamedens," said Hans. "The ones we fought at Mohacs were crack shots and fast too." He kicked an abandoned musket, it was certainly made in the Turkish fashion. "This lot couldn't tell the stock from the barrel."

"Something strange going on tonight," said another.

Peter looked out at the long grass as high as a man's waist. The trail of the retreating attackers was as clcar as a highway. He was about to order them into the grass when he heard a scream from the camp. Nuray, the attack had been a decoy.

Stanislaw could scarcely believe how well his plan had worked. The big lanky brute, guarding the Turkish princess would have to die and he would have to die fast.

Stanislaw was right on the edge of the firelight, only three strides away, when Sokol saw him. The swordsman give a savage warning shout, but he was too late.

the Krakowian horseman drew his scimitar and ran at Sokol.

Sokol swung his sword in a wide chopping ark.

Stanislaw ducked and he heard the whir of the blade as it swung just a finger's breadth above his head. From his crouching position Stanislaw slashed his sword forward against Sokol's unarmoured shins.

Sokol gave a grunt of pain and bought his sword in and down in a skewering motion hoping to pin Stanislaw to the ground like a needle through a spider.

Stanislaw rolled, again missing death by seconds.

Sokol fell to his knees, incapacitated by his leg wound.

Stanislaw jumped up and away from Sokol's final lunge.

Before Sokol to recover his position, Stanislaw sprang forward and split his skull with his scimitar.

Nuray had watched the battle in silence. Now she and Stanislaw locked eyes.

The Turkish princess said something in her own language and spat at him.

With one swift movement he stepped over to her, lifted her off the ground and threw her over his shoulder.

She screamed.

Ordinary horsemen would not have been able to ride at speed at night. But the tartars were no ordinary horsemen and they clung to their horses' necks, whispering words of encouragement in their ears. As they cantered along the narrow mountain rode, the leather and cloth bindings muffled the clop of their hooves to a gentle rumble. For Asra the night ride was a torment, gagged and bound to her horse, her body ached with pain. Eventually the road widened into a grassy plain and the company slowed to a walk.

Mustafa motioned his men to be silent as they drew up around him. With no sound other than scrape of wood on cloth he drew his bow from his holster and fitted an arrow to the string.

Asra heard the crunch of boots on grass and the excited chatter of men speaking a Slavonic tongue. She watched as a group of men dressed like Muslims seemed to grow out of the long grass as they approached. They halted and grew quiet as they became aware of the Tartar horsemen. A breeze blew from the north and she smelt their fear.

Mustafa's muscles bulged as he drew the recurve bow.

Asra heard the creak of the bending wood, the rush of the arrow's flight, the thud of its impact and the scream of the man as he fell.

Another arrow left the bow another man fell.

A small volley of arrows twanged and hissed, pin-cushioning the men.

Mustafa rode over to the nearest corpse and dismounted. "Here we have a riddle, seven Christians dressed as Muslims wondering in the night. Salim, see if any live. Uzgur, the whore knows many tongues. Bring her to me and let us see if she is of any use."

Two tartars held the prisoner, while Mustafa Khan and Asra stood. The rest of the troop remained mounted while their horses cropped the grass in the darkness of the early morning.

"What did the Christian say?" said Mustafa, his hand resting on his scimitar.

"He said that the Christians have turned on one another in their desire to win Nuray for themselves. She is now in the possession of Stanislaw of Krakow, who leads the Christian horsemen. They are camped yonder close to the pines and cliffs."

The tartars murmured curses, and gripped their weapons. The polish knights were their hated enemies. For generations they had fought them across the plains north of the Black Sea.

Mustafa nodded, and one of the men holding the prisoner drew a dagger from his sash and cut the Prisoner's throat. "Remount," ordered Mustafa, "we make for the pines."

"Mighty khan," with a fluidity and flexibility that came from years of practice, Asra, kowtowed before Mustafa and kissed his feet. "You are so powerful, so strong. I understand now that I deserved the punishment that in your wisdom and magnanimity you dispensed upon me. How could a mere woman presume to know more than a man such as you?" Asra kissed the soft leather of his boots. They tasted of dust, dew, and horse. "You were generous and lenient in your justice, fore my shrewishness I deserve to have been flayed."

Asra rose onto her knees where she looked up at Mustafa. He was a hulk, ten score lot of taught muscle dressed in leather, silk and steel. His hand rested on the pommel of his long heavy scimitar. Asra would have struggled to lift it, but she had seen Mustafa wield it as if it were a willow whip. She did not doubt that he could cut her in half with a single cut.

Mustafa looked back at her, his face hidden in shadow. "Enough of your grovelling. For your service and repentance you may go ungagged and unbound. But as is the will of God you must cover your face, remain silent and unseen."

"Your generosity and grace is great, and I shall do as you command," Asra bowed down again, "but I dare to ask for another boon, that I should be allowed to act as a woman should and that I be allowed to retrieve my prayer rug from the baggage and pray for your victory, that I may be allowed to anoint your wrists and ankles with oil of almond, and that when victory is done, I may be allowed to sit on your right side and serve you your ayran."

Mustafa removed his gaze from Asra to look up at the moon. "What say you Salim. Can we allow the woman her indulgences?"

Salim spoke quietly from where he sat astride his horse. "It is proper, my khan. Allah delights to see all in their in proper place."

Stanislaw hurried back toward his camp with the Turkish princess slung over his shoulder like a dead hind. She had spirit. She had shouted and cursed, bit and scratched, kicked and squirmed, but Stanislaw held her firm. He was a hunter, a prince and a warrior, and the more she struggled, and the more her scent of almonds and roses filled his nose, the tighter he gripped her. *What a jewel she was!* When he returned to Krakow loaded with booty he would ride through the streets to adoring crowds with her on his saddle afore him. Men would stare with jealousy at her porcelain skin glowing like white quartz, and think to themselves, *there goes Prince Stanislaw. How I wish I were he.* Women would blush at his gaze, and throw garlands of flowers before his horse.

He drew close to his own company. While he had been gone his men had been busy. They had stowed away the tents and cooking supplies onto the packhorses. The horses had been saddled and bridled and the men dressed for battle. The winged lancers were ready to ride during the night and his own horse, Thunderer, was saddled and awaiting Stanislaw to leap on his back carrying him and Nuray away from Peter and the Turks.

He was within shouting distance of his men but they had not yet seen him, when a stabbing pain interrupted his pleasant thoughts. Nuray had slipped her hand underneath his tunic and she now dug her sharp fingernails into the skin around his kidney, drawing blood. Stanislaw lifted Nuray off him and threw her into the long, waist high grass. Her silk Turkish trousers split through the middle seam. "By the Alchemist of Krakow," he said, "I'll take you now."

He unbuckled his sword and let it drop to the ground. He reached forward to grab the hem of her underwear.

Nuray kicked him in the face.

Stanislaw felt his nose break. It wasn't the first time and it wouldn't be the last.

"*Kahretsin pic*" said Nuray.

Stanislaw threw his hand over her mouth and held her head to the ground. With his other hand he drew a dagger from his belt and slid it over her tummy cutting away her lower garments at the waist, exposing her hill, river and cave. Stanislaw felt his desire rise through him. He unbuckled his belt.

The ground trembled to the sound of horses' hooves.

Stanislaw froze.

Riders were coming from the north, from the direction of the pass. There were shouts from the mounted sentries in Stanislaw's own camp. He lifted his hand from Nuray's mouth and rose to crouch on the balls of his feet. He watched in the moonlight with pride as his company formed a line then advanced in a pincer to intercept the two riders.

"Don't kill," the voice, though harsh and raspy, was that of a woman. She spoke a Slavonic tongue, course but approximate to the language of Krakow. "It is only I, a shepherd's widow and with me my daughter Vrba."

Stanislaw heard the mixture of relief and confusion in the voice of his lieutenant that he felt in himself. "What in the name of Heaven are you doing riding around the mountains at night."

"To be honest with you my good men, and I should say it is rather by Hell than by Heaven, we have come to see you."

"*Carodejnice,*" murmured some of the men.

"No," said the woman, "it is nothing more than desperation and our own human sins. Since my husband died I had to sell everything to feed my daughter and myself. We live in nearby in a mountain cottage; we had of course seen your arrival and journeyed through the night to seek you." The woman paused.

The men were silent, doubtless feeling as curious and perplexed as Stanislaw.

"Vrba has always been a pretty and lively girl," the woman continued in a clear loud voice, "and it started off just with kisses for suitors in exchange for bread and honey. But men seldom want for just a kiss. And my sweet Vrba can't say no to any man. And to tell it shortly, we progressed from honey to silver. And do great charity for

144

the paupers. Now as we know both full well, no chivalrous knight is so mean as to spare a scraping of silver for the girl who will repay it in love. Vrba, sweetest, take off your hood, show the men your face."

Stanislaw craned his head to get a look the girl.

Nuray had risen to her feet and eyed the sword that her captor had left to lie in the grass.

As Vrba threw back her hood, all that Stanisalw could make out was a faintly attractive profile and a head of long hair. It was not, he supposed, so odd that a whore would seek to make money from soldiers, but the place and timing was uncanny. It gave Stanislaw a prickle of fear.

"Don't be shy, my princes," said Vbra, her voice soft and husky. "But listen to me now if you wish to know me further. My father was a honourable man. He owned his own land and his own horses. I am a lady and I know that you have all read the rules of chivalry, and know the proper respect with which to treat me."

The riders nodded and murmured. It seemed that Stanislaw's men did not share his apprehension and indeed they knew the rules.

"Though it is only fair," said Vrba that you know what you are getting for your silver. Kisses are a boon, and each man here shall have one." Vrba kissed her hand and blew kisses toward the assembled cavalry. "I shall stay mounted on my colt, and each of you shall come one at time and as you ride past me, you shall lean forward and touch your lips to mine."

Stanislaw cursed quietly to himself. He wanted to get going and be clear of this place by dawn, and he had sworn he had just heard a thrush sing. But he couldn't walk among his soldiers and expose Nuray's body to his men. He turned to call Nuray to him. Nuray was holding his scimitar with both hands. Pointing it directly at him.

Peter threw the blanket over Sokol's body. He had been a good soldier and a good lieutenant, tough and loyal. Now he was dead and half his men were missing. He had fallen for an enemy trick and lost his Turkish princess. "We leave now," he said.

"We're not moving," said Hans.

"Hear, hear," said the landsknecht

Peter could feel his authority seeping away. "Janissaries hit what they aim for," he said, "those were no janissaries. They were bowlegged Polishmen. Stanislaw took Nuray. I've seen the way he looked at her. And he's escaping while I'm arguing with you."

"You can chase your princess my lord," said Hans. "But we're not coming. Thomas and the rest of them went off chasing skirt, and look what happened to them. We don't know. There are Turks, dragons, witches and worse out on this black night, my lord. The best thing we can do is fortify these wagons and build up the fire."

"I am your lord and paymaster," said Peter. "I have made you rich, and our wagons are filled with the wealth we have saved from the Turks. Have you forgotten what lies on the other side of the pass? Let me remind you! We are bound for Eisenberg where I am lord. Defy me and I shall not forget. Obey me and I shall forgive and make you all the richer when we get home."

"I have had men call me a coward, my lord," said Hans, "for being afraid of what comes out of the night. Those men are dead now. But I beg your pardon, for we mean you no disrespect. We're loyal to you and we'll swear it by saint Georg the dragon slayer. We don't want Mutiny. We just want you to stay with us and be our leader. But that doesn't mean leading us to our doom for a pair of wide dark eyes."

The other men murmured their approval.

"It was I," said Peter, "who led you to victory in the battle of Pavia. I killed Jean of Toulouse with my own sword beside Pavia's gates. Together we saw off the attacks of the janissaries at Mohacs and escaped that battle with our lives. Some may call you a coward Hans Shafer, but not I. I have seen all of you stand your ground against French knights, pistoleers and savage Muslims. We have stood against Hungarian bandits and Italian pikeman and every time we come out alive and richer. If we stay here now and let Stanislaw escape then we have lost. We will be here in the morning like sitting ducks for the Turks. When men are on foot they may move unheard, all the more so when they are few in number."

Stanislaw eyed the Turkish princess as she stood before him. Naked from the waist down, holding his sword with shaking hands, she was weak and the sword, heavy. With every moment he waited her arms weakened further. Soon he would knock aside the blade and tackle her to the ground.

"Now that each of you have touched your lips to mine," he heard Vrba, the whore's voice ring out as she addressed his soldiers in her rhythmic hushing dialect, "I hope you found me to your liking."

"Indeed I did." It was the voice of Macek. He was rich and popular with the men. "I will give a whole pouch of Hungarian silver for your lady's first favour."

"Oh come now," said Macek, "where is your chivalry? The lady wants silver and I'll double whatever groats you can scrape together."

Stanslaw sensed a brawl was brewing He had to act swiftly. He heard the hooves of horses. Nuray's hands faltered on the sword. Stanislaw leapt at her.

She dropped the sword and stepped away just as the horse charged at Stanislaw from behind. He shouted and rolled out of the way.

He then watched with incredulity as the old woman, who had slipped away from the lancers while they focused on Vrba, ride up to Nuray.

Nuray stared at the ugly woman on the horse.

"Greetings," the old woman spoke in the tongue of the Faithful.

"Greetings," replied Nuray who covered her woman hood with her hands.

"Come, said the woman climb onto my horse."

Nuray obeyed, the old woman kicked the flanks of the horse and began to gallop away to the north.

"Hey, stop there," The men were shouting. Vrba had turned her horse and spurred after the old woman."

"Lancers of Krakow," Stanislaw shouted, "to me!"

Across the open meadow, in the gathering dawn, the lancers galloped in pursuit of the women. The wind rushed through the feathered wings that rose from Stanislaw's saddle. It felt good to be on Thunderer's back, with his lance in its holster and his sword at his side. Heavy loads did not burden the women's horses and they rode with skill. But the horses of the lancers were bred for speed and strength and once they had broken into a full gallop they began to close the distance between the horsemen and the women. Stanislaw could almost reach out and touch Vrba's long hair as it blew behind her in the wind.

Just as Stanislaw was about to knock the whore of her horse, the women abruptly turned to the east and rode toward the pines and cliff behind.

The riders wheeled in pursuit.

In the pines the women began to draw away from the riders. They were surer of the stony ground and guided their horses deftly over the crooked tree roots, and ducked beneath the spreading branches.

One of the lancer's horses screamed as it stumbled.

A rider cursed as a branch lashed his face.

"There's no escape for them," proclaimed Stanislaw, "tread with care we want no injured horses. Spread wings to cut off their escape."

The lancers slowed their horses to a walk, fanning outward to form a line.

At length, Stanislaw who held the centre of the line broke out of the pines and came to a swathe of open rocky meadow between the pines and cliff.

The women had reached the cliff, dismounted from their horses, and had begun to ascend the cliff climbing a narrow winding stairway that lead to the mouth of a cave.

Macek was the first to reach the cliff. He made strait for Vbra who straggled a little behind the other two He reached high in his saddle and grabbed Vrba by the ankle pulling her down and lifting her onto his horse.

Stanislaw had eyes only for Nuray who was halfway up the cliff. Without even bothering to issue orders to his men, he dismounted, tethered his horse to a stunted pine, ran to the stairs and began to ascend.

"I caught the vixen," Stanislaw heard Macek shout, "and by Saint George, I'll be the first to bed her."

Among the lancers was a young man named Barek. He was known for his close kinship to horses. He was a breeder and a physician. He was the first to notice that the horses were behaving strangely like stallions do when they smell a mare on heat.

As robins, thrushes and finches sang, dawn's pale light gave colour to the world. The trail of the horsemen was easy to follow, a broad road of trampled grass. The Tartars, bows in hand, guided their nimble mares beneath the pines, the sound of their hooves, muffled by their cloth bindings. Asra followed in the rare, her hair wrapped in a scarf with only a slit around the eyes, her dagger tucked into her sash, her bag hanging at her saddle.

Mustafa held up his hand to halt the troop as they reached the edge of the pines.

Asra nudged her horse forward to peer at the scene beyond. A troop of Christian horsemen milled around in a state of disarray. Some had dismounted and were ascending the cliff toward a cave. Attached to each saddle were two wings built with wood and feathers. One of the riders had removed his saddle so that the wings lay spread out on the ground. Three men worked binding a naked woman to the wings. Others sat on their horses, watching on while their mounts grazed.

For the first time Asra saw Mustafa smile. "Draw," he shouted.

The tartars fitted arrows to their bows, took aim and drew.

"Loose."

The arrows hit the Christians, puncturing through chain and plate armour, and knocking men from their horses.

The Christian lancers, shouting curses and death cries, turned and charged with an unexpected speed and vigour, and it seemed to Asra that many were pulled into the charge by their horses. The heavy Christian war stallions seemed more intent on baring down on them than their riders, and much to the surprise of the men on foot their mounts joined the charge without them.

"Retreat," ordered Mustafa

Asra took a last glance at the frothing mouth and wild eyes of a leading black beast before wheeling her mare around and kicking its flanks to flee. The mares sensing the charging stallions needed no encouragement and bolted through the pines. Asra had to duck to avoid being knocked off her horse by an overhanging branch.

The mares and their clinging tartar riders quickly cleared the pines, but the lustful stallions were right behind, though their shaken riders struggled to control them.

"Kill them," shouted Mustafa.

Asra watched with awe as the Tartar khan clung to his bucking horse with his legs while releasing arrow after arrow into the Christians.

Asra walked through the battlefield. The Christian horsemen had been destroyed. Their stallions had been herded together and tethered to the pines. Their bodies had been dragged to the edge of the cliff. And here the Tartars worked, stripping the bodies of their valuables, piling the loot into little mounds. Murmuring prayers they cut the throats of the injured men and horses. Mounted sentries watched from the edges of the battlefield. A crow alighted on a corpse's face and pecked at his eye.

The battlefield reminded Asra of her childhood. It was her earliest most vivid memory, the Fall of Durrës. She remembered the Turks running through the burning city.

"Whore!"

Asra looked over her shoulder to see Mustafa beckoning her. The khan sat mounted on his horse. The naked woman still bound to the wings of a Lancers saddle. Was propped up against a pile of loot, beside him.

"Translate," Mustafa ordered as she approached. "Ask her what has become of Nuray."

Asra turned her attention to the woman. Her ankles were tied to the tip of the wings, her wrists were bound halfway down the wings, so that they pulled her shoulders back and her breasts out. Asra was drawn to the extroidnary whiteness of her skin that reflected the early morning sun. Despite the obvious discomfort of her bonds, she did not seem to be badly harmed. It appeared. Her wrists and ankles were bruised where the rope had been tightened, but there were no cuts where her clothes had been shorn away, and her splayed body appeared otherwise unblemished. Asra noted the strong legs of a horse rider.

"Water," said the woman in Latin.

"The woman begs for water." Asra deferred to Mustafa.

Mustafa nodded.

Asra uncorked her own water skin pressed it to the lips of the woman, and gently tipped the water into her mouth, pausing for her to breath. Asra allowed the last drops of water to spill onto the woman's chin before asking her if she knew where the Turkish princess had been taken.

"She has gone where you will never find her."

Asra relayed the words to Mustafa.

"Tell her," said Mustafa, "that I am a khan and the blood of the king of kings flows in me. Tell her that my word is iron. If I am satisfied with her words she shall die cleanly and unviolated and that she shall be buried according to her custom."

Asra relayed this to the woman, adding only that she believed Mustafa to be as good as his word. She watched the woman's expression when she realized her own death was a certainty.

"Well," said Mustafa, "has the woman made her choice."

"The princess has gone into the heart of the mountain, brought there by Iron Finger the witch. I am the witch's daughter and if you kill me my ghost will haunt you for the rest of your days. Dare not go into the cave for the home my mother is protected by her pet dragon which will consume you all."

"Nuray," Asra relayed to Mustafa, "was abducting by the woman's mother who lives in the cave on the cliff." Asra paused.

"Is that all?" asked Mustafa.

"No," said Asra. "In the cave is a great quantity of treasure that these women have accumulated from robbing travellers."

"Is that so. Ask her how deep the cave is."

Asra relayed the question.

"Deep," said the woman. "It is deep. It winds right down into Hell."

"It is deep and yet not so deep. One can follow the passage to the lair and return in the times it takes to prepare and eat a meal."

Mustafa narrowed his eyes. "It is a strange tongue. Some things take so many words to say and others so few. Ask her if there are any other dangers in the cave."

Asra relayed the question to the woman.

"Oh yes," said the woman, "there are blood drinking bats and serpents."

"Nothing but tricks to scare children," relayed Asra.

Mustafa leaned back and pulled on his beard. "Tell the Christian I am satisfied with her answers."

As Asra relayed this to the woman, Mustafa stood, murmured a quick prayer to the God of all Children of the Book, and cut woman's throat.

In the growing light of dawn, Peter and his remaining soldiers marched along the trail left by the horses. They were dressed in their full and colourful regalia of slashed satin and embossed breastplates. They wore their muskets, slung on their backs, their powder horns, tinderboxes and pouches of shot hung at their waists beside their short swords and daggers. Their long swords they carried in their hands, resting on their shoulders. Each man wore his lucky signs, a tress of a lover's hair, a rabbit's foot, a silver horseshoe, a peacock feather.

As they marched the world began to wake around them, the larks, swallows and finches sang, the bees, butterflies and hawk moths began to fly among the wild flowers of the meadow. A spider strengthened a thread on its dew-jewelled web. The pines rose in a dark green wall on their right, beyond that loomed the grey mountain cliffs. Somewhere in the distance a horse whinnied. Peter approached a corpse lying facedown in the grass. Arrows protruded from his back. The soldiers grasped at their lucky charms and murmured prayers to Georg the dragon slayer or to fair Lady Fortune.

"Light the wicks of your muskets," ordered Peter.

Asra kowtowed before Mustafa. "I have brought you your ayran, Great Khan." Asra raised her eyes to watch Mustafa's reaction. The Tartar khan had won a victory and Asra guessed he was in as good a mood as he was ever likely to be in.

He stared unflinching into Asra's face. "Your sweet looks and charms have no effect on me. Women are weakness. Desire makes men weak."

"Your ayran." Asra placed the wooden cup of fermented milk into Mustafa's hands.

Mustafa drained it with a single gulp, and then addressed the Tartars that had gathered around him. "We shall enter the cave and bring back Nuray and the treasures of the strange women. Ozgur and Salim shall guard the horses."

The Tartars murmured uneasily among themselves. They were horsemen, warriors of the open land, and none liked the idea of entering into a cave where they could not easily use their bows and would have to leave their horses behind, but none was prepared to challenge the word of their leader.

The landsknecht followed the trail of destructions through the pines, and arrived cautiously at the swathe of meadow that separated the trees from the cliff. They halted under the cover of branches thick with needles and looked out at the strange scene before them.

The slain Polish lancers were piled beside a heap of their looted possessions. The horses, both Christian stallions and Turkish mares, were tethered in separate herds. The battlefield was deserted but for two strange warriors. They wore pointed steel helms ringed with fur, their light baggy pants were tucked into high riding boots. They rode horses and carried bows.

Peter felt his heart race. Here were the dreaded Turkish cavalry. They had arrived silent as ghosts in the night. They had massacred the Polish lancers, here right on the boarder of his own county. But where was the rest of the troop.

"Advance and fire." Peter gave the order, stepped out from the shadow of the pines, aimed his musket and pulled the trigger. The wick ignited in the flash pan. The flaming wadding landed on the needle-covered ground.

Peter saw the face of the horse archer as he recognized the attack. He marvelled at the speed with which he strung and loosed an arrow, crying out, as he spurred his horse, away too late as the musket shot threw him from his saddle.

There was a scream from Peter's left and he turned to see that the arrow had hit home, and was buried in the thigh of four fingered Markus.

The tethered horses brayed with fear and pulled at their ropes.

The landsknecht advanced cautiously toward the edge of the cliff.

The birds sang, the insects chirped, the horses snorted but there was no sign of a living man or woman.

Peter was first to reach the cliff. He gazed up at the stairway and cave above. And in the morning light he thought he saw a familiar figure. Peter climbed the stair. And stood on the threshold before the mouth of the cave.

Here, propped up against the edge of the cliff, was Stanislaw Prince of Krakow, dressed in his hauberk of fine chain mail. His pointed helm lay on the ground beside him. With one hand he held his stomach from which an arrow protruded and blood seeped over his fingers. His face was pale and his moustache bloodied. It was clear that he was not much longer for this world.

Peter knelt beside the young man who had betrayed him and drew his short sword.

Stanislaw opened his eyes and fixed Peter with a bleary, death haunted stare.

"Where is Nuray you treacherous bastard?" Peter ran his finger along the edge of his sword blade, drawing a bead of blood.

"Peter," the lancer's voice was weak and shaky. "I took her from you. I coveted her. Forgive me. Burry, burry my men and I like Christians."

"Where is she?"

"A Christian burial, Peter, burry me according to the rites."

Peter couldn't help but feel a twinge of pity for the dying prince. He had betrayed him and brought catastrophe upon himself. Peter laid down his sword took out his kerchief and wiped the blood from Stanislaw's lips "It shall be done just tell me what happened."

"She was abducted by strange wild women. They led us on a merry chase and brought us to this cave. I tried to follow them but the Turks fell upon us and slew us. Then they too went into the caves." Stanislaw slumped back and closed his eyes. "Finish me Peter," he raised his hand to grab at Peter's sleeve. "Tell my father, I died a hero's death."

"It shall be done," said Peter. He picked up Stanislaw's sword from where it lay beside him, placed it in the dying man's hands, and cut his throat.

"We're not going my lord, and there's nothing that can be said that will change that." Hans kept his hands tight around the handle of his long sword. Have us hung when we return to Eisenberg for any of us would far rather face the rope than what the witch and dragon have in store for us. Only the dead enter that cave, Lord Peter, mark my words."

The other mercenaries nodded and murmured their approval.

"Lady Fortune has seen fit to leave us in possession of the battle field and with all the gold and treasures of our enemies," Hans continued, "we'll follow you to the Well at the End of the World but not into the Devil's hole."

Peter could see that his men would not budge, and he himself felt an odd foreboding about that dark cave. Too many strange things had happened that night. Too many people were dead. *Maybe Hans was right and a witch and a dragon had taken Nuray.*

Asra walked behind Mustafa as the Tatars made their way along the passage, deeper into the mountain. The men glanced nervously around them, ill at ease in the tight confines of the rock. It was only the trust in the khan that drew the men on.

In the flickering light of the lantern Asra watched as the effects of the arsenic she had poured into Mustafa's ayran took effect. He began to stumble. He vomited and dropped to his knees. Mustafa began to seizure and froth at the mouth.

Panic rippled down the line of soldiers. "The khan has been bewitched," one shouted. "We're doomed cried another." They began to run back they way that had come, stumbling and cursing, pushing and shoving.

Asra listened as their cries and shouts grew more distant. She straightened her gown, picked up Mustafa's fallen lantern, and continued with gentle steps along the passage. As she walked she sang to raise her spirits, she sang the sad songs of the harem, the songs of caged birds. She remembered what it meant to be free. That gave her courage and she walked on through the darkness without fear.

Peter and the landsknecht were ready for the Tatars as they burst into the blinding morning light. The volley of musket fire startled the flock of griffin vultures that were feeding on carcasses at the foot of the cliff. The cloud of gun smoke was carried by the rising warm air from the valley toward the mountain pass and its sound echoed like distant thunder in the valleys.

It took the best part of the day, for the mercenaries to prepare for leaving. They fetched their wagons, stripped the dead of their valuables and piled the loot upon them. They took the finest and most handsome horses filling their saddlebags with further loot. They buried the Christian dead in shallow graves in the peaty soil and left the Muslims to the vultures. No man wished to stay another night in that cursed place, so they mounted those horses that would take them and rode toward the pass. As Peter turned to leave he took one last look at the cave and thought of Nuray and he swore silently to himself that one day he would find her and wed her.

As they rode they sang the songs of soldiers, songs to raise the spirit and to keep their tired feet marching, songs, cruel sergeants, of gold and foreign women.

At length the mercenaries came to a mountain tarn, at which they hoped to fill their skins and barrels of water. But beside the tarn they found the corpses of their comrades, already stripped of flesh by vultures. They crossed themselves, clutched their lucky charms and hurried, thirsty, on their way while the light still lasted.

As evening came the weary mercenaries came to a pretty stone chapel, with an interior of whitewashed plaster. On the dais of the chapel was a shrine to the Holly Virgin. The men left offerings of looted silks and other trinkets, imploring the Holly Mother to guard them against evil before making camp for the night.

When the camp had been made the sound of bells drew their attention and a flock of sheep appeared, driven along the road by an old, blind shepherd. The mercenaries invited the shepherd to join their camp, which he did gladly. Peter paid him handsomely for a young sheep, and the soldiers feasted on roasted lamb. The shepherd took great delight in the tales of the soldiers.

"You did well not to enter the cave," said the old, blind man, "for those caves are the domain of the abbess of Saint Hildegard's Abby. They do not suffer men to be among them and there is no doubt that you would have perished undiscovered in the mountain's heart."

Book Five

The Miller's Wife

The 20th of September, Year of the Lord 1526

Countess Greta von Esienberg drank wine from one of the bishop's jewelled cups. She had been drinking a lot of wine recently to sweeten the woes of victory. All her friends were dead. Of her household only the female servants remained. She was now in possession of all the wealth of Eisenberg. She had done her best to dispense of some silver to ensure a net of patronage protected her position. She was, moreover, pleased to discover that the name of Eisenberg commanded some loyalty among the townsfolk, even if she was one by marriage only. She quickly acquired a retinue of boys turned guards and footmen who were happy for noble favour. It was two such young men, armed with halberds, which flanked her table as she welcomed Ule, chief burgher and head of the city's Lutheran Council.

Ule was a broad shouldered, short bearded, balding man dressed in a long yellow tunic and faded blue cloak pinned with a silver broach. The man was a silversmith but was devout, reasonable and a skilled accountant, having reviewed the ledger board of many a tradesman, farmer, merchant and lord. Ule was not glamorous but he was a competent.

"Wine?" Greta offered.

Ule shook his head and he seated himself before Greta. "Ale will suffice for me."

Greta turned to Magda who stood beside her with the jug of wine in hand. "Magda, sweet child. Fetch the good burgher a pitcher of ale."

Magda curtseyed and retired.

"Grain," said Ule flatly by way of introducing his topic. "Most is unground and the rain has destroyed much of the harvest and though it is not yet winter, in only three moons we shall have no bread for the townsfolk."

Greta frowned. She was of course aware of the shortage but had not realised its severity. Can we not bring in more from the countryside?"

Ule shook his head. "The Church was popular with the farmers and peasants north of the river. The countryside is in insurrection. What little grain they have they don't want to part with. Two tax collectors were murdered near swineherd's ford. Hungry folk are already turning to banditry and wolves have come down from the mountains."

"Wolves," repeated Greta, "isn't that the sugar plum atop the sweet bread. Have you found Lock yet?"

"Not yet," said the burgher, "but bounty hunters are searching and Captain Johann thinks he knows where to find him."

"Where?"

"Muhlborg. It has become the centre of the resistance. In their Castle the Muhlers have horded the largest grain and flour supply left in the land. Folk loyal to the old Church have gathered there and taken up arms in defiance of our rule. We must take Muhlborg seize the grain, capture Lock and break the resistance. With the help of your new guards…"

"Oh I see," said Greta cutting him off and raising her voice as she allowed her anger to surface. "I am to send my household to the slaughter again. What about the Lutheran militia? Why do they not take the castle?"

"Of course the Lutheran council will send what men we can spare and certainly cannon and some musketeers. But we must hold order in the city."

Magda had returned but she did not have a pitcher of ale in her hand.

Greta was about to berate the girl for her forgetfulness but saw the expression on her maid's face.

Magda knelt down to whisper. "You'd best come at once my lady."

"Can't you see," Greta hissed back, "I'm in audience with the town's chief Burgher."

"I know my lady but you'd best come all the same."

"You must excuse me," Greta said to the councillor. "An urgent matter has arisen that requires my immediate attention. My guards will see you to the gate." Greta rose and stepped towards Ule.

"Thank you your ladyship, but before I depart, may I know if you will be attending the iconoclasm?"

Greta turned to look at the burgher. "Naturally I shall. Have I not already approved the plans? I assure you that my commitment to the creed of Luther is iron strong and sincerely held."

"That is good," said the burgher, "I have come only recently to the light. Though I now understand that God has ordained our fates, and our new faith will lead us to the kingdom of heaven for the day of judgment will soon be upon us."

The sentiment struck Greta as unusual. Though her thoughts often wandered to her own place in heaven, she seldom contemplated the end of days. And when she did it was far distant not something that would affect her life. But she felt the urgency in Magda's grip so she nodded her agreement and left.

"What is it Magda?" said Greta as she left the audience room. "This had better be of great import."

"My lady," said Magda, "there is not a moment to lose. Lord Peter has returned. He is on his way here as we speak. We should anticipate that he shall be here at any moment. People say that he has slain a dragon."

Bishop Lock stood thoughtfully on the porch of the woodcutter's cottage, slurping sour pottage from a wooden bowl. He still hadn't gotten used to eating without cutlery, at least a knife or a spoon. As he licked the saltless turnipy paste from his lips the Lament of David came to mind, *The beauty of Israel is slain upon thy high places: how are the mighty fallen!* Though for the woodcutter's wife it was the greatest hospitality she could offer, Lock mused on how it was only extreme hunger that had driven him to eat the sludge.

Sonia came and joined him on the balcony slipping her arm around his waste. "Don't worry," she said sensing his mood, "Saint Francis chose the life of a beggar and see how revered he is."

"In certainty," said Lock, "if only more Franciscans followed the example of their patron."

The woodcutter approached from the edge of the fir trees. "You'd better be off," he shouted in a rough Latin, "The woodcutter's broad tanned face was dripping with sweat and he waved his axe in the air holding it near the bottom of the handle. "Soldiers are coming with dogs. Fly, fly."

As if to emphasise the woodcutter's words a dog bayed in the distance.

Lock dropped his bowl of pottage.

"Meet me at the edge of the woods behind the hut," said Sonia, "Ill fetch our things.

Yet again Lock felt the indignity of lifting up the hem of his long black cloak and running.

But a short time later Sonia ran to meet him. She was wrapped in a dark blue cloak, held about her throat with a silver broach beneath which she wore a skirt and bodice. Her hair was tied in a red kerchief. The red and blue paint on her wooden shoes had not yet faded and she carried their leather sack on her shoulder. As long as he had her he could withstand the cruelty of Fortune.

Together they ran through the damp dripping forest, past oak, spruce and linden. The only path they followed was that of least resistance. They wove past fallen pine and spruce whose branches jutted out like the bones of giants. They avoided clumps of saplings and ant mounds. They slid over rotting trunks. On and on they ran. Lock stopped to catch his breath sitting on a rotting linden log, ridden with bright orange fungi.

"Have we any wine?" he asked.

"Alas no," replied Sonia, "you drank the last of it three days thence."

"Water," said Lock, "have we water?"

"Yes," said Sonia, "I filled our skin from the wood cutters bucket." She opened the sack and passed it to Lock."

"But drink with care my lord for only Lady Fortune knows when we will next find a stream,"

"Lady Fortune," said Lock, "is a pagan goddess."

"Oh don't say that," said Sonia her face contorting in distress. "I always pray to her in the hope that she will turn her wheel to our benefit."

"It is of little matter," said Lock, "your assessment was in any case correct. We do not know when or if we shall come across a stream or for that matter a house or food. We are lost. And though we have evaded for now the stakes and fire of our persecutors, nobody knows if we shall ever make it out of these cursed trees." Lock stood and kicked the trunk of one of the low shade loving trees beside him. "And if we are not to keep walking in circles we must mark the way we have come." Lock reached up pulled one of the branches toward him. The branch broke easily with a tearing of bark and fibre.

"Oh your Excellency," cried Sonia. To Lock's surprise her expression shifted to shock and horror. "What have you done," Sonia fell onto her knees. She took out of the sack an apple, which she broke in half and laid at the tree's foot. She then stood and began to remove her kerchief.

"What are you doing?" said Lock unable to soften the frustration in his voice. "We only have three apples and precious little else."

Sonia stared back at Lock with a look he had seldom seen in her, determination and defiance. "I'm asking the elder mother for forgiveness."

"The what?" said Lock, allowing his misery to infect his tone with bitter superiority.

"The elder mother," said Sonia. "This is an elder tree and a very old one. It has a powerful spirit that can affect the goodwill of the forest toward us. And you have harmed it. I have given it the offering and will bind the wound with my kerchief. If we are lucky the spirit will forgive us. Cook told me so."

Lock decided he would take a stand. He was not going to allow superstition to cause the waste of a good apple and kerchief. "Trees do not have spirits. There is no elder mother, or good will of the forest. Cook is a stupid old woman. There are no goblins, werewolves or vampires." Lock broke another stem of elder. "There are no witches, no dragons, no giants and no talking animals." Lock broke a third stem of elder. "And there are no angels!" A forth stem of elder cracked in the silent forest. "There is only God and Aristotle."

Sonia began to cry. "Take it back," she shouted. "You pretend to be wise but you don't know. In the catacombs I made an offering to the kobolds that live there that they would guide you out alive. You wouldn't be here now if wasn't for them. You are endangering us with your ignorance and anger. Take it back and repair the damage you've done."

"No," said Lock, "you dare to call me ignorant. Ever since I first met you I wondered if it was possible for a human being to be more stupid."

"I hate you," screamed Sonia. "And I hope the soldiers find you." Her eyes brimming with tears she threw the leather sack at his feet and ran into the forest.

Lock considered running after her. But pride restrained him so he sat in the gloom and watched as a long black slug slithered across the leaf-strewn ground. Lock lacked the spirit to eat the broken apple at the foot of the elder tree.

The Kobold's Breaches was crowded. The disruption brought about by the Lutheran seizure of Eisenberg did not seem to have affected the townsfolk's taste for ale. And the return of Peter's company of mercenaries had created a sensation. Many ladies and young widows had gathered to partake of the soldiers' generosity and listen to their tales of distant lands. The ale flowed in a constant stream of earthenware jugs bourn by stocky barmaids. But not everybody that crowded around the tables came simply to hear the boasts and tall tales of the soldiers, but to find out what their arrival meant for the city's new order and Johann was sure that among the crowd were papal sympathizers.

The mercenaries, however, seemed uninterested in religion and politics, wallowing instead in a heavy lull of drunkenness and enjoying the appreciative female ears and eyes that surrounded them. Yet there were things of interest among the stories of the mercenaries, and to Johann it was the holes in their stories. One of the mercenaries had mentioned a name, Nuray, and had been about to say more before his companion had given him a hard look and he had shut his mouth. From there Johann had begun to discern something of the unspoken element in their tale.

Johann pushed his way through the ladies dressed in colourful gowns and high cloth hats. He hated them, the capricious whores, all they needed was a pretty new face dressed in slashed satin with sword and dagger and money to spend and they congregated like feral cats to the butcher. The women shrank away from him as he approached the mercenaries' table and banged his fist upon it. "What happened to the Turkish princess?" he shouted, the alcohol pervading his voice. The table fell silent all eyes rested on captain Johann. "The Turkish princess everyone was fighting over," said Johann, "what happened to her?"

"Good evening to you and well met, Johann of Eisenberg," slurred the young man at the head of the table who seemed to be the leader.

"Why," said Johann, "if it isn't Hans the bakers boy. I see you have become a man. The Turkish princess what happened to her?"

The women were silent there eyes fixed on Hans.

"She was taken into the dragon's lair."

A murmur of hushed excitement reverberated around the table.

"The dragon Steinbauch of the Pass of Eagles?" asked Johann.

"The very same," said Hans in low serious tone.

Johann sniggered.

Hans drew his dagger.

A woman on his right moved to restrain him.

"Do not bother yourself with me," said Johann as he turned his back on table. "You have told me all I need to know."

As Lock sat in the deepening gloom of the forest, he stared at the sack on the ground. There was precious little to eat and drink. But Sonia had dutifully packed his favourite Italian edition of Lucretius', *On The Nature of Things*. She had even remembered his collection of seals. Lock was not given to the self-mutilation fashionable among various holy orders, considering the practice of purging the flesh to be absurd, but for the first time in his life he felt a strong desire to hurt himself. There was only one person in the world it seemed who really cared about him and he had driven her away through his own boorishness, anger and pride. He didn't even have a knife with which to fashion a suitable switch to administer his own atonement. *Oh the wicked man writhes in pain.* Lock raised his gaze and found that he was staring into the yellow eyes of a wolf.

It had given no warning of its advance, padding silently over the damp forest ground while Lock wallowed in his own misery.

Lock and the wolf weighed each other up. Lock was a slightly overweight man in the twenty seventh year of his life with no stick or weapon. The wolf was a male but not an alpha. He was a youngster with something to prove and a decidedly hungry look in his lean jowls.

The wolf bared its fangs.

Lock glanced past the wolf to see two more emerging from the trees. To Lock's left a strong middling spruce was growing with a bow just low enough to pull himself up. He made a dash for it.

The wolf ran after him.

Lock managed to climb up into the branches of the spruce unharmed.

The wolf growled.

And the group of wolves moved to surround the tree.

"Do you think its good?" asked Greta, "Spoons and knives or just knives? The gown isn't made too formal with a ruff is it?"

"I'm sure his lordship will be overjoyed to see you."

Greta had given Lock's old bedroom, with its windows overlooking the church and square, a makeover. Gone was Lock's general clutter – books, paintings, broken quills and stacks of paper. Everything was now stowed on the ground floor where it awaited the iconoclasm. But Greta had kept Lock's bed. The wide goose down mattress on an oak frame replete with satin sheets, canopy and curtains, was, the best thing she had either slept or sinned on. On the wood framed walls she had hung bolts of calico. Lock's sofa had been replaced with stools to create more space and give the room a more Spartan look.

A wood fire burned in the fireplace and candles were fitted in iron holders in the room's corners. The windows were open allowing the vapours and sounds of the city to waft in. On a wooden table Greta had placed a leg of ham, a jug of wine and two silver cups. On the bedside table she had placed a copper clock.

Greta and Magda heard the sound of boots ascending the stairs.

"The ruff, it's too much," said Greta and she threw it under the bed.

Peter walked through the open door.

For the first time in five years Greta looked at her husband.

In some ways he was as she remembered him, a round, tanned thoughtful face, short brown hair, dressed in fine yet modest clothing. But in so many ways he was different. His boyish swagger and grin was gone. He had a scar on his cheek. He was leaner, stronger, exuded a sense of danger that she did not remember, and he looked like drank too much.

She curtseyed as he moved toward the table with the jug of wine.

Would he try and take her, she wondered. *Would he feel the same? Would he dismiss Magda throw her onto the bed and rip apart her fine dress?*

Peter quaffed his wine. "My lady" his voice sounded distant like he was talking to a stranger. "What has happened here? The city wall is decorated with corpses and I find you in the bishop's house."

Greta moved to greet her husband. She kissed his hands, refilled his wine and cut a slither from the ham, which she fed to his waiting mouth.

"My lord, how I have wished to have you by my side. Everything I have done I have done for us, us and, God willing, the heir that I shall bear you. There is much to speak of, but come, I am your wife. My first and only duty is to you. And now you have returned you may guide me in matters that are beyond my station and intelligence. Magda, fetch our lord another jug of wine."

Magda left the room.

"Come," Greta ushered Peter to the stool by the fire. "Let me loosen your tunic." Greta stood behind Peter and slid her fingers along the seam of Peter's tunic, unpicking the buttons. As her hands moved from his neck to his stomach, she felt some of the tension in his taut muscles ease.

As she neared the last button, Peter winced.

"What is it, Peter," she whispered his familiar name.

"It's but a bruise... Greta..."

"Hush now, let me remove your boots so you may stretch your toes and warm them by the fire." Greta knelt beside her husband, untied the leather thongs and pulled the fur lined leather boots from his feet.

Peter bent down and reached his hand to touch Greta's face. With his other hand he gulped more wine. "Greta, what has happened here?"

"Peter," she said, "I have become a Lutheran."

Peter drew back his hand and slapped her. He had not used full force, but enough to bruise.

Greta cried out in pain. In their younger days he had never hit her and she had thought it not in his nature.

"I had heard the rumours," said Peter, "But I had not believed them. My own wife, a heretic, bringing the wrath of God and excommunication upon us. While I was fighting for God's Kingdom you were consorting with the Devil."

Magda re-entered the room carrying with her another Jug of wine. If she was shocked at what she saw, she gave no sign.

"Leave the Jug on the table, Maid," ordered Peter. "You may leave us for the evening."

Magda curtseyed and left.

"You have every right to beat me," Greta whispered, "but know this I would never have deigned to disobey the wishes of my absent lord by converting to the faith of Luther had I known that he lived. For these past months I have wallowed in agony believing you to be slain by the Turks. Be gentle with me, my lord, and fair. Listen to what I have to say then judge me as you see fit."

Sonia cried as she stumbled through the forest. Night was approaching and it was already dark. Tired and hungry, Sonia threw herself down beside a tall straight oak. *There is no use crying,* she told herself after some minutes of weeping, *you'd better dry your eyes.* She wiped her eyes on the edge of her cloak, as she no longer had a kerchief. *Lock cannot have meant it. He has shown us how to experience God's bliss. He is a good man, but he reads too many books. He must not have meant what he said and did. He only did it because he was upset at us having to leave and not having any wine. I will give a prayer to the spirit of this oak tree and ask the fairies of the forest to help us.*

Sonia ripped off a piece of Satin from her dress and tied it to the twig of the oak. "Spirit of the oak, Please forgive the Bishop Lock for his ignorance as I forgive him for his cruel words. Help us and guide us so we come out of this forest without harm."

Having spoken these words Sonia felt much clearer about what she must do. She found a solid staff on the forest floor to ward off wild animals, and began to retrace her footsteps as well as she could back to where she had parted with the Bishop. She had not gone far though before she spotted a light twinkling through the tree trunks not all that far away.

Is it wrong to beg for a crust of bread from strangers when one is lost in the woods? Sonia asked herself. *Certainly not,* she replied, *most probably the fairies have guided us to this light for a reason.*

Lock could hardly imagine things getting much worse, cramped and chilled in the bows of a tree while a trio of hungry wolves sat waiting for him to fall. Then Lock saw the lights and mused that perhaps things could get worse. He watched as the band of three armed men carrying lanterns approached through the forest. They were led by a hound and followed by a laden donkey.

The wolves fled.

The men made their way to Lock's tree. They were dressed in hose, tunics and cloaks. They had crossbows strapped to their backs, and swords and daggers at their waists. One man was short and stocky, another tall and lean with a long pointy nose, the third was immensely strong and barrel chested. Lock dubbed them Gnome, Weasel and Ogre.

"We'd best make camp for the night," said Ogre, "that dog of yours has been following red herrings up every tree."

"Hold on to your reigns," said Gnome, "old Crack Tooth has found something. A sack..."

Lock watched as the man held up the sack he had left on the ground. The hound stood underneath the tree and began to bark.

"A book, some old seals, an apple."

"What's this," said Weasel, "The girl's kerchief tied round an elder tree. They were here. But why discard their belongings?"

"Because they left in haste," said Gnome. "They are no doubt lurking in the bushes near by as we speak."

Weasel skewered the piece of apple left on the ground with his dagger and held it up to the light. "If they left in a hurry, it was not on our account. The apple is well-browned and providing food for ants. It was some turns of the clock when they were last here."

Lock felt sure that it was just a matter of time before the soldiers realized that he was perched just above them in the branches and they would get him down one way or another.

Gnome fetched a bone from the donkey, which he threw to the dog that ceased to bark.

"Let the riddles wait for the morning," said Ogre. "The light is fading, and we're all hungry. We'll make camp for the night and continue the hunt in the morning."

The men seemed agreeable to this, and Lock watched as Gnome tethered, fed and watered the donkey, Weasel cleared the sleeping place, gathered wood and lit the fire, and Ogre skinned and butchered a young roe deer.

Sonia cautiously approached the fire and was surprised to see two women. They were wearing long black cloaks and wide brimmed, pointed black hats. One sat on a fallen log while the other stirred a cauldron that steamed as it hung from a tripod above the crackling fire.

Sonia stood on a twig.

The woman who was sitting turned and looked right at her, her face concealed by the brim of her hat. "Baba," she said, "there is a girl standing at the edge of the firelight."

The second woman stirring the cauldron turned to look in the direction of Sonia. "Come here, child."

Sonia hesitated. *Are these witches? It doesn't matter if they are daemons or not right now*, Sonia told herself, *I'll die if I don't have a bowl of whatever is in that cauldron.* Sonia began to walk toward the fire and the waiting women.

"Are you alone," asked Baba.

"Oh yes, yes," stammered Sonia, "I mean, I am now, I've lost the bishop, and my only apple. He didn't mean to be cruel. It just happened. And now, yes, I'm here. And oh I'm so hungry. Do you think I could have some stew? I would be so grateful. I'm not sure I can give you anything for it in return. But I feel if I do not..."

"Baba," said the first Woman, "It's Sonia Muller."

Peter made love to Greta yet somehow it felt listless. It was not the homecoming he had imagined. He had hopped to spend only a day or two in Eisenberg before pushing on to the schloss to enjoy some days of comfort, hunting, and his wife's embrace, which was after all, something he had long waited for. Yet now here he was in a looted town house, in the midst of a war torn city in a hungry country. He was drunk. He had forgiven her, forgiven her because he needed to. If Peter admitted the truth in that moment of sweating drunken coupling, then he would have told her that it was not her heresy that had made him angry, nor her usurpation of power or her popularity among the townsfolk. His true reason for anger was that she was not Nuray.

Basha watched as Sonia drank hungrily from the bowl of broth. The soup was made from chestnuts and wild garlic, flavoured with salt and lamb fat, which Baba always carried on her.

"It's so good," said Sonia as she placed the bowl on the ground beside her. "I knew the forest spirits were leading me here for a good a reason, to meet my sister."

Basha felt love for Sonia. She reminded her in some ways of Joseph. They looked similar, rounded face and features, kind eyes. They both had a naivety that nevertheless seemed to mask an odd wisdom. *How odd it was for them to meet her here in the very woods where she had met Joseph just two years ago.* She had been gathering mushrooms and he playing his whistle in the shade of an aspen tree. Then they had met as free folk, now she and Sonia were hunted exiles. There were differences of course between Sonia and Joseph. Where Joseph had been dreamy and thoughtful Sonia was bursting with chatty curiosity. "I can't believe you didn't know your brother," she said, dipping a bowl into the broth and giving it to Sonia.

"I told you," said Sonia, "my mother is a lunatic. She was obsessed that I should read and write and be uncorrupted by the world. From my ninth birthday I was locked in a tower. I got visits of course and could go out on holidays. But most of my life has been reading, writing, singing and staying out of the sun to protect my complexion. It was horribly lonely. All that changed of course when I became Lock's ward. He was such a holly and important person. It's just, well, I'm just so happy that it happened. But now... oh no. What am I going to do about the bishop? What are you doing in the woods?"

Basha shrugged, "Same as you. It's not such a good time to be a Jew in Eisenberg."

"I'm not afraid of Jews," said Sonia, "I asked the bishop about it, and he said there was nothing wrong with being a Jew at all."

"I'm sorry Sonia," said Basha, "The Lord Lock, well, I wouldn't bet my silver needle that he shall live. We saw him and watched him without his knowing." Basha lowered her voice. "I wanted to help him Sonia, but Baba saw that he had a demon on his back, a small crawling hairy creature that would give us ill luck. All I could see was that he looked beset by misery. Sitting on a log alone in the forest. Then we heard the hounds and soldiers so we fled.

Sonia began to speak.

"Quiet girls," said Baba, "there are lights approaching through the forest and I hear men's voices. Basha draw your cloak around you and help Sonia scramble into the branches of that oak. It would do no good for these men to find her here."

The smell of roasting venison and chestnuts wafted into the branches where Lock still clung watching the bounty hunters as they began to eat the first pieces of meat. Lock shifted his balance in the tree to give his sore rump a break.

The branch creaked and dry twigs broke, falling to the ground below, the hound leapt and barked.

"He's at that poxy tree again," said Ogre as he swallowed a mouthful of venison, "got a taste for martens does he?"

"I heard something up that tree too," said Weasel who stood and peered into the branches, "and it didn't sound like a pine marten or a squirrel neither. Pass me that brand."

Lock froze, clinging to the trunk

Weasel pushed the burning stick in Lock's general direction and in the glow of the flames he met the eyes of the soldier.

"By the Devil's golden hairs," said Weasel, "look what we have here, a fat little blackbird worth his weight in silver."

Lock scrambled higher into the branches as the bounty hunters gathered around the tree.

"Who'll be first up to bring him down?" asked Ogre.

"We could always just set the tree alight," said Gnome.

Sonia watched from the branches of her tree as five men approached the firelight. They were, she supposed, brigands. They carried cudgels and bows. They were bearded and clad in skins and furs.

Baba stepped toward them pointing her stirring spoon. *"Gimel vav dalet lamed vav bet samekh yud vav!"*

A shiver ran down Sonia's spine. The words were spoken in a deep guttural voice. They conveyed a feeling of power that did not seem to belong to the gentle old woman who minutes ago had been stirring a cauldron of soup.

The men stopped, lowering their cudgels and bows.

"Who dares to disturb us?" said Baba in Latin.

The leading man, dressed in a wolf pelt, leant on his bow. "We want no trouble with witches." His tone and body conveyed a cautious confidence, Baba ruses had given him pause, but he appeared more curious then deterred. "But those who travel the forest path must pay the forest tax."

"Witches?" said Baba assuming a raspy and unthreatening tone. "We are but poor Jewesses," Baba curtseyed, "forced to flee the city. The only payment I can offer you is a bowl of soup. Though come, taste. It is seasoned with foreign spice and Russian salt."

Greta could not sleep, and not because of Peter's drunken snores in the bed beside her. She was staring in glum terror at the clock, counting the seconds as the minute hand moved steadily toward the hour of midnight. How could she have forgotten? Surely he would not come. Surely Magda had had the forethought to send him a message. Surely he had heard that Peter had returned and he would not try and visit her tonight. Not this night. For the love of God, not this night. Her face was tender and swollen where Peter had hit her. She had seen a different side to him. And she did not want to think of what would happen if he found a strange man knocking on their bedroom door.

The clock struck midnight.

Greta traced the patterns sewn into her hangings trying to calm her racing heart.

Then she heard a gentle knock.

It would do no good to ignore it. He was here now.

She slid her feet as quietly as she could off the bed and onto the floor. Slowly she edged off the bed so that she stood naked and on tiptoes. A floorboard creaked. Peter's breath changed. And the knock came again a little louder.

Greta glanced at the floor at the pile of Peters clothes, on which lay his sword and belt. She crept to the door, her fingers rested on the latch. "Luke she whispered not tonight. You have to go. Please go."

Luke's voice came as a low rumble from the other side. "Just a crack my lady, so that I may see your beautiful eyes, just a crack and I swear I shall be off."

"No," Greta whispered back, "are you a lunatic? My husband is asleep. His sword lies close beside him. I shall send you word but for now go."

"Drunk men sleep like corpses. Just the briefest peek, for it is the sight of you in candle light which gives meaning to my life."

"Stop it," said Greta, "just go."

"I think," said Luke, raising his voice just a notch, "that if you send me away so unsatisfied I shall make such a noise that I shall wake the count. For what value is my life if I can't visit you."

Greta Glanced at Peter. He lay on his back, his breathing heavy, regular. He certainly seemed to be deeply asleep. "So be it," she whispered but just a glance.

The scrape of the iron latch and the creak of the door seemed in that moment so loud that it would awaken Hell. Behind the gap was Luke's smiling face.

He slid his hand through the crack so that she could not close the door without jamming his fingers. "One kiss, One kiss," he said, "The lord sleeps deeply. Just one kiss."

Lock had climbed as far he dared resting in the crown of the evergreen tree. A cold autumn wind blew from the north and ruffled his hair.

"I should think twice about it if I were you," said Lock in his western educated dialect. "Eternal damnation is not something to be shrugged off."

"I don't believe you," said Ogre, straddling a branch a yard beneath Lock and running his finger along the edge of his katzbalger short sword. "I've been baptized again. If you lot are right I'm damned anyway. But if the preacher's right I'm headed straight to the land of glass and gold. Whichever way I'm going, killing you won't make the difference."

"Then why don't you," said Lock.

"You're worth much more alive than dead," said the bounty hunter, "the countess will want to do something public. I would rather not risk your neck by pulling you off that tree. Come down and I'll clap you in irons."

"You make it sound so inviting," said Lock, "forgive me if I would rather go falling out of the tree and breaking my neck in this perfectly nice forest than to be publicly tortured and burned."

Gnome and Weasel who were positioned at various lower junctions of the branches snickered.

Ogre shrugged. "Either way we are taking you alive. It's up to you whether you get hurt or not. As I said nothing personal." He reached into his belt bag and took out a clock. "I'll give you a half turn of the clock to make up your mind."

In that moment of surreal despair all Lock could think about was the absurdity of his being given thirty minutes to make his decision. It seemed like an inordinately long amount of time. *Why not grant him only one minute and be done with it?* Ogre was evidently a patient man. "It sounds very reasonable," said Lock, "may I get an extension if I keep you entertained."

"I should think not," said Ogre, "But entertain away. We like a good story don't we, men?"

"We do," said Weasel, "especially stories about monks fucking. Know any of them?"

"They're my favourite," said Lock. "But before I begin I wonder if any of you would be so kind as to give me a bit of meat to chew on."

The soldiers became so engrossed with Lock's story, and Lock himself was oddly enjoying the attention that nobody noticed as the brigands crept close to the tree. The first thing Lock heard was a creaking noise which he mistook for branches swaying in the wind. Then he heard the twang of bowstrings and his story was cut short by a volley of arrows. Gnome and Weasel cried with anger as they fell from the tree.

"Fuck you," said the Ogre, as an arrow took him in the shoulder. The clock dropped from his fingers. The sound of cudgels impacting on flesh, bone and iron sounded from the bottom of the tree, the hound whined and the donkey thrashed at his tether.

Silence followed.

"Lay out the bodies," said a voice, in a Latinate tongue.

"My lord bishop."

Lock was silent, not daring to believe his ears.

"Do you forgive me for abandoning you, my Lord."

Greta lay on the floorboards, barely daring to breathe. The sound and smell of her and Luke's exertions seemed so loud and so pungent as they panted and sweated on the floor, their sinful humours spent. Peter, it seemed, still slept. The fear had somehow made it all the more devine. But with every moment that Luke lingered they risked discovery.

Luke withdrew from her river and shuddered as he emptied his millpond. He tenderly kissed the bruise on Greta's face. "He will come to our way of seeing things," he whispered.

"I don't know," said Greta, "He's loyal and he and Lock were friends. He could reverse everything we've done."

"Bring him to the church tomorrow. I'm sure he will see the light. From what I have heard he is also a material man. Material men will see sense."

"I shall do as you say, my love."

"And worry you not, my beauty, for the townsfolk are true believers. Their loyalty to their faith is higher than their loyalty to your husband."

"Hush now," Greta moved her finger to Luke's lips. "Go now. Tomorrow I shall bring Peter to you."

As Greta latched the door behind her and returned to the bed she looked at Peter and saw that his eyes were open.

"What are you doing," he asked in a groggy tone.

Could he not smell Luke's sweat on her?

"I awoke from a dream my lord. I had to pass water."

The next day, 21st of September, Day of the Moon, Year of the Lord 1526

Peter woke. He felt sick. Magda brought him a bucket of warm water and he washed in it. He condescended to allow Greta to trim his hair and beard. When he looked in the mirror, he thought he would have taken a little more off, but it was a fair job. He dressed in his finest red hose, and black doublet slashed with red satin. He donned a black cloak and pinned it with the iron broach of his house. Breakfast was bread, butter, saffroned fledglings, and honeyed plums. It was a little rich for his personal taste but he appreciated the effort as well as the gold and silver dishes. The best thing though was the fresh apple juice. It really took the edge off his hangover.

Greta broke the silence. She was dressed in a pointed high hat with vale to disguise her bruise. "I've more than doubled the size of our domains."

"By seizing Church property," replied Peter. "If you declare yourself a heretic you don't just make an enemy of the Pope, but of all Christendom, and soldiers will be sent from the emperor and… " Peter had been about to say the king but the king was dead. He had been there when he died. Peter stalled. "And the common folk they will turn against you they believe the priests. As should you."

Greta bowed her head in submission to her husband's superior wisdom. "You are of course right but times have also changed." She looked at him imploringly, "Peter, I've been writing with Ferdinand in Vienna. It is of no matter to him. The emperor is planning an invasion of Rome to break the pope's power. Ferdinand is the real power in the east and he wants our help against the Turks. He has claimed the throne of Bohemia and he has no wish to cause rebellion there by suppressing Protestants, as he told me himself. Lutheranism is sweeping the world. People are reading the bible for themselves and they can see there is nothing about popes and bishops in there."

Peter tried to channel his anger at Greta for her refutation of him, but he could only remember Krum, who had died at Mohacs, laughing at him, what was he had said – *I'd not have taken you for a holy fool.* Peter smiled. "My mother warned my father against me marrying a bohemian girl. Nothing but trouble, she'd said. How long have your people been protesting?"

Greta smiled a tired smile back from behind her vale. "Longer than most people remember. The whole world tried to destroy us and they failed."

Lock woke from uneasy dreams, to the sound of singing birds, the bites of flies and ants and the smell of Baba cooking breakfast. He had been rescued from bounty hunters only to be captured by Romanian brigands.

Breakfast was venison cooked in a sauce of herbs, salt, honey and ale, served with roasted chestnuts. Sonia made a great show of serving the five brigands their meal, which they accepted with gracious compliments and appreciative glances at her figure.

"It is rare to find such beauty and goodness together in a girl," said the leader of the brigands as Sonia spooned the meat onto his wooden bowl.

Sonia giggled, and gazed back at the brigand with what Lock supposed was genuine pride. "Did you really slay that wolf," said Sonia pointing at the brigands pelt. "That must have been very dangerous."

Was she flirting with him? Lock felt an unfamiliar feeling of envy creep over him.

Basha ate her breakfast in the shadow of her hat. Avoiding the occasional glances of the men.

After Baba had cleared the dishes away, Lock cleared his throat. "We thank you, fair folk of the forest for saving us. But now we must bid you farewell. For we have a long journey ahead of us."

The chief of the brigands ran his fingers along the smooth wood of his cudgel. "The bishop of Eisenberg is too important a personage to simply be allowed to walk free. But I know not what to do with you. So I have decided that you must come and see the patriarch. He will decide the fate of you and your companions."

After the women had cleaned the bowls and cauldron, and the brigands had loaded their loot upon the luckless donkey, they began their march through the forest. They followed a dark little river that meandered through stands of birch, alder and willow.

The main topic of conversation on the road was the subject raised by Sonia of whether Baba was really a witch or not. Baba claimed that was matter of perspective at what one really meant by a witch. When Sonia pressed her on whether she could do magic, yes or no? Baba admitted that she could and under that definition could be classed as a witch, but that the magic she did was good, and so if it was possible to be a good witch that was her. Sonia then gave Lock a look that seemed to say - *I told you there were witches. You told me I was stupid and look there you go, irrefutable proof.*

Lock didn't contradict her, instead when they broke for a rest beneath an old hollow oak, he willingly consented to have Baba exorcise a demon, which he apparently had been carrying on his back, which she did by chanting over him in the secret language of the Jews. Lock even laid some of his mid day bread at the foot of an elder tree, and mumbled an apology.

Sonia was ecstatic, and she kept pestering Lock asking him if he felt any different now the demon was gone. Lock honestly felt better and had no trouble telling her that he felt as light as duck down. The chief of the Brigands, who told them that from there on they must be blindfolded, interrupted the jolly mood.

Peter walked, escorted by his wife and a troop of halberdiers, through the streets of Eisenberg. The city had changed during his long absence. Despite the fact that it had just experienced a violent upheaval, the place seemed full of people, including unfamiliar faces and the sounds of unfamiliar tongues.

"You keep the city in good order," said Peter, as another band of musketmen stopped to salute them. "How do you pay for them?"

"With the Church's looted silver we pay the iron guild to forge arms," said Greta, "But they are the Lutheran militia. They fight for God, and we provide them with naught but their daily bread, milk, ale and lodgings."

"Who commands them?"

"Johann, but final military decisions rest jointly with, with the Lutheran council, and with," Greta paused, glancing at the repairs being made to a burned-out house, "and with you. I also employ a number of household men."

"Johann?" said Peter, "Why not Friedrich or somebody else."

"Peter," said Greta, in a tone that he was getting used to, "Everybody's dead, you and Johann are the only noblemen left. The noble widows and orphan girls are getting betrothed to burghers."

They were quiet for a while as they walked down the rutted cobblestone North Road toward the Square of Flower Sellers. Peter's mind didn't linger long on Death. He had got used to living in his shadow. His gaze drifted from a pamphlet nailed to the beam of a wood frame house and the man leaning against the wall, reading. That was what was different. There was print everywhere.

Greta noticed his look "The Lutheran council has commissioned the iron guild to build two new presses and a paper mill is being built beside the iron works. We sell broadsheets for three grouts a piece."

"Are the guild masters also Lutherans?"

Greta nodded. "They're devout men, all members of the Lutheran council."

"I'm sure they were more than happy for the commissions," Peter murmured.

Greta stopped walking and paused beside a beggar propped against a house wall. His face was lean and the bones of his neck and chest protruded out from his skin. "No," said Greta as she dropped a handful of copper grouts into the beggar's bowl. "Swords and books are not a problem, but food is."

Lock, Sonia, Basha and Baba walked blindfolded along the forest trail. The walked in single file, holding a rope pulled by a Brigand. Sonia walked first, then Basha, then Baba and last of all Lock. Every so often the rope puller would shout out an obstacle, such as *root or bolder*. Lock, going last, tripped and stubbed his toe more often than the women, who, to Lock's consternation, seemed to navigate the path in the darkness without complaint.

"I'm grateful, lord, for the support you gave to my son. You have ever been a friend of Jews and a Jew remembers her friends." Baba spoke to Lock in the Germanic dialect of the Jews. It was a close enough approximation of Lock's mother tongue that he could converse with her in a language, that the Latinate speaking Brigands could not understand.

"I'm glad that there are at least some that think of me fondly," said Lock.

"Would you take advice from a woman?" asked Baba.

"I would take advice from a talking ass at this point," Lock cursed as he stumbled over a tree root.

"Your acting," said Baba, "as if all is lost and you are already on your way to the gallows."

"I see little reason to think otherwise." Lock's feelings of bitterness returned to him.

"You must know that Herr Muller and the villages north of the river have remained loyal to you. I do not know why you decided to flee to a cottage in the woods rather than seeking refuge at the miller's castle, but I guess well enough that it has something to do with you and the miller's daughter."

Lock silently thanked God that they were all blindfolded and the old woman could not see him blushing. "I..."

"Hush, I am not your judge. But I do want vengeance on the townsfolk, for the slaughter of our people. You must swallow your pride. Among the villagers loyal to you there are skilled huntsman and stout labourers. You must rally them. The townsfolk will come for the grain. You must defeat them."

"I know nothing of warfare," lamented Lock as he stumbled into a tree trunk.

"Stop moaning," said Baba. "You are a clever man. God gave you good head. Now use it. If you think your enemies are cleverer than you, they certainly shall be. Now think how Fortune has blessed you. Last night enemies surrounded you. Now they are dead. The Latins have helped us once. They may do so again."

"I think its more likely they will sell me to the Lutherans."

"Use your head," said Baba. "Pick your words carefully when you are brought before the patriarch."

Peter glared at the Lutheran priest as both men stood on the dais of the church that had been stripped of its fine wealth. Greta sat in the pews. Peter understood that Lutherans weren't supposed to have priests. But this man was a priest nonetheless. Peter could see in him a churchman's education.

Preacher Luke, spoke, his dialect was almost Eisenberger. "Consider me your ally and your confidant. I have many ears and eyes throughout the city. And I am willing to lend those eyes and ears to your service. I have many preachers who carry word on the street and friends among the free print houses and I swear to you my total allegiance and fealty."

"If I agree to join your cult?" said, Peter his fingers tracing the line of his crucifix that lay buried beneath his shirt and tunic. Peter dropped his hand to his sword pommel. He'd call the preachers bluff. "As any skilled horse trader will tell you, one does not buy a horse without first looking it in the mouth. I have promised my wife that I will consider your proposal so what can you tell me about the politics of the city. Who should I trust on the Lutheran Council?"

"I can tell that we shall work well together," said Luke. "The real politics of the council is about who is to claim the remaining Church property that has not yet been divided. Thanks to the countess the lion's share has already been claimed the by von Esienberg domain. Lock's townhouse and all the agricultural land south of the Forest Bridge now belongs to you. The burgers and guild masters have had to content themselves with the money of the churches and Jewish houses. There is only one really important prize that remains — The Abbey of Saint Hildegard the Virgin." Luke paused.

The abbey, Peter had been thinking of it and it lay always in his mind. *How strange the preacher now also spoke of it.* He remembered the words of the blind shepherd. *That is not the dragon's lair. That is the secret door into the holy abbey.* The abbey, that was where Nuray was. "I had no idea," said Peter.

"Your Kinsman, Johann, is secretly plotting with Eldritch of the iron guild," continued Luke, "To seize the abbey and claim conquerors rights by dividing the spoils amongst themselves. Eldritch is building a cannon capable of knocking a breach in the abbey walls. "

"Those bastards," muttered Peter.

Luke bowed. "My lord."

Peter hesitated. He imagined himself seizing the abbey. Surely under the threat of cannon fire, the nuns would surrender. Perhaps they could continue in some form or another, but he would rescue Nuray from them and take her at the front of his horse. The abbeys gold and relics could be taken to his treasury and he would cover his mistress and his wife in gold.

As the cold water of the baptism splashed off the crown of his head, Peter genuinely felt changed. He felt guilty like a sinner and yet somehow free. Now there was work to do. First he would take the Mullborg and secure food for the town and quell the rebellion in the northern villages. Then he would take the abbey.

The blindfolded column began to climb and at length came to a halt. The brigands removed the blindfolds from the prisoners who blinked in the late afternoon light. Lock gazed up at the brigand's fastness. What he saw was a strong palisade with a heavy portcullis gate, built from sharpened oak logs. Lock sniffed the air. The smell of wood smoke had never seemed so sweet. It was dry inside.

Guards at the gate pulled on ropes, the portcullis slid upward, and the brigands escorted them inside. They walked through muddy lanes and past wooden cabins built on low stilts. Lock watched as a woman skinned and gutted an elk with a small axe. A group of children ran down the street kicking an inflated bladder. The brigands greeted the folk as they passed. A group of dirty children followed the prisoners.

Others stared. At length the brigands brought them to the gates of a church. It was built like the other cabins but larger and Lock took a moment to admire the onion shaped wooden dome that rose from the steep roof. *So, thought* Lock, *the brigands are Romanian schismatics.*

As they approached Sonia gasped, Basha and Baba drew back and Lock had to stifle a scream. In front of the church, a huge brown bear lapped at a basin of ale.

The brigands laughed. "Fear not," said one, " Daniel thinks he's a man. He won't hurt you unless you slight his mother's honour."

The women were led off by the brigands to be quartered elsewhere. Lock was left to wait with a guard outside the church where he was at length allowed in, and ushered to a fur draped stool beside the fire.

Seated before him in the warm smoky room were three men, dressed in fur cloaks with high square hats of black fur. One man had a brown beard another black and the third man, seated in the middle, looked to be of venerable years and his long grey beard reached to his waste. Lock guessed that he was the patriarch.

"The bishop of Eisenberg," said Long Beard after Lock had warmed his hands. "The last time that we had such exalted company was at the head of an army. Though I was just a boy I'll never forget it."

Use your head. Lock bowed in a gesture of submission. "My predecessor was not a tolerant man. I on other hand believe in reconciliation between the two Churches of East and West."

"Sweet words come easy to beggars," said Brown Beard.

The patriarch held up his hand to silence him. "The countess is offering two chests of silver for your capture. Can you best that?"

"The Lutherans can not be trusted," said Lock, "They are fanatics. They love your Church no more than mine and once they've done with me. They'll come for you. I can't offer you a ransom and but I can offer something better, an alliance."

"You want us to kill Germans for you?" said Black Beard.

Lock blew his nose on his kerchief. "If the Lutherans are defeated I can offer you legal title to all the forest on the north bank of the river to be held by you as prince and belong to your people ad infinitum. I will draw out the maps and treaties myself. You shall have also your share of loot from the defeated army I should hope that that should more than top two chests of silver. Why settle for the smaller sum?"

"And how do you intend to defeat the army of the countess?" said Long Beard.

"The northern villages remain loyal to me. I will rally the fighting men at the miller's castle. The Lutherans have little grain. They must acquire Muhlborg. They will march to take it. Your men know the forest road better than others. When they march north, our combined forces will ambush them, and destroy them.

The man with black beard smiled. "I like the man's bravado."

The patriarch rose and motioned to his companions to likewise. They walked out of Lock's earshot and conferred among themselves.

"We want sixty barrels of meal, twenty barrels of ale, and a barrel of cheese, from Muhlborg's stores. And we want it in advance," said Long Beard.

"Done," said Lock. The miller would no doubt baulk at the loss but Lock felt he could hardly refuse.

the next day, the Day of Refuge

After morning prayers Lock, Sonia, Baba and Basha, set out from the Brigand's fastness toward Muhlborg. They were escorted by two bowmen, who led them blindfolded for some hours through the forest. At length they heard the sound of a trickling brook. Here, beside a stand of mossy elm trees, the brigands removed their blindfolds, bid them luck and departed.

"I know where we are," said Basha excitedly. "This is the Selberbach. I know the way to the mill. It was beside this stream that I first met Joseph."

"And where they found his body," said Baba grimly.

Lock was gazing thoughtfully at the flowing stream. Sonia was overcome with a sudden feeling of joy and hope and stepped beside Lock, slipping her hand into his. "Isn't it wonderful. I really feel that Lady Fortune has turned her wheel in our favour. Of course my family will protect us. Muhlborg is pretty much impossible to be taken by attack. Trust me. I know. I spent most of my life in the tower and I spent many hours looking at the walls and trying to imagine how somebody might get through to rescue me."

"Hopefully," said Baba to Sonia, overhearing her words, "your family will also welcome the in-laws of their late son."

"Don't be unkind, grandmother," said Basha, "The miller will be pleased to know that his grandchild still lives within me. He will no doubt also welcome the bishop and be overjoyed to see his daughter return so worldly wise." Basha inflected the last words with a barb of sarcasm directed at Lock, looking over at him and raising her eyebrows.

But Lock was not listening to the conversation. He was thinking about Joseph's murder and his promise to Sonia that he would do Justice by him. All his woes seemed to stem from his hearing of that act. There was a web of actions and intentions. And somehow Joseph's cruel and unusual murder was entwined with that. *Who had murdered Joseph and why?* Lock felt if he could understand that he could understand some truth, a hidden piece of the story, something that had nothing to do with Martin Luther. It was on this river that

Joseph had met his love and been killed. Then again perhaps he was just distracting himself from the cold dread he felt at the thought of facing Sonia's mother.

"Its not the miller I'm worried about," said Baba. "It's his wife."

Peter met Johann in the town house parlor, in which Peter displayed some of his trophies, a French knight's helm, a Janissary's scimitar, a Tartar's bow, and a strange wing made from wood and feathers. He kept a chest of jeweled broaches, buckles and pins on display beside his carved wooden thrown.

"Wine?" Peter motioned for the maid, Magda, to serve his unpleasant cousin.

"No, thank you," replied Johann holding up his hand to halt the maid. "I only drink ale."

Peter nodded to Magda who hurried off to bring a jug of ale. "What kind of soldier turns down fine wine?" asked Peter.

"The kind that enjoys killing, I suppose," said Johann.

The bland frankness of Johann's reply caught Peter off guard. In the heat of battle Peter did enjoy fighting and killing, but the memory of it, the memory of it haunted him, the smell, the blood, the sound. It never went away. Peter shuddered and slugged his wine. He hated the demons of bloodshed and yet here he was planning another campaign, a campaign against peasants, folk who should be his own subjects. He hated the war, yet craved it, and the focus of the campaign kept his mind from wandering to his broken hearted desire for Nuray and the ghosts of past battles. Perhaps after five years it was all he knew. And here his cousin spoke with such confidence about enjoying killing. *But did he really know what it meant?* Peter shrugged and poured himself another glass. "When can I inspect the troops?" he asked.

"Outside the Forest Gate when the bells toll six," replied the captain. "I've rounded up a few Jews and miscreants we can use as target practice."

Peter understood the logic. Shooting at living people demonstrated the nerve of troops in a way that shooting at scarecrows could not, and executing people would convey a message of ruthlessness and power. Lord knows he had seen enough people die. But the sickly pleasure, with which Johann clearly anticipated the action, compelled Peter to oppose it. "Have them shoot at straw men," ordered Peter.

"As you command," Johann delivered his words with a knowing sneer.

186

"The river is too flooded to move our forces by barge," said Peter, "So we must take the north road and cross the Eisen at the Forest Bridge. I understand that Eldritch has completed the construction of sixteen pound culverin."

"Hammer of God is her name," Johann smiled, "She's beautiful, Lord Count. She'll have the walls of Muhlborg down in a day."

"Good, if God wills it, we shall not have to fight and the northern villages will surrender." Peter enjoyed watching Johann's smile drop as he contemplated the prospect of a bloodless campaign. The captain then began to irritatingly pick his teeth with his fingernail. "I have a boon to ask of you, my lord?"

"Speak," said Peter.

"I have reason to believe that a certain Jewess, has taken refuge at Muhlborg. I wish to claim her as my share of the spoils."

"Were you really kept in a tower all your life?" asked Basha as the two girls peed together behind the trunk of an ash tree.

"Yes," replied Sonia, "though I did not know it at the time I believe I was very unhappy?"

"May I ask your age?"

"I'm fifteen replied Sonia," as she wiped the last drips of pea from her loins with her kerchief.

Basha whistled, holding up her white underskirt with one hand while also wiping her pee on her black handkerchief. "And you have been out of this tower how long?"

"But since spring," said Sonia dropping her skirts as she stood.

"I see," said Basha, "but you can read and write and have many skills. Who taught you?"

"Mother. I can read Latin and Greek. I can play a psalter and sing. I can recite the psalms, draw and write calligraphy."

"Impressive," said Basha, who was looking through the trees to where Lock, Baba and the donkey appeared to be conversing in low tones.

"Sister?"

"Yes Sonia?"

"Were you and my brother in love?"

"Yes," said Basha as she turned to look back at the strange girl, "I feel as if I need to defecate. Will your join me."

"Certainly," said Sonia.

Sonia and Basha moved further from the path before stopping and squatting behind a stand of rowans.

"I can see why my brother liked you," said Sonia you're very pretty and knowledgeable too, and you know magic."

"And I liked your brother. That is why I carry his child."

"What was it like?"

"What was what like?"

"To be touched by a birch fairy?"

"I'm sorry?" Basha was the first to rise.

"Touched by a birch fairy, isn't that how you got pregnant?"

"What are you going to do?" Baba picked the thorns from a branch of wild rose. "You think old Wolfgang Muller's wife won't find out what you did with her daughter?"

Lock cringed into his cloak.

"It is good that you have a conscience. But you've got to act like a man. The girl is of age and you are the lord bishop. You are their ruler. If you act like it, they will not dare to question you."

There was a moment's silence as Lock digested Baba's words. "Thank you," he said with genuine gratitude.

Baba smiled. "Yahweh knows, I have no interest in your crimes. But I foresee that you will face some kind of reckoning. However you convinced Frau Muller to hand her precious daughter over to you is beyond my reckoning. I should very much like to hear that story."

"She was persuadable on the point of furthering Sonia's education beyond the limits of her own knowledge."

"So I've gleaned," said Baba, "but you know I've met the woman too. I've never known a mother to look so ragefully at the news of a son's wedding. Not to mention she locked her own daughter in a tower for half her life."

"It's the truth," said Lock plaintively. "I talked with Frau Muller long, when I was inspecting Muhlborg and I enjoyed her hospitality. She herself has an education. She was the youngest of three sisters. The other two are sisters at the Abbey of Saint Hildegard the Virgin, and when she would be allowed to visit them they would teach her to read, and she had gone to some trouble collect a small library, all religious texts in Latin of course. You know why she locked her daughter in the tower? So that she could copy books and learn to read and write. She wanted for her daughter what she could never have for herself, a full education. One better than even the abbey could give. When I told her of my education in Koln and that I was not opposed to the education of girls, that was enough for her to suggest that I tutor Sonia."

"You make her seem so reasonable," said Baba, "yet think about what she did. She imprisoned her daughter and forced her to copy out the same books day after day. It's cruel."

"Regrettably, there were no French romances," muttered Lock.

"The woman is a lunitic," said Baba. "I believe that she is somehow responsible for my son in law's death."

Peter looked at the forces that Eisenberg could muster. They were arrayed on the parade grounds outside the Forest Gate in four columns of infantry: three columns of the Lutheran Militia and one smaller column of Peter's veteran landknecht, somewhere over three hundred men in total. Of the Lutheran militia there was one column of pikemen, one column of matchlock musketmen and one elite column armed with wheellock muskets. Wives and families of the soldiers, as well as sweethearts and onlookers, had gathered on the city wall to watch the spectacle, cheer, wave kerchiefs and blow kisses.

Johann shouted orders. The matchlock musketeers knelt and worked at their tinderboxes lighting charcloths from which they lit the wicks of their matchlocks. They then marched forward, forming a line. They tamped their powder and then their shot, knelt, braced the stock of their muskets against their shoulders and fired at the line of straw men. One man screamed as his musket misfired spraying burning powder into his face. The audience on the walls cheered. When the smoke cleared the straw men had taken a hit, their billowing clothes torn by the musket shot.

Then came the turn of the wheellock column and the first column rather inelegantly hurried to make room as the inpatient wheellock musketmen, keen to show off their skill to the women on the wall, rushed forward. Peter was impressed. They fired without the need to strike a flame, the iron wheels of their locks turned against a piece of brimstone when they pulled the trigger. There were no misfires. And another volley riddled the straw men. The crowd whooped and cheered. Next the pikemen advanced slowly in a block formation until they reached the straw men which they poked with their pikes, looking rather foolish when they retreated, to a less enthusiastic applause.

Johann looked pleased with himself. "With these weapon's we will make those peasants into sausages," he said.

"Let's hope we don't have to," said Peter, and he stepped forward to give his own men their orders. Their job was to finish the straw men off. Peter noted that despite being poked with sticks and filled with lead they were for the most part still standing. The mercenaries advanced, dressed in their most expensive silks, jewels and feathers, strutting rather than marching to the shouts of their female admirers. They spread out into a pike breaking formation. They drew their longswords, which the held near the bottom of the handle to give maximum reach and weight. They attacked with swinging blows, intending to chop through the middle poles of the straw men and nock them to the ground.

Peter had to admit that the result did not look very heroic. The straw men were built from tightly bound straw, which in many cases resisted the chop of the long sword. The mercenaries were in their frustration reduced to cutting the ropes that bound the straw with their short sword before hacking through the poles, which Peter could not help but think had been driven unnecessarily deep into the ground. None of this stopped the townsfolk from cheering.

Finally the new cannon was loaded, and after three shots, the engineer was able to bring down a little wooden tower. The crowd whooped. Women streamed from the city gate to mingle with the soldiers as their discipline began to ebb. They were happy, and Peter supposed they had a right to be. They had performed well. They had defeated the straw men and the only casualty was a burned face. The men beamed with pride as the women praised them.

Peter turned to look at Johann. The captain scowled at the merry making. "Isn't it disgusting he remarked."

The sun was setting as the four travellers left the forest and entered a land of rolling open fields and hamlets. Country folk watched them pass with curious unfriendly stares. This land had belonged to the Church and the tenants had paid their taxes to Lock. Though in truth he had only once visited it. There was something about the insular provincialism, the rural poverty, and the illiteracy of it all that made Lock detest it. His feet ached and his leather shoes were giving way, and he just wanted to get there now, even if he was killed on arrival.

"Isn't it lovely," said Sonia "they way the light plays on the corn flowers in the evening."

Lock only grunted in reply.

The last light was soon obscured by rain which soaked the travellers to their under garments.

It was well after nightfall when they arrived at the gate of Mulborg. Lock could see what Sonia meant when she had described the place as impregnable. Built by one of Lock's ruthless predecessors to protect grain supplies from rioting peasants, Muhlborg was part castle, part mill and part fortified village. It was built with one wall flush against a fast flowing stream, which powered the mill wheel and provided the borg with running water. It was strategically placed close to the River Eisen so that barges could take grain downriver to the city. It's walls were five times the height of a man, and built of brick and stone. The church, which backed onto the wall, resembled more a keep than a place of God and was fitted with firing ducts. At the back of the borg, Lock could just make out a square tower that rose like an ominous finger from behind the battlements.

"Well," said Sonia whose merry tone sounded forced, "here we are. Welcome home."

After a quick conversation with the gatekeeper the travellers were ushered through the narrow stone streets to Herr Muller's quarters built against the borg's back wall and beneath the tower.

Sonia and Lock's arrival was greeted with warmth and enthusiasm, while Baba and Basha, largely ignored also took their places by the fire. Lock and Sonia were given fresh clothes, Lock taking a fine set of the miller's own hose and doublet, which though a little tight was not a bad fit. Sonia squeezed into one of her mother's high cut gowns. Servants soon laid a table with ham, bread, salt and honey. And Lock and Sonia sat down to eat with the miller and his wife. Conversation was muted, with both Lock and Sonia concentrating on the meal.

Herr Muller began to discuss aspects of the harvest and contents of the cellars, but after a kick and hard look by his wife, he professed his loyalty to Lock and declared that Muhlborg was at his disposal. Lock swallowed a piece of ham and thanked the miller for his loyalty, adding, he would be well rewarded for his support.

When the meal was finished Frau Muller suggested that her husband take Lock out for an inspection of the borg's defences. Herr Muller dutifully relayed this request to Lock who obliged.

But a short time later the two men stood behind a parapet on the castle wall, watching the rising moon race between the dark billowing clouds above the full and fast flowing Eisen River.

"Ninety seven, huntsmen," Herr Muller replied to Lock's question. "They've lived by their yew bows since they were boys. They can hit a hare on the run and shoot with enough force to pierce the heart of a boar at fifty paces."

"That sounds promising," said Lock.

"And you have no need to muster them, I have already called them to the borg, where they have been enjoying my ale, bread and cheese for these past two weeks."

"It is good that you are amply supplied with those commodities," said Lock, wondering when he should breach the subject of the brigand's payment.

He was just about to raise the issue when the two men were interrupted by a third man, who approached carrying a lantern.

"Oh?" said the miller, "Brother August I am glad you have found us. Lord Bishop, let me introduce Brother August. He's a monk, and his advice has been most valuable."

The tonsured white robed monk, bowed to Lock in acknowledgment of his high rank.

"To what order do you belong?" asked Lock surprised to see the monk.

"The order Saint Bernard your Excellency."

"A Cistercian? And where were you ordained?"

"Altum Vadum, Hohenfurth."

"I see. It is in the south of Bohemia is it not?"

"Yes, your Excellency"

Lock was going to question the monk further to discover what he was doing in Eisenberg. But the miller interrupted him.

"Regarding the battle plans, Lord Bishop, the townsfolk will come for our grain. But they'll never take Muhlborg. The villagers will take refuge inside, the bowmen can defend the walls and we have enough grain to last the winter. Without adequate provisions the townsfolk will return hungry to the city. What do you say?"

Lock remembered the battle of Eisenberg and Brother Felix's assumptions of victory. "And what if the Lutherans bring a cannon? Will the walls hold? Will the huntsmen hold their nerve against musket fire?"

"They must," said Herr Muller, "the walls and bowmen are all that stand between us and the townsfolk. Would that we had a thousand men armed with pike and muskets. But we must work with what Fortune has given us."

"What if they weren't all that we had?" said Lock. "What if we could muster three times that number, ambush the Lutheran's in the forest and then march to Eisenberg and reclaim it?"

"Then I would say that we are indeed blessed," said Herr Muller, "but where are these men?"

"In the forest, I was rescued by a band of forest brigands. They speak a strange Latin tongue. They are formidable woodsmen and bowmen. They have agreed to fight for us but at a price."

"The forest folk are godless heathens," said the miller. "There is nothing to be gained from talking to those thieving dogs."

"They are not heathens, but schismatics who say their mass in Greek," said Lock.

Herr Muller looked unconvinced "What says Brother August? Should the forest folk be trusted?"

"My monastery was sacked during the Hussite Heresy," said the monk. "I would gladly enlist the help of any heathen if it would gain us a greater chance of victory."

Lock smiled. "Is it agreed then? Shall we follow Borther August's council?"

Herr Muller dithered, his gaze shifting between the two other men. He swallowed and then nodded. "Who am I to question the decisions of wiser men."

"Then I shall leave with the huntsmen at dawn," said Lock. "Oh and I shall need provisions for the forest folk to secure their alliance," he added as if it was an after thought.

"Sonia," my dear child.

Sonia couldn't help but feel a strange terror as she watched her mother cross the floor to where she sat with Basha and Baba at the fireplace. Sonia felt like such a different person from the girl that had been unlocked from the tower and entrusted into Lock's care just a few months ago.

"My poor, poor child. I shudder to think of the things you have been exposed to in this heresy and upheaval?" Frau Muller's wooden shoes clapped on the flagstones as she approached. Her face showed aged prettiness, her eyes conveyed an ambitious intelligence, and her arms and shoulders showed the strength of a working woman. "I trust that no harm has come to you?"

"No harm has come to me," mumbled Sonia, "other than the blisters on my feet."

"Praise be to God," said Frau Muller. "And what," she turned to glare at Basha and Baba, whose faces were hidden beneath the brims of their hats, "is the company that you are keeping... I do not approve of Jews and Jewesses."

"But Mother," protested Sonia raising her voice and meeting her mother's gaze. "This is my sister, your daughter, Basha. She..."

Keeping one hand on her tummy. Basha raised her finger two her lips.

Frau Muller scratched her chin and turned to look grimly at Basha. "I see, so the miserable little witch has come crawling back to wreck more ruin upon us. My husband may not believe the rumours but I have no doubt that it was your foul magic that killed my son."

"It's not true," Sonia stood and shouted. "Basha loved Joseph. She would never have done anything to harm him."

"You!" Frau Muller grabbed Sonia by the wrist, twisting her arm. "What has happened to your temperament? I thought I taught you that young ladies, speak only when spoken to and do not offer their opinion about things that they know nothing about. It seems that the lord bishop has allowed you too much freedom. But you are in my house now and I shall not be spoken to with such impudence." Frau Muller groped at the keys that hung from her girdle. "I think a little return to the tower might remind you of your manners. As for you," she turned to the Jews, "I have not the power to turn you out of this house. But if you are to stay then you will have to earn your keep. You may sleep in the stables and tomorrow you may clean the latrines."

"What brings you to Eisenberg?" Lock enquired of Brother August as the two men drank ale in the borg's courtyard, *what a shame the miller did not keep wine.*

"In truth," replied the monk his hand moving toward a leather satchel attached to the belt of his habit, "I come in search of you."

"Really," said Lock, "I hope it wasn't to borrow a book. My collection has probably already been burned by a rabid mob of philistines."

"No," the monk grinned, "Actually, I'm fairly certain, I've come to bring you a book. A few weeks thence, a merchant arrived at our Monastery. His humours were inflamed and he was suffering from a fever. We treated him at the infirmary but to no avail. He was taken by Lord Death. We found among his possession a letter and a package addressed to you. We had heard rumours of the heresy in Eisenberg and the Lord Abbot believed that the letter might be of urgency. I volunteered myself to bring the letters to you and to be of any assistance that I could." Brother August drew out of his satchel a letter and a package that indeed appeared to be a book wrapped in a strip of flax linen. "I bring further tiding. A company of ragged peasant pikemen are traveling toward Eisenberg from the west. They terrorised a few villages but the Bohemian lords kept them on the move and when I departed on my mission to seek you out they had been driven into the mountains around the King's Pass. I am here to aid you in anyway in which I am able."

"I thank you," Lock replied. "I shall always remember the friendship of Hohenfurth."

Sonia sat in the dusty room of the tower. The room seemed to have hardly changed since she had left it. The narrow window facing the river let in a little starlight. Her books still sat on the shelves where she had left them. Her bed was made just as she had left it. And her embroidery stuff was stacked neatly on the table. The door was, just as it had always been, locked and bolted from the outside. She tried to raise her spirits by thinking of the bishop and warming up Hell. But she found she wasn't in the mood. *It's no good crying,* she told herself. *We'll just have to put on a bold face and ask the fairies for help. I really hope that mother is not too cruel to Basha and Baba as she's definitely wrong about them. I know mother is only trying to do what she thinks is best for me. Maybe she'll be able to see reason. Lock always says that reason is one of the greatest forces in the world. I do hope poor Lock's feet are better. He really was complaining so terribly about the pain on the way here.*

Sonia heard the sound of feet climbing the stairway to her room. She knew the sound. It was her mother. She straightened her skirts and stood upright on her bed.

The lock rattled, the bolt was drawn back and the door pushed open. Sonia looked upon her mother's stern face. In one hand she carried a bucket of water, in the other a willow switch.

"Here's your water for washing child, and a towel to dry you."

"Thank you, mother," replied Sonia, "I'm terribly ashamed for raising my voice to you."

"So you should be," said Frau Muller, her face remaining hard. "But you understand that everyone must take responsibility for their actions. It is the will of God. It gives me no joy my child but you must be punished for your actions. Lift your skirts and bend down. You may take hold of the table.

"But mother..." said Sonia.

"Defy me further and I shall be forced to punish you further, child. Now lift your skirts."

Sonia clenched her teeth as the first the first lash of the willow whip slashed across her bum.

Lock sat in the bedroom that had been offered him. The straw of his bed was fresh as was his bucket of water. He read the letter.

> *My dear Lock, I am thrilled that you should grace me with your communication and remember with great*

fondness our discussions of philosophy. I went to some trouble to investigate your queries as fully as I was able. A witch hunter going by the name of William was indeed resident for a short time here though his brutality soon earned him an unpleasant reputation. But I was unable to discover more for the whole province has been in revolt, peasants with all kinds of heretical notions have been murdering noblemen and declaring all men equal. Thankfully the armies of the nobles have acted quickly to quell the trouble.

Incidentally your little country has been arousing a lot of interest among reading folk, here, as the local press commissioned a run of copies of this book. I hope you have the time to have a look at and perhaps let me know if there is any truth to it...

Lock carefully unwrapped the book. It was a reasonably small volume bound in cow leather the embossed title read, *The Travels of Brother William.*

some days later, the 25th of September

"What's the difference between war and murder?" asked Johann.

The column was resting beside the river but the stand of oaks gave no relief from the pounding rain. Everything was soaked. The river was a brown rushing flood overflowing its banks. The water had soaked through Peter's tunic and undershirt and dripped off his leather hat. He watched as men and horses struggled to pull the cannon through the mud.

"In war," Peter, wet and miserable, was not really in the mood for conversation, "men kill for noble causes, for their country, for their king, or for God, for glory, wealth and conquest. Murder is a sin and a crime. Battle is virtuous and honourable. Any child can tell you that."

"Do you really believe that?" asked Johann as he sat on a log, sharpening his sword. "Any child has not been in a battle. But you have. Tell me how virtuous did you feel cutting men or even women down, spilling the blood of strangers? You know what I think?"

Peter didn't reply. Johann's question had dragged his mind back to the places it tried to ignore, the screams, the violence, the stench, and worst of all the joy of it.

"I think," said Johann, "people kill each other for wealth. Murder or war its all the same. The difference is power. You see people like us, we have power, so when we murder we call it war. But people without power can not be allowed that privilege so when they kill we call it murder, and hang them for it."

"Are your men not wet enough?" Peter watched the Lutheran Militia. They were standing in the flooded banks of the river pouring water over each others heads from their bowls."

"They're baptizing themselves," said Johann. "Preparing for the end of days. And their ascension to heaven."

Lock was regretting his plan, as he blew his nose on his kerchief. The cured leather of his coat kept out as much water as the stick hut that served as his shelter. He had an excess of phloem and needed fire desperately to increase his yellow bile and therefore restore balance to his humours, but fire could not be risked even in this weather.

The Lutheran army was on the move. Peter had returned, and was leading it himself with a vanguard of his veteran mercenaries. Their scouts had been spotted as close as the forest bridge and the inevitable battle that Lock was daily growing more pessimistic about was getting closer. How could he and a handful of bowmen, defeat an experienced general like Peter. He was a fool following a whim on the advice of an old Jewish woman who knew nothing of warfare. Herr Muller had been right. They should have stayed at the Castle. The ambush was a forlorn hope. They would be outnumbered and cut pieces. Maybe he should order the retreat now while there was still time. A raindrop dripped from his nose. "God deliver me from this soaking," he said aloud.

"You should be grateful to the rain."

Lock looked up and saw Brother August as he stood in the entrance of the shelter, holding Lock's breakfast, a bowl of ale a hunk of bread and stick of dried boar meat.

"The enemy will be feeling the rain more then us," said the monk. "They are marching through it. It will make their scouts cold and lazy. Your plan is bold. I admire it and I believe it could work but they men see you looking so dejected and they doubt themselves. You must speak to them and raise their spirits."

Lock looked miserably out at the rain, "Very well, come then help me to my feet."

Sonia whiled away the hours sewing little figures into a white sheet. She sewed a picture of Lock, and herself. She had then moved on to Basha and Baba and was now embroidering the donkey. Her bum still hurt from the lashing. But the swelling had begun to go down. The door to her tower was pushed open and her mother entered with a tough looking washerwoman.

"Mother," said Sonia as she dropped her embroidery and fell onto her knees. "I'm sorry that I defied you. You are of course much wiser and knowledgeable of everything than me."

"It is of no matter, my child," Frau Muller walked forward and stroked the cheek of her daughter. "Rise. You have been punished and forgiven. My concern now is for your good. I have bought you some warm milk, honey and stewed apple."

Tears welled in Sonia's eyes. "Oh thank you, thank you, mother. Thank you for your kindness. May I come down from the tower?"

"Not yet my sparrow and before you sup we should like to have a look at you. Do as we say now child."

"Yes mother."

"Now lie on the bed and lift your skirts."

Sonia's heart moved from joy to surprise and then to apprehension but she obeyed.

The washerwoman knelt in front of her legs and pulled away her underwear while her mother watched on."

Sonia moved her hand instinctively to cover the gates of Hell.

"Don't squirm, my sparrow," said Frau Muller, "we won't hurt you."

Sonia retracted her hand.

The washerwoman pulled back the gates of Hell with her finger and thumb. With her other hand she probed the Devil's passage. She then withdrew her fingers.

"She's been violated. There is no doubt of that, my Lady, and on a regular basis I would say."

Sonia sat up and straitened her skirts. "I don't what you mean by violated but this is my holy Hell. Bishop Lock himself taught me the holy ritual of putting the devil back into Hell. And I must say it has done me much good."

Frau Mulher gave Sonia a long look. Then sat down on the bed beside her and placed her hand on hers. "Oh my poor, poor child. You have been badly used. There are things in this world I have shielded you from, but it seems from nothing but my desire to help you I let you walk into the wolf's lair."

"Mother, what on Earth do you mean?" said Sonia.

There was a brief relent from the rain and Baba and Basha worked to clean the excrement from their clothes. Two days of cleaning out the latrines had left their silk robes smeared with the village's defecation. Dressed only in her undershirt and skirt, Basha felt bitterly cold as she scrubbed her robes in the freezing stream, her body aching from the hard labour.

"Some warm welcome we have received from your in-laws," said Baba.

"Joseph's mother never liked me," said Baba. "But I never thought her to be so cruel."

"The death of one's children changes people," said Baba.

"Well," said Basha, "I suppose that we should be grateful we are not to be hung. And truth be told, I feel that after my imprisonment by captain Johann I could survive anything. But it is my child that I fear for. The cold and work it can not be good for him."

"Stand up, child," said Baba, "and let me see your figure."

Basha stood.

Baba whistled. "Yes the child is showing, growing by the day I should think." Baba touched her hand to her grandchild's belly.

Basha yelped at the cold touch.

"Oh the little thing is alive and kicking."

Somewhere nearby a person sneezed.

Basha turned to look over her shoulder. It was the miller, watching them from the shade of a pear tree.

Baba stood up and called over to the miller. "Don't just stand and watch, man. Come over and meet your grandchild."

The miller rather bashfully walked toward the two women.

"So," mumbled the miller, "you are Basha the beautiful."

Basha watched as his eyes roamed over her body.

"I can… I can see why my son loved you."

Baba visibly rolled her eyes. "Yes, yes, my granddaughter is a pretty little plum that all men like to ogle at. But she is also carrying your grandchild. And I would have hoped that for the love of your son, you would have taken greater care of her. She is nearly blue with cold. And she needs decent food as she's eating for two."

"Of course, of course," said the miller.

Basha sat by the roaring fire in the miller's room, eating a rich bowl of pottage. A crucifix hung on the wall beside a painting of the miller himself. A table in the room was piled with papers covered in tallies. He had a brass clock a sword and a hunting bow. He sat on a stool with legs crossed watching Basha eat. There was an intensity in his gaze that made Basha feel uncomfortable, but she did not know what to say and so ate in silence.

"You met Joseph in the forest?" said Herr Muller.

"Yes, father. I was gathering mushrooms and he was playing his reed pipe."

Herr Muller came to the fire and stood momentarily over Basha as he removed the pot of hot ale from the fire. "Drink," he proffered her a tankard.

"No," said Basha, touching the silk of her hat that hung on the iron rack by the fire to see if it was dry. "I may not."

"I see," the miller returned, to his standing position by the table, and took a gulp from his tankard. "You married?"

"Yes father, we married in the birch grove, in the spring, before the leaves had grown. We were crowned with forest flowers."

"Was… was the… the wedding…"

"Yes, father, we were married as Jews."

Basha and Herr Muller were silent, listening to the tick of his clock and the splashing of the rain.

"Father? " Basha turned in her chair to look at the miller.

"Yes." He spoke quietly, an acknowledgement, barely more than a breath.

"Did you love my husband?"

The miller wiped his eyes on his shirt. Took a draft of ale. Opened his mouth and closed it. Basha could see that the sorrow of his loss hurt him.

There was a quick sharp knock at the door.

The miller sprang to the alert. "Quick he whispered take your things and get into the chest. She can not find you here."

Basha grabbed her still damp hat and robe, opened the lid of the oak chest and jumped inside, squeezing up against a pile of the miller's shirts and hose. "

The miller closed the lid, shutting her into complete darkness.

It was hot and stuffy inside the chest and Herr Muller's clothes definitely needed a wash, but she could hear everything through the cracks in the wood.

"My Little rabbit," she heard the miller rumble.

"Drinking again, I see," came the voice of the miller's wife.

"As you see me."

"It is no matter." Basha heard the sound of her mother-in-law's feet as she clacked across the wooden floor. "Have you been taking to cooking pottage alone in your room?"

"I fancied a little something," replied the miller.

"Why didn't you ask the cook to fix you something?"

"I..."

Basha bit her tongue and cursed silently to herself as Herr Muller stalled.

"I... felt like cooking."

"That is surprising given the size of the omelette I spooned into you mouth but a few hours thence."

The miller said something that Basha did not catch.

"Have you seen the Jewess?" Basha heard the sound of Frau Muller's feet come nearer. "She is a witch and a devilish woman. Sonia has told me that the old woman even confessed to witchcraft." The lid to the chest creaked above Basha as Frau Muller seated herself on it. "I know not what evil thing grows inside her that she claims is our flesh and blood, or what manner of devilry she used to seduce him, but of this I am sure, she is the cause or our son's death. When evening comes I shall lock them at the base of the tower so that they may not make wickedness in the night. But the young witch is not to be found."

"I'll send out the word," said Herr Muller. "She will be found."

"She had better. Let me know when she is brought in."

Basha heard Frau Muller rise from the chest and walk to the door.

"Wife." Even from within the chest Basha could detect the pain in the man's voice. "Do you think that I could see Sonia?"

"Not yet," replied his wife. "She is absolutely indisposed, and you should watch your greedy appetite."

Basha heard the sound of the door close.

For the hundredth time that day Peter cursed the pounding rain. The landskencht were in a sour mood. They had refused to set up wet tents and had crowded into the baggage wagons where they huddled among the supplies of food, ale and powder. Alone among his men Peter had set an example by setting his tent. But he stood no chance of lighting a fire in the soaked ground. The rain had slowed their march to a crawl. Peter had hoped to cross the river Eisen and camp at the edge of the forest, but the wagons and cannon had been continuously stuck in the mud. Worse at a number of points the streams had flooded the road and they had had to cut temporary bridges. Despite his greatest care, two barrels of powder had gotten wet and had had to be jettisoned. Moral was low, and a number of men, particularly among the Lutheran militia, had imbalanced humours and had taken fever. Peter would have marched back but they had already come too far. If they straggled back now they would be defeated without seeing the enemy. *At least,* he thought, *no enemies would be out in the rain and his advance was most likely undetected.*

"What of the road ahead." He proffered, Udo, the scout, a cup of wine from his personal supplies. Udo took it gratefully. Peter had known him since he had first left Eisenberg with his army He trusted the man with his life. He had once been a farmer's son and the lands around Muhlborg were his home. "We're not far from the forest bridge, but at the pace we are going we will not reach it until noon tomorrow afternoon. Once we cross the bridge we'll be in their land."

"Surely you don't expect anybody to attack us in this weather."

"Probably not," agreed Udo. "But I wouldn't be surprised if we were spotted."

"What sort of folk live in the forest?"

The scout shrugged. "Swine herds, woodcutters, huntsman, som
say there are brigands who have a fastness where the forest meets the
mountains. Witches and vampires are also said to dwell… "

"And they're loyal to Lock?" Peter cut in, "I mean the huntsman,
wood cutters and such."

"If they're loyal to anyone its to the miller, he gives them bread
and justice. But they won't take kindly to an army of townsfolk as
they call us, marching into their land."

Peter sighed. "I made a mistake A small force of horsemen could
have torched Mulhborg and been back to the warmth of a tavern by
now. Curse the heavy cannon. But we will have to make the best of it.
I need you to take twenty of our fittest men and cross the bridge in
the night. If there are enemy there, we cannot be blind, if we are to
be ambushed we must know where."

The 26th September, Day of the Battle of the Bridge, year of the Lord 1526

The rain had receded to a drizzle. The banks of the river rose to rocky cliffs, from which the forest grew thickly and through which the brown floodwater rushed. The bridge was built of stone with neither walls nor railings. It was thicker at the banks and rose in an elegant curve to its narrowest point in the middle of the river, just wide enough that four men could walk abreast, and that the wheels of a wagon would not pitch into the torrent. No one knew who had built the bridge. It seemed as old as the forest itself.

Peter gazed at the opposite bank. It was thick with greenery, willows, birches and alder, undercut with thickets of nettle along swampy margins. It looked entirely uninhabited and yet an army could be hiding on the other side and he would not see it. Though cross it he supposed he must. The speed of advance was of the essence. He needed to get his soldiers somewhere dry and soon.

"You saw no sign of any enemy?" asked Peter.

Udo shook his head. "Nothing, the north bank is clear."

"Did you find any people?"

Udo nodded "A swineherd's wife. She complained bitterly of the weather, and swore frankly that she had seen neither hide nor hair of fighting men. The huntsmen, she told me, were feasting out the bad weather at the miller's expense. And... oh... it is of no matter my lord."

"What is it Udo? One does not begin a sentence in a military report and then take it back."

"She warned against crossing the forest bridge."

"Why?"

"A troll has apparently taken up residence under the bridge and it must be placated with the flesh of a pack animal."

"Oh for the love of God, don't tell Hans. I have no intention of loosing a horse to superstition.

"Who'll cross first?" asked Johann, who had walked over and peered suspiciously at the murky autumn forest.

"I shall," said Peter. "My men are the most experienced. If there is anything waiting for us on the other side we shall face it. Once we have secured the opposite bank the pikemen may cross, followed by the musketeers, then the cannon, the baggage wagons, and finally yourself with the rear guard."

Johann looked like he wanted to protest, but Peter gave him a cold look and the captain nodded, and returned to get soldiers in to marching order.

Peter stood silently with Udo for a few moments before he broke the silence. "If there is great big troll underneath the bridge, how come we can't see it?"

"It lives beneath the water," replied Udo. "Its form is not dissimilar to a monstrous frog."

"I pity Sonia," said Basha as she swept the last of the moulding rushes from the bowman's bedroom floor. The bowman was a dirty man, as the rushes had not been changed in over a month. In one corner they stank of urine and many had begun to rot while discarded chicken bones intertwined with them. "Locked in that tower, unable to see her father or talk to anyone but her evil mother."

"Save your pity for yourself," the old woman coughed and spat out a glob of phloem. "At least she's warm and dry. I'll warrant she eats better than the gruel we're fed too. I'm convinced that Frau Muller is trying to work us to death. And Yaweh knows, I'm getting sick."

Basha finished the job pilling the rushes into a handcart and shoving it out into the street.

A stable boy who was about nine years old waved out to her and ran over. "A message for the Jewess," he said.

"Yes," replied Basha.

"You're wanted in the miller's quarters." the boy whispered to her, "and try and look discreet."

"Discrete?" asked Basha.

"Try not to be seen," said the boy.

"Oh, thank you," said Basha. "I shall go directly."

Basha turned to leave and confer with Baba.

"Hey," said the boy, "aren't you going to pay me for my message."

"With what should I pay you?" asked Basha.

"With a kiss," said the boy.

Basha laughed and kissed the boy on his cheek and set off immediately.

She followed the way that the miller had shown her, down a

manhole by the south wall and through the cellars filled with sacks and barrels. She followed the sacks and barrels to the end, after which she climbed a short flight of stairs. She passed through an unlocked door and arrived within Herr Muller's stone house, in front of the door to his chambers. The door was ajar and Basha pushed it open.

The miller looked up at her from his papers and his jug of ale and motioned her to come inside, and close the door behind her. The smell of roasted lamb stuffed with sage and mint assailed her nostrils. It reminded her how hungry she was, having eaten nothing but a thin wheat gruel.

"You must be hungry. Please eat."

Basha washed her hands in a basin of cold water and Herr Muller watched her eat.

"Did you sing for Joseph," he asked after she had finished the lamb.

"Yes," replied Basha.

"Could you sing for me."

Basha began to sing.

Lock watched as the enemy column crossed the bridge. They appeared as a procession of colourful cloth moving behind the gaps in the trees. Men variously cursed grumbled and grunted as they clapped along the cobblestones, formed into lines and waited their turn to cross, as the drizzle gave way to cloud. It had seemed like miracle they had not been seen. But The Brigands and Huntsmen moreover had disguised themselves with skill and care smearing their faces with mud, while sewing autumn to their cloaks and thanks to the swine herd's wife they would not be expecting them. "Hold your fire till the front of the column reaches the hollow oak" Lock whispered the order but the huntsmen beside him heard the reminder and passed it down the line.

Peter and his men crossed the bridge in good order, and the cobbled forest road continued on before them. They fanned out into the surrounding forest but saw no sign of enemies. Peter gave the order and rest of the column began to cross.

Peter who, was leading the column, paused to admire an ancient hollow oak. His mercenaries formed the vanguard. Behind them marched the musketmen. The pikemen had just crossed the bridge, while the wheellock musketeers, cannon, wagons and rare guard, commanded by Captain Johann, were still stretched out on the bridge.

The enemy struck. A volley of goose-fletched arrows flew, from the direction of the forest. The arrows smashed through cloth and armour, tearing muscle and puncturing organs. Men screamed and fell.

Peter threw his back to the oak tree's trunk, and his men did likewise as the arrows hissed between trees.

Peter swore. He watched as two successive volleys took their toll on the tightly packed column of musketmen, slashing through cloth flesh and bone. Peter thought quickly. He needed to close with his enemies and quickly, giving time for the column on the bridge to form up and support. If the musketmen could hold their nerve and fired back at their hidden enemy it would give the Peter the cover he needed to engage his longswordsmen. He judged from the volley that he had the advantage of numbers. If he could engage the bowmen long enough to allow the pikemen and wheellock musketeers to get into position he could overwhelm his attackers.

"Musket men turn and prepare to fire." Peter shouted the order over the sound of the rushing river and the screams of the injured. He offered a silent prayer that Johann's drilling had done its job, and turned the townsmen into soldiers.

The musketmen made a fair attempt of forming a line but struggled to light the wicks of their muskets in the wet, and while they fumbled with their tinderboxes they continued to fall under the barrage of arrows, while the column stalled on the bridge.

Peter could not wait. "Smear yourselves in mud," he commanded to his mercenaries. "We'll advance on these bastards tree by tree."

As Peter and his men crawled from tree to tree, the musketmen finally managed to advance and fire a volley in the direction of the enemy. But a combination of wet powder, fear, and ill discipline caused them to fire haphazardly and despite the crash and smoke, Peter heard no cries of fallen foes.

"Quick," shouted Peter, "rush them."

Peter's men ran at the enemy line with drawn swords. He could see the enemy. They were dressed in furs and leather and wore long beards. They reached for more arrows, notched them and drew back their long bows."

"To cover!" Peter shouted.

But several of his men were too slow to avoid the well-aimed arrows that hit them with such force that it knocked them to the ground. Peter listened as the bowmen renotched their bows, but did not fire. The bowmen knew where they were and were marking them.

Peter was pinned. He glanced back toward the bridge. The withering arrow fire had broken the musketmen who had dropped their arms and fled into forest. The commander of the pikemen had done his best to get his men into ranks and make room for the column to move off the bridge, but with the musketmen broken Peter guessed they would soon receive heavy fire from the enemy archers. "Get yourself to those cursed pikemen," snarled at Udo, "and get them to charge. We can overwhelm the rats but only we show nerve. You failed me once. Don't fail me now."

With a grim expression Udo left to fulfil Peter's order.

Lock watched as the pikemen lowered their weapons and charged, stumbling over the uneven ground. They were led by a swordsman in colourful attire, who screamed a war cry as he ran. The brigands and huntsmen launched arrow after arrow into the attackers. Their line thinned but they charged on, following the swordsman. He drew closer and Lock could see the sweat dripping from his brow. A huntsman launched an arrow. The bowstring twanged and an arrow slashed through the swordsman throat and he fell. The pikemen broke, running weaponless back toward the bridge and the baggage wagons.

"Now is the time," said Brother August quietly to Lock.

Lock drew his sword. It felt cold and awkward in his hand. "Pursue," he shouted.

The huntsman and brigands grabbed their cudgels, drew their swords and surged over the mossy ground in pursuit of the pikemen.

Peter cursed as the pikemen broke and the far flank of the enemy rushed after them. It was now or never. "Charge," he ordered.

The Landsknecht charged from behind the trees at the momentarily distracted bowmen. Some were able to draw and loose.

Peter closed with the nearest brigand. He was strong and hairy. He dropped his bow and seized his cudgel, swinging it at Peter. Peter ducked, closed, and opened the man's stomach with his short sword. With the smell of death and the sight of gore, Peter felt his old demons return, the joy and the disgust.

With swinging and jabbing longswords the landsknecht opened up the brigands flank and they began to flee.

Peter stepped over his fallen enemy and ran on in pursuit. Perhaps winged Lady Victory would smile on him after all.

The brigands rallied to resist the pursuing mercenaries.

The mercenaries closed.

Peter swung with his sword.

A broad shouldered brigand parried.

There was a horrifying bellow. The brigands parted and a monstrous brown bear charged the mercenaries. He knocked one to the ground with a swipe of his paw and gored another. The brigands shouted war cries, raised their cudgels and closed in on the shocked mercenaries.

In his mind Peter heard the ghostly voice of his old Lieutenant, Sokol, *run, run or die.* "Retreat," Peter ordered.

The mercenaries fled.

The brigands, distracted by the action on their other flank did not pursue, but turned their attention to the baggage wagons.

Any residual feeling of elation at the thought of victory did not last long for Lock as the messy business of close combat at the edge of the river began. It was dirty bloody and visceral. Lock found he was of little help, having no stomach for fighting. But the huntsman and brigands did not need him, and the fighting soon gave way to execution, binding of captives and division of loot. They pushed the cannon into the river and they threw the piles of dead and injured townsfolk in after it. The next day their bloated corpses would float through Eisenberg. The townsfolk would pull those they could from the floodwater while widows would line the riverbank.

Basha finished singing and the miller cried.

Greta moaned as her lover brought her to bliss.

"I should go," said Basha as Herr Muller wiped the tears from his eyes.

But she spoke too late for there was a knock on the door. Basha hid herself again in the chest and again she heard the sound of Frau Muller's shoes on the floor. She heard the sound of Frau Muller's hand slap across her husbands face.

"You pig," Basha heard her say. "You think I wouldn't find out that you were hosting the Jewish whore to private little rendezvous. Oh she is a wicked, sinful creature, trying to pull you into her web just like she did with our son."

The miller mumbled something that Basha did not catch. But she heard the mocking laugh that followed. "You fancy the little witch don't you? Thought you would grease your pole with a little Jewish lard? Look at you. You are as guilty as a stable boy at confession. Well did she open her devil flesh for you? Did her river flood its banks for you? Speak man. Has the cat taken your tongue?"

Basha heard Herr Muller protest his innocence.

"Been fattening the whore up on roasted lamb have we?" continued Frau Muller unperturbed by her husbands protestations. "She's here now isn't she? Where is she hiding?

Frau Muller walked to the chest and lifted the lid.

Herr Muller simply sat with his head in his hands as his wife dragged Basha by her hair from the chest and spat in her face. "You evil creature. I have caught you in the act of whoring yourself to my husband for scraps from the table. What do you have to say for yourself?"

"I think only of your grandchild growing within me, mistress," replied Basha. "Our lord had called for me and I attended him. He laid no hand upon me, nor did I desire him to."

"Liar!" Frau Muller threw Basha onto the floor. "That thing that you carry inside you is no blood of mine. I took you in from kindness and I see how it is repaid. But I know now what to do with Jewish witches. You shall burn. I shall lock you in the keep until the necessary arrangements have been made."

It had ceased to rain and the donkeys which had left the brigands' hideaway loaded with bundles of rope and arrows, now laboured under heavy burdens of barrels of ale, salted pork, and sacks of valuables looted from the fallen soldiers.

"I consider that I have fulfilled my side of the deal," said the patriarch as the last barrel of salted pork was loaded onto a donkey. "We have shed enough blood for your war. We will return to our mountain fastness."

Lock nodded warily. "I am forever in your debt. May there be rapprochement between our faiths. Though it shall always remain a mystery to me that you speak among yourselves in Latin but hold mass in Greek."

"What will you do now?" asked the patriarch.

Lock watched as the huntsmen broke open a barrel of ale and began to swig back its contents with tankards taken from the defeated enemy. When he had set out from Muhlborg he had imaged crushing the enemy and then marching on to Eisenberg, but without the brigands his force seemed small and weary. Lock himself was wet tired and hungry. "I shall take the wagons and the prisoners back to Muhlborg," replied Lock, "and bring them news of our victory."

"May your road be uneventful," said the patriarch.

"You know many of the folk who spend their days in the forest," said Lock as the patriarch was turning away. "Tell me did you know Joseph the miller's son?"

"I did," said the patriarch over his shoulder. "The only decent German I've known, a great hand for music, and a way with animals. It was he who brought us the bear cub."

"You don't happen to know who killed him do you?"

"No, but I would wager it was jealousy. Why else would one kill in such a horrible fashion?"

"And who would be jealous of Joseph?"

The patriarch shrugged. "Joseph was wed to Basha the Beautiful."

Lock watched as the patriarch moved away to join the column of brigands. There was one person he could think of who had showed very odd attention to Basha, nor was he the person to flinch from committing violence. Lock had hoped to find his body among the fallen, but the wily captain Johann was nowhere to be seen.

Brother August approached. "The wagons are ready to move, Lord Bishop. If we make haste we shall make it to the first hamlet before nightfall."

At least the rain had stopped, thought Peter, as he stared gloomily at the fire of silvery beech logs, *at least I, and my best fighting men, are still alive.*

"It seems wrong sir," said Hans, "after all we've been through fighting French knights, Turks, hussars, surviving the fever, and the swamps, facing witches and dragons to be defeated by brigands led by a drunk bear. I won't be able to go back to the Kobold's Breaches now. The ladies will laugh."

"I wouldn't worry about that. You'll probably have a larger number to pick from now their husbands are all dead," said Peter humourlessly.

Hans's face lit up with genuine joy. "You believe so, my lord."

"You can count on it. Women are now the only thing Eisenberg has a surplus of. Without the supplies from Muhlborg we won't even have the food to get through to spring, and we need to hole down for the winter. Hans?" said Peter, something suddenly occurring to him, "don't you believe the bear was a forest demon? I thought you lot believe every bit of superstitious nonsense you hear."

"Halt," the sentries voice carried through the trees.

"Fear not," a voice replied from the darkness. "It is I Johann, cousin of the count."

"Advance and be recognized," the sentry replied.

Peter gave an involuntary shudder. The death of his cousin had been one of the only silver linings to the whole disaster.

"How did you survive?" asked Peter coldly, when Johann had joined him by the fire.

"I feigned death," replied Johann.

"I see," said Peter "and have you anything to show for your cowardice."

"Information," murmured Johann, "I watched and I listened."

"And what did you learn?"

Johann began to pick his teeth with his long fingernails. "The enemy army was an alliance of huntsmen and peasants loyal to the miller and Latin speaking brigands who had moved into the forest from over the mountains. Lock had promised them title to much of the forest if they supported his army. But now his force has split. The brigands have returned to their fastness. And Lock is on his way back to Muhlborg with our wagons and prisoners. The enemy is vulnerable. Their forces have split and they believe they are already victorious."

"We are less than forty men," said Peter. "They are right to think us beaten."

"How well do you know Muhlborg?" asked Johann.

"I've been there twice," said Peter, "enough to see the strength of its walls."

"On the north face of the borg," said Johann, "where the walls are highest, the stone is rough cut, a man might scale it, and if he had the advantage of surprise, might with a small band take the castle."

Book Six

The House of the Lamb

the day after the battle, 27th of September

The bells of Muhlborg had just tolled six, when Lock and Brother August arrived, with the bowmen, wagons and prisoners. Lock had to admit that he felt rather proud of himself. So much for those who had doubted him, now he was a conquering hero. He would deliver the wagons to the store, and prisoners to the keep, before marching up to Frau Muller's chamber and demanding that he see Sonia. No longer bothered by his cold, he held his head high as he approached the gate.

He was greeted by a guard who stood on the parapet. "What news?"

"Fair tidings," shouted back Lock. "The heretics have been routed. Tell the women to pluck the choicest swan they can find. We may all feast and sleep easy tonight."

The guard smiled, infected by Lock's exuberance. "Sounds like you have a tale to tell." The chains rattled and the portcullis rose.

Such was Lock's good cheer that he didn't notice the two stakes and pyres in the village square, so enamoured was he by the attention of the village folk that rushed to kiss his robe.

"What are you doing?" asked Basha.

"What does it look like," replied her grandmother. "I'm feeding the mice."

"How can you be so calm?" said Basha. "Frau Muller is about to have us burned."

"Would it make things better if I were to panic? I can no more breakout of this house than you can. Besides, perhaps the mouse lady can help us. She seems to know the way in and out of here well enough."

"How do you know it's a she?" said Basha.

"Well," said Baba sprinkling the last of her bread on the ground. "I've been watching this mouse since we've been locked in here, and its tummy seems to be growing by the hour. I think the mouse is with child."

"Grandmother," said Basha, "can't you put your mind toward getting us out of here?"

At that moment they heard the sound of a heavy key turning in the lock. Both women turned to watch the door. The door swung open.

"Basha, Baba." the hairy face of the miller pushed inside. "Everybody is in the great hall, listening to the bishop's tale. Now is your chance. I will not have my grandchild's blood on my hands. Come make haste."

Lock had tired of telling the story for the third time. He had gone to some pains to embellish his own role in the battle. *Not,* as he told himself, *out of any false vanity but to avert from the problems of heaping too much praise on the schismatic brigands.* He was just taking the opportunity to serve himself another side of swan, when he felt a tug at his arm.

"If you please your lordship." It was a stable boy. "If you please your lordship, Mistress Sonia would very much like to see you. She awaits you now in the small parlour."

Lock smiled, *what a perfect evening.* "I shall come forthwith."

The small parlour was a square stone room at the base of the tower. The stable boy led Lock to the door that was ajar, before running off into the dark streets. Lock pulled the door gently open and slipped inside. The room was bare, lit with a simple iron chandelier. The only decoration was a large wooden crucifix, depicting a particularly hairy and emaciated Jesus. *What a strange religion I preside over,* thought Lock, *we worship a torture victim and ritualistically drink his blood, while elevating pain to the highest virtue.* Sitting before a table was the miller's wife.

"Close the door, Inga." she said.

Lock turned and saw a tall solidly built woman close the door behind him, turn a key in its lock and return it to the pockets of her apron.

"You are a fraud and a sinner," said the miller's wife. "You had your dirty, shameless way with my daughter. What do you have to say for yourself?"

Lock looked at the woman across the table and then back at the woman who stood by the door. It was the moment he had feared, but rather than feel fear he felt liberated that the moment had come. He felt courage. "Yes I took advantage of your daughter's innocence. Yes I talked my way into her embrace. But do I regret it? Nay, it was the best thing I ever did... "

"Stop," said the miller's wife. "Sonia, you may enter."

A door at the back of the room opened and Sonia stepped out. Tears were streaming down her face. "You... mother's right... And it's all lies? I swore that it was the truth. You mean to say that there is no Benedictine monk? There was no divine ritual? You've been making fool of me this whole time." Sonia's voice shook with emotion. "I hope you burn in Hell." Sonia turned and ran.

"Wait," Lock called after her retreating footsteps, which rang out on the tower staircase. "I've been wanting to talk to you. I..."

But Lock didn't finish his sentence. Inga punched him in the temple, knocking him off balance. He only just managed to catch himself on his hands as his head spun from the blow.

"I think you've talked enough," said the miller's wife.

The landsknecht crept through the mud to the base of the north wall of Muhlborg. Peter, his long sword strapped to his back and his katzbalger strapped to his waist, felt out the handholds among the stone from which he might climb. The ascent was gruelling. Three times he nearly slipped from the wet crumbling stone. Near the parapet he had to pull himself up with one arm cursing the extra weight of his long sword. When he reached the top he let down a rope and soon the other men quietly joined him. It seemed that once again Lady Fortune was smiling on him. The night was dark and cloudy and the parapet empty of men. He drew his short sword and began to descend the steps into the village. His men behind him, he followed the bend of a stone cottage, turned a corner and ran into a man carrying a lantern and accompanied by two women in long dark robes.

Everybody froze.

Peter looked Herr Muller in the eye and saw recognition in his face.

The miller opened his mouth to speak.

Peter stabbed him in the throat with his short sword, killing him instantly.

The women fled.

Basha and Baba caught their breath beside the effluent trench in a dark corner of the south wall. Basha straightened her hat. Baba rested her sack on the ground.

"What are we to do now?" asked Basha.

Baba shrugged. "Not the main gate. There is no worse place to be when there is a fight about. Besides I don't think either of us are able to raise the portcullis. The miller was taking us a secret way no? The same way he took you when he was spying on us by the stream. You know how to get there?"

"Yes," said Basha "It goes under the north wall. But it's no good. It is barred by a locked iron gate bolted deep into the stone."

"Then we must go back and search the miller's body for the key," said Baba.

"What if the soldiers have already taken it?" asked Basha.

"Then all the worse for us." replied Baba.

No alarm had been sounded since Peter had stepped over Herr Muller's body and he was able to march his men right to the doors of the big hall. A drunk bowman stood outside leaning against an old, well pruned maple. A woman sat on the tree roots by his feet drinking ale from a brass tankard.

The Bowman stared, dumbstruck, as the landsknecht with drawn long swords emerged into the lantern light.

The woman screamed.

The bowman looked to his bow leaning against the wall of the hall.

Peter shouted and charged.

He dodged the woman who threw herself at his feet, and skewered the bowman in the back as he ran for the door. While Peter pulled his sword out of the dying man's back, Johann threw open the door and the landsknecht rushed inside. By the time Peter had entered, the battle was already over. Five men, a monk and one woman, were bleeding to death on the floor. The survivors, men and women alike, huddled in a corner. The room stank of fear and defecation, but beyond that the scents of the cosy evening still lingered, the scent of ale and roasted swan, wood smoke and women. And though the immediate sounds were groans and rattles of death, accompanied the slurping suck of swords pulled from bodies, it seemed to Peter that he could still hear the sound of laughter hanging in the air. Peter and Hans exchanged a look. Johann played with the monk's head pushing it backward and forward with his foot.

"Leave the dead be," ordered Peter.

Johann stood to attention.

Peter stepped forward so he stood in front of his men and motioned to the survivors. "Women, stay where you are. Men, beside the fireplace. Move or we'll kill you as you are. That's it. Move along. Good. Now, anybody who tells me where the bloody bishop is and who else I have to lookout for gets to live."

Basha patted down the body of Herr Muller. As silently as she could she lifted from him a heavy ring of keys, a bone handled dagger and his ruby set wedding ring. "Come," said Basha, as she slipped the items into her sash bag, "let us make haste. I saw him, grandmother, among the soldiers. Johann, I recognised the way he walked. I would recognise it anywhere. I hate to think what would befall us if he found us here."

"Fear not, my little Babashka. We shall flee. Your son was conceived on a carpet of spring flowers before the birch leave's bloomed and he shall be born on a bed of soft autumn moss. So I see it and so it will be. But, child, we must seek vengeance for the wrongs done to us. The Christians killed your father. The Christians killed your lover and your lover to be. All our kinfolk are either dead or lost. And we ourselves are lucky to not be burnt."

"But, grandmother," Basha pulled away from Baba's hand and glanced nervously over her shoulder, "How could we take vengeance? We are but two weak women." Basha began to bite her fingernails.

"My granddaughter, could you find the way to the granary?"

Basha pulled her fingers out of her mouth and whispered. "You don't know him like I do, for the grace of Yahweh. Every moment I stay is terror."

The old woman reached out and took the young woman's hand. "Be brave, Basha the Bold. Be brave."

Sonia watched the sacking of the main hall through window of the tower. She watched as Peter impaled the bowman in the lamplight. The enemy were among them again but this time she didn't have the will to care. She was almost happy to see them come. Her grief over Lock's betrayal hurt like a rock in her stomach.

Her mother reached out and put her hand on her shoulder. "Come, child. We must flee before the heretics put us to the sword and use you foully."

"How shall we escape and to where will we flee?" Inga stood by the door, arms crossed over her apron, her carving knife hanging at her belt.

"We shall take the secret tunnel at the base of the tower and seek refuge at the Abbey of the blessed Virgin. Come, child."

"I'm not coming," said Sonia. "I hate you and I want to die. Lock was a liar, and he deceived me and used me. But at least he was kind to me. He was kinder than you ever were. I don't know if he ever loved me. All the time I thought that the way I felt was to do with the grace of Heaven but I realise now that it was love. I only want now to see Lock, and listen to what he has to say, and if I am found and killed by the soldiers so be it."

Frau Muller dug her fingernails into her daughters shoulder. "The soldiers will not kill you, child. They will rape you. Do you know what rape is? I thought not. You thought you had been to Heaven? Well then you would know Hell. You are coming with us. Inga, prepare to bind Sonia."

"Yes, my lady."

It took Peter time to break through the blockaded door of the small parlour at the base of the tower, by chopping away the wood of the door with his sword. Peter had been expecting to find the small parlour deserted with Lock and the last holdouts taking refuge in the tower. But to his shock he found, illuminated by a still lit chandelier, the naked body of a man dangling from a rope bound to his wrists. The rope was leveraged off a hook on the ceiling and held fast by an iron stanchion to the wall.

The body moved, twisting on the rope, so that Peter could see his face. His hair was matted with blood, his nose was broken and his front teeth were knocked out. And on the floor below mingling with the teeth and blood was a single testicle that looked like it had been cut from the man's scrotum with surgical precision. Recognition spread across the man's face in the form of a manic grin. It was Bishop Lock.

"For the love of God, Lord Peter," gurgled Lock as more landsknecht pushed their way through the ruined door.

Peter laughed. "I came to arrest you," said Peter, "not save you." But he cut the rope.

Lock crashed, cursing, to the ground.

"Hans," said Peter, "Guard the bishop. Though the Lord knows I can't imagine he'll try and escape. I'll see if I can find somebody to tend to his wounds. He's no good to us if he bleeds to death."

"Yes my lord," Hans grinned.

"What will you do Grandmother?" asked Basha after the two women had unlocked and hauled back the trapdoor which led to the grain store.

Baba fumbled in her sash bag. "This grain is what they are all fighting over, for without it the Christians will starve. Well," she pulled a package from her bag wrapped in cloth from which Basha heard squeaking from within, "may they starve." Baba unwrapped the package to reveal a young family of mice. One by one she gently dropped them into the dark, onto a bed of grain. "And may you," Baba addressed the mice, "have many more children, and children's children, and may you never be in want of grain."

After the last mouse was dropped into the granary, the two women lifted their skirts and ran. They ran up a flight of steps to a low parapet on the wall. They ran along the unlit parapet until they arrived back at the north wall. Stumbling in the dark Basha found the trap door to the secret passage. The two women heaved it open. The hinges were well oiled and it made little noise as it thuded onto the ground thick with straw and rushes. Basha stepped onto the first step. Her leather shod feet made no noise.

"Halt," a gravelly voice spoke from the street behind. "Don't even think about running." It was the voice Basha had been dreading. "A fat whore and an old witch wouldn't get far. And if you struggle or run I'll hurt you when I get you, like you've not been hurt before. That's it. Turn around now. Come here and kiss my boots and I may spare your child."

the 1st of October, Day of Service, Year of the Lord 1526

Brunhilde, abbess of Saint Hildegard the Virgin, looked into her lead-glass mirror. She had come to own her ugliness, her warts, her disfigured nose, and her lazy eye. Men had never desired her and for many years she had hated them but now she had only contempt. Her passion was for knowledge and this was the basis of her power. She had come to the abbey twenty years ago and as a young novice she had shunned the other sisters and explored the labyrinthine caves, carved deep into the cliff that made up the larger part of the abbey. Many of these passages and rooms had been long abandoned, as many of the younger generations of sisters preferred the gardens, houses and orchards between the cliff and the abbey wall. But it was in the old dusty rooms that the treasures of the abbey were hid among the tombs of ancient abbesses, or perhaps they had one been high priestesses, bedecked with gold girdles. There were magical relics of untold power and rooms of vellum books, and papyrus roles. The abbey was old indeed. How old Brunhilde did not know but of one thing she was certain, its rulers had always been women.

Nuray, Bright Moon, lay naked on the bed behind her and Brunhilde tilted the mirror to admire the sight. The Turkish princess lay legs slightly spread her hand resting on her vulva, her body flushed with exertions of lovemaking.

"I am to meet with your countrywoman forthwith," said Brunhilde in Arabic.

"She will want to take me back to the pasha," replied Nuray. "To think that I once desired his attention."

"And you wish not to return to your country?" the abbess queried, and if she was honest to herself the question had a little vanity in it.

Nuray laughed. "You are joking! Go back to being the property of some man? Every man I've ever known, has ignored me, worshiped me or wanted to hurt me. I can't decide which is worse. I want nothing more in the world than to stay here with you. That is of course," Nuray took her own turn to fish for complements, "if you'll have me?"

"I should be loath to let you go," said Brunhilde, "I need your help with those Arabic books, I've been working to translate."

Guarded by two strong sisters Asra was led into the audience room. It was carved high into the cliff and had a balcony that opened out above the hills and valleys below. Sitting in a wooden throne sat an ugly woman. Beside her was a female clerk. On the other side a sister who wore a sword like she knew how to use it.

"You were caught," said the abbess in Latin, "stealing from the pantries and squatting in an abandoned cell. What do you have to say for yourself?"

Asra prostrated herself on the floor. "Only that I am guilty and plead for your mercy."

"Stand up," said Brunhilde, "I am not the Popess. A subtle inclination of the head and a modest curtsy is proper practice. You are lucky that you are a woman or your punishment would be harsh indeed. As it stands I am inclined to act with leniency provided you give an honest account of your purpose and how you came to be here."

Asra stood. "I have come to bring the Lady Nuray back to her husband. I followed her trail into a cave from the Pass of Eagles. For many days I wandered hungry in the darkness until I found my way to the inhabited parts of your great abbey. And I heard from the talk of the sisters that my journey might not have been in vain for Nuray is said to be held captive here. I can offer you a great ransom for her return."

"Nuray is free to leave as she wishes," The abbess replied. "But she has converted to Christianity and wishes to join the sisterhood and stay among us, chaste and wed to God."

Asra inclined her head as she had been told. "I see," the parlour was silent for a moment, but then Asra spoke, "if she is free to go, then may I see her alone and see if she may be persuaded to leave with me, of course the ransom would still be paid."

"You may see Nuray. I certainly would not wish to stop the two of you from reuniting. I have no need of your money, but I do like a good wager. You may see Nuray and if you persuade her to leave then you may both go with my blessing. I will guide you back to the Pass of Eagles and I shall furnish you with provisions for your journey. On the other hand if you fail to persuade Nuray then your service is forfeit to me. You must swear to serve me faithfully until such a time as I release you from your vow or taken by Lord Death. Do we have a wager?"

Asra considered the offer. Nuray did not speak the languages of the Christians. Did she really want to give up her country or her God to live among these primitive women? The abbess was looking and she had to make a decision. "I accept your wager."

"That pleases me," said the abbess, "you may refer to me as superior."

"Yes, Superior," replied Asra.

"The soldiers that accompanied you," said the abbess. "What happened to them?"

" I had them killed them, Superior, because they disobeyed me."

"You called for me, lord," said Lock as he limped into the small parlour, the agony of the pain in his groin shooting through his abdomen. The wound had healed but the pain remained. Lord Peter had added some touches to the room. The crucifix was noticeably absent and heavy sacks of loot were stacked in the corner beside some barrels, presumably ale.

"I'm bored," said Peter. "I have to wait for the river to go down so we can take grain and supplies by barge back to the city. Entertain me."

"Forgive me but I feel like I left my sense of humour behind on the torture rack along with my left testicle," said Lock

Peter laughed, "You really are hilarious."

"I clearly made some disastrous career choices," said Lock, "I should have pursued a career as a dancing dog. Everybody loves performing animals. Say, is that wine your drinking?"

"The finest Hungarian red you'll ever try. Come have a bowl and tell me something to make me laugh. By Georg the Dragon Slayer, I have had few enough these days."

Lock winced as he lowered himself on to a stool. "Have you heard the one about the monk who tricked a young lady into sleeping with him on certain nights by pretending to be the archangel Gabriel?"

Greta stood on the parapet of the Forest Gate and watched as the migrant caravan drew up to the walls in a dirty and unkempt mass. The men were unshaven with long hair and wild beards. The women, who appeared to be the majority, wore no hats and their dirty locks fell over their ragged peasant shifts. They sang as they advanced, herding their goats before them, some flagellating themselves with willow whips.

"They are pious folk," said Luke his hand resting gently in Greta's. "They have come seeking refuge and protection."

Greta removed her hand from his. "They look like a rabble. How will we feed and house them?"

"Do not be so quick to judge. Though they seem rough and uncouth their hearts are pure in their love for God. There are many empty houses in Eisenberg, and now that we have lost so many of our strong men they shall help to rebuild the city and establish the kingdom of God that we strive to create."

"Don't tell me how to judge," said Greta, "I'm the countess of Eisenberg. And in my husband's absence I rule."

"Look at me," said Luke.

Greta looked at her lover. His broad handsome face was smiling.

He touched her gently on the cheek. "Greta, I love you. You saved my life and I owe you mine. My life, myself they belong to you. By all means we should keep the gates closed and make arrangements to send these folk on their way."

Greta burst into tears and embraced Luke. "I'm sorry," she whispered in his ear. "Of course we must let these people in. God knows what should become of them on the South Road. It's just been so hard. Everybody dying, the procession of widows, and you have been so busy and visiting me only for fleeting moments. I almost forgot why we are doing all of this."

Nuray scooped up another plum, baring her teeth as she cut into it before plucking out its pith with her fingernails. She began stripping the flesh from the skin with her teeth and swallowing it. The Turkish princess was certainly not looking worse for wear. Her face had an attractive glow, and she moved with a sensual confidence that Asra had not been expecting.

Asra cleared her throat.

Nuray placed the skin next to the pith in a little wooden bowl. "There is no need for you to speak," she spoke with the tone of a princess addressing a servant. "I know all. You have made a wager with the abbess and wish to take me back to my husband. Well you have made a bad wager. You may as well seek out the abbess immediately and swear your oath of allegiance. I have nothing more to say to you."

Asra prostrated herself on the floor. "Forgive me your highness, but may I be allowed some words with you. We are both far from home and have doubtless been through many difficult trials. Do you really wish to stay among these unwashed savages? If you are frightened of any retribution on yourself that came from any unwanted violation of your chastity, I assure you that no one need know. You can return to a life of power and luxury. Your every need will be attended to and you shall be loved by one of the most powerful men in the empire."

Nuray laughed. "You may rise. Every need of mine will be attended, will it? That should make a welcome change from my previous experience of marriage. I was nothing but a caged falcon. To be admired but not used, a slave to a man. Oh I had needs as all folk do and to think that I had once desired my husband's touch. He ignored it for his books, for his stars, his hunting and his hash. Every time he had another excuse, another holy day, but the truth was that he never had time for my pleasure. I was driven mad by boredom and denial of my desires. Since then I have seen how men love women and spurn the thought that I ever entertained desire for their attention. They think only for themselves and consider resistance and anger to be an invitation to their pricks. In so much as you are considered it is only as a kind of jewel to bedeck their crowns. They have no notion of first stimulating the waters and inducing fever in the skin, believing that women's flesh is naught but cured hide to be stretched taught over their thrusting tent polls. Their hearts are full of envy but they seek only to possess. But now I have found a lover who knows how to treat me and I find paradise several times a day and more often at night. Why would I forgo bliss and freedom for a silken prison? Waste my time no longer. The abbey may be under threat and the abbess thinks that you may be of use."

"What is to become of me?" asked Lock as Peter refilled his goblet. Both men were drunk and in good cheer.

"Public execution," said the count of Eisenberg. "I'm sorry."

"Not as sorry as me," replied the bishop. "Is there not any other option?"

"I think not," said Peter. "You are a symbol and the people must have something to show for the loss of so many lives. I promise you it will be quick and relatively painless. There will be no torture."

Lock raised his arms in gesture of mock supplication. "Such grace."

Peter slammed his fist on the table, drunken anger rising in his voice. "Look, I didn't choose for things to be this way. But they are. We cannot run from our fate. My fate is to lead a new Lutheran county and..." Peters voice shook and he stopped talking.

"Don't leave me hanging," said Lock, "go on."

Peter smiled weakly then chuckled.

Lock took a sip of his wine. "Forgive me. I am drunk on this fine wine of yours and I feel most genuine gratitude for your mercy. It could really be worse. I could be in a dungeon without any wine. But tell me, what is your fate? I can't quite work it out. The story of your adventures there's something you've not told me. What was it really that the Lutheran preacher offered you? It was something that you could not refuse. It was your fate. What was it? Speak to me as a friend. Tell me. Lighten your heart. I am at your disposal and I am a terrible sinner which makes me all the better to absolve you."

Peter's mood swung from anger to affection. He stood and pulled Lock to his feet embracing him in a crushing hug. Tears rolled down his face. "Nuray," he said, "Nuray, Bright Moon."

Lock extricated himself from Peter's grip and pushed the soldier back into his chair. "Who is Nuray?"

"A woman like no other," said Peter.

The abbess looked at the two supplicants before her, the last audience of the day. Before she retired to enjoy the kisses of the Nuray. The supplicants were Frau Muller and her daughter. They had fled the attack on the Muhlborg and sought refuge at the abbey. It would not be long they had told her before the men would come for it as well. The audience had a peculiar awkwardness. The daughter looked like she wanted to talk and the mother would look at her in a threatening way until she began to fidget with her apron. Brunhilde had just endured another uncomfortable silence when she decided something had to be done.

"I should like to talk to your daughter alone," said the abbess. "Leave us."

Frau Muller looked like she was going to protest, but thought better of it. She curtseyed and left.

When the sound of her shoes on the stone floor had faded, Brunhilde spoke. "What was it that you wanted to tell me but did not want your mother to hear?"

"Are you a mind reader?" asked Sonia with genuine surprise. "How did you know I wanted to speak to you alone."

"No," said the abbess severely without a hint of a smile. "I am not a mind reader. Now speak to the point for my time is precious."

"Of course your highness," said Sonia, "I... I have a boon to ask."

"Speak and it shall be considered."

"I wondered if you might move me to another place. Maybe give me something to do."

"You wish to be separated from your mother?"

"I hate her. She is cruel and evil. She has destroyed what I love most."

"Watch your tongue." replied the Brunhilde. "It is neither seemly nor virtuous to talk about your mother in such a way."

Tears rolled down Sonia's face. She dropped from her stool on to her knees. "I beg you. Please don't make me stay with her. Take pity on me."

"Stand up and dry your eyes. I have no wish to know the reason for your hatred of your own mother. But I have heard you can read and write Latin. Is that true?"

"Yes, indeed." Sonia dried her face on her kerchief. "The bishop himself praised my skills in calligraphy. He said I had a steady hand and a good eye."

"Did he now?" said Brunhilde, "you knew the bishop?"

"Yes," said Sonia, "I was his ward."

"How interesting. Would you say the bishop is a good man?"

Sonia paused. Her hand strayed to a lock of her hair. "Yes," she said, "yes, he is a good man."

"Let me see if I have the right of it," said Lock. "You abducted a Turkish princess in Hungaria. You held her with the intention of ransoming her but you seduced her over a bucket of wine?"

"That was no ordinary wine," Peter shouted.

"Of course, magic wine made by an ancient sorcerer for the king of the Tartars. You fell in love with her and were bringing her back to Eisenberg as your mistress. But after an extraordinary night of confusion and bloodshed you lost her to the abbess of St Hildegard's abbey, who took her through a tunnel under the mountain. You know that this is the tunnel to the abbey because a blind shepherd told you so. Believing you had lost your love you fell into a melancholy that not even the caress of your sensible wife could cure. But when you spoke to the preacher, he told you of Lutheran plans to dissolve the abbey. This fanned the embers of hope in your heart. You could seize the abbey and carry off your love with the sanction of God. You embraced your new religion with zeal. But first you had to crush resistance, which means killing me in public. Do I have the right of it?"

"You have the right of it." Peter slumped into his chair. "You must think me a terrible fool."

"Indeed yes," said Lock.

Peter sat up in his chair, grasping for the handle of his short sword.

"But most understandable," Lock hastened to add, "I was wondering if you had considered a more traditional approach to courtship. If we suppose that the lady is in fact in the abbey, might you not approach the sisters and ask to speak with her? You could woo her. In my experience women like to be wooed."

"What do you know about women?" asked Peter sullenly.

"I know but a little," said Lock, "but enough that it will bode far better for your happiness if you can convince her to come with you willingly. Now if you will consider to hear me out. I have a proposal for a different plan which I hope will be to the benefit of all concerned parties."

"I'm listening," said Peter.

"First," said Lock, "I convert to Lutheranism. Don't look at me like that. It's perfectly reasonable. If the grandmaster of the Teutonic order can convert, so can I. Personally I think Luther makes a lot of sense albeit it is all rather boring. I mean who really believes that the Eucharist transmutes into the actual blood of Christ on being imbibed. But more to the point why does everybody care so much, all of a sudden? Everybody knows that the Church is a den of worldly depravity. That's what makes it appealing. In any case I consider myself already converted. Luther is both moderate and reasonable. I can see you are concerned for your claims on my property. But have no fear. As a sign of my change of faith I shall sign over, by legal contract, all Church property to the noble house of Eisenberg. This will help to strengthen your claim and help with the recognition of your new county with foreign lands. As a sign of your magnanimity for my generosity you will spare my life, and swear me to your service, an oath of which I should be willing to take forthwith. In my service to you I should act as your financial adviser. Money as you know is my business. I shall work tax reforms that shall be needed to refill the state's coffers. The charismatic young preacher can continue to take care of the religious needs of the community, which should keep your wife and his followers happy. Now as concerns your fate. Once we have returned to Eisenberg, you will call off the preparations for attacking the abbey. Instead you shall ride with a small escort and a letter of introduction written by me that will encourage the peaceful handover of the princess. There will be peace in the county and if we are in a position we may assist Ferdinand with his war against the Turks."

"Fantastic," replied Peter. "I can see you are right. I shall accept your oath of allegiance forthwith. But I shall not pardon you yet. I shall set a date four weeks from now, and if you have proved yourself as good as your word, then you shall be pardoned."

"I shall be honoured to give you my oath of allegiance. And I shall be happy to present myself to you in a month's time for your judgement. But before I do I have one more boon to ask of you."

Peter tapped his fingers on his chair. "Go on."

"Before the war began there was an ominous murder. Joseph, Herr Muller's son, was horribly murdered. His body found dismembered beside a stream not far from where we both sit. The death was blamed on Heinrich the Jew, the boy's father in law. Though the accused has since been killed in battle, I'm convinced of his innocence. I ask that you allow me to do justice by apprehending and trying the true murderer."

"On saint Georg's sword I wasn't expecting that. What the hell is the point of it all? The county is riven with war and upheaval. I killed the boy's father in an act of war. The remaining Jews are facing banishment for treason. People have been slain in their hundreds."

Lock felt the acute pain in his wound as he poked the rushes on floor with his toe, his gaze fixed on the ground. He also felt a different kind of pain, and it had nothing to do with cuts and bruises. It was the tearful face of Sonia that haunted him. He heard her last words that she had spoken to him over and over again – *I hope you burn in hell*. He missed her and realised how much he had loved her. And her disappointment and his shame tore through him like a scythe. He raised his gaze to meet Peter's eyes. "I promised the woman I love I would see justice done for her brother's death."

Peter shrugged. "I suppose we must hang murders. If you know the culprit then name him."

"I don't," said Lock, "know the murderer yet but I will discover him."

the 4th October, Day of the First Frost

The level of the river was slowly starting to drop as the unseasonably cold dry weather set in. The maples, poplars, and oaks, which had been green but a few weeks before had now turned yellow, brown, and red. Only the willows spear shaped leaves remained green, while the berries ripened on the old village yew.

Peter had set up his tent and throne in a meadow beside the river and surveyed his troops that stood to attention. Of the five hundred men he had commanded at Mohacs only thirty remained. Their clothes had been washed by the village women, and though faded, their brightly died Flemish hose and Venetian silk tunics made them look appropriately resplendent for the occasion. Each soldier displayed his wealth on his person, with gold and jewelled brooches, rings and pendants. They carried long swords and had muskets slung over their shoulders. Hans bore Peter's standard, a wild boar above crossed tongs and hammer. They may have only a handful of men, but they were veterans, survivors and Peter was proud of them.

On the opposite side of the meadow, the commune elders and yeomen of the former Church lands had gathered to swear fealty to Peter, service in return for protection. The peasants were dressed in drab woollen hose with sheepskin cloaks and boots. They wore their beards long, and their faces were lined and tanned, weathered from wind and rain. They spoke a mixture of Germanic and Ruthenian and smelled of sheep, earth and hopsy ale.

Lock, dressed in one of Herr Muller's finer outfits, stood to Peter's left. Johann stood to his right and scowled. One of Peter's men blew a trumpet, and the first peasant walked forward and knelt before Peter on the frosted ground.

Greta looked sternly across at the eighteen-year-old who was now the captain of her guardsmen. The Lutheran militia may have been slain and the granaries near empty but order must be kept and if that meant recruiting boys and arming them with what weapons the city still possessed then so be it.

"How are our guests, the holly men and women, settling in?"

"Well enough your ladyship," replied the lad, "they have moved into the abandoned north quarter around the square of flower sellers. They have taken to making the repairs with vigour. There have been no reports of stealing and everything has been paid for either in silver or in kind." The lad shifted a little on his chair, proud, but still a little awkward in his breastplate and satin doublet that marked him as a guardsman.

"Go on," prompted Greta, "I can see from your scrunched nose that you have something more to report."

"Well, it's nothing really, my lady. Just oddities really, rumours."

"Oh I love oddities and rumours, go on indulge me."

"Well," said the lad, "I have heard said that they share clothes, and that they also took down the walls between the houses and sleep altogether on the floor. They baptize themselves three times a day. And I have heard that they covert not the smallest possession but hold all things in common."

Light shafted in from the window slit high above them. Sparrows sang in the courtyard. A wooden trap door, bolted from below, led to the turret house, a stone billet built into the castle's wall where Johann had set up his quarters.

"What does he do with you?"

"He talks to me," said Basha, "although it's really more to himself. If I speak it just makes him angry. But sooner or later he gets out his dagger and tells me to strip. And then he just sits there sharpening his weapons and looking at me. Sometimes he threatens me. He says... oh Baba you don't want to know."

"Sure I want to know," Baba licked her lips, precious little else to do in this elevated dungeon, then listen to the depravities of a Christian."

"He says he'll cut my cunt out."

"Yahweh," Baba cursed.

"Sometimes he cuts me on the legs and back, but not deeply. You know I think he's afraid, afraid of Jewish magic maybe. He desires me but he cannot bring himself to touch me. It's terrible madness."

"I suppose that's why he hasn't killed me. But just leaves me here out of sight like a big black spider under an iron cup," said the old woman.

"Baba, don't say such things"

"Shh. hear that? The Christians are returning from their ceremony."

Basha felt a familiar cold dread fall over her. Soon she would be called for.

"What do you think would happen," said Basha sensing the reaction of her granddaughter, "if you told him no."

"Strip," Johann sat in his chair his feet on the table, a fire burning in the hearth. He seemed in an even fouler mood than usual. The festivities had clearly not gone according to his plan.

Basha hesitated. Up until now it had been her only act of defiance.

"Get on with it or I'll cut you bad"

The words rested on Basha's lips, *No*, her hand began to shake. She looked at the rage in Johann's face, the hatred, so much worse than usual. Maybe if she defied him now he would overcome his fear. He would cut her. He would harm her child. Her resolve broke. Just as it had on that first evil night, when she had kissed his boots and he had taken her gold. She went to that unfeeling part of herself, the part where she had let her heart die. She moved mechanically, taking off her hat, letting it drop, unfastening her cloak, letting it drop, unbuttoning her shirt, letting it drop, unbuckling her skirts, letting them drop.

"You whore," Johann spoke under his breath.

A key turned in the lock. The turret house door was shoved open.

Johann startled and turned to face the interruption.

Basha made no move to cover her nakedness.

Manfred Lock, accompanied by one of Peter's soldiers, Hans, entered.

"How the hell did you get in, you son of a bitch?"

"I borrowed the keys from his lordship." Lock's eyes met the dead stare of Basha. Lock showed no expression.

Basha picked up her cloak and covered herself.

"You should have been hung in a cage and fed alive to ravens," said Johann to Lock.

"One can never tell the way that Lady Fortune's wheel will turn," said Lock, "I rather like my new position in the service of his lordship. I did not see you at the Lutheran mass I gave. I read from the book in Germanic. The men rather liked it."

"What do you want? I'm busy."

"So I can see," said Lock. "I shall speak to the point. I intend to have you hung."

"Do you now," said Johann his hand reaching for his dagger. "On what grounds? I have fought for the new faith. I am a nobleman and you are an opportunist and a papist."

"I have a mandate from the count, to prosecute the murderer of Joseph the miller's son. I shall prove your guilt in having killed Joseph and have you hung as a murderer."

"Outrageous," said Johann, but his face was calm. "The Jew killed Joseph. He was seen leaving Eisenberg, heading for the woods with a loaded donkey on the night of the murder. He would stop at nothing to prevent the marriage of his daughter to a godly Christian so he murdered him in cold blood. I was drinking with the city guard. A dozen men can attest to my whereabouts."

Johann's answer surprised Lock. He had expected Johann to react with surprise that Lock was pursuing the matter, or to question, like Peter, the necessity of pursuing a case of murder in the aftermath of a bloody war. Johann's answer was that of someone who had thought, and still thought, carefully about Joseph's death. "I am surprised to hear you talk so confidently about your whereabouts on that specific night more than three months ago. Surely they are the words of a man possessed by guilt?"

Johann spat, "I have a good memory and you can prove nothing. I care naught for his death, but I did not kill the boy."

"Perhaps not, but you have a motive." Lock pointed to Basha who stood covered in her cloak trying to make herself invisible in the corner of the room. "Jealously over the possession of Basha the beautiful. I am going to relieve you of your captive."

Johann stood and drew his sword. "Get out of here you blood sucker. The count swore the Jewesses to me before we even set out. He will keep his word. And let me warn you there is more than one power in Eisenberg and you would do well to watch your back when we return to the city, lest you find a knife in it."

Hans drew his sword.

Lock backed toward the door.

the 15th of October

"See what you can find out," said the abbess to Asra as they watched the sisters gather apples in one of the orchards enclosed by high lichen covered walls. "Find out where the power in the city is, what they plan and when. What are weaknesses are, their strengths are, and anything that might save us from the rumoured dissolution of our order."

"I shall do as you say, Superior," Asra curtseyed.

"Take this with you." The abbess passed a sealed letter to Asra. "It's from one of my new clerks, and is if possible to be delivered to the once bishop of Esienberg, Manfred Lock. I know not what has become of him."

Asra took the letter and slipped it into her sash bag. "I shall leave for the city before nightfall."

"Is there anything more that you require?"

"Yes, Superior," I would require a smock and cloak such that a peasant girl might wear, an old pony such as a broom makers widow might sell. I require soot and dung to blacken my hands and face, and give me a pair of silver spoons for my dowry.

"Do you know anything about Hell?" Hans the long swordsman asked over his shoulder at Manfred Lock, adviser to the count, as they walked beneath the eaves of one of the wooden slate-roofed houses. "Do they teach you about it in bishop school?"

"It's a terrible place," replied Lock. "It begins deep beneath the earth, deeper than the deepest cave. It has nine levels in descending order of evil and torment. There are seven levels for each of the deadly sins, plus two more. The first level, Limbo, is for the good pagans who never heard the word of Christ. It's actually a fairly pleasant place..." Lock paused he had know idea what Lutheran doctrine would mean for the sixth hell. "The sixth level is reserved for heretics, it's a place of excruciating torture. Each sufferer is interned into a flaming tomb, alive but in pain for eternity."

"What's on the bottom of Hell, my lord?"

"The ninth hell. It ss reserved for those guilty of treachery, the worst human sin. There, the sufferers are frozen for eternity, unable to breath encased in ice. And in the very frozen centre of hell, in the centre of the earth itself, is Lucifer, who betrayed God."

Hans shivered. "I knew an old soldier who had met the Devil. I never look into the eyes of a goat. Will you hear my confession?"

Lock did not at first reply as the pair drew closer to the crowded Square of Flower Sellers, where the prophet Luke was preaching. He knew that Lutheranism disavowed the practise of confession, believing that all souls were predestined to their fate.

"Yes," Lock whispered as he stood on tiptoes to peer above the crowd where he could see Luke standing on a barrel, his hand raised toward heaven. "I will hear your confession."

"Hear ye, brothers of Christ," Luke's deep rich voice carried through the plaza. "The Kingdom of God will soon come to us and it shall begin here in Eisenberg. In this year fifteen twenty-six, a child shall be born, that shall be the second Christ. Eisenberg shall become the new Jerusalem. We shall know no hunger. All men shall be equal and there shall be bliss on this earth."

A hurrah ran through the crowd.

Luke stepped down from the barrel, and the excited crowd began to slowly dissipate.

"Come on," said Lock, "let's see if we can talk to him."

The mercenary put his hand on his sword hilt and began to push through the crowd.

A knot of chatting townswomen parted to allow them through.

Lock and Hans found Luke surrounded by some of the pious peasants from the west who had taken refuge in the city. He was speaking to them in hushed tones.

Luke caught Lock's eyes and motioned his people to wait as he stepped forward to greet the ex-bishop.

Lock extended his hand and Luke took it in a firm grip.

"You were good," said Lock.

"You liked it?" the preacher smiled. He was obviously not immune to the sin of vanity.

"I'm quite jealous," replied Lock, "of your conviction and the power of your voice."

"My gratitude," said Luke. He had a warm pleasant face and tousled sandy hair, "but I'm sure you did not come here with an armed body guard to pay me such compliments. How can I assist the advisor to the count?" The last words were spoken in a sneer.

"You are astute," said Lock, "We shall deal to the business forthwith. I have been given a mandate from the count to investigate the murder of Joseph the miller's son." Lock studied the face of the preacher to gauge his reaction.

If the preacher knew anything he hid it well, for his face showed only mild surprise. "I had no idea the count had appointed you sheriff."

"He hasn't. My authority to investigate it is a boon form the lord. It is a personal matter to me and it concerns my honour. May I query you on the matter?"

Luke glanced behind him at the waiting people. "So long as you shall not make me miss my prayers. But I hardly see if I can be of help. I know nothing of the matter."

"No, I thought as much," said Lock, "the only reason why I thought I would speak to you is that you arrived in city around the same time as the boy was killed. It's just an excuse to talk to you really. Do you mind if I ask you about the night that you arrived and what brought you to this land?

A ripple of anger crossed Luke's face. "I hardly see what business it is of yours. But if you must know I was on quest to bring the word of Luther to the Kingdom of Hungaria. I was tricked by bandits who beat me and took all I owned from me. But God led me to Lady Greta's house where she saw fit to show mercy to me and saved me from death."

"Where your mission was at least partly successful as you soon converted the countess into an ardent Lutheran."

"My Apologies," said Luke, "but I have no time for this banter. I must depart. May God be with you." Luke turned his back on Lock and Hans."

"Does the countess know you're not a Lutheran?" Lock called after him.

The preacher paused mid step. "What do you mean?"

"Adult baptism? The ends of days in Eisenberg? All men shall be equal on this earth? Far too radical for Luther. Tell me, what do the Lutheran princes do to Anabaptists?"

"You're a liar," said Luke.

Peter left the city, riding with twenty-nine of his mercenaries. Lock had begged Peter to leave him at least one man, so Hans, who was on good terms with the bishop, had remained in the city. Muskets were slung over their shoulders, their swords hung at their waists and their slashed silk doublets shone in the morning sun. A group of women waved them off from the city wall, but Greta was not among them.

His wife, mused Peter, had seemed distant and preoccupied. When he had told her that he was leaving for a few days to seek solace at the schloss, she had simply nodded and encouraged him without question. He was grateful for Greta. She had been an able ruler in his absence, rationing flour and maintaining order. But the thing that had most consumed Peter's thoughts was how to reconcile Nuray with Greta. He had decided he would bring Nuray to the schloss and set her up there with servants and guard, and spend his time between the schloss, and the city. *But what if Greta decided she wanted to stay at the schloss?* He hadn't worked out all the details. First he had to woo her. Then, once she was in his possession he could work something out. The thought of having her once again sent shiver of anticipation running upward from his stomach to his heart.

He tapped his saddlebags where the letter from Lock to the abbess sat in its leather casement. The breeze was cool on his face as the horses' hooves rang out on the cobbled road. They would ride west for a few miles until they were well alone on the forest road, then they would head south, across country, breaking camp for the night in the hills. The next morning they would skirt the open land around the city as they looped back to connect with the South Road, from which they would make haste toward the Abbey of Saint Hildegard the Virgin.

Asra prepared herself for her mission. First she stripped herself of her fine Turkish clothes, and applied the mixture of soot and dung to her body. She then pulled on the grey flax shift, and platted her hair. She belted the shift with her old sash from which hung her jewelled dagger and her sturdy leather bag. She clasped the cloak with a plain iron broach and pulled the pointed hood over her head. She combed the pony's hair and sang to it before loading the wiling beast with the brooms and provisions. She led the Pony from the stables and paused to consider her reflection in a sunlit pail of water. She was as invisible as she could be.

The clocks of the church tower struck six and the sound of bells rang through the city startling a flock of starlings which rose like a cloud from the pointed, dark, slate roofs. The gatekeeper stepped out of the gatehouse and onto the parapet as he prepared to close the gate. The last of the women had returned from the orchards laden with fruit for the morrow's market, and the evening light lit the fields of the Eisen Valley with a deep red. It was a beautiful cold autumn evening. The

South Road wound through the gentle country, flanked by fruiting plums until it disappeared in the blushing haze of woods that coated the foothills of the southern mountains. The scene was animated by a flock of storks that flew southward, across the gatekeepers view. If he were a painter, the man mused, he should like to paint that scene. It was a wondrous thing the way a painter could capture a landscape, immortalise that moment.

The sound of hooves on cobbles drew the gatekeeper out of his revere and he turned as a rider approached from within the city. He was cloaked, his hood obscured his face and he rode at a fair speed. He kept his head down and gave no acknowledgment to the gatekeeper who watched him as he galloped through the open gate and rode away to the east along the south road.

Lock couldn't sleep. Instead he paced his room, pausing every once and a while to cut another slice of bread and cheese. He had appropriated one of the more intact houses in the old Jewish district and spent his first allowance granted on him by Peter to hiring a young widow as a housekeeper. The woman was comely and Lock had considered whether she might be persuaded to share his bed. He was, he supposed, now that he was Lutheran, eligible to marry, a side effect of his conversion that he had not at first considered. He further conjectured that his new status as an eligible bachelor may have brought with it unforeseen pitfalls. Back when he had been bishop and before that a student no lover had expected Lock to marry them. It had been good honest sin from the get go.

On the other hand it seemed that whatever the religious beliefs of the people, dissolute and licentious behaviour was rapidly on the rise. People were kissing, nay nuzzling, on the street. Just a few hours earlier Lock had seen a man, one of the zealot migrants, caressing and embracing two women who clearly wore nothing beneath their shifts and skirts. Rumours had been abounding of religious gatherings that mixed drink with religion and descended thereafter into orgies. And it was not confined to the religious zealots that had flooded the city. Women who had previously been of good character were indulging in the great moral loosening. Lock supposed the sexual liberation taking hold had something to do with the frequency with which Lord Death stalked the city. He had read how in times of plague, when corpses piled up in shallow graves, had precipitated an air of desperate celebration, feasts and wild abandon.

Once Lock would have been intrigued by the moral laxness and taken the opportunity himself to glut his earthly pleasures, as he had done in those Halcyon days in the Pope's court in Rome. But Lock was a changed man and the moral loosening only served to sadden him. Not because of any newly discovered righteousness of faith, nor because he begrudged the people their pleasures, but because when he thought of lust and love his mind inevitably led him to think of Sonia, and he would feel the pain in his scared scrotum. He would muse on the look of anger at his betrayal on her face. He would wonder where she was and his heart would hurt worse then his wound. He would see her in his mind's eye, hear her voice and he would cry. It was a slow heartbreak and the only way he could dull the pain was to pursue his case to find the killer of Joseph. It gave him something to occupy his restless mind and quiet his screaming heart. It was something he could do for her. He had an inkling now of the truth and, if he was right, it pertained to much more than the life thread of a single man.

Lock opened the shutters and let the cool night air enter his room. He needed something to take his mind off the loops it kept leading him in. He lit a candle and picked up one of the only books left in his possession, the Journeys of Brother William. He began to read.

The candle had burned to a stub and the flame was beginning to gutter. Lock reread the lines. *It was around this time that I discovered the works of Saint Hildegard, herself. Not only was she an accomplished philosopher and theologian, but a great mystic. Her work, Visitations of the Angels, tells of a series of mystical visions and apocalyptic prophecies. My days of peace and study were however drawing to a close, as my lover and patron, the abbess, told me that she was with child. Little did I know it, but this would herald the end of those glorious years spent in that heavenly place.*

The candle's flame shuddered and died. The room went dark. Lock closed the book. It was an unnatural hour to be awake and he was about to remove his clothes to finally try and find some sleep, when he heard a creak on the stairs. Perhaps it was just the house creaking as old houses did, but Lock's brushes with Lord Death had made him weary. He slipped quietly to his feet and crept to the wall where the sword he had taken to carrying about with him hung. There was another louder creek, and Lock saw a dim light seep from beneath the door. Somebody was indeed climbing the stairs to his room and wished not to be heard. Lock flattened himself against the wall and watched as the lockless door was pushed open with a violent shove.

A man rushed into the room Holding a lantern and sword. His hair and beard were ragged.

Lock put his leg out. The man cursed as he sprawled onto the floor. Lock considered stabbing him, but fear and squeamishness of killing got the better from him. He ran down the stairs and out the door while his would be murderer was still picking himself up.

the next day

Peter emerged from the tree line on to the South Road, several hours after dawn. It was a great relief to himself and his company to have reached the road. They had had to walk the horses along the thin winding trails of swine herders and occasionally cut their way through bristling hawthorn bushes. The road itself was not much, uncobbled and just wide enough for a wagon or two knights to ride abreast. The stony mountain soil did however offer good grip for the horses' hooves, and prevented the road from becoming too rutted.

"Do you know where we are my Lord," asked one of the mercenaries.

"Certainly," replied the count pointing with a gloved finger along the road that began to wind steeply up a wooded hill. "He travelled this road on our journey from the Pass of Eagles. On the other side of that ridge is Hermit's Valley. The road runs beside a stream and there is a fair meadow beside it. There is an abandoned hermitage there where we can rest and water the horses."

As the company ascended the ridge the beech and oaks gave way to birch, rowan, and pine. The forest seemed to glow with red berries and yellowing leaves. At length they arrived at Hermit's Valley and at the old hermitage. It was a ramshackle collection of abandoned wood and stone buildings, a house with a makeshift roof, a storehouse, stables for animals and a stone chapel. Gnarled and overgrown apple and pear trees grew in and around the buildings, beyond which stretched the meadow. Peter had just sat down to a cup of wine and a honeyed dumping, when the sentry called out to him. "My lord you had best come and look."

Peter cursed, threw down the wine, and rose.

"What do you make of that, my lord?"

Peter stared down the road before them. In the distance, where it descended from the wooded slopes, people were emerging. A merchant caravan?" asked Peter.

The sentry shook his head. "Look at the way they are marching, no riders among them, but I think I can see pikes."

Peter stared as more of them emerged. "By the teeth of Devil you're right. We must find out who they are."

"Lord, look." Another mercenary caught Peter's arm and pointed back at the road they had come. Another group of pikemen were emerging from the trees and moving to block any retreat.

"Ready your muskets," Peter ordered.

Turnip Nose led his column of pikemen from the front. Once they had all been peasant lads. Now they were soldiers of God. They were dressed in simple undyed shifts and carried pikes of ash and cudgels of plum. They were survivors of wars in the west and had marched through many lands to get here. They were hardened by Fortune and unafraid of Death for they knew they were destined for the Lord God's Kingdom.

The knot of horsemen advanced down the road to meet them. At a hundred paces they dismounted and formed a line of musketmen.

"Halt." A man who Turnip Nose supposed was the count of Eisenberg rode forward to meet him. "I am the count of Eisenberg these are my lands. I demand to know who marches in arms on my road."

The pikeman held up his hand and the column stopped its advance. He then stepped forward as if he would address the nobleman, but then turned his back on him and faced his troops. "Do you smell that?" he shouted, "It's the reek of the Devil's shit, coming strait out of his arse in the form of this old man's mouth."

The pikemen laughed.

Peter felt his blood boil, "Surrender yourselves and you shall be spared."

"Your mother," said Turnip Nose, "was ploughed by a toad. You better run old man. Because you're about to meet the Devil in Hell." He turned back to his pikemen. "Kill all nobles."

"Kill all nobles," the pikemen chorused in reply.

"What are we to do?" one of the mercenaries replied as Peter returned from the parley.

"Kill all those sons of witches," said the count.

"We are out numbered six to one," said another soldier.

"Six dirty farmers to one of the finest soldiers in Christendom. I call that food for poets."

The pikemen advanced in a tight formation.

The mercenaries fired a volley of muskets. The volley was well directed and several pikemen fell. But with only thirty men the volley lacked the volume to halt the enemy advance.

"Prepare to charge," ordered Peter.

The landsknecht threw down their muskets and drew their long swords. The weapons were designed for breaking apart ranks of pikemen, and that was their expertise. The mercenaries dodged the outstretched pikes and impacted with the enemy. Their swords could be held by the handle with two hands and swung in wide arcs or held by the ricasso, the unsharpened bottom of blade to shorten the sword's length in close fighting. First they used them in powerful cleaving arcs and they cut, sliced, severed and skewered their attackers and the bodies quickly piled up around them. It was a devastating attack.

Peter paused in the work of slaughter to pull his sword out of a man's ribs. He felt exhilaration and the sweetness of vengeance as he looked around for the man in with a turnip shaped nose He would kill him next. Ordinarily, he thought, he should have already won. The force of the attack should have sent the enemy fleeing. But they were a strange enemy they seemed possessed, without fear, and they cried out as they died for God to take them, and that His Kingdom was near.

Georg was the first fall, too slow in withdrawing his sword from a man's chest he was bludgeoned by a cudgel. The enemy pressed forward. The landsknecht dropped their long swords and drew their short swords, but one by one they were torn down by weight of numbers, or skewered on pikes.

Peter cut the throat of the man in front of him, but the dead man gushing blood was held upright by the force of bodies, pressing the dead man's face into his own. Peter stumbled backward, tripped on a rock and fell onto his back. *I'm going to die,* he thought, and as he felt a pike pierce the skin of his chest he thought not of Nuray and the night when they had drunk the wine of dreams and she had transformed before his eyes into a monstrous cat. The words of her prophesy rang through his mind, *you will die with a sword in your hand.*

"You wanted to see me." Greta was flanked by two young halberdiers, dressed in the livery of the house of Eisenberg. She kept her face deliberately cold and still, as she sat in the parlour of what had once been Lock's house.

The man who bowed before her had changed since she had last seen him. He seemed older, less fat and less arrogant. But he was still irritatingly ingratiating. His speech sounded as if it bordered on sarcasm and he still spoke with a knowing superiority, as much as he tried to hide it, which made Greta want to run him through with her dagger. This was the man who had been in ultimate command when Felix the black monk had massacred the nobles and the townsfolk. For that she would never forgive Lock. That he had weaselled his way out of execution by his faux conversion, which made a mockery out of the true Lutheran vision, was a bad enough. That he could now saunter before her in audience, knowing that he was under the full protection of her husband was hardly to be believed but his trial was still due. He had not yet been pardoned and Greta would do her best to see him hang.

"I fear for my safety," said Lock.

"Don't we all," replied Greta, "Fever has broken out in the city, and we have not the physicians and the infirmaries to deal with the sick."

Lock felt a grudging respect for the countess. She was an able and determined administrator, much more so than Peter. Lock felt certain that if it were not for Greta the city would have fallen into anarchy. She kept the wall manned and the city patrolled. Looters and thieves had been arrested. Taxes had been collected and much of Lock's previous wealth had been melted down and minted into coins by the iron guild. Greta had drafted many of the city's widows into work, cleaning out the sewage trenches, digging graves and repairing houses. Even so, Lock could see that worries lay heavy on Eisenberg's de facto ruler. The death of the king and the fall of Hungaria had combined with the collapse of the Jewish trading network to cut the city off from trade and no merchants had visited the city since its Lutheran ascendancy. There was now a range of shortages from cloth to salt. Most of the miners were dead and the mines remained closed. Only one iron guilt master, remained alive, and Eisenberg had little to trade even if merchants came. The city was filled with foreign religious zealots, and though grain had been brought in from Muhlborg, it was hardly enough, and the prospect of famine lurked in the times to come. Many artisans and specialists had also perished creating a shortage of tailors, physicians, turners, masons, painters, and tanners.

"Somebody made an attempt on my life last night."

"Did you report it to the captain of the guard?"

"You want me to report an attempt on my life to captain Johann? With all likelihood he is behind the attack. I wondered if I may be allowed to stay in some discreet room of your house until the day of my trial. It seems to be the safest place in the city at the moment."

"I think it unlikely, as all the rooms are accounted for. Look here, you may have my husband's favour. And when he returns I am sure that he will offer you lodgings to your liking. But until that time you will make your own arrangements for your safety." Greta having so dismissed Lock felt instantly better. In truth she didn't morn Peter's decision to seek a retreat at the schloss. He had left her with a free hand to administer Eisenberg and she liked to do so unimpeded by his meddling. The lord count had seemed most preoccupied since his return from Muhlborg and had paid her little attention. Besides Peter's absence made it easier for her to spend time with her lover, Luke. She felt good and that made her a little generous. "But you do have my curiosity. You believe Johann was behind the attempt on your life. What brings you to think so?"

"I believe," said Lock, "that it is to do with the investigation."

"Investigation? Oh yes the murder of Joseph the miller's son. A most odd thing to pursue amid all the death we are surrounded by. How is that going?"

"It goes well and yet not so well. I can almost grasp something yet it is shadowy and indistinct. When I try to grasp it, it dissipates. Tell me, you knew Joseph did you not?"

"How did you know?"

Lock shrugged, "A hunch."

Greta sighed, and roiled her eyes. "Yes I did know him. The gamekeeper introduced him to me. He played beautifully on the pipes. We used to employ him to entertain sometimes. He knew the Travellers and would bring them to our court."

"I heard he was a man both lovely and virtuous, beloved by man and beast alike. Would you not like to see justice done to his killer?"

"I would," replied Greta. "Now get out, I have much to do."

The halberdiers stirred and lowered their halberds.

Lock bowed and hastily retreated.

Asra rode her pony following the mountainous South Road toward Eisenberg. The road from the abbey had been steep, treacherous and unfit for wagons. The heavy summer rain had bought slips that had consumed whole sections of it. She had been kept awake the previous night by the bellows of stags and the yelps of jackals. The trail had its beauty – the open meadows were rich with crickets, bees, spiders, snakes, and autumn flowers, while larks and song thrushes flitted through the trees that were a magnificent sea of red and gold that was beautiful and unfamiliar. She kept her mind occupied by singing the melancholic women's songs she had learned in the harem. They were songs of love, but a love that was ever denied to a harem girl.

At length she came to a meadow that had clearly been a camp for a large number of people. The grass was flattened where they had slept. The surrounding woods had been plundered for fuel. But other than burned down fire pits and shallow latrines, the people had left little for Asra to identify them, though she supposed they travelled for the most part on foot, for there was scant evidence of horses. She considered leaving the road, but seeing the steep and treacherous slopes of the hills she thought better of it. "Who would harm a poor peasant girl," she said to the pony and continued cautiously on her way.

She smelt the battlefield before she saw it. And when she did arrive she swiftly led her pony off the road and waited in the lee of a boulder to see if any living soul was still around. The pony grazed on a juicy sow thistle. Crows and harriers alighted on the ground. The thrum of flies attracted to the dead meat grew louder. Asra yelled out the name of God. It echoed in the hills. But no response came. It seemed the blood soaked ground was abandoned. Asra left the pony grazing and moved out to investigate the battlefield.

Whoever had been victorious had tried to give the dead some kind of Christian burial. But the soil was nothing but a thin gravely layer above the rock. The result was a mound piled in front of a large wooden cross, held in place by a cairn of boulders. The soil barely covered the bodies and the crows and harriers were scratching at the mound. In an around the hermitage Asra found little of note, a burned out fire, a pile of half butchered horses that had had the choicest meat cut from them and a pile of stinking excrement.

Eventually her curiosity got the better of her, and she returned to the burial mound. She was a believer, one of the prophet's faithful, and she had no fear of Christian ghosts. She chased away the birds and used a staff to lever the bodies off the mound. Each seemed to have been buried as he had fallen, in plain, bloodied peasant shifts not unlike her own. They belonged to men who took little care of their appearance, with hair uncombed and beards untrimmed. The only thing she found of interest was a little wooden sheep attached to a string, this she put in her bag.

As she dug deeper she began to come across other bodies, men that were dressed in colourful silks and wools, and boasting a variety of trimmed beards and oiled moustaches. Their buttons and broaches had been cut from their clothes. All looked like strong and violent men. *What kind of soldiers would not also loot such valuable clothes? The kind that doesn't want them.* Among the dead was a man dressed more richly than the others, his cloak still clasped with a heavy iron broach that had perhaps been left for the low value of the metal. She held the broach up to the light and recognised the insignia of the house of Eisenberg. Asra looked at the dead man's face. She was sure it was the body of the count. She took the broach and put it into her sash bag. A cold wind blew from the mountains and Asra shivered. It was time to leave.

It was some hours later when Asra arrived at the soldier's camp, a collection of tents and wagons, arranged on a meadow between the road and a stream. Whistling softly to herself, Asra as bravely and innocently as could manage, continued on her way.

A sentry, who was dressed much as the bodies had been, simple and rough, stopped her. He carried a cudgel as long as Asra was tall, and as thick as her thigh at its end. "Who are you?" he demanded.

"A good and simple girl," Asra replied in her best peasant dialect. "I was the wife of a broom maker but he was possessed by a terrible little devil, and, bless his soul, he was taken by Lord Death. Now I am to take what I have and join my brother in Eisenberg, where God willing I will take a new husband. I can offer two silver spoons as my dowry."

The soldier gave Asra's dirty face an assessing look. He then glanced back toward the camp, where the interaction on the road was attracting the interest of others. "You'd better come with me to King Turnip."

Asra followed the soldier through the camp, where men turned to stare at her with wolfish looks. At length she was brought before King Turnip. He was dressed like the other men, different only in that he wore a carved wooden sheep on a silver chain. The man might have been handsome were it not for his ragged appearance and bulbous broken nose.

The sentry introduced Asra.

"You are looking for a husband?" said King Turnip.

"That is so," said Asra who fell on to her knees, "I have but one pony, and a pair of silver spoons as dowry. And I should be grateful to any good man who would claim me as his own."

King Turnip stepped forward, cupped her cheek and chin in his large calloused hand, lifted her head and gave her face a critical appraisal. He then lifted her arm and felt her wrist. "You're a little thin," he said, "but I'll wed you nonetheless."

"Oh thank you," said Asra, "I had no idea I would be so fortunate as to meet my husband on the road."

King Turnip gave her a lopsided grin. "You should know that we are brothers of Christ. We covert nothing, not even our wives. If you are to be my wife you must be baptised a fresh, as a sister of Christ."

Asra rose and curtseyed. "I know only that a wife must always obey her husband, whatever his wishes," she replied. "I ask only that I may first visit my brother in Eisenberg, to ask his permission, for that would only be right. You must agree. I shall leave you with my dowry as a sign of good faith."

King Turnip scrunched his face, and Asra thought for a moment that he might refuse her, but he didn't.

two days later

Basha and Baba did not know why they had been summoned. They sat in the parlour in awkward silence while Johann paced the room. It was different from his usual routine of threatening and tormenting Basha. Something was about to happen, and Basha felt a rising sensation of excitement and terror.

At length there was a knock on the door and Johann rose to open it. Six men stepped inside. Among them was the Lutheran prophet who had been seen in the summer preaching in the Square of Flower Sellers. The others with him were wild looking men, unshaven and dressed in ragged clothes, yet they carried themselves with pride despite the apparent poorness of their condition.

The preacher's face had a warm friendly appearance and Basha could not help but feel her spirits rise as his eyes made contact with hers. "We have come for the Jewesses," he said.

Johann, his hand resting on his sword pommel, eyed the preacher with suspicion. "And you swear you can remove the witchcraft and curses from them?"

"The power of Jewish devils is no match for the power of God. When I have finished with her you may do with her whatever you will without fear of witchcraft."

Johann rubbed his hands with undisguised anticipation.

"But it is certainly beyond my ability to dispel her evil powers while she is still with child. For now her power is at its strongest. But by the look of her you shall not have to wait long and I must bring her into my care forthwith, for I must begin the invocations needed to cleanse her spirit."

"Very well," Johann nodded toward the women, "I've bound their wrists nice and tight."

"You are a thoughtful man," replied the preacher, "I trust you will use the time to organise the expedition to the abbey."

"If only God willed it," replied Johann, "The countess won't let me take the city guard. And Peter has in any case forbidden it. I have no men."

"God does will it," said the preacher gently. "The wealth of the abbey belongs to the new Kingdom of Jerusalem. Leave the countess to me. She is a sister of Christ. And you need not worry for men, for on the South Road you shall be joined by an army of God so nothing can stand before you and your destiny. As for the count, I tell you in confidence that you shall not hear much from him again. Take your guns and march south."

Johann smiled "I shall look forward to wetting my sword between the legs of the young nuns."

The preacher wrinkled his nose in disgust at the captain's crudeness.

Asra rode her Pony down into the lowlands of the Eisen Valley. The only change she made to her disguise was to wear around her neck the wooden sheep, given to her by King Turnip. She travelled through fertile lands of gardens, fields, orchards and hamlets. The road became wider and cobbled. The village folk paid her little attention and at length she drew near to the East Gate of the city. Here, she was joined on the road by a group of women. They were clearly of the same cast as King Turnip, her husband to be. They were barefoot and with wild hair. They carried baskets of mushrooms.

"Blessings sister of Christ," they greeted her as they recognised the wooden sheep around her neck. They clasped their hands in hers.

Asra returned the greeting.

One of the women nodded. "All the peoples are equal before Him. It is only the love we feel for Him within our hearts that shall redeem us. And He shall walk among us again and the Kingdom of Jerusalem shall be made afresh."

The group, in a mumbling chant, repeated the last sentence.

Asra hastened to join them.

Everybody laughed.

"We are known as the three mice," said one of the sisters. "This is Brown Mouse, on account of her brown hair. This is Hungry Mouse on account of her appetite, and, I, they call Good Mouse because I never forget to say my prayers. What do you they call you?"

Asra looked around for inspiration, her eyes settled on the collection of brooms she had loaded on the Pony. "The call me Sister Broom, she said, because I am a fair hand at making them."

"A fine skill," said Good Mouse, "my own father was a broom maker."

"Are you coming to the House of the Lamb tonight," asked Brown Mouse.

"I should like to," said Asra. "I have come from the battle in the south but decided to leave the men and make my way to the city. To join the sisters of Christ here."

"Is it not a fine city?" said Good Mouse. "So strange to think that this town of all the others is destined to be the new Jerusalem."

"I heard of the battle," said Hungry Mouse. "It is the beginning of the coming of the Kingdom. The wicked, the covetous and the rich shall be destroyed. You must come with us to the House of the Lamb. And tell us all about what happened."

Lock sat on a stool outside the Kobold's Breaches. He had taken up residence in the tavern solely because it was the place where Hans the mercenary also billeted. If he were going to be attacked again it would do to have a sturdy fighter within shouting distance. Lock sipped his beer and grimaced at the taste of the week bitter ale. It was surely a drink for peasants. He looked up from his ale and noticed that a ragged looking boy about eight years old was looking at him.

"Give me a groat and I'll clean your boots," said the boy.

"I have no need for clean boots," replied Lock. "But you can have a groat for what it's worth to you in anycase."

The boy approached and Lock dropped a copper groat into his dirty waiting fingers. The boy promptly deposited the groat into a large pocket sewn into his shift.

"You may go," replied Lock as the boy lingered in front of him.

"You're the bishop aren't you?" said the boy.

"I was the bishop," Lock replied, "now I'm just a bookkeeper."

"What's a bookkeeper?" asked the boy.

"I count things and write the numbers in a book."

"I can count." It was a second child that had spoken, a ragged girl about the same age as the boy, and holding the hand of a much younger child. "Can I have a groat too?"

"What are three twos?" asked Lock.

The girl scrunched up her face and counted on her fingers. "Six."

"That was easy," grumbled Lock as he fished another groat from his pouch.

"Is bookkeeping a good job?" asked the boy.

"Oh very good," said Lock, "It requires a good head, you see."

"Better than a blacksmith?" The boy looked sceptical.

"Much better than a blacksmith," said Lock sternly, "no risk of burning oneself."

"Do you know any stories asked the boy?"

"I know one or two."

"Any stories about Egypt?" asked the girl, "I know all about Egypt."

"Is that so?" said Lock.

"Yes," said the girl, "the Egyptian told me himself, and he's been all around the world."

"Who's this Egyptian?" said Lock.

The girl was about to speak but the boy nudged her in the rips and she shut her mouth.

"Mimi hungry," said the young child.

Lock sighed and dug into his pouch for more groats.

As the boy led Lock through the streets of the old Jewish quarter a whole gang of ragged barefoot children joined them. The Jewish quarter had not been rebuilt after the battle and had the worst damage. Many of the houses were burnt out ruins, nothing more than piles of ash, slate and charred wooden frames. A pair of swine grazed on the flowers that had grown on the ruins. The children seemed at home here and shouted to each other as they danced along the abandoned street plying Lock with questions.

At length they came to a house less damaged than the others. It was cone shaped, and built of stone and mortar, and abutted the cliff of the Eisenberg hill. The children led Lock through the broken door and into a crooked stone parlour. There sitting in the corner in a bed of blankets and cushions was Jango, Prince of the Travellers. Lock recognised him from the night before the battle. Heinrich the Jew had introduced him as his son. Lock remembered him as confident and handsome. He remembered the glint of his pistols and the swish of his silks. But the young man before him now was changed forever. His leg had been amputated and the left side of his face and body was badly burned.

Jango smiled and greeted the children that crowded around him, and grimaced at Lock.

"Come to hang me," said Jango. "I won't stop you."

"The day I hang one of Heinrich's sons is the day I stop drinking wine."

Jango paused to stare at Lock, "You're the bishop. How come they didn't kill you?"

"It's a long story," said Lock.

"I'm not going anywhere," said Jango.

Lock seated himself on the stone floor and began his story. Some of the children stayed to listen. Others left to play on the street.

When Lock reached the part of his story when Sonia, Baba, Basha and the brigands rescued him, Jango sat up in his seat. "Basha is alive."

"It is true," said Lock, "She lives still, but I fear she is in great danger." Lock told Jango of the battle of the Muhlbog, Basha's recapture by Johann and his own subsequent entry into Peter's service.

"That bastard," Jango reached for his sword, "take me to him and I'll kill him."

"I too wouldn't mind seeing the captain of the guard die," said Lock "and I too want to save mother, daughter and child, but I have not the power to demand that Johann hand her over. Nor can you, a rabble of children and I storm the city barracks. But I wonder if you could not help her in another way. When last I saw Heinrich before he died, I asked him about Joseph's murder. He told me that the Travellers knew something, that one of the wives of Zafir, your mother, I believe, told him that he would be found beside his father's farm, and so he was. Now forgive me that I do not believe in fortune telling. Tell me what do you know of Joseph's fate."

Jango slumped back onto the bed and sighed. "I should have told her long ago. I only wanted to protect her."

Luke and Greta sat side by side in the grand bed, nestled among the crumpled sheets and sheepskins. It was getting colder.

Greta pulled on of the blankets around her breasts and shoulders. "You want half the city guard to attack the abbey? I must disagree." Greta had been happy to receive Luke. She loved him and she was tired of hiding her love. She wanted to walk with Luke through the streets, to sit beside him at feasts, to laugh with him, to greet lords and ladies with him on her arm. She was tired of playing the part of Peter's neglected wife. Her love for Luke was so strong that she had considered poisoning Peter. But she had inwardly berated herself for the terrible thought. "The sisters have done nothing to hurt us. Besides, Peter has called off the attack."

Luke reached his hand out to Greta's, working his fingers into her clenched fist. "I'm sorry, Greta. I should have told you when first I heard. But I didn't want the news to darken your mood. Peter is dead."

"What?" Greta turned to face Luke. She felt no sorrow. She had already grieved for him when she believed him dead at Mohacs. Instead she felt relief and hope clouded with disbelief. *How many times had Peter cheated Lord Death?* "How do you know?"

Brigands attacked the Lord Peter and his band on the South Road. They robbed them of their possessions and murdered them. Their bodies were discovered by a brother of Christ who was taking that road to join our community."

"What was he doing on the South Road?" Greta murmured.

"The brother found a letter on his body, signed by Lock. It seems that Peter was infatuated with a Turkish Princess who is a captive of the abbess. Peter was on his way to make his case for her handover."

In truth Greta had been too consumed with her own infidelities that it had not crossed her mind that Peter was himself similarly inclined. Greta wriggled over in the bed to snuggle into Luke. "My love, perhaps it is time to stop hiding, to take us into the light."

Luke nodded. "Perhaps you should accompany me to the House of the Lamb. Together we shall break bread among the people of Christ."

"Oh yes," said Greta, "Let us go to the House of the Lamb tonight."

Asra went with the women to the House of the Lamb. It was really a block of houses, but all the internal walls and divisions had been knocked down, leaving a skeleton of pillars and beams. The affect was rather like that of a large smoky barn. A wooden gallery ran along the side of building where the second story would once have been. The floor was covered in a thick layer of straw and rushes. A heard of goats were penned in on one side of the house, while cats and chickens ran amok in the area that Asra supposed was for dining, as it was filled with rows of tables and stools. Cooking fires and ovens burned next to a collection of work tables on which were piled various foods, apples, turnips, course greens, and bread. It was here that the women headed and deposited their baskets of mushrooms.

"Was there anything that you coveted?" asked Hungry Mouse.

Asra, not knowing quite what was meant, shook her head.

"My skirts were what I found difficult to give over to the community." The girl happily chatted on. "I had a red Flemish skirt. It was my mothers. I still get to wear it some times. But I remember the first time I saw another sister wearing it... well I had to punish myself for my covertness. But when I finally let it go I felt the most amazing sense of holiness."

"There must have been something that you coveted," piped up Brown Mouse. "I had a silver locket. But after I gave it over to the community I released what a weight it had been sitting there around my neck."

"Yeah go on tell us," said Good Mouse. "You must have coveted something."

Asra thought about the question. In truth she had never really felt that she had possessed anything. She barely remembered her Christian parents and at the harem they had had fine things, jewels and clothes, but she had never really thought of them as her own. When she had become a spy and had become rich, she had thought little more of the wealth she had accumulated, than as a means to an end. It was power that she desired, perhaps because she had been so powerless. Her mind drifted to what she carried on her, her sash bag in which she carried the girl's letter to the Bishop Lock.

The girls noted her gaze and the hand that reached toward her bag.

"That's a nice sash bag," said Hungry Mouse.

"What have you got in there?" asked Brown Mouse.

"No secrets between sisters," intoned Good Mouse.

"It... in it are things I need to show to..." Asra thought desperately about who these strange people might have as a leader, "to somebody important."

"To Brother Luke?"

"Yes."

Hungry Mouse withdrew her hand.

"He'll be along later," said the first girl, "I'm sure he'll want to speak with you."

For the rest of the day Asra stayed with the three girls. First they had joined others for prayer, in a kind of area for bathing. It was really a collection of big water barrels clustered around an open fire. The women had then stripped and immersed themselves in the cold water. After they had dressed and warmed themselves by the fire the girls showed Asra the sleeping quarters, which were at the far end of the house. It was heated and lit by several open fires and had a raised wooden floor covered in straw, rushes, sheepskins and goatskins. There were even a number of pillows, cushions flax sheets and woolen blankets. Nobody was asleep at that hour, but the sleeping quarters were nevertheless busy. Women worked sewing, spinning and mending cloth. Some men were cutting firewood and feeding the fires. But others drank what Asra supposed was beer from a range of cups and bowls. Men and women snuggled together in groups quietly kissing and caressing in the shadows.

"I wonder what man I shall lie with tonight," said Brown Mouse. "I hope it will be Eldred, I know I mustn't covert him, but he is gentle."

"I'll be happy with any man at all tonight." said Hungry Mouse, "there seems to be many more sisters than brothers these days."

"I want to lie with Brother Luke," said Good Mouse, a look of determination on her face. "I have before you know. He is amazing, so close to God."

Asra felt creeping fear. *Would these girls expect her to join them in some kind of cultic ritual that involved sharing lovers? How would she respond?* She was at once repulsed and intrigued. She had not lain with a man since she had left the sultan. She was not averse to fulfilling her pleasures with a stranger. But she liked to do so on her own terms and in a private place of her choosing, not in a great barn with a hundred onlookers.

The girls left the sleeping quarters and worked to prepare food for the community, cutting vegetables into large cauldrons of spiced and salted pottage. Gradually the dining area began to fill as groups of people took their place at the rows of tables. Asra stayed with the cooking group, trying not be noticed. Other women delivered cups of ale, and the hubbub of Germanic rose louder. Soon Asra was scooping pottage into bowls. Other women took the bowls and began to deliver them to the tables.

Asra and her party were relieved of their jobs and took their own turn to sit at a table. They were joined by a group of three men and one woman. The two groups were familiar with each other and they shared some joke that Asra did not understand. Conversation, however, quickly moved to her, and Good Mouse filled the others in on Asra's story. Asra was grateful to have finished her bowl. She'd never liked pottage and was wondering if she would ever eat her favorite lamb head stew again, when a hush descended on the hall.

"He's here," whispered Brown Mouse. "Brother Luke."

"And look who he has bought with him," whispered Hungry Mouse.

Good Mouse rose to help clear the bowls from the table.

Asra watched Brother Luke. He was handsome, with a broad friendly face, and sandy curly hair his clothes were nice but he wore no jewels and did not carry a sword. At his side was a rather beautiful brown haired woman who wore a fine dress inlaid with gold. The couple took their seats at the head of a table. Brother Luke and the woman were positioned in such a way that they could look right at Asra. Asra's met first the woman's gaze and then the man's. They broke eye contact and when Asra looked again. Brother Luke was talking to Good Mouse. Their eyes met again, he beckoned her to approach.

Brown Mouse nudged her. "Go on, I expect Brother Luke will

want to see what you have for him."

Her heart racing Asra stood up and walked around the table. People shuffled in their stools to let her pass. She curtseyed to Luke and his lady, and he indicated that she should sit in an empty seat at their table. The woman had a stern and regal appearance. And Asra recognized her as a member of the nobility. Her heart went out to the woman. She seemed more out of place than Asra, and she knew it. She was fidgeting uncomfortably and did not know where to rest her eyes. Her distaste for the pottage seemed to outweigh her hunger for she did not eat, but drank ale with an expression of little pleasure. It was only love thought Asra that could have brought her here.

"Who are you?" asked Luke.

Asra inclined her head, as she had learned to do at the abbey, "I have been at the battle in the south, Brother Luke."

"Battle in the south?" the woman repeated with interest.

A little wave of irritation passed over Luke's face. I think I had better have a word with you alone," said, Luke.

The woman looked like she was going to protest. Luke murmured something conciliatory to her that Asra did not catch.

Asra followed Luke through a small door behind the kitchen and out into a courtyard filled for most part with sheep.

"Tell me who you are and what you are doing here, no riddles."

Asra considered attacking the man. She had a dagger strapped to her waist beneath her skirt. But the man was strong and watchful and seemed to read her thoughts.

He held out his hand. "Give me your bag."

Reluctantly Asra handed it over.

One by one the man emptied the bag of objects, Peter's iron broach, a handful of coins, and the letter to Lock stamped with the seal of the abbey. She watched as Luke read the story in the objects. Then opened the letter read it quickly, crumpled it in his hands and threw it to the ground.

"You have come from the abbey to spy," he said softly. "You are an enemy of God's Kingdom."

Asra reached for her dagger.

But the man was faster. He grabbed her by the arm and twisted it around her back forcing her on to the ground. He pulled her roughly to her feet and forced her along the edge of the courtyard toward a stone outhouse. He drew a key from his belt, unlocked the door, shoved her inside and locked it. "I'll deal to you later," he said.

Greta clasped and unclasped her fingers feeling ashamed and uncomfortable. She had imagined something different. She was the Countess of Esienberg, the ruler of the city. She was born of a Bohemian noble house and accustomed to deference. Greta was a celebrated public figure, and her Viennese gowns had set the fashion of the province. She was used to being looked at, but from a position of authority and superiority. When she had envisioned herself as making her relationship with Luke public it had been at a master table not on a peasant stool, and had been among people dressed for the occasion, not these plain shifts and unkempt hair.

The girl that Luke had introduced as Sister Good Mouse took her hand in a manner that was far too familiar. "I've never spoken with a noblewomen before," said the girl in an accent that Greta could not place. "But I've known a few bastards. I used to think all nobles were evil. My grandmother told me that if I didn't say my prayers a nobleman would come and capture me in a net. Some girls I've been known, they've caught by noblemen out hunting. They're not afraid to spare the lash when they find a common girl. But Brother Luke taught me better. Not all nobles are evil. They have only been born into evil. And if they choose they can enter the light of truth just as simple folk can."

"Luke told you that?" Greta's curiosity overcame her discomfort.

"Oh yes." The girl's face expressed a solemn earnestness. "The evil of covetousness and power."

Greta was about to press the girl further when Luke arrived from whatever business he had had with the strange dark girl. He slipped his arm around her and kissed her cheek. "I must lead the group in prayer," he said, and before Greta could say anything more, he climbed onto the table and cleared his throat.

The congregation shuffled, scraped and clattered as they arranged themselves to watch him.

Luke's sermon was short, and it seemed to Greta that he was missing out parts of his usual performance. He dwelt on the virtue of patience before moving into a condemnation of infant baptism, stressing the importance of will in the acceptance of God. It was not a subject that Greta had thought much on, but the condemnation was obviously grain for the mill, for the congregation cheered and thumped the tables.

After prayers, Luke took Greta by the hand and led her to the far end of the strange smoky hall, to the sleeping quarters. The rest of the congregation followed the couple.

As they reached the edge of the communal sleeping area, Luke put his hand around her waste and whispered to her, "you must leave your material possessions behind here. Do as I do." Luke began to strip removing his doublet, shirt and hose so that he stood naked."

"You want me to expose myself before all these people?" said Greta with horror.

Luke moved so that he stood before Greta and his eyes met hers. They were the eyes she had come to love. He reached out his hands and cradled her head. "Trust me."

Greta glanced around her. The other people paid little attention to her as they stripped, the curves and textures of their bodies illuminated in the low smoky light. *Trust me.* The words echoed in her mind. She realized how tense she felt. She would trust and would let go, what else could she do? And she pulled at the knots of her gown, until it fell in a silken pool at her feat. A turmoil of emotions rose through her. She felt arousal at the naked closeness of her lover, She felt fear and anticipation, shame and vulnerability but running through it all a simmering anger.

Luke withdrew and two other women seized Greta's hands. The congregation began to chant and Greta saw that the women were forming a large circle. The chanting began to increase and one woman pulled her and they began to run around the open fire, its light reflecting off their bodies. Greta felt herself caught up in it, she ran, her sweating hands entwined with the two sisters. The chanting lost its rhythm and instead became a chaos of sound, screaming, wailing singing chanting and one after the other Greta lost the hands of the women, slowly the men began to join them, leaping and bounding around the fire. Greta could not bring herself to sing like the others but she ran, around and around, dodging legs and feet. She began to pant and sweat. Strong arms gripped her. She knew it was Luke from his smell. He pulled her from the dance and threw her onto the straw.

Asra was surprised to discover the outhouse she had been locked in was neither uncomfortable nor uninhabited. Two Jewish women had watched with surprise as Brother Luke had pushed her inside. One woman was very pregnant, the other quite old. The room was decked with straw. A fire burned behind a hearth on to which was laid bowls of food and pitchers of water.

The pregnant woman came and helped Asra to her Feet, "Basha, daughter of Heinrich," she introduced herself politely.

"Miss Broom, servant of..." Asra paused wondering how much she should reveal to these women, "Of the abbess of the Saintly Virgin?"

"You are sworn to the abbey?" Basha threw her hand over her mouth in horror. "Oh I have terrible news. The townsfolk plan to attack the abbey and they have a cannon to knock down the walls. The battle will be lead by a terrible man and I fear for the women there. He is to be joined by some strange army of Christians beyond the city gates. You must warn them. I believe he means to march forthwith."

"I shall," said Asra and she reached into her shift, where her lock-pick rested, firmly intertwined with the rough flax cloth. She moved over to the door and ran her fingers over the rough iron keyhole. "The Christians will retreat to their sleeping quarters to indulge in their debaucheries, and I shall slink like a black cat from their clutches."

Basha watched as the strange woman inserted a metal hook into the keyhole of their prison and worked away on it until the lock clicked, and she pushed it open, letting in the starry night and the smell and sounds of sheep. Baba sang softly to herself as she platted a little doll from the straw.

The strange woman turned and looked at Basha and Baba. "Will you come?"

Basha gazed out past the woman and into the dark night. She felt the pull of freedom, the desire to feel the wind on her face, but she touched her belly. Her child would come any day now. Here she may be a captive but she was well fed and warm. Even if she escaped the House of the Lamb she would have to wander the city and also escape its walls, and then where would she go. She felt sure that the preacher and his people would not let her go that they would find and bring her back and make her life and the birth of her child more difficult. "I dare not," she said at length.

"As you wish," replied the woman, and she stepped out into the night and closed the door behind her.

another two days later

Lock breakfasted in the Kobold's Breaches, treating himself to pickled eel in a redcurrant and egg sauce. It was the early afternoon and most of the tavern patrons were enjoying their beds. He was rapidly depleting the gold that Peter had given him, and he had sworn to cut down spending, but when eel had arrived on the menu he felt he had little choice. Lock was halfway through his breakfast when he noticed that he was being observed by a cloaked and hooded woman sitting over a plate of bread and butter in the corner of the room. Their eyes met.

The woman with a slight nod of her head beckoned Lock to join her. Lock sighed and looked back at his greasy half consumed eel, how remarkable that these creatures generated spontaneously from mud, an animal without sexual organs. The woman was probably a new working girl trying her luck with a man who could afford a proper breakfast. Yet there was something intriguing, urgent perhaps, about the girl, and Lock feeling suddenly quite self-conscious, gathered up his knife and platter and seated himself opposite her in the corner of the room.

"You are the Bishop Lock," asked their girl in oddly accented Germanic.

Lock eyed the girl again, she was a beauty and had a foreign look to her, but there was a hardness and unreadable quality to her. For no particularly good reason he thought suddenly that this must be Nuary. *But why would the Turkish princess have come alone, and to him, and where was Peter?* "I was," he said.

Asra looked across at the bishop, feeling distinctly unimpressed. He was a rather fat man in his twenties with a tired looking and unexceptional face. He seemed moreover rather easy to read, oscillating between ascetic interest in her proportions and his disgustingly smelling breakfast. Asra would never understand the Christian obsession with fermenting their food. Nevertheless, she had promised she would deliver the man her letter. It was after all a letter that had nearly got her killed.

"I am Asra, Servant of the Abbess of Saint Hildegard's abbey," She reached into her sash bag and drew out the folded piece of paper. "I have something for you."

Lock unfolded the paper. It was crumpled, the seal was broken, and it looked as if sheep had soiled it. *My good Lock,* the letter read, *I pray to Lady Fortune that this letter finds you alive. I believe I understand all now, and I am greatly ashamed of my foolishness, but I am no longer angry at you for your deception. I know not how you truly felt toward me but I know now that it was not Heaven's bliss that you evoked in me but earthly love. I tried to hate you for what you did but I cannot. My heart is broken. But I want you to know that I forgive you. I do not know if I shall be able to love again, and I have barely the will to warm the gates of Hell...* Lock felt a lump form in his throat.

The girl who sat across from him had clearly read the letter and gave Lock an irritatingly knowing look. "I have news which will not be to your liking. Your liege lord is dead."

Magda wiped Greta's tears from her face with a kerchief.

"It was a like he was a different person." Greta choked back another burst of sobbing. "I thought I knew him but that man who took me in the House the Lamb. He felt like a stranger."

Magda began to comb her mistress's hair.

"You are no stranger to love Magda?"

"No my lady."

"He hurt me Magda he forced my gates. I did not think he had it in him, I thought that he had a gentle soul, but he covered my mouth with his hand, and left me upon the straw to be ogled at by peasants." Greta burst into tears. "You know what they were doing," Greta bit back the lump in her throat. "They were copulating in a mass like a net of eels. Without shame, Magda, without shame. And they believe that they do the will of God. They do not believe in marriage. They say that to marry is to covert and they believe that nothing can be coveted, only shared."

"Fear not my lady, the preacher Luke shall not set foot in this house as long as I run your household."

"And that is just the terrible thing," said Greta, "I love him still. I desire him to return. I keep telling myself that it somehow was just a bad dream, that the Luke that I love is the true Luke and that he has been bewitched by some foul magic. But the more I think about it the more I torment myself."

"My lady."

"Yes Magda."

"Johann is ordering the city guard to leave the city with him on a conquest to the abbey and the chief burgher wants to see you about the pox that has broken out. And Lord Lock has been insisting that he needs to see you, something about his pardon."

Greta rose from her chair and turned to face Magda. "For shame! You think I could sit in an audience hall, when I have been violated before the eyes of peasants. I no longer care for the city. It was all lies." Bitterness welled up in Greta. "Let the guardsmen go. I shall not leave my room."

yet another two days later

Johann was in high spirits. He was the general, answerable to no one but himself and he was impressed with the way his small army had marched. The city guard may have been composed of many smooth cheeked boys. But they responded to the whips of his sergeants, and in truth Johann rather liked the way that his superior age and strength allowed him to mold his soldiers in a way that he could not have done with hardened veterans. Early in the march two boys had left the column without permission to gather apples. And Johann had taken pleasure by hanging them from an ash tree. After that there had been little disobedience. Johann had taken to riding up an down the column, whip in hand, keeping a look out for any misdemeanor that might give him reason to administer the lash. The beatings that he had received at the hands of his father had made him tough, and these boys needed toughening, as much they needed anger because that would make them deadly. Some of their sweethearts had tried to follow the column but Johann had driven them back. Young men he knew were hot with lust and while he drove them forward with the whip he would reward them with women to rape.

So were Johann's thoughts happily occupied when he arrived at the camp of the Army of God, a troop of tanned peasant pikemen, led by an ogre of a man with a battered turnip of a nose.

two days travel

The abbess held court in the apple orchard seated on a stool, surrounded by baskets of ripe fruit while the waning sun crossed the stone wall that had protected the abbey since any could remember. Her eyes traced the line of the ivy as it climbed the aging masonry.

"The enemy is marching," Asra reported. "They are a joint army comprising the city guard, and a troop of polygamous feral peasants."

"They are bringing a cannon you say?"

Asra bowed. "The enemy is confident they can breach the abbey walls."

The high-ranking sisters that had gathered in the courtyard, whispered to each other in worried urgent tones.

"The lord Peter was on his way to try to negotiate the handover of Nuray but he and his soldiers were killed by the communalist peasants en route. The countess still rules the city for now, but she is in love with the prophet of the peasants. I could not tell how deeply she is under their influence. I can say only that she looked uncomfortable."

"And what of the bishop?" asked Brunhilde.

"A waste of time," said Asra, "He had the ear of Peter but Peter is dead. His only friends now are beggars and children. He talked a lot but told me nothing we did not already know: the fall of Esienberg, the sacking of the miller's castle." Asra allowed her gaze to soften as she recalled her meeting with Lock. A gentle breeze rustled the leaves of the apple trees.

Brunhilde lent forward, "Your thoughts?"

"When I was in the House of the Lamb," said Asra, "I was imprisoned in a kind of stable for sheep. There I met two Jewish women, one heavy with child. I tried to persuade them to come with me when I had picked the lock, but they dared not, fearing that they should be caught. I confided this to the bishop. And he clearly knew who the women were. It was news to him that they were held at the House of Lamb, and yet he was unsurprised. He responded by jumping to his feet. And shouted *Ha so the time is nigh; a flock of sheep, now that's too much.* He seemed pleased with himself as if he had been proved right about something. He entreated me to return to the House of the Lamb, and try to move the women elsewhere. I refused thinking it better to return to you forthwith. I have the bishop's letters, one addressed to you and the other addressed to Sister Sonia."

"Give me the letters."

Asra curtseyed and took letters from her sash bag and handed them and her dagger to Brunhilde.

Burnhilde cut open the seal of the first letter with the dagger and read. *Your grace, I humbly present myself as but a man, yet one who I hope shares your desire to bring peace in this land. Esienberg has been taken over by a cult of heretic Anabaptists. I have reason to believe that they will stop at nothing to destroy your abbey. Even if you defeat the army that is marching toward you, and I have heard enough about witches and dragons in the mountains to believe it possible, the city will still stand against you. But I believe that even now there is still time to act to turn the heretics out of Eisenberg. Though it may sound strange, much of it rests on the fate of a Jewess and her child. Your servant was able to enter and flee the House of the Lamb before. She can do it again. Send her back to Eisenberg. Charge her with rescuing the Jewess and taking her somewhere safe. In this way we will remove the crown from the Devil.*

The Abbess crumpled the letter in her fist and closed her eyes. She saw in her mind's eye the enemy camped on the road before the wall. The thunder of the cannon, the smoke, and the pounding of iron on stone until the walls crumbled and men surged on to the sacred ground burning and destroying all in their path.

The abbess opened her eyes to see that the assembled women were watching her, awaiting her decision. They trusted her. They expected her to save them. What could she do – attack, defend the walls, flee? Or was there another possibility? The other sisters, perhaps with the exception of the Sister Librarian, knew not what she knew, that the abbey was far older than its walls and had in those times of yore survived the wanton greed of men.

Asra curtseyed. "Superior?"

"Yes."

"May I ask you a question?"

"You may ask."

"Why did you kill the count's men in the Pass of Eagles and why did you risk your own life and the lives of others to capture Nuray?"

The attending women began to murmur among themselves.

Brunhilde held up her hand to silence them. "I killed the count's men to repay a debt and captured Nuray because I found her beautiful."

Brunhilde met with Sister Sonia in her cell, a small cave not far from the larders. She watched as Sister Sonia read the letter in the candlelight. As she neared the end of the letter, the girl's face broke into a joyous smile.

"Oh thank you," Sonia wrung her hands with gratitude. "This is more than I could have wished for."

"You wish to leave the abbey and marry this man?" Brunhilde kept her ugly face, cold and stern.

"Yes, I mean, no," Sonia dithered before Burhilde's gaze. "I mean I should like to, but I also do like it here."

"Do you?" said Brunhilde. "You have made vows. Chastity may be an over valued virtue but men have no place in the life of a sister. I shall be loath to let you go for your skills of reading and writing are exceptional. The librarian has wisdom and a keen mind, but her eyes are failing. I should like to set you to work in the library. You will be allowed to write one last letter to your lover. He requested a book from you did he not. You may copy from that book and give him what assistance he needs. After that you shall not hear from him again." It gave Brunhilde satisfaction to deny the girl the love of a man.

"Must I never talk to him again?" Brunhilde could hear the pain in the girl's voice.

"If after three years has passed you still desire to seek him out you may do so," Brunhilde liked to think of herself as fair but not cruel.

"Thank you," said Sister Sonia, though joy at her response was muted.

"One more thing before I leave you to your prayers. Do you know of the Jewesses of whom your man speaks?"

"You mean Baba and Basha? Well of course, Basha is my best friend and sister."

the next day

The scriptorium was a spacious cave carved from the soft stone into a colonnaded hall. The writing desks, stools, dais and banks on which the candles rested, were all integral to the room, carved from its stone. Two pale skinned copyists leaned over their books in the dim yellow light.

"Sister Sonia?" Sister Librarian looked down on her from where she sat on the dias, a large leather bound book laid out before her.

Sonia nervously folded and unfolded Lock's letter. "I have orders from the abbess to begin work as a copyist."

"Yes," Sister Librarian observed Sonia quietly for a few moments. "I've been expecting you. I know of your assignment."

Sonia quickly slipped the letter back into her sash bag.

The librarian smiled. "How cruel of Sister Superior. Writing is a difficult and thankless job, noble though it may be. You'll go blind before your time, and miss the kiss of sunlight on your skin."

Sonia did not know what to say to this so she nodded meekly.

The librarian pointed to an empty desk. "You may take your place..."

Sonia opened her mouth.

The librarian lifted her eyebrows. "There was a particular book you were to copy was there not?"

Sonia fidgeted. "Visitations of Angels, by Saint Hildegard."

The librarian rose, "I shall fetch it for you. You may wait at your desk."

one week later

Asra and a score of other women descended the abbey wall by rope in the cover of darkness. The enemy had arrived at noon. They had made no attempt to besiege or surround the abbey. Instead they had blockaded the road and set up a bridgehead on a rocky outcrop. Here they had positioned their cannon to concentrate their fire on the main gate. Asra had seen the effect of cannon fire before, and she understood the commander's confidence. The abbey walls would not last more than a couple of days against the coming bombardment. Then the soldiers would march through the breach to slaughter any resistance.

Asra waited until the last of the sisters had descended and gathered on a steep stony slope, that descended from the bottom of the abbey walls into a gully thick with spruce. All the escapees, but Asra, were women who had pleaded with the Sister Superior to be allowed to escape before the bloodshed. Asra had accepted her command that she should lead the women to safety and she was grateful to Sister Mushroom Gatherer who could guide them, but she felt uneasy at the responsibility. Brunhilde had refused to allow any fighting sisters to accompany them, keeping them all for the Abby's defense. *One or two might slip past unnoticed, but a band? Something could always go wrong.*

The mushroom gatherer led them expertly down the crumbly slope, and Asra thanked Allah when reached the spruce without incident. She had doubtless been worried for nothing. The enemy commander had not had time to send men to climb into the gully, and if he had tried they would have been seen from the walls. The mushroom gatherer soon found her trail and women descended as quietly as they could manage in the deep dark.

Johann and a dozen hand picked men waited in the darkness. Johann had been certain that the women would try and escape like rats from a sinking ship. And the Devil take him if he would let them get away. The greedy whores were no doubt at the very moment attempting to take their treasures and their youngest girls away from his grip.

Mountains and high cliffs closed the abbey in to the south, east and west. Only to the north could an escape be made. Either along the rode or the spruce clad gully below it. With this in mind Johann had split his forces near the bottom of the climb toward the abbey. He had taken twelve of the toughest men with him to follow the line of the gully. While the rest under Turnip's command would encamp at the main gates and begin the bombardment.

"Can't we make a light, sir?" one of the men grumbled.

"Shut your mouth or I shall see you hang," said Johann, "the fat little sows are coming and we will cut them from chin to trotter."

As they descended toward the bottom of the gully the land flattened out a little and the spruce became larger and spacer. Asra heard them before she saw them, the crack of breaking sticks. A band of heavy men advanced at a walk emerging them from the dark spaces between the trees. Her eyes, adjusted to the darkness, could make out their hulking shapes looming closer with every step. The other women screamed and attempted to flee. Asra stood as if frozen, her hand resting on the pommel of her dagger.

The first man bore down on her. He was unprepared for her fast response and she killed him swiftly with her dagger in his heart. Another man stumbled on a tree root as he ran at her, catching himself on his hands. She severed his spinal cords with a jab to the nap of his neck.

With two dead men at her feet, Asra turned to look around her. Most of the men had rushed past her in their attack but now they turned to stare at her. Asra looked at the enemy and they looked at her. One of the men was holding a sister. He lifted her off the ground by her hair as she screamed and he cut open her belly with his sword.

Asra fled.

the 3rd of November, the Day of the New Dawn, Year of the Lord 1526

It was a dim, dawn that seeped through the cracks in the wood, illuminating the stable. A cock crowed. The sheep bleated. Basha screamed. Baba sang. And a tiny baby boy was born.

Brunhilde, the abbess watched from a cave high in the cliff face as another cannon ball crashed against the weakened wall. The captured sisters who had tried to escape had had their bodies mutilated and had been left on the road to rot before the abbey gate. Her hands reached for the cross that hung on her neck. She did not often pray, believing God was distant and took little interest in the doings of such short lived beings as people, but now she began to pray, entreating the Lord and his angels to save the abbey. The abbey had stood for hundreds of years. She could not let it fall. She had done all she could. Now she could only pray.

Lock looked with melancholy at the thin pottage that slopped around in the wooden bowl. The city was falling apart. The countess had ceased to govern and the city guard that had not left with Johann kept close to her residence. In the vacuum the cult of the House of the Lamb ruled the streets. Bands of armed religious zealots wandered from house to house, appropriating food and valuables. Lock spent more and more time in the Kobold's Breaches, close to Hans and his long sword. But he was running out of money and running out of time.

"Do you know why goats have short tails?" asked Hans.

Lock shrugged. "Can't say I do, pray go on."

"An old soldier told me, that it was the Devil that created goats and once they had long tails but they all caught in the brambles as they wandered looking for plants to feed on, so the Devil bit off their tails, so they could move more freely. That's why goats have short tails."

"Hey, lord."

Lock looked down and saw that a child was pulling on his cloak.

It was one of his little friends who brought him information for money.

"What is it?"

"It's happened," said the ragged breathless boy, "I thought you would like to know at once. The baby has been born at the House of the Lamb. They're preparing for something and gathering wood for pyres and torches. They're all talking about the Day of the New Dawn."

"One of the cultists is entering the tavern," Hans cut in with low sharp whisper. "She's looking over at us and approaching."

Lock turned his chair to see a female figure dressed in a baggy shift and cloak walk head down toward their table. She lifted her head and met Lock's eye. It was Asra.

"The abbess has answered my pleas," said Lock as he made room for her on the bench.

"She has," Asra remained standing, "I am to attempt a rescue of the Jews. She drew a letter from within her cloak and slid it across the table to Lock.

Lock broke the seal and opened the letter. *My sweet Lock since I received your letter I feel a great weight of shame lifted from me. You tell me that you loved me truly. And for this I can forgive the way that you kept me in ignorance. But as for your offer of marriage, I ask that you allow me more time. My heart yearns for you but I am a novice now at the abbey and I have my own vows to think of. Perhaps if there are brighter times in the future, then you may call me yours. But for now it shall suffice to know that you love me. Regarding the book you were asking after. You will be pleased to know that I have pursued it with all urgency. And it is most peculiar for one of its copies was missing and the librarian was totally distraught. But fortunately there is an older copy, and terribly yellowed with time it is and I have taken it upon myself to copy it. I came across the page that will interest you as you have said. And I have thus enclosed it with this letter.*

Lock looked up from his letter and around at his companions, the hardened swordsman the street child and the Turkish spy. "Sister Asra, you must go forthwith for I fear that our time is close to out, and now it is three you must save and not two. Young David," Lock turned to the boy, "I need you to take a message to Jango."

"And me?" the mercenary stroked his trimmed waxed beard.

"You will come with me to see the countess," replied Lock. "It is time for her to pass judgment on me, to pardon me, or hang me."

Johann stood beside the Cannon and breathed in the taste of black powder as the explosion deafened him. He watched as the ball crashed into the wall. The wall shuddered. It then rumbled as stone and masonry tumbled down in a wide breach. It had taken him longer than he had thought, but he had been in no rush. He doubted more women would attempt an escape after they had seen the fate of their friends. Besides, he had learned from torturing them that the abbess meant to fight and that pleased him.

Johann drew his sword. He felt his heart race at the anticipation of violence and the shrieking of women. It would be a day to remember.

Greta stood on the balcony of her house. Watching the cold clear day. Many of the trees had shed their leaves, the sun rose lower in the sky, and the shadier corners of the steep black roofs of the city were still coated in frost. The sound of chanting brothers and sisters of Christ carried on the still air.

A knock on her door pulled Greta out of her revere, and she turned her back on the view. "Enter," she commanded.

The door was pushed open and Magda entered, and bowed, "My lady?"

"Speak, Magda."

"My lady, Lock has arrived at the doors of the house. He has with him the last man of Peter's old soldiers. He says it is the day of his trial and demands that you either pardon him or hang him."

"And the fool expects me to pardon him, but being rid of that arrogant walking codpiece is perhaps the only thing that could lighten my mood. Bring them into the courtyard and have my throne brought there. Tell Lord Lock I shall attend him in time. Tell my captain to make sure all men are armed and ready and to assemble in the courtyard. I still have my regiment of halberdiers do I not?"

Magda smiled. "Yes my lady. They shall be happy to have orders."

"And send word to Luke. Tell him that I forgive him, that I love him, and that I am ready to put myself fully in the hands of God, but that he must attend me forthwith."

Yes my lady.

"Be fleet Magda. For I shall need your help with my dress."

Johann ran unimpeded through the breach in the abbey wall, the shouting mass of soldiers behind him. He had expected to meet some resistance, and had been relishing the prospect of slaughtering women, followed by a surrender and a rounding up of any that were hiding at which point looting and rape could begin. Unfortunately the space between the cliffs and the outer wall was a maze of walled orchards in which there was not a woman, nor anything else of value to be seen.

"Keep with me," ordered Johann, as he led the snaking column closer and closer to the great overhanging cliff.

At length they came to the yawning entrance to the caves, carved into a broad smooth arch. No light issued from within and there was something ominous about it that made Johann stop. The column fanned out as his soldiers joined him on the threshold.

Fetch, candles and lanterns." Johann barked to his lieutenant.

Lock and Hans knelt before Greta who, flanked by a dozen Halberdiers, sat on her throne in the cobbled courtyard of the house that had once been Lock's. Two dozen more halberdiers stood to attention around the edge of the courtyard. Close to the stables the members of Greta's household that had gathered to see what would unfold. Lock recognized among the servants a number of noble widows and their children.

"You are here," said Greta, "to answer for your crimes, for inciting armed insurrection against the rightful rulers of Eisenberg, and," Greta narrowed her eyes, "for the crime of atheism. What have you to say for yourself? Rise and speak."

Lock rose and began to pace. "I shall answer, my lady, those charges brought against me you make your decision I intreat you to listen to what I have to say for I have proof, Countess, of the guilt of Luke the preacher for the murder of Joseph the miller's son, and for being the head of a sinister conspiracy that means to dethrone you."

"Do you now?" said Greta, fixing Lock with a critical gaze, before turning to Magda who served the countess water. "Should I listen to what he has to say?"

Magda snuck a look at Lock and Hans, "Surely there can be no harm in listening to what they have to say."

"Very well," said Greta, "I shall hear what you have to say but I think you must agree that it would be unjust if the man you so accuse could not defend himself from the accusations you bring against him. It is fortunate, therefore, that he is here to answer them." Greta murmured an order to a guardsman who left the courtyard for the house. "If I find you false," Greta addressed Lock, "than I shall hang you."

A few moments later the halberdiers parted and Luke the preacher entered the courtyard he smiled at the attending soldiers and onlookers and took his place on a chair beside Greta's thrown. "I have no doubt," the preachers rich voice carried through the courtyard, "that whatever lies this corrupt old atheist has come to poison your ears with shall be swiftly dismissed by your wisdom."

Lock's heart fell. Was Greta really so blinded by love to not see what was happening to the city? Lock looked up and caught Greta's eye. Her expression conveyed that look that he admired in her, a curiosity and intelligence, but marred by a hardened grimness that was unfamiliar.

"You may begin," she said.

Lock felt tongue-tied. He had been rehearsing this for days, but suddenly he did not know where to begin. It was not how he had imagined it, standing here in front of these people with the man he was accusing sitting comfortably before him, smiling calmly. *And where for God's good grace was Jango?*

Hans the mercenary assessed the strength of the halberdiers. Standing to attention while holding a heavy halberd built strength. They also appeared to be well paid by the countess. Doubtless they would fight if ordered to. *Could he cut his way out if he had to?* His Long sword was strapped to his back, but it would be his katzbalger short sword strapped to his waste that he would go to first. *Draw quickly, close quickly* "You'd better be able to talk your way out of this," hissed Hans to Lock.

"I don't know where to start," Lock hissed back.

"At the beginning."

"This tool of the Devil has nothing to say," said Luke coolly.

Shouts and an altercation at the courtyard gate drew the court's attention.

Lock turned to look and saw, the black hair, the handsome face, the torn colorful silk clothes, and wooden crutches of Jango, Prince of the Travellers. Two guardsmen blocked his entrance into the courtyard with lowered halberds. Lock fell to his knees and addressed Greta. "I beg that this man be allowed to pass within," said Lock, "Though a foreigner he is a man of noble blood and a witness to the crime of which I speak."

"Halt," Greta's voice carried on the still, cold morning air. The guardsman stood to attention and Jango drew himself up on his crutches. "State your name and business?" Greta called.

"I am Jango, son of Zafir," shouted the cripple, "and I come to tell the truth."

"You may enter," said Greta, "I knew your father."

The guards parted and Jango hobbled past Lock and Hans, past the watching crowd, and alert guards, toward Greta's throne. He had made himself as resplendent as he could for the occasion. He had made an effort to clean his silk robes. He had shaved and oiled his moustache and hair. A pair of pistols and jeweled dagger rested in his sash. Jango made the best he could of a bow. He glanced at the assembled folk before pointing a finger at Luke. "It was he." The Traveler spoke in a rough Germanic that was much like the tongue of the Jews. "It was that man who murdered Joseph. I saw it with my own eyes." He raised his own dark scared face to meet Greta's gaze. His wide brown eyes met hers and lingered. She recognized him. He had played the fiddle at her feast.

Luke began to protest, but Greta silenced him.

"Tell me what happened," she said.

Jango drew himself up on his crutches. "It was a moonlit night. Joseph met that man of his own will and he reminded Joseph of a deal he had made. The price had been Joseph's first born child, which the man would raise himself."

There was a murmuring among the onlookers and guards leant in to whisper to one another.

"Greta raised her hand to bring order."

" Joseph refused to hand over his flesh and blood," continued Jango. "He said he would no longer abide by their agreement and that he would take his family faraway from the madman. Then he," Jango pointed at Luke, "flew into a rage, struck Joseph with a cudgel and beat him to death."

"Lies," said Luke, "absurd lies by a pagan accomplice of the bishop."

"If it is true," said Greta "then you must tell me how you came to witness this act."

Jango looked at the ground and was silent.

"You see," said Luke. "He lies."

Lock watched as his witness bit his lips and closed his mouth. "Jango," he shouted, "Tell them. Do it for her."

"I followed Joseph with two of his brothers," said Jango, "to spy on him because I loved his wife, Basha the beautiful."

"All the more reason for him to lie," said Luke calmly, "no doubt he was the murderer himself."

Jango reached for his pistols. The guards closed in with their halberds. Jango raised hands and fell on to his broken knees. "I am Jango, son of Zafir, and I swear to all that is holy that, what I say is truth. We were not able to save Joseph from the murderer's club. But we seized the murderer, for he knew not that we watched. But we had not the heart or stomach to slay him in cold blood as he had killed Joseph, and I curse myself everyday for my cowardice. Instead we stripped him naked and left him to die in the wilderness."

Lock who had been closely monitoring Greta's face, noticed the mask of indifference slip. She glanced at Luke. Her face showed shock. The Traveler's words had touched something. *Was that how Greta had first found him, naked in the forest?* But the loss of composure only lasted a breath.

"That may or may not be the truth," said Greta, "but reach for your weapons again in my presence and you shall die. Now speak. What happened then?"

"We wanted to bring Joseph's body to his family but were afraid to be blamed for his murder, so we cut Joseph's head from his body, so that he may be lighter and carried him to the outskirts of his father's lands. I was so ashamed that when Basha's father came for word of Joseph we told him only what we could in riddles."

Luke opened his mouth to speak, but Greta silenced him. A part of her heart had died that night in the House of Lamb, and in its stead sat cold iron. She knew that she would hang somebody that day. She had thought that it would be Lock, but the story was too strange to be false and somehow she could believe it to be true. She pictured in her mind's eye the look on her lover's face when she ordered him to be hung from the hanging tree and the tender part in her heart that still loved him cried out against it. She wanted to hear more and feared to. Of one thing she was certain. She would not allow herself to cry.

"Don't forget," Luke whispered the words, in the voice she knew from her pillow so that only she could hear them, "Don't forget the night of the battle of Eisenberg."

How could she ever forget? It haunted her dreams.

Basha held Baby Joseph wrapped in a kerchief to her breast. Her body was week and torn, and exhausted, but she was alive and she held to her bosom a living creature that she loved with all her heart. The women of the House of the Lamb had not been unkind, bringing warm water for her to wash and goat's milk for her to drink. And for a blessed moment she had been left alone with the baby and with Baba.

"He's a strong one," said Baba, looking over her daughters shoulder at the face of her grandchild. "He's crying like an expert and he will be doing his first poop in no time."

Basha smiled.

"And you've done well too," continued the old woman, "I've known hardened mothers that have screamed louder than you on their third."

"Grandmother," Basha broke down into tears that mingled with laughter. "I don't know what I would have done without you."

"Hush now," said Baba, "the Christians are approaching."

The door to the stable on which they sat on the straw was pushed open and half a dozen sisters of Christ entered, one of them holding a sharp pair of sheers. "It is time for the ceremony," she said, "we have to cut the baby Lord's cord."

"You can't do that," Baba stepped between the Christians and her daughter. "They could both die from the blood loss."

"It is the will of God," intoned the woman, undeterred. "We shall bind the cord to reduce bleeding."

Lock struggled to read the countess's face. The court was silent. *What was she thinking? Was she wavering?* Lock decided he must push on with his tale. "I," he said, "am a Lutheran like you."

"Silence." Greta's voice was cold. "I will not be spoken to about Lutheranism by the man who ordered the massacre of the nobles and their households. It was on your orders was it not? Where was your faith in Luther then?"

The venom in her voice was such that Lock shut his mouth and stood, speechless.

"Forget us not the massacre of the loyal townsmen at the forest bridge." Luke pointed a finger at Lock. "Do you deny that you instigated it?"

"Speak, curse you," said Greta "What have you to say for the blood that is on your hands?"

The Members of Greta's household and the noble widows that gathered to watch exchanged whispers and gave Lock dark looks. The front rank of Halberdiers lowered their weapons.

Lock bowed low. "I will always regret that I did not do more to prevent that terrible tragedy." Lock lifted his hands in supplication to the countess. "But let me say," he raised his voice as Luke tried to interject, "that the papal troops were not the only ones who knew what would happen when a mass of cavalry charges a line of pike and musket. Luke," Lock now pointed his finger at the preacher, and projected his voice and loud and clear as he had learned, "knew, because he had fought in Swabia and in the Black Forest two years thence and incited the peasants to rise against the nobility where he advocated the communalisation of property and the destruction and execution of the nobility. It was here that he met William the Witch hunter, a man whose penchant for violence had always proved helpful to him. There is no doubt, that Luke was overjoyed at his success in urging the hated nobles to their deaths at the hands of his other enemies. Blame not their death on me but on him who tricked them to it. For Luke is no Lutheran. He is a radical heretic. Is it not true? Have you not seen so for yourself?"

"See how he twists words," Luke rose from his seat, "to turn a victim to perpetrator."

"Silence." Greta turned on Luke. "I have seen enough of your Kingdom of God to doubt my own heart. Speak Herr Lock. What more can you tell me of this man?"

For the first time that morning Lock felt real hope. Greta would listen and Eisenberg would be returned to order. "I can tell you," Lock raised his voice above the excited hubbub of voices, "that he is the bastard son of a wandering monk who died before Luke came of age. That monk was an accomplished writer known as Brother William, who wrote a popular account of his travels, which was printed in Munich, the city where he died, and where the young Luke found himself destitute and without family." Lock paused to catch his breath. The court had fallen silent the guards and onlookers listening with curiosity.

Luke did not reply but stared defiant at the court.

"Is it true?" Greta turned her face toward her lover.

"I do not deny it, for I am not ashamed. I know not by what evil means this wizard has employed to divine my past, but I am no killer."

Greta turned her eyes back to Lock and for the first time he saw in them surprise and something akin to admiration.

Lock forced himself not to smile. It would do him no favours to look smug. So with his face set in a serious expression he pushed on with his tale. "Luke was no peasant. He was literate and well spoken. And the injustice of his condition weighed heavy upon him. It was thus in the alehouses of Munich that Luke became drawn to the most radical preachers. But in his charisma and conviction he soon outstripped his mentors. For he knew something that they did not, Hildegard's Prophesy, he had read in his father's keepsake, a book written by the saint. The end of days was coming soon and with it Luke's destiny. Luther's words were spreading. Princes were renouncing the pope, and poor harvests filled the towns with hungry simple folk. And they flocked to Luke's message of the destruction of the princes and bishops, the distribution of their wealth, and the second coming of Christ. They sacked towns and slew lords and soon it seemed that nothing could stop them. So much the sadder when the retribution of the nobles fell upon them." Lock turned to face Luke, who sat face and body still as stone. "How many died?"

"Uncountable thousands, torn and cut to pieces, acts of purest evil." Luke's voice was steady but Lock thought he saw a twitch in the preacher's expression, a shadow of loss passing over his face. The bells of the city tolled noon.

Disguised in a peasant shift, her hood shadowing her face, Asra watched the Square of Flowers Sellers from the eaves of the House of the Lamb. In the middle of the square were several wagons each harnessed to a pair of donkeys. On each wagon was built a pyre of brush and branches. On one of the wagons the pyre was built around a stake and bound to the stake were Baba and Basha. Around the wagons were piles of weapons, pitchforks scythes, pikes, knives, shields, bows, cudgels and torches. The brothers and sisters of Christ that filled the square spoke to each other in an excited hubbub.

The bells of the great church tolled noon. Asra shifted her gaze up toward the hill, the church, and the house of the ruler.

"He has come," somebody in the crowd, shouted.

And the cry was taken up by the brothers and sisters of Christ, and rang through the streets. The crowd surged toward the pile of weapons. After each had taken their pick they began to march up the hill toward the gate of the inner city. The men whipped the donkeys and the wagons rumbled along the street.

Asra joined the flow of people. As she made her way closer to the wagon on which the Jewish women were bound, she saw that riding on the wagon was also a woman nursing a tiny baby.

Greta had expected to feel rage, and grief, instead she felt cold resolve and a clear mind as she quelled the ember in her heart that had loved Luke. "What did you do then?" she asked the preacher.

"I could not lead my people to the slaughter," said Luke, "so I took them to refuge in Bohemia."

"Yet ever in your exile," sad Lock, "your mind strayed to the place of your birth, did it not, to Eisenberg and the prophesy of Hildegard? And how did the prophecy go?" Lock reached into the breast of his tunic and pulled out a leaf of paper, written in Sonia's small neat hand. "In Eisenberg the son of Christ shall be born again, mothered by a

Jew and fathered by a Christian of humble name, conceived beneath a roof of leaves." Lock replaced the paper back into his tunic. "Tell me how did you come to know of the marriage of Joseph the miller's son and Basha the Beautiful? I cannot believe that it was coincidence anymore than I believe it was the hand of God. Was it in the spring of yester year when you left your followers, and your soldiers and wandered over the mountains and came to Eisenberg where dwelled as a hermit in the woods? There you spied, did you not, on both the Jewish and Christian folk. You observed where Basha the Beautiful would gather wild garlic beside the stream. And you also befriended a curious and handsome Christian whose young mind was open to persuasion."

"It was my destiny to bring them together," Luke's tone and expression had changed, from surprised and innocent, to righteous and defiant. "Joseph was the man through whom the seed of God would pass. His soul was pure, as the animals that loved him knew. It was written even in his name."

"Was it also your destiny to slay him?" Lock shouted above the muttering crowd.

"All that has come to pass has been destined. And your persecutions will only make me stronger." Luke rose from his seat.

"Order." Greta's voice was cold and the halberdiers eyed Luke with interest. "I wish to hear the rest of Herr Lock's tale."

Lock bowed to the countess. "Who would not wish to be the vehicle that God would use to bring Himself into the world and marry the most beautiful woman and the mother of God? It was all too much for young Joseph and he agreed to all the terms, did he not? Nor was it a hard thing to put Joseph among the blue bells and the wild garlic, beside the flowing stream, to play his pipe, to his play his part, and woo the Jewish maiden. How perfectly the plan did go was scarce to be believed but Lady Fortune was yet to turn her wheel. Joseph told nothing of his pact to Basha. He could not face her wrath and sadness, for he loved her as much as any man has ever loved a woman. He told you so on the night of his death that he would tell her the truth and they would flee and take their child far from you. It was something that you could not countenance. This was your life's work, your destiny. The child that Basha carried was indeed He. You believed it and believe it still. When Jango and his brother stripped and left you in the forest you thought that all might be lost but it turned out to be a blessing in disguise, for you made it to the schloss of the house of Eisenberg, where you invented the story that you told her ladyship!

"So it was that you gained official sanction to begin your plans to prepare Eisenberg for becoming the new Jerusalem. But ever you were worried that Basha and the baby would evade you so you made a deal with the Devil, Captain Johann of the city guard. You soon discovered that the one thing that the Captain coveted above all things was Basha herself. And so you promised her to him and gave him the hope that he could have her but you played his fear of Jewish magic to keep her safe. Thus you kept Basha and her growing baby where you needed her. Having won over her ladyship, you then made your move against the one man who could stand in the way of your new Jerusalem, myself, the corrupt Lord Bishop Lock. You played the nobles off against the Church, and succeeded as you watched them slaughter each other. The return of Peter gave you pause. But you soon bound him to your ends with the lure of his love and, when your army of peasant soldiers arrived from Bohemia, you had him slain. Now you are poised to put all things in common, even women, to loot the houses of the rich and share the spoils with the people. Your baby is born and Jerusalem is nigh. There shall be no nobility and no property. All things shall be equal before God. All that remains to be done is to burn the baby's mother, loot the abbey of your mother, and get rid of us."

The crowed booed Luke.

A halberdier positioned close to the courtyard gate, shouted a warning. The eyes of the court turned in his direction. Black columns of billowing smoke rose from the outer city. In the distance the court could hear the chanting of the brothers and sisters of Christ.

"You are too late," Luke's voice was loud calm and clear, "You may martyr me now, but you can not stop God's will." Luke fixed his eyes on Greta who returned his gaze with a cold stare. "I had hoped that you would join us," he whispered, "in the glorious new Jerusalem. And even now He is not without forgiveness. I came to you when you called me, unarmed and in trust. Renounce your wealth and power and join me in love and God." Luke held out his hand.

"You lied to me," said Greta, and then turned to address her halberdiers. "Bind this traitor tight and take him to the stables. Prepare the horses and carriages. We are to leave the city forthwith. And we shall hang him form the first tree on the forest raod."

Asra followed the mob as they began their cleansing of the city. The houses of those whom they deemed to be impious or covetous were stormed and set alight. They dragged the wealthy townsfolk from their houses, slaughtering them, bludgeoning them or cutting them to pieces. They stuffed the looted food, cloth and metal into sacks, which they threw onto the wagons, while paintings, books and sculptors were thrown onto the pyre at the feet of Baba and Basha.

The mob began to thin out as they moved through the streets. As the group around the pyre wagon surged through the gates of a mason's house, Asra saw her chance. Only three men remained on the street to guard the pyre.

The first man rose to greet Asra as she approached. Asra assessed him. He was strong. He had seen hardship. But his sword was still in its scabbard. Asra drew close. She pulled out her dagger and thrust it through his eye into his head. She drew her knee up to her chest and pushed the dying man off her blade. The next two men drew their swords and began to close in on her. She waited for them. The first man made a sideways chop at her. She rolled under the chop rising up from beneath and cutting out his groin. The man fell thrashing and screaming in pain, as he quickly weakened from blood loss. *Allah be praised.*

The third man dithered. Asra watched the fear and uncertainty play on his face. He threw his eye back to the woman with the baby and the two Jewish women bound to the stake.

Asra moved before he could. She made a jab at his throat, he parried, keeping her at length. She feinted low, crouching. He moved his sword to parry but she turned her crouch into a spring and threw herself on him knocking him to the ground and cutting his throat.

"Don't move," said Asra to the woman with the baby, "or you will follow your men folk. Asra climbed the pyre and cut Baba and Basha loose.

Basha leapt from the pyre and snatched her child from the woman's arms.

Shouts resounded from the mason's house ss three women dragged the mason and his wife onto the street.

Johann led his men deeper and deeper into the catacombs of the abbey, the light of the lanterns playing on the smooth sandstone. At length he came to a great underground hall, adorned with wall paintings of saints and angles. From here many smaller passages ran off in every direction. The hall was eerily empty. The eyes of the painted figures stared from the smooth walls, their images shifting in the guttering light of the lanterns. When the men heard the attack, it was like an avalanche of pattering soft shod feet.

The women streamed out of the passages, attacking without light and fell upon the men with swords, knives and daggers.

There had been no room in the passages to bring pikes. Some men carried muskets but there was no time to fire a volley. Many were so surprised that they dropped their lanterns. Others raised their swords and cudgels. Many were cut down in the darkness before the eyes of the saints. The mass of men panicked. They tried to flee and were stabbed in their backs. Their blood pooled on the hall's floor and their cries echoed through the caverns.

Johann placed his lantern by his feet. "Fools," he shouted, "cowards, they are but women. Stand your ground and fight them."

But he had no time to berate his breaking army. Three women set upon him. He drove his sword through the breast of the first, and as she fell she took his sword with him. The second woman he punched in the face, downing her so that she fell on the ground at his feet. The third woman slashed her dagger across his face, opening a cut from cheek to brow. Blood flowed into his eyes and mouth. He drew his sword from the dying woman and slashed at his assailant cutting into her thigh.

"Come on you whores and witches, I'll slay the lot of you." Johann crushed the chest of the woman before him with his boot. Quickly the lanterns were being extinguished and it was only from the shouts and moans of the dying that he could tell in the chaos, that the fight was not going his way. Three more women attacked him. They he also killed though he lost a finger. He took pleasure in their deaths, from the smell of their deaths, from the sounds of their death rattles. Beneath the craze of battle he felt the simmering of lust. He killed another woman, skewering her with his sword.

Now his was the only light left burning. And the sound of his army had dissipated. His light reflected off the faces of the women who surrounded him. Their expressions were grim set. Their robes were white. Johann began to laugh, laughter to mask his fear. "Come at me you devils and I shall fill your cunts with steel." So were the last words of Johann von Eisenberg the Cruel.

Asra, Baba, Basha and Baby Joseph hid under a hay cart while a mob of fanatics ran past.

"How do we escape the city?" Asra whispered when the sound of their shouts and the clack of their feet had receded.

"The smuggler's door," said Baba, "by the north wall. It is locked, but I have seen your skill with picklocks, and I'm sure you could open it. It opens onto the River Eisen and there, if it has not been taken or destroyed, is a little boat that may take us across the river."

The women fled, running through the deserted streets, through wafts of black smoke, avoiding the mobs by hiding behind doorways or in the dark corners of alleyways beneath the carved eaves of the houses. So they came, Basha holding the baby tight to her breast, to an abandoned shack that lent against the south wall. They pushed the door open. Baba cleared the rushes from the floor, beneath was a wooden trap door, locked with a heavy iron padlock. Asra set to work on the lock and at length it sprang open. They descended to an underground waterway where a little boat was tied to an iron stanchion. They boarded the boat, Asra cut the rope, and the current carried them from the city walls.

Greta's column consisted of some fifty odd halberdiers, three carriages filled with noble women and children, and two wagons filled with baggage and supplies, on top of which rode the female servants. Lock, and his friends walked near the rare, the halberdiers were placed in three clumps between the carriages and wagons, and Luke was bound and escorted by four solders. Once she had made it out of the city and onto the west road she would have him hung from a tree and she would watch his face while he choked to death. Greta was leaving the city and she was not coming back. The coachman touched his whip to the horses and Greta watched from the windows of the covered carriage as the column began to roll through the smoking city.

As they made their way through the inner city, children, women and men fleeing the wreckage of the cultist mob joined the column, pressing close behind the baggage wagons. Older children carrying younger children gave frightened stares toward the overhanging buildings and the narrow streets between them. Some of the refuge seekers wept. Others chattered wearily among themselves. Smoke rose from the outer city and the column rolled on.

Greta's carriage passed the sight of the massacre of the noblemen and through the narrow North Gate and onto the streets of the outer city. Here, among the houses of the merchants and tradesmen, the carnage wrought by Luke's followers was greater. A tailor's wife wept over the body of her dead husband, and son. His cloth and tools of his trade scattered on the street. Household animals came to feed on the dead. A black cat pulled on a man's entrails. A cock dipped his beak in a pool of blood and drank. A group of swine devoured a corpse. A lost looking cow fled, its hooves clattering on the cobblestones. Once Greta would have felt sick at the smells and sights that now assailed her. But she had seen so many such sights of late, that she paid them little heed.

The column came to a crossroads. Ahead, to the west was the Square of Flower Sellers, the House of the Lamb and the area most controlled by the cultists, beyond that was the Forest Gate and the West Road. To the right of the column the road turned eastward, running through the Jewish Quarter between the river and the cliffs, before coming to the River Gate and the East Gate. To the left of the column ran the South Road. It was narrower than the other roads but still wide enough for a wagon or carriage to pass with ease. The coachman slowed the horses.

"Drive on," Greta commanded, "Let us not linger here. Straight through the Square of Flower Sellers and the den rebels to the Forest Gate. That is the swiftest route."

"The road is blocked, my lady," replied the coachman, "by a burning wagon.

The column ground to a halt. Servants and refuge seekers murmured to each other. A hungry child began to cry. The halberdiers gripped their halberds and glanced nervously around them.

"Looks like trouble up ahead," said Hans to Lock as he peered at the smoke that rose from the head of the column.

Lock and Jango followed Hans as he weaved around the wagons and carriages toward the crossroads. Lock heard the thrumming of drums and the clanging of spoons banging on iron pots. Hans drew his long sword. The halberdiers gripped their weapons and looked nervously up at the intersecting streets. The sound drew closer and Lock watched as a mass of brothers and sisters of Christ emerged at the top of the steep, cobbled South Road. They crowded, drumming and singing, around a wagon on which a pyre was built. Around the pyre was piled much plunder from the town. The mob threw flaming torches onto the pyre. The flames grew and the black smoke of burning wood and pitch billowed upward toward they grey sky. Lock watched as the cultists strained as they pushed the wagon. As they reached the top of the slope the flaming wagon began to roll in the direction of the column. It careened down the hill, leaving a trail of ash and debris behind it. Men shouted, women screamed and the children ran. They pyre disintegrated as the wagon collided with a carriage. Horses reared and screeched. Flaming wood and debris fell across the street.

The followers of Luke came armed and screaming in the wagon's wake. Jango dropped his clutches and fell onto his knees. Hans drew his long sword. Lock resisted the urge to run.

The cultists charged. Hans used the long sword in wide cutting arcs. He cut down two burley sword-wielding brothers of Christ. But the attackers made no attempt to close with Hans or with any of the halberdiers. Instead they surged past the defenders and between the wagons to where their prophet lay bound and immobile in the sweltering heat of the fire. They mobbed the Halberdiers that guarded him pushing them to the ground and stabbing them. They lifted Luke onto their shoulders and bore him aloft.

"Stop them." Greta had dismounted from her carriage, her voice carrying through the chaos of the battle. The halberdiers began to close in on the cultists. But the brothers and sisters of Christ did not stay to fight but hurried away into the smoke filled streets carrying their leader with them.

A gunshot resounded in Lock's ear and he turned to see Jango, leaning against the wall of a house a smoking pistol in his hand. "I hope I hit the bastard," he said.

18th of December

Hoarfrost covered the trees of the Vienna garden in delicate icicle blossoms. Ferdinand Hapsburg, Duke of Vienna, brother of the emperor, surveyed the Lady Greta. She was dressed in a cloak of Flemish wool, trimmed with Muscovy fur. Past the bloom of her youth she was yet beautiful and grim.

"You want me return your county to you?" he said.

"I do."

"You understand the political situation?"

Greta inclined her head. "Though but a woman I am not ignorant of such things. The Kingdom of Hungary has fallen. King Lajos is dead. And his birthright by marriage passes to the emperor, but the emperor is busy fighting his war with Rome while his mind is on the riches of Spain, so really it belongs to you. But it is only in the north in Bohemia where you rule. For in the valley of the Danube the Turks rule under their vassal, John Zapolya, but Eisenberg is in the borderlands and belongs only to rabid heretics. It could be yours, yours and mine."

"You are most astute," said the Duke, "But there are things that you have not thought of. I know not the sultan's plans. But when the spring mud has dried I believe he will wage war on us again. My brother has left me with little enough soldiers. Does it truly serve my interests to send them thither with you."

"Iron," said Greta, "you need my iron."

John Zapolya clapped Lock on the back as he greeted the bishop in the castle parlor in front of a roaring fire. Zapolya liked Lock. He was exactly the kind person he needed in the new Kingdom of Hungaria, men of the world, pragmatists who understood the benefits of accepting Turkish rule.

"I've been thinking over it," said Zapolya, "and I've decided when the snow thaws I shall send you north with a troop of hussars. We're training them in the Turkish way, you know, fast, light. Not like the bloody heavy knights that got themselves killed at Mohacs. I'll reinstate you as Prince Bishop of Eisenberg and we'll start selling the iron to the Turks."

"Must I go?" Lock mournfully swilled his mulled wine. "Pest is awfully comfortable, peaceful and tolerant. The women are clean and not of so pungent an odour. The wine is sweet and of a good price, and the climate, well..." Lock stared out the window at the gently falling snow. "Well in summer I've heard it's balmy. Oh to see Pest in the summer time."

Zapolya laughed. "No, no I won't hear of it. You're just the man I need in the north."

Suleiman the Law Giver, Caliph of Islam, and the most powerful man in the world, surveyed his trusted spy, Asra. Her sun darkened skin did not detract from the beauty of her face as she bent to pour the sultan his tea.

"You were unable to bring Bright Moon back from the barbarians?"

"She would not come, Prince of the Faithful. She dwells among the savage women and shows no inclination to return to her people."

"What if I were to send a troop of Janissaries. Could I not force her return?"

"The caves of the savage women are deep and labyrinthine. Not one of the Christian soldiers made their way out alive."

The sultan stroked his beard. "But you know these caves and you could lead the men to her."

Asra arched her chin up to meet the eyes of the sultan. She then fell onto her knees and prostrated herself before him. "Oh Prince of the Faithful send me not to Eisenberg but take me with you to Vienna."

The End

Historic Note

Esienberg is a fictional place and its inhabited by fictional people. Yet in its construction I wanted to convey the spirit of the diverse milieu of east-central Europe in early sixteenth century, with its overlapping jurisdictions, languges, cultures and beliefs. The Eisenbergers typify the medieval Ostsiedlungen, in which German communities founded towns as far flung as Transylvania and the Volga River.

Bishop Lock typifies a strand of sceptical late medieval humanism that was prevalent among some members of the catholic clergy up until the hardening of the catholic Counter Reformation in the late sixteenth century. The Travellers represent the thriving nomadic Roma communities, who lived for the most part, from horse-trading. The representation of the Jewish community, which also colonised Eastern Europe from Germany in the middle ages, I portray as witch and wizard like. By the late middle ages Jews had become firmly linked in the popular imagination with magic, and in the Hungarian Empire Jews were required to wear pointed hats by law, which is one theory as to how the iconic witches' hats came to be. Love apples were a thing, rich people indeed smothered their food in saffron, and persistent pagan beliefs meant that Lady Fortune was one of the most popular deities of the period.

The Ottoman Empire decisively defeated Lajos, King of Hungary in the battle of Mohacs, 1526, making him one of the last European monarchs to die in battle. German mercenaries did fight in the Hungarian army, which was comprised mostly of heavy knights. Mohacs was the last hurrah of the medieval knight, and the period was one in which medieval power balances were being overturned by the effectiveness of pikemen, musketeers and cannon. German landsknecht mercenaries, such as those comanded by Count Peter, were at the forefront of this change. The defeat of the Hungarian king brought the line of Ottoman control to the edges of modern day Austria and Slovakia. Crimean tartar regiments, decedents of the Mongolian Golden Hoard, fought as irregulars in the Ottoman army, particularly on the Ottoman boarder lands with the Polish-Lithuanian commonwealth. Pope Clement VII was one of the most militarily active popes in Catholic history, and he sent papal soldiers to fight alongside Lajos at the battle of Mohacs.

The period was one in which the protestant reformation was rapidly spreading and was not contained to the north and west of Germany. Princes converted to Lutheranism as far south as the Tyrone in southern Austria and as far east as Transylvania and East Prussia. Luke's story was inspired by the real events in southern Germany, in particular the "Peasants War," of 1525 where the reformation moved beyond noble control. Peasant unrest combined with radical theology exploded into general revolt. The revolution collimated in the seizure of Munster, 1534, where the city was indeed taken over by a polygamous communalist cult of Anabaptists before being brutally suppressed. I apologise for villainising such peasant movements, as polygamous communalism is not something I am against per se.

As to the Abbey of Saint Hildegard. Sadly, I know of no communities of warrior nuns who lived in networks of caves. Yet abbesses could indeed be powerful landowners and political actors and the abbey in the book is perhaps how the real Hildegard, Saint Hildegard of Brenen, would have liked an abbey to be.

Printed in Australia
AUHW020954130121
339637AU00006B/13

9 780995 139824